THE BETRAYAL

THE UNBROKEN SERIES: RAINE FALLING

SHAYLA BLACK
JENNA JACOB

DREAM WORDS LLC

THE BROKEN

THE UNBROKEN SERIES: RAINE FALLING PREQUEL

THE BETRAYAL

THE UNBROKEN SERIES: RAINE FALLING ONE

A DARK ROMANCE SAGA

NEW YORK TIMES BESTSELLING AUTHOR
SHAYLA BLACK

USA TODAY BESTSELLING AUTHOR
JENNA JACOB

THE BETRAYAL
The Unbroken Series: Raine Falling (Book 1)
Written by Shayla Black and Jenna Jacob

ISBN: 978-0-9911796-8-8

THE BROKEN
The Unbroken Series: Raine Falling (Bonus Prequel)
Written by Shayla Black and Jenna Jacob

This book is an original publication by Shayla Black and Jenna Jacob

Copyright 2021 Shelley Bradley LLC, Dream Words LLC

Cover Design by: Rachel Connolly
Edited by: Chloe Vale and Shayla Black

Excerpt from *The Break* © 2021 by Shelley Bradley LLC and Dream Words LLC

Previously published as *One Dom to Love*

The characters and events portrayed in this book are fictional. Any similarity to real persons, living or dead, is purely coincidental and not intended by the author. All rights reserved. No part of this book may be reproduced in any form by an electronic or mechanical means—except for brief quotations embedded in critical articles or reviews —without express written permission.

All rights reserved.

THE BROKEN

A DARK ROMANCE SAGA

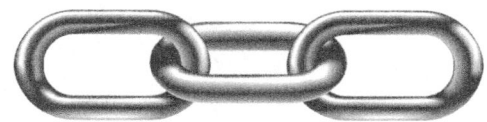

THE UNBROKEN SERIES: RAINE FALLING PREQUEL

NEW YORK TIMES BESTSELLING AUTHOR
SHAYLA BLACK
USA TODAY BESTSELLING AUTHOR
JENNA JACOB

ABOUT *THE BROKEN*

Three **Broken** people.
Separate.
Adrift.
Damaged.

Raine loves Macen.
He burns for her…but she's off-limits.
Until his best friend, Liam, says he wants her for himself.
And their fiery collision begins…

An innocent runaway, her tormented savior, and the shrewd player embark on an epic, passionate journey of rage, jealousy, forgiveness, and love to become **Unbroken**.

Raine

Six years ago
September 1
Los Angeles

Raine Kendall held her breath as she waited for Macen "Hammer" Hammerman to touch her. He prowled closer. She swallowed, her insides feeling jittery. In seconds, his hands would be on her.

Then it came, his touch. She jolted when he cupped her shoulder, just as she had the first time. Except when his fingers curled around her now, it wasn't fear that made her tremble.

"Precious?"

She loved the way he called her—and no one else—that.

Raine leaned closer, her heart racing, as he studied her for a long, silent moment. She resisted the urge to fidget under his intense hazel stare. "What's up?"

He set a guiding hand at the small of her back and led her into his office, gesturing her to the chair opposite his big desk. "Sit. Let's talk."

Her insides pinged with foreboding. She was a seventeen-year-old runaway, and he had taken her in off the streets three weeks ago. Who did that out of the goodness of their heart? Only a saint. Admittedly, she didn't know Hammer well. So far he'd been great...but he was hardly a contender for a halo or his own holiday. And why would a bachelor with a busy life volunteer to finish raising an almost-grown kid with a chip on her shoulder?

The short answer? He wouldn't.

Damn it, once he tossed her out, where would she go? Back home was *not* an option...

Raine sucked in a calming breath and prayed for the best. So far, Hammer had fed, sheltered, and comforted her, never taking his watchful eye off her. And true to his word, he had kept her safe from—

No, she refused to think about *him*.

God, she didn't want to leave here. For the first time in years—maybe a decade—she felt blessedly safe. How would she give that up?

Maybe she could make a pitch to convince Hammer to let her stay. Everyone had a price, right?

She froze, feeling incredibly stupid. No, naive. *That's* what this chat was about. Hammer intended to tell her what he wanted in return for all the consideration and care he'd shown her. He hadn't asked her for anything—yet. But of course, nothing in life was free. Everyone wanted something.

The only thing she had to give him was her V-card.

It was probably a fair price for taking on the role of her strong, stalwart protector. And it wasn't as if climbing between the sheets with him would be a hardship. He was fucking gorgeous. And Raine suspected he'd make it good since he seemed thorough and capable in everything he did. Besides, she'd be lying if she said she wasn't curious.

At least she now knew why high school guys had never interested her. They were boys. Macen Hammerman was a *man*. Sure, he was older than her, probably by a dozen years or so. And he owned a kink club. Apparently, he liked to spank women or whatever. She didn't completely understand that stuff. But he'd definitely proven dependable, patient, concerned, tender, and completely hands-off.

At least until now.

Raine wasn't really down with selling herself. But if she had to choose between his bed or the streets? No contest. She'd pick Macen. She would just respect him less.

She sat, watching with clammy palms as he rounded the desk to his own chair. The heat of his hand was like a brand on her skin.

It wasn't the first time his touch had lingered with her.

The night he'd taken her in, she'd stumbled into the alley behind his club, Shadows, too injured to go on. It had been hot. Though the concrete had reeked of urine and rotting garbage, Raine had preferred the gag-worthy stench over the swagger of local pimps searching the dark streets for fresh flesh to peddle. Nor had she wanted to tangle with the drug dealers seeking another customer to addict. Two blocks away, she'd seen a gang initiate a new member by beating the hell out of him, then passing his resistant girlfriend around for the rest of them to use.

Raine had run as far and fast as she could, given her bruising and what she suspected were cracked ribs. She'd hidden, crouched in the dark safety behind Hammer's dumpster, where the light overhead looked as if someone had thrown a rock and broken the bulb. There, she'd dry heaved, since she hadn't had actual food in her belly to lose. The involuntary spasms had hurt like a bitch.

That had been nothing compared to the heart-stopping moment Hammer had opened his back door, trash bag in hand, and caught sight of her.

Heart thudding, breath all but stopped, she'd felt terror roll through her when he bent to cup her shoulder. She'd expected the worst. He'd been nothing but gentle as he'd offered her a hot meal.

She'd refused—immediately and more than once. But Raine was learning fast that Hammer could be very persuasive. And he persisted until he got his way.

He'd coaxed her trust with a cold bottle of water and a protein bar, talking with her in the alley for hours as if he had nothing better to do. Finally, her adrenaline had worn off and exhaustion had overcome her. He'd carried her inside, ignoring her protests, then given her some soup and a Coke. Next thing she knew, she'd awakened in an unfamiliar bed—alone and fully clothed. Hammer offered to take her to breakfast at the diner down the street. There, he'd cajoled her until she admitted why she'd been hiding behind his club. Not the whole story, though. God, if he really knew, he'd see her as a freak show and a charity case all rolled into one. But after the bits she'd shared, he hadn't treated her any differently, simply given her more of his kindness.

She'd been hanging out at Shadows since, reluctant to leave.

Would today change everything?

"Raine, school starts next Tuesday. What do you plan to do about that?"

Of all the things she'd thought Hammer might say, she'd never expected that. "School?"

"You have to think about your future."

And he didn't mean in his bed?

"Macen, I can't go back there. It's too close to—" Raine couldn't finish her sentence, couldn't think about the monster who would find her. He would take her…and no one would stop him. "I'll get my GED and find a job. Then I'll repay you and get out of your way."

"A GED is a good start, but you're too bright not to go to college."

Was he crazy? No, it probably sounded simple to him. He seemed to have money. But she couldn't keep sponging off him, especially before she heard what his support would cost her. "It's too expensive. Hardly anyone in my family has their degree." Her sister was well on her way, Raine supposed. But she hadn't heard from Rowan since she'd waved goodbye and headed to London for her amazing university experience almost three years ago. God knew where her older brother, River, had gone or what had become of him. "I'll get by without one."

Hammer glowered. "No."

One word; that was his whole answer. Raine shouldn't be surprised. Most of the time, he listened with open ears and offered wisdom, but he sometimes acted as if his word was law. He definitely had a bossy side.

"Yes. I need to get a job so I can start reimbursing you for the food and the roof. Then I'm sure you'll want me to get a place of my own."

"Do you know what kind of money you'll earn in a job that requires no education? What sort of apartment do you think you'll be able to afford?"

She shuddered. Everything was expensive in LA, but that wasn't his problem. "I'll figure it out."

"How, by selling drugs or your body? Without a good education, you'll have few other alternatives." Hammer stared, tapping his fingers on the desk slowly, considering her. "I have an idea. Hear me out."

Here came the pitch, where he told her that if she'd just take off her clothes and keep his bed warm at night, that would be payment enough. He had probably waited so long to proposition her because he'd wanted her bruising to heal. After all, who wanted to do it with someone black and blue?

She shot him a cynical glare, hating that she'd let herself hope Hammer was above taking advantage of her. But he was a man, so apparently not.

"You don't have to say anything else. I get you." She stood and headed toward the private bedroom attached to his office, surprised to find she was shaking. Should she take off her clothes or wait for him to do it?

"Where are you going?"

"The bedroom. You want me to pay you with my body, right?"

"No. Never." Thunder rolled across his face as he gripped the desk with big hands. "Sit down."

Raine didn't understand the reason he was pissed off, but she quickly complied. In fact, she always did her best to please him. She wasn't sure why. Maybe because she owed him? Usually, she just told people to kiss her ass.

As she slinked back to the chair, embarrassment stung. "Sorry. It sounded like you were propositioning me. You really don't want me to repay you with my virginity?"

He clenched his jaw. "I didn't pluck you out of the alley for sex. I took you in so you'd have a chance. You want to repay me, Raine? Go to college. Make something of your life. I'll help you."

Seriously? "You're not even after a blow job? I've never done it, but I can get on my knees."

Macen's gaze dropped to her lips. She tingled. The air turned thick. Her breath caught. Was he reconsidering?

"No. I want you on your feet. Where do you want to go to college?"

Like all he had to do was snap his fingers and he could make that happen?

Raine sat back in her chair, staring. "You're serious? Higher education with no strings attached?"

That would be an amazing gesture. No one had ever believed in her. Well, maybe her mom, but...

"There *are* conditions," he clarified. "But nothing sexual. How are your grades?"

"Decent enough, but I can't accept more of your charity. And I don't want to start my life saddled with student loans. I'll just get a job and support myself."

"You don't need a loan, Raine. And I'm not offering you charity. You'll work for me while you're going to school."

She blinked. This man barely knew her, and he was offering to save her. Why? As far as she could tell, he wasn't any sort of philanthropist or caped crusader taking troubled teens in off the street. Since he apparently hadn't offered her a roof because he wanted to get his kink on with her, what was his deal?

Raine could only think of one other possibility; he pitied her. She swallowed a lump of frustration. No way would she ask him if he felt sorry for her. She didn't want to hear the answer.

"Hammer..." To Raine's horror, she started crying.

"Precious..." His voice was painfully soft. "Let me do this for you."

"Why?" She swiped a hand across her wet cheeks.

"It sounds like you haven't had many breaks in your short life. I can change that."

He wasn't wrong. How nice would it be to have one advantage?

She sighed. "What kind of work did you have in mind?"

"First"—he looked slightly sheepish—"you must have noticed I can't cook. At all."

That was the first time she'd heard Hammer admit he sucked at something. And as far as she could tell, he never apologized for anything. He could be damn stubborn...but under his bluster, he could also be terribly kind.

She hid a smile. "Yeah, you nearly set the kitchen on fire the other morning. And you make lousy coffee."

"Well, I can count on you to be honest." He chuckled. "You're fantastic at both. So you can take on those responsibilities."

"That's easy. I like to cook. And I love to bake."

"I've noticed. Those apple spice muffins?" He all but groaned. "The best."

"Thanks." Her lips curled up with pride. She couldn't remember the last time someone had complimented her.

"It's good to see you smile, precious."

"You talked about a job, Hammer. The going rate for a few home-cooked meals is next to nothing. School is way more expensive than that."

"I wasn't finished. I also need reliable help around here. Inventory and secretarial assistance are in short supply. I could use a hand preparing the club each night before opening, so tasks like stocking the coolers with chilled water and filling the bins with clean blankets. And the equipment must be sanitized and stored properly."

Okay, so he had more responsibility in mind than a little kitchen duty, but it still didn't sound like a fair exchange. Her considerable pride told her to refuse his handout. Except…what if he really did need help around here? He'd stuck his neck out for her when no one else had. He had faith in her when no one else did. He cared for her well-being when no one else would.

She owed him.

"Of course I'll do it. But how am I supposed to cook and tidy up for you from a dorm room?" A place like that honestly sounded horrible. The last thing she wanted to do was share space with vapid girls whose only worry was how their hair looked and which jock to flirt with. She would have nothing in common with them.

"You'll stay here."

"Really? I can?"

"Absolutely. I'll need you nearby. And it's not safe for you out there."

A smile spread across her face. This deal got better with every second. "That would be great. But are you sure you're getting your money's worth?"

"I will. You'll get a business degree with a focus on accounting and finance. I know my limitations; keeping the books is one of them. And if I never had to work on the club's taxes again, I would be thrilled. Trust me, you'd be doing me a favor."

Now he was talking. That was a real job people got paid decent money for. Maybe he didn't see her as merely a charity case.

"You've got a deal."

"Excellent. I expect you to take care of the paperwork to get your GED. Let me know when you need money and how much. You can start at the local community college while you figure out what four-year university around here you'd like to attend. Then we'll work on getting you accepted."

Suddenly, the future Raine hadn't wanted to face because she'd merely been surviving looked lots brighter.

She had so much to be thankful for now, and she owed everything to Hammer, who apparently *wasn't* like other guys. Obviously he liked sex. Duh, he ran a kink club. But he wasn't demanding a piece of her ass. Maybe he wasn't into jailbait. After all, a statutory rape charge would be bad for business. Or maybe he just wasn't into her…though she'd thought she'd caught him looking once or twice.

Then again, it was possible she'd read him all wrong. It wouldn't be the first time.

"Thank you so much." She shot to her feet, resisting the stupid urge to launch herself into his arms in gratitude, but he kept the desk squarely between them. "I won't let you down."

The smile that stretched across his face was benevolent and proud. It did something to her heart.

"I know you won't. But I've got a few rules. Sit."

Raine sank to her chair again. "I'm listening, sir."

He froze. Then he squirmed and cleared his throat.

Had she said something wrong? Was he worried she couldn't be obedient enough? *Please let his rules be easy to follow.* The way she felt right now, she never wanted to disappoint this man.

"First, I'll be giving you a cell phone so we can stay in contact. We'll figure out transportation when it's time for you to go to school. Do you have a driver's license?"

"No." Dad hadn't wanted to give up his control of her enough for that.

"Then I'll teach you. If you make friends at school and want to go out, curfew is midnight. I expect to always know where you are and who you're with. It's the easiest way to help you stay safe."

Most people her age would chafe at his demand. It sounded pretty freaking parental. But honestly, it had been so long since anyone had given a shit about her that she didn't mind. If it helped keep her past from catching up with her, she could check in. Besides, she wasn't much of a social butterfly. "Okay."

He sighed, steepling his fingers and staring at her over the long tips. "I've been honest with you about the purpose of my club. You're a minor, Raine. I'm taking a huge risk by letting you walk through the door at all, much less harboring you here. Until now, I've managed to separate you from the play space, but if you're going to help me prepare for the evenings, you'll be seeing the rest of the club and all its equipment. I'm sure you'll have questions. You will ask me and no one else. Is that clear?"

"Yeah. Totally." But it was sex. How hard could it be to figure out?

"I've also advised all the members, especially the Dominants, that they're forbidden to approach you or talk to you, much less lay a hand on you. In fact, they're not allowed within ten feet of you. No one here will touch you. No one."

Especially him. That's what he meant.

He'd more or less already turned her down tonight. Not that she'd been panting for it or anything. But his blunt refusal kind of stung. She was hardly a troll. Maybe he just saw her as a stupid kid. Whatever. The weird pull she felt to him would go away. She was only curious because he was hot and he knew about life and sex and all that. But obviously, he wasn't feeling it for her. Fine. He didn't have anything special, like a magical penis. And it wasn't as if he'd ever be the love of her life. She didn't believe in that shit. But she'd settle for friends.

So why did she feel oddly disappointed?

She shrugged. "All right."

"It's important you understand that rule, Raine. The club members know you're off-limits."

"I got it. Geez... What else?"

He paused. "Every November, I travel to New York for a few days. I usually leave on the fifth and return on the eighth. I'll cut my trip a day shorter this year if you'd like. But you'll be safe here. I'll make sure of that."

Raine wondered why he went back there at the same time every year. Friends? Standing appointment? Kink convention? She was curious but it was his business. It would be a little weird to be at Shadows without him, but if Hammer said she'd be safe, she would be. Besides, she rarely saw people associated with the club except that Beck guy. She avoided him because he seemed intense and kind of scary.

"I'll be fine," she assured. "Do what you need."

"Good. Then it's settled." He rose to his feet. "You can start work next week."

"Sure. Thanks." She bit her lip, then turned back to him in all sincerity. "Really."

He gave her a clipped nod, then slipped into the private suite adjoining his office. Raine floated out on cloud nine. She would get an education. She would have a place to stay that wasn't sorority central. She'd get to live with Hammer. Finally, she had some hope for the future.

Smiling, Raine made her way to the kitchen. He might have suggested that she start her new responsibilities next week, but they both had to eat tonight. She'd rather not suffer more takeout or whatever he tried to whip up. He might be more experienced in many ways, but her cooking was way better.

As she slid some seasoned chicken in the oven and readied squash for baking, she heard the clicking of stilettos on the concrete in the hall behind her. Who was that?

Raine whirled to find a stylish woman standing in the doorway. Looking a few years older than Hammer, she had the casual elegance of someone who had lived and felt comfortable in her skin. Raine envied her easy polish. The woman's champagne tresses looked artlessly tousled. Her berry lips had been painted with precision in a shade that was sexy without being overt. A black sheath clung to her graceful curves and stopped a few inches above her knees. The woman's patent shoes looked designer, seductive without being hookerish. She even carried a chic red clutch.

In short, the woman looked completely put together—something Raine feared she never would be.

Realizing she was staring, she wiped her hands on her apron. "Can I help you? The club isn't open yet."

"I'm a bit early." Her eyes lit up as she looked at her watch. "Traffic was lighter than normal. I'm here to see Hammer."

Why? But Raine was afraid she knew the answer. Hammer fucked this woman, didn't he? His business was sex. And she'd seen boxes of condoms in his personal space.

Something ugly slammed into Raine's chest. She'd never be half the woman this amazing bombshell was. No wonder Hammer had zero interest in having sex with her. Why would any man want a silly little virgin when he could have this goddess?

"Um, he's busy." Maybe if she wasn't forthcoming, the woman would go away.

Raine didn't want to think about why that idea made her happy.

"I'm sure he'll get unbusy for me. He never keeps me waiting." The woman looked her up and down, ending the scan with a speculative raise of her brow. "Are you his…little sister?"

She and Hammer looked nothing alike, but clearly the woman was trying to decide why someone so young stood in his club, in his kitchen.

"Employee." *Why, are you his mother?* "He can't cook."

Even the woman's laugh sounded refined. "Well, his skills lie elsewhere, after all."

Obviously, this woman would know. And Raine didn't like that at all. "Did you need something?"

"Can you tell me where to find him?"

"I…" Raine refused to speak the words that would send her to Hammer's bed.

"Oops. I almost forgot…" The woman reached under her dress and tugged on something. With a shimmy and a wriggle, her panties came down her sleek, spray-tanned thighs before she stepped out of the satiny undergarment and stuffed it in her purse. "There. That should make Hammer happy. Now, where can I find him?"

Raine closed her gaping mouth and resisted the urge to punch her. Was this bitch serious, dropping her drawers in the fucking kitchen?

The sound of sure, masculine steps resounding down the hall saved her. Hammer appeared a moment later, smiling at the blonde. "Erika, good to see you. Lost?"

The woman's eyes lit up with heat and anticipation. "Eager."

He smiled and settled a hand at the small of her back. "I'm ready. Let's head to my…office."

Raine knew where they were really going and what would happen there. Suddenly, she was desperate to stop it. "Dinner will be ready in fifteen minutes."

"Keep mine warm. I'll eat later," Macen tossed over his broad shoulder as he led Erika out of the kitchen, shutting the door behind them.

Leaving Raine alone to cry tears she didn't understand—a cycle that would repeat itself over and over for the next six years….

Hammer

Fourteen months later
November 7

Thick clouds rolled across the cold November sky, matching Hammer's dark mood. The bitter wind lashed his face as he stared at the familiar gravestone in somber silence. As always, his Irish pal Liam O'Neill stood beside him, offering his steady support through this annual vigil of contrition. But Hammer could never really atone; he knew that.

"The flowers you brought are lovely," Liam offered. "She would have liked them."

Probably. Sometimes, it felt as if she'd left a lifetime ago. And sometimes, it seemed like yesterday.

Hammer nodded at his best friend because he didn't know what else to say. He hated thinking about her loss. He hated talking about it even more.

It also sucked that he and Liam only saw each other once a year now, when Hammer flew back east so they could share a few grim smiles and bittersweet recollections during this terrible ritual.

They'd been inseparable back in the day, solid through the best and the worst of life. Then time, circumstance, and some really regrettable decisions had changed everything. Still, despite the distance between them, he loved the bastard like a brother.

Liam turned to him. "Did I tell you I brought flowers for her birthday?"

"You did."

"That day was sunny with a tease of spring in the air. She would have been pleased."

Hammer nodded. "She never liked winter."

"No." Liam didn't offer another comment, like he was at a loss for words, too.

The silence stretched on. Macen hoped they had finished dutifully paying homage—at least for another year—to a past that could never be undone. After all, nothing could purge the remorse staining Hammer's soul. Did Liam feel the same? Hammer didn't know. They'd never talked about the end.

Instead, he had escaped to the opposite coast, moving from New York to Los Angeles. After that, things had never been the same. Today especially he missed the unguarded camaraderie they'd once shared.

In the old days, he would have confessed to Liam that his mind wasn't here at the cemetery but preoccupied by his desperate desire for Raine. In the last year, she'd gone from being the too-young runaway he'd taken in because she tugged on his heartstrings to the budding siren who had tied him up in agonizing knots of lust.

But he said nothing. In fact, he'd never mentioned the girl to his best friend.

It was on the tip of his tongue to ask for Liam's advice on coping with this potent need for the girl-woman living under his roof. He remained mute. He didn't want to share her even verbally. Besides, too much water had washed under their bridge for such soul baring.

Not to mention the fact that O'Neill had his own problems—big ones.

Hammer had kept his opinion of Liam's fiancée to himself. Not his igloo, not his ice queen. And if he delved into Liam's problems, his old pal would only do what he did best: deflect the questions and dissect Hammer instead.

Macen wanted to avoid that at all costs.

He clapped Liam on the back. "Ready to go?"

"If you are."

Hammer merely nodded.

Wordlessly, they plodded across the frozen ground. Usually, Hammer looked forward to this part of their observance, when his Irish friend stayed true to his roots and took him to some pub where they'd imbibe a pint—or ten—and forget…at least for a while. This year, he wished he could skip it and fly home.

Was Raine all right? Did she miss him, too? Were the club members obeying his rules?

He'd left Pike, a trusted dungeon monitor, in charge of Raine's well-being. If any Dom so much as breathed in her scent, Pike would not only carry out Hammer's strict, hands-off, castrate-any-bastard-who-touched-her policy, he would revel in it. But that wasn't fucking enough, and not knowing how she was doing was turning him inside out.

God, he hated how much he ached to see her right now.

"So, where are we getting shitfaced this year?"

Liam smirked. "As long as the drinks are stout and we get bloody pissed, does it matter?"

"Not really."

"Then I'll call for a ride and find us a friendly pub."

Hammer nodded. Since he couldn't skip this drunkfest, he might as well enjoy it. "How's Seth?"

Liam focused on his phone. "As you can imagine, our friend Mr. Cooper is busy, but when we have time for a chat, he seems good, if a bit more of a homebody these days."

At least someone is happy. But Hammer didn't say that; he'd only sound as bitter as he felt. "Glad to hear it."

"I'm hoping to join him soon." Liam pocketed his phone. "Uber is on its way."

Another pause. Another awkward silence.

Hammer grimaced. He really didn't want to delve into Liam's mess, but what kind of friend would he be if he didn't try? "So…marriage, huh? Are you really sure you want to take the plunge?"

"Oh, aye. I am."

"You've thought about all the things you'll be giving up, right? You've always liked…variety."

"Not anymore. She's perfect for me, mate."

Hammer didn't see it. In fact, he'd bet Liam had merely fallen prey to Gwyneth's pretty face and lithe body. "What about the lifestyle? You're a Dominant. Submission is not her thing, man."

"There's a hungry sub inside her, and I'll find it."

Hammer raised a brow at his friend. If that crazy bitch was any sort of submissive, then he was a fucking virgin.

"Don't look at me that way," Liam protested. "With a little time and effort, I know I can coax Gwyneth's deepest desires."

Maybe her deepest desires for Gucci and Vuitton, but cuffs and spanking benches? "From one Dom to another, I've seen no hint of a submissive lurking inside that"—*catty, calculating, conniving*—"woman."

"If you spent more time with her, you'd see her potential."

At Liam's earnest tone, Hammer somehow managed not to roll his eyes. It had only taken him an evening with the couple to know that Liam's future wife wasn't what his friend needed.

"Why don't you stay a few more days, Macen, get to know her a bit better? We can have dinner tomorrow night at that little Italian place you like over on Mulberry Street…then see where the night takes us."

Hammer knew what that meant and couldn't shake his head fast enough. "I can't. Sorry."

Bailing made him feel more than a little guilty. Sure, he'd like to save Liam from making the biggest mistake of his life. But the man was too blinded by lust to hear that Gwyneth was a straight-up narcissist, incapable of loving anyone but herself. Instead, Hammer stayed tight-lipped. That conversation was a fistfight in the making, and he was hesitant to say anything that might drive a bigger wedge between them.

Liam's mouth pressed into a glum line. "I understand. I've the feeling you're eager to get home to something. Or someone. What aren't you telling me?"

A fucking shit ton. But how could he explain to Liam an obsession he didn't understand himself?

Fifteen months ago, when he'd found Raine hiding in the alley behind his club, he'd taken one look at her, seen the fear and defeat in her pretty blue eyes, and felt a fist squeeze his heart. He'd had no idea how long she'd been living on the streets, but some asshole had obviously used her as a punching bag, and he'd felt an undeniable urge to save the terrified waif.

At first, she'd been skittish, unsure if she could trust him. She'd masked her fear behind bravado and sarcasm, but Hammer hadn't been fooled. Instead, he'd done his best to be patient, gentle, and coaxing. Slowly, it had worked.

Then all too soon his concern had become…more. At first, he'd dismissed the pull he felt as mere need to protect her. After all, without him, she was a child alone in the world. But as the months passed, she'd begun to blossom, no longer bruised, scrawny, or skittish. Maturity and confidence had turned Raine from a striking stray to an alluring woman.

Now she was eighteen. Since her birthday, he'd been exercising his considerable restraint and existing on cold showers. No matter how many times he reminded himself that he was thirty and had no business wanting her, the fact that she now was legal taunted and tempted him every fucking day. Her skimpy outfits and flirtatious smiles only threw kindling on his blaze. Still, she was too damn innocent to be subjected to his Dominant desire to drag her beneath him, lay his mouth over hers, slide slow and deep into her virgin pussy, and claim her for his own.

How the fuck could he want to save and defile the girl at once?

God help them if he ever gave in. He'd unleash the gnawing beast inside him, and it would destroy them both.

Sure, he knew prettier women, more sophisticated and educated ones. Hell, he had sex with them, willing himself to be satisfied with her substitutes. But none had Raine's intriguing mix of sharp wit, fragile soul, and wide-open heart.

He had no idea what to do.

Finally, Hammer turned to his best friend and lied without even blinking. "Nothing."

Liam frowned. "Are you sure? You seem distracted."

Time to change the subject.

"Hey, since I can't stay, why don't you visit LA? Call it an early bachelor party. What kind of best man would I be if I didn't give you a big send-off?" If he could persuade Liam to come out west, maybe he could introduce his friend to some soft, lovely subs who might change his mind about marrying that soul-sucking shrew. "There are tons of things to see and do. We could spend a few days checking out Disney,

Malibu, Hollywood… I know dozens of amazing restaurants and nightclubs."

Liam had never taken him up on his invitations to visit in the past. Hammer couldn't think of a single reason he'd change his mind now. On the other hand, if Liam came to Shadows, Hammer would have to explain Raine. It was probably goddamn selfish, but he hoped Liam refused again. He didn't want his old pal anywhere near her.

"A bachelor party sounds fantastic, mate. I know you'd throw me a legendary bash. But you're coming a few days before the wedding in April, right? We can do it then. I just don't want to leave my girl now. I hope you understand."

Unfortunately, he did.

"Sure," he said as they hopped in the arriving Uber and headed to a pub.

The rest of the night was a blessed blur, and despite the cabin pressure of the plane playing hell with his hangover the next morning, Hammer was all too happy to be winging his way back to LA.

By late afternoon, Macen strode through the doors of Shadows. A million and one tasks no doubt awaited his attention, but for the first time in years, he wasn't drained and looking to drown himself in tequila after paying his annual penance in New York. All he wanted was Raine.

Striding through the dungeon, he scanned the room, itching to lay eyes on her. Three days away from her was two and a half too many.

He skimmed a cursory glance over the members, his heart beating a little too fast with anticipation. It wasn't as if she would run toward him and leap into his arms like some romantic movie. They wouldn't even touch. Their reunion would be nothing more than a few cordial words and a smile.

Safe.

Chaste.

Empty.

With an inward curse, he shoved down his rising desire and reminded himself that, when it came to Raine, he had three simple rules: Keep your hands to yourself. Keep your dick in your pants. See rules one and two.

He took a slower pass over the dungeon but still didn't spot Raine. Then he caught a whiff of cinnamon and apples mingling with the usual scents of leather and sex in the air. A smile tugged at his lips. Of course. She had known he was coming home today. The little vixen was busy in the kitchen whipping up a batch of his favorite apple spice muffins. He turned and headed her direction.

He'd only taken a couple of steps before the hair on the back of his neck stood on end. The stares of the club members pricked like needles. He'd been so focused on finding Raine, he'd missed the anxious undercurrent humming around him.

Something was wrong.

He tossed a glance over his shoulder, seeking the source of his disquiet. No one would meet his gaze except Kenneth Beckman, Shadows' most enthusiastic sadist and one of his good friends.

When he caught sight of Beck's grim expression, Hammer stilled. Alarm bells rang in his head.

Beck glanced toward the kitchen, and Hammer turned his gaze to follow. Raine stood in the portal, her long, inky tresses framing her delicate face. She met his stare for a moment. Guilt glimmered in her blue eyes. She quickly jerked away, turning her back on him.

No smile. No welcome. No unpracticed flirtation.

Apprehension burned through him. What the fuck had happened?

Raine usually wore her feelings for him on her sleeve. Now she barely looked at him. And the spitfire he had left three days ago? Long gone.

She disappeared into the kitchen, leaving Hammer frowning at an empty doorway while a million unanswered questions rolled through his brain. Before he could chase her down and interrogate her, Beck stepped into his path.

"We need to talk," his burly, tattooed friend muttered in a low, grave tone. "And no, it can't wait."

Annoyed, Hammer craned around Beck to look at Raine. He scowled at the wilted line of her spine. That worried the hell out of him.

"I'm listening."

Beck shook his head. "Not here, dumb ass."

That made Hammer zip his gaze back around. Yeah, it was serious. "My office. Let's make it quick."

Without another word, the two strode down the hall to Macen's private quarters. After closing the door behind them, he pinned Beck with an impatient glower. "What?"

Scrubbing a hand through his dark hair, his friend exhaled heavily. "I have to tell you something because nobody else will. But before I do, you have to promise you won't lose your shit."

"Spill it before I beat the fuck out of you."

"You'd die trying," Beck quipped. "It's about Raine."

Macen had guessed that, but his stomach pitched when Beck confirmed his suspicion. Somehow he managed a blank expression. "Go on."

"While you were gone, she and Zak got together."

Hammer froze, a dozen images assaulting his brain that all made him want to commit murder. "Got together…how?"

"C'mon, do I really have to explain how to insert tab A into slot B? They had sex."

Hammer rocked back on his heels as if he'd been sucker-punched. As the words rolled through his brain, rage, hot and atomic, exploded inside him. She'd given that motherfucker her virginity?

Hammer should have known by Zak's leering glances that the prick would try to slide under his radar and get to Raine one day. Now Macen wished like hell that he hadn't gone to New York. But he owed the dead the respect he hadn't given her in life.

Damn it.

"Where is he?" Hammer pounded his fist on his desk. "I'm going to kill him."

Beck sighed. "This is why no one wanted to tell you. You have to calm down."

"I don't have to do anything except murder that fucking bastard."

"Stop being so dramatic. As much as I'd enjoy cheering you on because no asshat is more deserving, you can't do that. Besides, you'd look shitty in orange."

"I'll settle for castrating him. Slowly. With a dull, rusty knife."

Beck sighed again. "I get it. Zak fucked your woman but—"

"She's not mine. I'm just protecting her from shitbags like him."

"Oh, please... Anyone with eyes knows she's yours. But you refused to grow a pair and fuck her yourself so—"

"Shut up," Hammer barked because Beck didn't understand. "Where is Pike? He was supposed to be keeping an eye on her."

"Home with the flu. I offered to fill in for him, but last night I had my hands full."

"Full of what, tits and pussy?" Rage pressed in on Hammer until he thought his head might explode.

Beck scowled and clenched his fists. Good. Hammer was ready for a fight.

"I had to break up a brawl in the parking lot before the cops showed. By the time I mopped that up, Zak had culled the princess from the herd. But Raine is legally allowed to make decisions about her body and sexuality."

"Until you slipped up, she didn't have any sexuality! Are you a hundred percent sure that she and Zak..." Hammer couldn't bring himself to finish that sentence.

"Well, I caught them leaving a private room together. Zak was zipping his pants, and Raine looked shell-shocked."

The mental image from those words pelted Hammer's brain. He didn't want to believe it. "That doesn't mean they had sex."

Beck gritted his teeth as if digging for patience. "I confronted Zak later. He admitted they had. I reminded him that Raine is totally off-limits. His exact reply was, 'I guess she didn't want to be Hammer's little virgin anymore.'"

Instant, violent fury shot through Macen. He suppressed the urge to ram his fist into a wall—barely. If Raine had meant to punish him for not accepting her subtle sexual invitations, it had fucking worked.

"So..." Beck went on. "When I found Raine crying in the kitchen, I figured the asshole wasn't lying."

"Crying?" Bile rose in the back of Hammer's throat as another possibility occurred to him. "Did he force her?"

"Would I have let him live? Look, as much as I loathe that cocksucker, I don't think he's a rapist."

"But you don't know that."

"C'mon… Think about it. Zak likes the chase. Seduction is a game for him."

True. So that son of a bitch had used his forked, silver tongue to talk Raine out of her panties. "I'm going to kill him."

"Why do you seem surprised? He's been working Raine for months. And he gave her the one thing she craved—the one thing you've refused to: a man's desire. In your absence, he finally had the chance to wear her down."

Hammer wanted to rip the door off its hinges, race to the dungeon, and wipe the floor with Zak. No, he hadn't expected Raine to stay a virgin forever…but damn it, he'd ached to be her first—more than he wanted to admit.

Now he'd never have that chance, though that was probably for the best. He was the last man she should ever give her innocence to.

Hammer frowned. "Did you talk to her about it?"

"Every time she sees me, she backs up ten feet, so no."

"Which means you don't know anything for sure?"

"Dude… They fucked. Accept it."

He glared at Beck, a heartbeat from tearing everything in his office apart with his bare hands, the man included.

His friend's voice softened. "Sorry. You've had your balls in a twist for months. You want her, and she sure as hell hasn't hidden how much she wants you. Why didn't you man up once she turned legal? What did you think would happen if you kept treating your woman like a child?"

Hammer had sworn to himself that he'd gladly release Raine to the man who put her on a pedestal and made her his queen. Someday. Years in the future. At the very least, he'd expected her to bestow her virginity on someone who would value the gift, not a player who treated women like a trophy in a competitive sport.

He rounded his desk, dropped into his chair, and scrubbed a hand over his face. "Where is that weasel-dicked son of a bitch?"

"You can't go out there and confront him."

"The fuck I can't. This is my club. He broke my number one rule."

"I meant that Raine probably needs you more than Zak needs his ass kicked. I think she's beating herself up."

"But that rat fucking bastard seduced her when he knew damn well—" Hammer bit back the rest. "Zak is a dead man."

"And if you're locked up in prison, how are you going to protect Raine from the next guy who seduces her out of her panties?" Beck pointed out. "Look, the damage is done. All you can do now is tear up his contract and escort him off the property. But don't go out there half-cocked, because I'm not posting your bail for murder."

"I didn't ask you to."

"But someone needed to remind you, and I drew the short straw today. Ever heard the phrase *don't shoot the messenger?*"

Beck was right.

Hammer sighed. "Thanks for having the balls to tell me what happened."

"Sorry, man. I know it hurts." Beck clapped him on the back in sympathy. "So what will you do to Raine?"

Hammer's scowl deepened. "Do to her?"

"You know, are you finally going to change things between you? Or are you going to keep setting her on a shelf like some goddamn doll?"

"She can't handle me."

"So you're not even going to try? You're just going to keep wasting your time with all the other subs? Everyone, even Raine, knows what you do with them. Hammer away at 'em, right? If you're this pissed off about another man laying his hands on your precious, but you're not willing to take a hard look at your choices, I can't help you."

"I didn't ask you to, so fuck off."

Beck shook his head as if he'd tried, but Hammer was hopeless.

Once the sadist had gone, he stood and paced. Looking for calm was pointless. Whatever his fuckups in this situation had been, they didn't mitigate Zak's sins. Those couldn't go unpunished.

Wrenching open his office door, he stormed down the hall and into the dungeon. Across the room, Zak was halfheartedly flogging a sub. Hammer suspected the manwhore had joined Shadows not to engage in the power exchange but to tag as much pussy as possible.

As he strode Zak's way, Hammer barely resisted the urge to wrench the flogger from the asshole's grip and beat him. Instead, he crossed his arms over his chest. "Let's talk. Outside."

"I'm busy," Zak pointed out with a wave of his hand. "You can wait."

Hammer clenched his jaw. "Now."

Without waiting for Zak's reply, he released the carabiner hooks from the sub's cuffs, snatched up a blanket, and wrapped it around the girl before leading her to a couch where several other subs sat.

"Take care of her, please," Hammer instructed the girls, ignoring Zak's protests.

"Yes, Sir," one murmured.

As soon as she was settled, he grabbed the cocksucker by the arm and hauled him to the back door.

"What the fuck?" Zak growled. "Why are you embarrassing me in front of that sub?"

"You broke my rules." Hammer dragged him into the alley, shoved him against the dumpster, then lunged until they stood nose to nose.

The rat bastard smirked. "Oh, so this is about Raine? Before you bust my balls, you should know she wanted it. Give your overbearing daddy complex a rest."

Zak hadn't begun to see his daddy complex in action. "Shut the fuck up or you won't like what happens next."

"You plan on taking a swing at me, old man?" Zak taunted.

"No." One swing would never be enough.

"Look, it just happened. We were talking, you know? Then one thing led to another, and we fucked." He shrugged. "It was no big deal."

Zak was wrong.

Hammer's hands curled into fists. "Shut up."

"C'mon, man. She—"

"I said shut up."

"I only plucked what was ripe for the taking. Since you weren't going to plow that field, you had to know someone was going to run his tool through her soil. Why not me?"

Hammer's control ripped off its chain. Zak had just dug his own grave.

"She was strictly off-limits."

"Why?" Zak cocked his head. "Oh, because you wanted to be the first inside that tight, juicy piece of virgin pussy, isn't that right, *daddy*? You're jealous I beat you to it."

In a fiery red haze, Hammer threw a brutal right hook to Zak's jaw.

The asshole flailed back, landing with a thud on the ground, howling like a bitch. "Jesus!"

Macen was done talking. He leapt on top of Zak and wrapped his fist in the shitbag's shirt, then punched him again. Then again. And again, until his knuckles throbbed and blood slicked them as it spewed from Zak's mouth and broken nose. Until the prick did nothing but cower and whine.

Hammer only stopped when he felt another hand clamp down on his shoulder. "That's enough."

Beck. The man's familiar voice barely penetrated his rage.

"Go away."

"You can't kill him."

Oh, but he fucking wanted to.

"I'm saving you from yourself." Beck tightened his fingers on his arm. "Let him go, Macen."

It took every ounce of his restraint to unclench his fist and stand over Zak's prone body. Breathing harsh, he glared at the douchebag. "If you ever try to see or talk to Raine again, I *will* finish what I started. I'll smile as I cut off that cock you're so proud of and shove it down your throat. Then I'll bury your body where no one will ever find you. Do I make myself perfectly clear?"

Zak tried to scowl. "You threatened and assaulted me. I'm calling the cops."

"I *dare* you. Won't they be interested to hear that you had sex with one of your little sister's friends a few weeks ago. What was she, barely sixteen?"

Zak reared back in shock. "How did you—"

"Know? I have ways. Don't fuck with me. Or I'll hunt you down and make you wish I'd killed you today. You got it?"

Zak nodded, whimpering as he rose slowly, then limped down the alley.

Beside him, Beck sighed.

Reluctantly, Hammer turned the sadist's way. "I'm fine. You can go in now."

"No, you need a few minutes to cool off before you talk to Raine. She needs you."

Yeah? How was he supposed to talk to her without losing his shit?

As Beck turned away, Hammer plopped onto the cement steps by the back door, wiping the crimson dripping from his knuckles on his bloodstained shirt.

The dumpster beside him caught his attention. He could still feel the heat of that August night he'd taken Raine in pressing all around him. She'd been huddled here, hiding and hoping no one found her. After he'd cut through her wall of defiance and reached the fragile, shivering girl behind it, he'd known she was in trouble and that no one else would help. So he'd offered Raine a safe haven, figuring that, one day, she would spread her wings and fly. For the first time, Hammer was forced to consider what he would do when that day came. He could no longer imagine his world without her.

"I'm fucked," he said to his retreating friend. "Aren't I?"

Beck hesitated. "Admitting it is the first step."

Then the door slammed, and Hammer was alone with his heaping regret.

When had everything gone wrong? After he'd first taken Raine in, he'd done everything he could to gain her trust. Eventually, they'd settled into a harmonious if odd coexistence. It had been all right.

Then…she'd turned eighteen.

He'd given her a surprise party because he'd wanted to make her happy. His fatal mistake.

Under the guise of taking her to dinner, he had sent her shopping with his credit card and told her to buy something pretty. When she'd returned, bags in hand, he'd urged her to get dressed while the guests secretly arrived. When he went to retrieve her for their "reservations," Raine had opened the door in a candy-apple-red minidress that clung to her every curve, accentuated her plump breasts, and ended with a slit at her lush hip. The sight had punched Hammer in the gut.

He could no longer deny that she'd become a woman. Or that he'd been fighting his desire for more than a while.

But the worst had been her blue eyes shining with hero worship and a plea for his approval. No avoiding the fact she ached for him to want her. To love her.

He'd been so fucking tempted to give in.

And he'd been a tortured bastard ever since.

Not much had changed…until today.

Standing, Macen exhaled with a heavy sigh. He needed a shower and to ditch his blood-splattered clothes. Then—somehow—he had to have a calm discussion with Raine, despite the thousand-pound weight that lay on his heart.

After a hot shower and a self-pep talk, Hammer pushed down his feelings as he trudged down the hall toward the kitchen. He stood in the doorway, watching Raine stir batter in a bowl. She swayed with each stroke of the spoon, and he couldn't not look at her pert ass…the one Zak had probably cupped in his hands as he'd tunneled inside her. Hammer closed his eyes and counted to ten, silently chiding himself for reigniting his temper.

"It smells delicious as always, precious," he called out to her.

Raine jumped and dropped the metal bowl on the counter with a little yelp. "Macen."

Her breathless tone rolled over him. Was that the same tone she'd cried out with when Zak had shoved his dick through her hymen? He gritted his teeth.

She put a hand to her chest. "You scared me to death."

"Sorry. Are you all right?"

"Fine." She didn't meet his gaze. "Did you have a good trip?"

"The usual. I'd rather not talk about it."

"You didn't want to last time, either." She anchored a hand on her hip. "Why do you go every year?"

"That's not what we need to talk about, and you know it."

"Don't," she implored. "You just got home. Why don't you sit and relax? You can pilfer some of my goodies while I slide in another batch."

When she gestured nervously to the batter, Hammer raised a brow. "Rumor has it, Zak already pilfered your goodies."

He struggled to keep the savagery from his tone.

Raine tensed. Guilt crawled across her face. But in typical Raine style, the defiant minx banked her expression and lifted her chin to meet him head on.

"It doesn't matter."

"It should."

"It's my body to give away and he wanted it." She gave him a meaningless shrug he didn't believe.

"When I first took you in, I told you all the men here, especially the Doms, were off-limits, remember?"

"I was a minor then, Macen. I'm an adult now. Maybe you hadn't noticed."

How could he not? She had all the trappings of womanhood—a saucy attitude and curves for days—yet in so many ways she was still a girl. "Legally, yes. But were you really ready for what happened?"

"It's done. I'm fine," she insisted.

He saw right through her. The slump of her shoulders and the way she hugged herself said she regretted it like hell.

"What made you choose Zak? Or did you give it any thought at all?" he snapped, then wished he hadn't.

She bristled, and he realized that he'd hit a nerve. A selfish part of him wanted Raine to suffer right alongside him. But her haunted eyes told him she already was. If he chastised her again, she would only put distance between them. That was probably for the best…but it would kill him.

He stifled the urge to bring her closer. No, to strip her naked, run his tongue over every inch of her satiny flesh, and show her in no uncertain terms that she was his. But he couldn't. He'd only hurt her more because Hammer knew that, unlike Zak, he had the power to crush her. And he'd already abused a woman's trust once. He lived with the scars of that tragedy every day.

"Someone wanted me, Macen." She sounded tired suddenly. "Someone attractive who made me laugh. He thought I was pretty. I thought he was hot." She waved him away. "It doesn't even matter. I don't grill you about all the women you fuck. Take your muffins and leave."

Damn. She'd scored a direct hit.

"Did he hurt you?"

His concerned whisper disarmed her, and tears filled Raine's eyes. "No."

"Did he wear a condom?"

"Yes." She barely managed to get the word out as she dropped her head. Tears dripped to the floor. Seeing her so broken tore his heart in two.

Without a word, Hammer pulled her to his chest, then wrapped her in his arms. Raine melted into him and fell completely apart.

Swallowing his eviscerating regret, he focused on what she needed. Sighing, he closed his eyes and rested his chin on the top of her head, holding her close.

"Shh, don't cry, precious. It's all right." He dropped a chaste kiss on her forehead.

It would be…but things had changed between them irrevocably. The knowledge that she was no longer an innocent to be sheltered at all costs lay between them. Hammer had to keep reminding himself that her lack of virginity didn't make a fucking difference. She still wasn't ready to handle his needs.

After several solemn minutes, Raine inched back, eyes swollen, cheeks mottled. "I'm sorry. I got your shirt wet."

"It's nothing," Hammer assured. Cupping her chin, he forced her gaze to his. "Why don't you go back to your room and take a nice, long bath?"

"I need to slide in this last batch of muffins for you," she whispered, as if unsure her peace offering was enough.

"I'll take care of them."

"You? Cook?" She tried to laugh but choked on a residual sob.

Hammer flashed her a mock scowl. As their gentle teasing warmed his heart, she sent him a watery smile. Relief slithered through him. Whatever happened next, she was the same Raine. Now he had to suck up the disappointment that she'd given Zak what he'd wanted so badly.

After she slid the muffins in the oven and set the timer, Hammer promised he would remove them once they finished baking.

"You're sure you got this?" She set the fire extinguisher on the counter. "I'm leaving this here. You know, just in case."

"Get out of here. Go take your bath."

As Raine exited, Hammer rolled the tension from his shoulders. Glaring at the clock, he mentally counted off the minutes until he could extract the muffins, lock himself inside his office, and drown his disappointment in a bottle of Patrón. Sure, that would get him through tonight. But what would happen when she tempted him again? Worse, how would he survive if she ever truly fell in love with someone else?

LIAM

Nearly five years later
August 31
New York

"So now that we've left Graffiti, I have to ask... Who are you and what have you done with my friend?"

Liam O'Neill watched as his pal, Seth Cooper, skated a hand across the laminated table at this dive of a twenty-four-hour diner and reached for his sandwich. Liam yanked his plate away. "What does that mean? And you've got your own meal. Keep your hands off my food."

"What did you say?" Seth was faster, snagging up half of his sandwich and shoving it in his mouth with a smirk. His cheeks bulged as he all but inhaled it.

"Choke, you bastard." Liam shook his head with a laugh. "It would serve you bloody right. And if you touch the other half, you'll lose a hand."

"Spoilsport." He mumbled around the ham and cheese. "Now, seriously. What's going on?"

"Nothing." Seth taking his food was one thing, but dissecting him? Hell no.

"Yeah? That scene you did tonight with Dominique was awfully...intense."

Liam raised a brow. "Meaning?"

"I watched you work her over with that single-tail. It isn't your usual, man. At least not until recently."

"Are you accusing me of sceneing when I'm not in the right frame of mind?"

"Nope. I'm accusing you of having unresolved feelings about your divorce."

Liam glared. "Are you really going *there*? We could talk about unresolved feelings all night. You first."

"I've been working through that shit for a long time, and you know it. So stop deflecting and talk to me. I'm your friend."

"You are, so stop acting like my shrink. It's been nearly a year. I'm fine." Well, mostly. "So stop worrying. I simply gave Dominique what she said she needed."

Seth swallowed down the last of his bite and wiped his mouth with a napkin. "I know she's a masochist, but you're no sadist. If the need to give pain was in your psyche, you would have been dishing it out for years. Instead, it's like you flipped a switch and went from melting subs with pleasure to whipping them into blissful agony. The change in your MO has me worried, man."

With a scowl, Liam devoured the remaining half of his sandwich, chasing it down with a swig of beer and using the moment to craft his words. "I discovered I'm good with a whip. Why does that require explanation? After all, I seem to recall you're decent with one yourself."

"How about I give you my theory?" Seth put in. "When you found your ex-wife in bed with two guys—"

"Fuck you."

"Fuck you, too," the brash New Yorker tossed back. "We can trade fucks all night, but I'd rather you think about what I've said."

"Gwyneth has nothing to do with what happened at the club tonight."

"Bullshit."

"She doesn't," Liam growled. "There's nothing wrong. People change."

The last thing he wanted to do was rehash everything weighing on him. Most days, he felt like the cocky Irishman he'd once been. Other days… Well, didn't everyone deal with anger, frustration, and regret from time to time? Admittedly, he had more of that than he used to, but he was doing all right.

Maybe, but if Seth had noticed his means of coping, maybe he'd ventured too far to the "dark side."

"Look, I'm choosing subs who seek pain because it's filling a need in me, too. Everyone is happy."

Seth scoffed. "You're not."

"I'm enjoying giving a woman her pleasure of choice. If you can't say the same, maybe we should review the birds and the bees."

"Oh, now you're a fucking comedian?" Downing the last of his beer, Seth set his mug on the table. "Can it. Have you seen your ex since that benefit you were forced to attend with her last fall?"

"No, thank god. I haven't even heard from her since she moved back to London." He pushed his plate away. "Can we not talk about her? It makes me queasy."

"I believe that," Seth shot back. "Look, there's nothing wrong with being righteously pissed off about what that bitch did to you. Maybe what you need is time to chill. Why not take a vacation? A change of scenery might do you good. Hey, maybe you should go see Hammer, work over some of his subs. You say he talks about how great Los Angeles is. I'm pretty sure it's going to fall into the ocean someday… but you should enjoy it until then."

Liam grinned. "I've never seen a grown man so afraid of an earthquake."

"Yeah, make fun, asshole. I like my ground stable, thank you." Seth glowered. "Seriously, visit Hammer. The weather here will turn cold in a month or two. You could take in the warmth and new sights out west. Relax. Get away from all the reminders."

The notion of leaving everything behind for a while was tempting, and Seth made it sound so easy.

"I don't know…" Liam said to the big blond Dom.

"Sure you do. You can run your business from most anywhere. I'll stop by your brownstone every so often to make sure it's still standing. And I can take care of your casuals while you're gone."

Liam sat back, considering. He had this feeling, a tingling at the back of his neck, that he should listen.

"Maybe I'll go for a wee spell." Since Hammer had asked him to visit more than once, he shouldn't mind the company. "I've not seen him since he came for his annual visit last November." And Macen had seemed off then. The last few years, actually. Liam worried that, while he'd been dealing with his own shit, he'd let the man's troubling aloofness fester. "Maybe while I'm there, I'll get up to that lodge I inherited and check on the place."

"Absolutely. And while you're in Cali, get a suntan for me."

"Thanks." He clapped Seth on the shoulder. "I just might."

They paid their tabs and exited the booth. Liam hadn't taken two steps before his mobile rang. He slipped it free from his pocket and glanced at the screen, then scowled over his shoulder at Seth. "Jesus bloody Christ. Why is my mum calling in the middle of the night?"

Seth laughed. "She's so uncanny it's scary. You know that, right?"

Did he ever…

Striding out the door, he tapped the screen to accept her call. He'd been avoiding Bryn O'Neill for weeks because he'd suspected she intended to dispense her brand of sage advice. But he could probably use it now...even if she wouldn't make it easy to understand. "Hi, Mum."

"Hello yourself." Her sweet Irish lilt traversed the three thousand odd miles between them as clearly as if she stood before him. "'Bout time you answered. Anyone would think I pester my own son senseless just for a chat."

"You don't. I'm sorry."

"Nothin' to be sorry about. I only call because I care. We all do."

Liam rubbed at the back of his neck and tried not to sigh aloud. "I know. Thanks for that. I'm fine."

She scoffed. "If you were, I'd not be ringing you in the middle of the night and you'd not still be in limbo. Seth is right, son. Head west. Go see Hammer. It's time."

He didn't bother to ask how she knew about his conversation all the way from Ireland. "Mum..."

"Your future—"

"Is something I'll figure out in good time." He sighed.

"Aye, you will," she agreed. "So let me remind you that sublime happiness can be had, but not until you take a step in the right direction."

He shook his head in frustration. "You always speak in riddles. What does that mean?"

She laughed, and the sound reminded him of home. "Take that first step and you'll find out. If you do, you'll start a whole new adventure." And she sounded positively giddy. "Now I've got to run. Love you. Your father and the rest of the brood send their love, too. Bye, son."

"Give my love back to them. Bye, Mum."

Since his oddly wise mother often seemed to know precisely what he needed, Liam took her advice. The following week, he stepped off a plane at LAX and headed down to baggage claim to find Macen Hammerman waiting with a smile too stilted to be real.

Whatever had bothered Hammer during his annual visits to New York troubled him even more here. Liam was determined to get to the bottom of it.

They gave each other a brotherly beating on the back. Despite Hammer's reserve, Liam still felt the bond they shared, once deeper than best friends. It was good to be standing next to the man somewhere other than a cold graveside. Liam suspected he'd done right in coming here.

Hammer looked tanned, healthy, and sophisticated in his smart suit and tie—like a walking advert for sex. The smile lines around his eyes only added to the man's allure, if the admiring stares he drew were any indication.

They claimed Liam's luggage, climbed into Hammer's Audi, and left, enveloped by the golden California sun. He could get used to that...

"Thanks for coming to get me. I could have rented a car and driven out to you," Liam said as Hammer wound his way south through the traffic and headed for Shadows.

"Fuck that. Of course I'm going to pick you up. The rental company will deliver your car tomorrow." Hammer zipped around a slow-moving van and powered ahead. "Your room at the club is ready and waiting. Any particular reason you decided to visit now? Don't get me wrong; I'm glad you're here. Just curious."

"I only see you in November, and it's always a quick trip. Your visits the last few years have been even shorter. I've missed your ugly mug. Besides, I'd like some California sun before the New York winter sets in. Good enough?"

Hammer nodded. "We've got plenty of sunshine and warmth."

"Excellent. How's the club going?"

"It's always packed. Great members. You'll like them."

"Has any special sub caught your eye?"

After a pause, Hammer sent him a tight smile. "You know me, man. I do what I can to help them all."

Liam laughed. "It's a hard life, mate, but someone's gotta live it."

"Damn straight." Hammer gave him a fist bump. After a minute of quiet, he turned a sober gaze Liam's way. "You didn't want to talk much about it when I saw you last fall, but was it a particularly nasty divorce? I can't imagine that she-devil taking her claws out of your hide without first scratching every penny out of you."

"She was about as cold and calculating as you suspected. Suffice it to say I'm done with commitment. Once was definitely enough. And I'm assuming there will be plenty of desirable distractions at Shadows?"

"Absolutely. You'll like Monica. Gorgeous, eager to please. Right up your alley. And then there's Eden…"

As they made their way to the club, Liam listened with half an ear, wondering who was responsible for Hammer's aloofness. It likely wasn't either of them.

When they arrived, Shadows was tucked discreetly into an industrial part of town, blending in with its neighbors, appearing nondescript. No one driving by would pay the building any mind. But once through the private entrance, the place was everything Liam had expected and more. Clearly, Macen had spared no expense.

As the man showed Liam around his pride and joy, he was thrilled to see Hammer's visions in brick and mortar now fully operational. Thankfully, his friend had put tragedy behind him and found some contentment on the West Coast.

Liam wondered if he might find the same for himself.

"This is bloody brilliant, Macen. It's exactly as you envisioned when we discussed the possibilities over a dram or two in New York years ago."

Hammer held a door open for Liam that led from the dungeon. "Some things had to be adjusted slightly for practicality and purpose. But overall, it came together exactly the way I wanted."

"It's a lot bigger than I thought it would be. Certainly bigger than Graffiti."

"The building had good bones to start with, which allowed me to turn many of the original offices into private rooms for the members. That's where we are now." Hammer gestured to a stairway as they walked the corridor. "Security is tucked neatly between here and the dungeon. All the public places and playrooms, except for my suite, are under surveillance. And down here is the kitchen."

Macen traversed a long hall, then stepped aside and held one of the double doors open to allow Liam through. *Kitchen* was an understatement. As with every other part of Shadows, it was modern, well laid out, functional, clean, and bright. Any chef would be pleased with such a space.

But the decor wasn't what caught Liam's eye. No, it was the raven-haired woman with the alluring heart-shaped ass who washed dishes at the sink.

As Macen sidled up beside him, she turned to them, blinking and startled.

Instant lust zapped Liam as if he'd been punched in the chest. She was petite. Intense blue eyes. Lush mouth. Painfully young.

When she smiled in welcome, his desire—among other things—swelled. Her dazzling warmth burned him. She was a gorgeous, wee thing.

Fuck, how soon could he talk her into bed? She'd be a great balm to help him forget his divorce…

Her gaze zeroed in on Hammer, her expression filled with worship. "Macen, you're back."

Liam froze. His old friend only let those closest to him call him by his first name, and never in that breathy tone.

Curious now, he turned to observe Hammer, stunned to see his mate stare at the brunette with hunger. The tension between them bubbled thick.

Who was she? Clearly not just another female in a long, long line of them.

Was she the cause of Macen's disquiet?

He hadn't taken this girl to bed yet; Liam would bet his life on that. But it was only a matter of time.

He smothered his disappointment.

Hammer finally ended the awkward silence. "I didn't expect to find you here."

"You know me." She shrugged. "Since I've taken care of the payables and the restocking, I came here to relax."

Hammer smiled—the first genuine one Liam had seen on his face in years. "As always."

His mate had learned this beauty's habits. Just how well did he know her?

"Who's this, then?" Liam asked.

"Uh…yeah." Hammer turned grim as he shuffled closer to her. "Precious, meet one of my oldest, dearest friends, Liam O'Neill. He's just arrived from New York."

Hammer towered over the woman. Hell, they both did.

Liam stepped forward, hand outstretched. "Hello, Precious." Though that must be her club name, it fit her. "Lovely to meet—"

"No," Hammer bit out. "Her name isn't precious."

"It's Raine." With a hint of a laugh, she sent him a long stare from under her thick lashes. "Nice to meet you."

In all the years he'd known Hammer, Liam had only once ever heard the man call a sub anything other than *girl*. The fact he called this one *precious* shouted Raine's importance.

The relationship must be developing. Maybe that's why Hammer hadn't mentioned it yet. But even a blind man could see they were gone for each other. The air between them sizzled and hummed.

Liam arched a brow in his friend's direction.

Macen didn't meet his gaze, merely clapped him on the back. "Why don't I show you to your room?"

"Wait," Raine called. "I'm starting dinner. Any preferences?"

The domestic question, spoken as if she'd uttered these very words a thousand times, stunned Liam. If they were a couple, why hadn't he heard about it?

"Don't bother. Since it's Liam's first night here, I'm going to take him out. We'll be back before the club is in full swing. Can you make sure everything is ready?"

Her shoulders drooped with disappointment, but she nodded. "Of course."

"Thanks." As if he couldn't get away fast enough, Macen turned and grabbed his arm. "Your room is this way. Let's drop your luggage and go."

Liam wanted to keep observing Hammer with his…what? Raine's ring finger was bare, but she was definitely someone to him. Girlfriend? Sub? Significant other? "I don't mind staying in, mate, if you and Raine already have plans. Or we could bring her with us."

"Oh, I-I wouldn't want to intrude…" she demurred.

But she did—badly.

Hammer scowled. "It would be better if you stayed—"

"Nonsense," Liam cut in. "I'd love to have you join us, lass."

"Really?" She might have said the words to Liam…but she looked at Hammer with pleading eyes. "I already have the dungeon set up for tonight."

Hammer sighed. "Fine. We'll go out."

Liam frowned. If Macen cared about Raine—and he had no doubt the man did—why the reticence? Why the cold shoulder?

A huge smile lit her face. "Okay. Should I change?"

She made a vague gesture to her oversized T-shirt and short shorts, which exposed her sleek thighs. Liam did his best not to gawk at her.

And Macen couldn't quite bank the heat in his stare. "Quickly. Wear your yellow dress. Cream-colored heels. Hair up."

"All right. I'll be ready in five." Raine shouldered her way past them and raced down the hall.

Hammer watched her go as if he couldn't stand not to look at her.

Liam turned to his friend. "So…you and Raine. How long has this been going on? She's a beauty and obviously besotted with you."

Hammer gave a sharp jerk of his head. "She's my employee. There's nothing going on."

The lie rolled so smoothly off Hammer's tongue. Anyone who didn't know the man well might believe him. Liam wasn't fooled. His old pal wasn't merely being dishonest with him; he was lying to himself.

Liam had seen Hammer during some of the most intimate moments of his life. Granted, in the past. But Macen would never look at Raine with such longing if he wasn't at least half in love with her. Clearly, he hadn't yet acted on his feelings.

"So she's not your sub?"

"Raine isn't a sub at all."

Was Hammer blind? Liam had barely met the girl two minutes ago, and he knew better.

"And she's off-limits to everyone," Hammer added.

"Is that so?"

"Yes."

"Even you?"

"Especially me." Macen peeked around the corner, into the hall. The coast must have been clear, but he still lowered his voice. "I took her in as a runaway. She's had a rough life, and she's got a fragile heart. I do my best to give her the roof, job, and encouragement she needs."

Runaway? The woman was admittedly young, but she looked in her early twenties. Why would Hammer imply she was some sort of rebellious teenager who'd suddenly left home to run wild?

"You took her in off the streets? That's kind of you."

Hammer relaxed, as if this was a topic he could warm to. "She had nowhere else to go."

"How did you two meet?"

His expression turned grim. "I found her injured and hiding behind the dumpster in the alley out back one night."

He could hardly imagine the vibrant siren he'd seen inhabiting Hammer's kitchen huddling behind the rubbish. His mate had obviously done well as her protector, but Liam had no doubt Hammer ached to be her lover. Yet his friend was denying himself. He knew why—and Hammer's guilt would serve neither of them.

Liam also knew now why his pal had been reluctant to welcome him once he'd finally agreed to visit.

"Poor thing," he muttered. "She must have had a time of it."

"You have no idea." Empathy and pain crossed Macen's face, along with concern. Longing. Love.

Bloody Christ.

"How long has she been living here with you?"

Before Hammer could reply, Raine bustled around the corner, wearing a sunny summer dress with wide straps that hugged her unexpectedly lush breasts, accentuating them with a bow beneath. A pair of off-white strappy heels gave her a few inches of height. Red gloss slicked her lips, making her look somehow vampy and innocent at once. She'd piled her inky hair into an artless bun at her crown.

Interest stirred again, but Liam did his best to extinguish it. When he turned to Hammer, however, he found the man sucking in his breath and staring as if he'd rarely seen anything so beautiful.

Raine curled her arms around her middle self-consciously. "Do I look okay?"

"Absolutely lovely." Liam smiled her way.

Macen merely cleared his throat. "Fine. I'll drive."

When he brushed his way past Raine and hightailed it out of the kitchen, Liam watched disappointment crush her. He wanted to rail at Hammer. How could the man hurt her so thoughtlessly?

"Shall we?" He gestured toward the door.

She pasted on a stilted smile. "Thanks."

When she made for the door, he caught an eyeful of her nearly bare back. Other than a bow at her nape and a narrow strip of fabric across her shoulder blades, nothing impeded his greedy stare from touching all her glowing pale skin. Liam swallowed back lust.

Out of habit, he settled his palm at the small of her back. Instantly, he wished he hadn't. Soft. Supple. So sweet. Even her musky lily scent teased the devil out of his nose.

Though the ride to the restaurant wasn't long, it felt endless and uncomfortable. Hammer remained stubbornly mute and surly, turning up the volume on the radio a bit too loud to allow conversation. Liam stared at the traffic, noting the number of times the man reached down to adjust his fly. Unfortunately, Hammer wasn't the only one. Raine's scent wafted through the vehicle. Behind him, Liam swore the girl's breath caressed his skin. He could *feel* her there, so close.

But so far out of reach...

Finally, they arrived at a steakhouse on the ocean. As they were shown to a table directly over the beach, Liam marveled at the view. Despite the fact everything so far had been unexpected and uncomfortable, he was glad he'd come to California. At least he finally knew why Hammer's behavior had been so off lately.

"Wow." Raine's eyes widened and danced as she took in the sight of the sea rolling in a few dozen yards from their table. "Look at that. I've never been to a place this nice."

Vague guilt twisted Hammer's mouth. He hid it behind his menu until the cocktail waitress took their drink order.

Raine enjoyed a white wine while he and Hammer sipped beers. They ordered, appetizers came, and alcohol flowed. Finally, so did the conversation. Soon, they all started laughing about a female patron with her freshly groomed poodle in a Vuitton carrier. Her orange spray tan, collagen-overdosed lips, and designer clothes made her look like an Instagram-ready Oompa Loompa.

After fine steaks, Raine took a picture of him and Hammer smiling and clinking beer mugs.

In that moment, he had no doubt he'd come to the right place at the right time for the right reason.

Before dessert and coffee arrived, Hammer excused himself for the restroom.

Liam seized his moments alone with Raine. "So tell me about you. When did you meet Hammer?"

"About six years ago. He's probably told you the story about how he took me in." Her gaze flitted away in embarrassment before she pasted on a bright, fake smile. "But things are much better now. He's been really kind to me."

Six fucking years?

Hammer had never—not once—mentioned Raine in all that time. He'd never even hinted the girl existed.

How the bloody hell had Macen managed to keep his hands off of her for so long? Since Hammer was neither blind nor stupid, he must know how Raine felt about him.

"You were a teenager then?" Liam asked.

"Seventeen."

"It must have been a dreadful time," Liam murmured softly, then fished for more information. "How long have you been Hammer's girlfriend?"

She looked startled. "No. Oh, no. We're not..." She blushed. "We've never...um. No."

As he'd suspected.

Liam sat back in his seat and resisted the urge to shake his head. How long did Hammer expect to hoard her? A glance around the swanky restaurant proved he wasn't the only man intrigued. Easily ten others stared at Raine with more than passing interest. She didn't seem to notice even one, but rather appeared suddenly fascinated by the napkin in her lap.

"So he's not your Dom, either?"

"No." A little frown creased her face.

A wealth of meaning—and longing—lay in that expression.

God, she had a soft innocence, the sort that drove a man to protect and corrupt her at once. Liam definitely wouldn't hate giving it a try.

But his friend needed her far more.

"Does Hammer already have a collared sub, then?"

She looked away, obviously uncomfortable with the subject. "I think that's a better question for him."

"I haven't seen much of the man since he left New York. After he moved here, I worried about him, and I'm hoping you can help. Does he seem happy?"

Raine shrugged uneasily. "I don't know much about his personal life. In fact, you're the first of his friends outside the club I've met. It seems like you two might be close, but he's never said anything."

Ever? In six years? "So he's never mentioned me, his best friend?"

She shook her head. "Sorry. No."

"He's never mentioned you, either, lass."

She sipped her wine, trying not to look crestfallen. "That's no surprise. I'm no one to him."

Liam barely managed not to gape. How the devil had Hammer convinced her of that whopper? Probably through his tomcatting and seeming indifference. *Stupid bugger…*

"So…what brings you here from New York?"

A not-so-subtle change of subject.

Hammer reentering the dining room saved Liam from answering her. Instantly, the man's stare lasered in on Raine, as if reassuring himself that she was unharmed and untouched. Still his, despite the fact he'd never taken her for his own.

That had to change.

Hammer needed to admit his feelings for Raine, and Liam would happily assist, especially if it gave him a necessary diversion from his own problems. All he had to do was tuck away his inconvenient interest in the girl and persuade his old mate to claim her.

Until today, Liam would never have called Hammer a jealous man. About Raine, though? Macen was both shockingly protective and possessive. Liam had every intention of using that against his old friend, until Hammer was forced to take the girl as his own—or lose her to another Dominant all too happy to treat her right.

Like him.

Watching them through the rest of dinner, Liam hid a smile and began to form a plan…

The End

Ready to see what happens when Liam enacts his plan? Start the epic, dark romance journey with Raine, Hammer, and Liam in The Betrayal now!

Two friends. One woman. Let the games begin...

The Broken

THE UNBROKEN SERIES: RAINE FALLING PREQUEL

The Betrayal

THE UNBROKEN SERIES: RAINE FALLING ONE

TWO FRIENDS. ONE WOMAN.
LET THE GAMES BEGIN...

NEW YORK TIMES BESTSELLING AUTHOR
Shayla Black

USA TODAY BESTSELLING AUTHOR
Jenna Jacob

ABOUT *THE BETRAYAL*

Two friends. One woman. Let the games begin...

Raine Kendall has been in love with her boss, Macen Hammerman, for years. Determined to make him notice her, she pours out her heart and offers him her body—only to be crushingly rejected. When his very sexy best friend, Liam O'Neill, sees Hammer refuse to act on his obvious feelings for her, he plots to rouse his pal's possessive instincts by making Raine a proposition too tempting to refuse. He never imagines he'll fall for her himself.

Hammer has buried his lust for Raine for years. After rescuing the runaway from an alley behind his exclusive club, he's come to crave her. But tragedy has proven he'll never be the man she needs, so he protects her while keeping his distance. Then Liam's scheme to make Raine his own blindsides Hammer. He isn't ready to give the feisty beauty over to his friend. But can he heal from his past enough to fight for her? Or will he lose Raine if she gives herself—heart, body, and soul—to Liam?

Chapter One

Early November

Raine Kendall knew it was going to be a terrible day when she managed to have her heart broken before noon.

Up and ready for work an hour early, she strode down the hall and lingered outside the boss's office, juggling a mug of steaming coffee in one hand and a plate with her fresh-baked apple muffins in the other. Macen Hammerman, the owner and Alpha Dom of the private BDSM club, Shadows, wasn't roaming the dungeon with a devilish smile, barking orders at her, or staring into her soul with those intense hazel eyes. His door was closed.

She paced. Should she knock and see if he'd awakened yet or wait until he appeared? Raine gnawed her lip in indecision.

Then the door opened. Her head snapped up, a warm smile in place. But it wasn't Hammer who emerged. Instead, a woman stood there, looking like everything Raine wasn't: tall, blonde, willowy. And totally satisfied. The smile curling her swollen lips belonged to a woman contented by a string of multiple orgasms given by a very capable partner. Like Hammer. Besides his surname and the fact that his word was law around here, Raine had heard the other subs had given him that nickname for a reason.

"You're blocking the door," Marlie said with an annoyed huff.

Raine scrambled back as the other woman clutched her black Chanel bag and sauntered closer, wearing a gorgeous pair of Pradas that made her sinful legs look even longer. When had she started spending the night?

Behind Marlie, Hammer appeared in the doorway, his rugged face flushed. He'd thrown his dress shirt over one brawny arm, his thick biceps bunching as he zipped his pants. His salt-and-pepper hair was mussed, as if Marlie had run her fingers through it repeatedly. His lips were red as well. Raine had no doubt he'd kissed the other woman with a hard passion that had made her toes curl. His wide shoulders hung loose, his lean, muscled body fluid. Relaxed. Sated.

As Hammer looked up, Raine's gaze locked with his. He stiffened. Regret flashed over his face before he quickly banked it.

Pain made her chest implode. The muffins and the coffee fell from her numb fingers to clatter at his feet. Jealousy stabbed her, along with a betrayal she had no right to feel. The cherry on top of the whole shit sundae was the pity in his eyes.

Hammer wasn't hers. He hadn't been for a single day of the entire six years she'd lived and worked at Shadows. He never would be. But she wanted him to be. Desperately.

Raine couldn't look at him now, so she bent and scooped at the soggy remains of Hammer's breakfast littering the marble tiles, feeling as if she had disintegrated, much like the mess she now cleaned.

Throat tight, she swallowed. Why didn't the damn floor open up and swallow her whole? Why did she keep humiliating herself over this man? He'd shown her in every way possible that he didn't want her. He was probably wondering if he was going to have to learn Greek or Klingon to make her understand.

"Clumsy girl." Marlie rolled her eyes as she stepped over Raine and out of Hammer's office and private bedroom, into the dungeon's corridor.

"Marlie," Hammer snapped. "Your attitude is unbecoming for a proper submissive. I've trained you better. Apologize to Raine this instant."

His stern voice never failed to melt and make Raine anxious to please. Hearing it directed at the other woman crushed her even more.

Marlie murmured a breathy, "Yes, lover. I mean, Sir. Sorry about that, Rai-Rai."

Raine almost retched on the bitch's thousand dollar crystal-studded stilettos. Instead, she looked up to see the leggy blonde blow an air kiss at Hammer before striding away. Raine jerked her gaze down again and focused on cleaning up.

What did Hammer see in that bitch? Well, besides a tall, model-thin figure, a perfect tanning-booth glow, and blonde tresses that spiraled artlessly toward her pert ass. Raine blew back a strand of her straight raven hair, stared at her pale hands with their short, capable nails, and wanted to cry.

Hammer crouched beside her. "Raine? Let me get you a towel, precious."

"Thank you." Her voice sounded fragile, like glass about to shatter.

He paused briefly before turning away to his private bathroom. Once he'd gone, she choked back a sob, but couldn't stop a scalding tear from dripping down her cheek and onto the floor.

God, how pitiful was she? He'd never love her. She had to pull it together before she made an even bigger fool of herself. While she was at it, she also had to face a few facts. Hammer had submissives sinking to their knees before him, eager to serve his every whim. He was hardly a monk; she knew Marlie wasn't the first woman to leave his bedroom with that satisfied glow. Sadly, she wouldn't be the last.

But Raine had never been so close to Hammer shirtless, looking so vital and strong, so disheveled and sexual and...

She had to get out of here.

He returned with a towel and bent to help her. Gathering up the pieces of the shattered coffee mug, she cupped the china in her hands, praying he was too busy helping her to notice her tears.

"Sorry I'm so clumsy."

"You're not clumsy. Accidents happen." He mopped at the mess with the towel.

Accident? They both knew it hadn't been. But he just had to be kind, didn't he? He couldn't be a complete douche bag and give her an easy way to hate him.

"I'll take this to the kitchen and throw it away."

"Stay," he commanded. "Give me the china, precious. I'll take care of it."

Raine hesitated. How badly she wanted to heed that powerful voice. But Hammer was her boss, not her Dom. He didn't want her devotion.

On shaking legs, she stood. "I've got it."

Eager to be gone, Raine turned away. Holding back her tears was becoming hopeless. What the hell could she say to him? *I'm in love with you, Macen. Please pick me!* God, that sounded stupid—and impossible. The man who'd always said that monogamy gave him hives, who never shared his inner thoughts with anyone, who was smart and sophisticated… Yeah, he would never desire the runaway he'd plucked from an alley, huddled beside a dumpster, years ago. He saw her as a little sister, so she needed to give up her hope of being his lover. Dry her tears. Move on.

But how the hell did she make her heart stop wanting him?

Hammer grabbed her arm and turned her to face him again, frowning. "Raine… Thank you for the breakfast, precious. I'm always proud when I see the desire in your heart to serve."

"Well, I tried, but it looks like Marlie already served you in the ways that count, so I'll take my pesky self, along with the china, and leave." She didn't wait for his reply, but jerked her arm free and hustled for the exit.

Thank god Hammer didn't respond. Ten seconds, then she'd be out of this hallway. She could hide in the kitchen and fall apart privately. But she wouldn't wait that long to call herself twenty kinds of idiot. *Stupid, stupid, stupid.* When was she going to learn?

Hammer hadn't noticed her when she'd turned eighteen. Twenty-one hadn't registered with him, either. For some reason, she'd really hoped twenty-three would wrap its hands around his throat this past summer and choke hard until he saw that she was no longer that lost little homeless girl he'd rescued years ago. But no. She would always lack sophistication and that intangible something that came with world travel and fucking a different person every day. She'd never be what he wanted.

Raine tightened her fingers. The shards of china cut into her skin until she bled. Who cared? As red seeped over the white porcelain, she forced down an internal scream and kept walking.

She was relieved Hammer could no longer see her face.

While she made her way down the hall, a shadow emerged from one of the open doorways. She glanced up to see Liam O'Neill, Hammer's Irish friend who'd come from New York, darkening the portal. His stare zeroed in on her, his expression somewhere between concern and pity. Urbane and gorgeous—and immediately popular with the subs when he'd arrived a couple of months ago—he watched her with a shrewd, all-seeing gaze that she'd come to know well. There was no way he wouldn't see her tears.

Damn it.

He opened his mouth to speak, but Raine couldn't deal with anymore of his questions about Hammer now, or worse, his compassion.

"Excuse me." She brushed past him and ran for the kitchen.

H ammer begrudgingly allowed Raine to walk away. As much as he wanted to comfort her, he let the girl leave with her dignity.

But goddamnit, Raine wore every emotion on her face. He'd always liked that he could read her so easily—until now. The devastation in her tearful blue eyes dropped him like a sound kick to the balls. The bite of her caustic quip didn't wound nearly as much as the remorse flooding his veins.

He'd always tried to shield her from his sexual exploits with other subs because he'd feared she would be crushed. Hammer hated to be proven right.

Marlie's gloating hadn't helped. The superficial shrew played at being submissive because she liked a little bondage with her sex. But as a Dominant and owner of one of the most successful BDSM clubs on the West Coast, he had a responsibility to train the submissives. That included punishing and rewarding them for their actions, be it beneath his hand or beneath his body. That responsibility had no bearing on his feelings for Raine. He'd much rather have spent last night giving her all the pleasure he'd dreamed of, in every way he'd imagined giving it. Unfortunately, if he ever touched her—even once—he'd seize her mouth and claim it. His greedy hands would tear at her clothes until he could stroke her soft body and suck her nipples raw. When she panted and begged, he'd thrust his rigid cock unmercifully into her swollen cunt until she threw back her head and screamed his name.

Hammer swallowed a thick knot of lust and raked a hand through his hair. He couldn't do any of those things. But he could save Raine from himself. He might be what she wanted, but she knew nothing of the demons lurking inside him that ensured he'd never be what she needed. So he let her believe he saw her as a child, not a sexy woman who'd grown into the focus of a neverending lust he couldn't slake.

If she managed to break his self-control, god help her. He'd be the worst fucking mistake of her life.

He'd destroy her.

As Raine retreated, Liam stepped from his private room, watching her delicate figure with a speculative stare. He had no idea what was running through his friend's mind. But even though she'd dismissed Liam and walked on, jealousy whacked Hammer in the face like a two by four.

The moment she rounded the corner, Liam turned to him with a disapproving frown. He wore a lot of those lately.

"If you're worried about Raine, don't be," Hammer insisted. "She might look upset, but it's for the best."

Liam approached him, that crafty mind of his obviously working. "Best for who, mate? You're tying yourself up in knots over that wee lass. I've watched you both since I came here, and even a blind man can see you have feelings for one another. Why won't you act on them? You could have her any way you want, if you've a mind to."

"It's impossible, man. Corsets and stilettos aside, Raine is built for picket fences, babies, and minivans. You know Juliet slammed that door shut for me years ago. I'm not going near it again."

Compassion softened Liam's face. "Not another soul here knows you like I do. We've been through the mill together, you and I. How long are you going to let the past haunt you? Put it behind you, mate, or it will suck you dry. Believe me, I know. If I hadn't done my soul searching in the past year since my divorce, no doubt I'd still be a bleak bastard."

Liam was probably right, and Hammer had tried to come to terms with everything, but... "Well, I'm glad you got your shit together. You're a better man than me, I guess."

And damn, didn't he sound bitter?

"Bloody hell. Not better, just more determined to move on."

"Don't you think I've tried every way I can think of?" The impatient sweep of his hand mirrored his pissed-off mood. "Drinking it out of my system. Talking it out. Fucking it out. Nothing works."

"You haven't tried Raine. And don't tell me you don't want that girl. I see the way you protect her, the way you watch her. You crave her so badly, you can nearly taste her. But you deny yourself, as if you're paying penance for an act that wasn't your fault."

Liam just didn't understand.

"That's your way of looking at it."

His friend sighed, tapping an impatient hand on the side of his leg. "If you won't consider yourself, think of Raine. She pays the price for your distance, too. You're ripping her heart to shreds. No other Dom here will touch her for fear of your wrath. At least try to live up to your responsibility and give her what she needs."

Macen swallowed hard. "First, she'd have to finish growing up."

"She has. You just don't see it. I don't think you want to." Liam laid out the ugly truth. "But if you won't take her under your wing, you've got to let her go."

Hammer knew he'd been unfair to Raine, but release her to another man? Some asshole who might truly hurt her? God, Hammer already felt half dead—and that would finish him off.

"How about you stay the fuck out of this?"

"Not this time. Eight years is a long time to grieve." Liam patted his shoulder. "Why do you keep such a tight grip on your guilt?"

"So I don't make the same mistake twice."

"Juliet chose her path without even talking to you, mate. You couldn't have known."

"I should have. I knew everything else about her, down to the last miniscule detail." But nothing changed the fact that he hadn't known how Juliet felt until it was too late.

"I probably should have known, too. I spent a fair amount of time with her. But she didn't communicate with either of us. You can't take all the responsibility for her feelings. You couldn't read her mind. It's time for you to move on and find happiness."

"Yeah? You think Juliet would agree?" Hammer challenged.

"Your misery won't bring her back, but I think Raine could save *you*." Liam stared at him calmly, as if he wasn't dissecting his life with a few pointed words.

No way he would ever confess everything he felt for Raine. If he did, Liam would never stop pushing for the impossible.

Macen looked away. "It's too late to save me."

"That's crap! Stop burying yourself with Juliet. If you don't start thinking about your future, you're going to wind up cynical and alone."

"I think it's a bit late for that."

"Not yet. But you keep dipping your wick in every hole except the one you want, trying to drown your guilt and run from your feelings. Haven't you figured out, mate, that you can't? Raine cares enough to help you face your fears."

"No." *God, no.* Down that road lay disaster. Better to adore Raine from afar than to risk destroying her completely.

"So you just plan to keep fucking every skirt that swishes past, even though you're miserable. Even when Raine loves you? Brilliant. How do you think that makes *her* feel?"

Lousy. Wounded. Insecure. He was a fucking heel.

"Whose friend are you?" Hammer bristled as Liam held up a mirror to the broken pieces of himself he'd long avoided.

"Always yours, which is why I'm trying to bloody help you. Is she a virgin, then? Is that your problem?"

"No, she's not a goddamn virgin!" Hammer gritted his teeth. "She took care of that behind my back years ago."

"Do you doubt that she's submissive? Have you ever scened with her or let any other Dom give her a go?"

"Of course not! But fuck, certainly you can see it. You've watched Raine. She's a natural. She tries so hard to please."

"Well, then I see no reason not to give her what you both want, but if you're set on self-destruction, you should be fair. Sit her down and tell her that you're not interested. Let her find someone else to satisfy her."

The visual that went with Liam's words overloaded Hammer with fury. There wasn't a Dom in the place who wouldn't kill to have the beautiful girl spread across his bed, legs open, ecstasy softening her features. He'd been fending them off for years.

"She's not ready."

"Raine isn't…or you're not?" Liam raised a dark brow at him.

"You don't know her like I do. No other Dom would understand… She's impulsive and has volumes to learn about tempering her will. And her mouth. She has major trust issues, so the brat's claws will come out when she feels challenged. Anyone else we know would try to 'fix' her attitude with a red ass, and they'd fail utterly. I have to protect her. Yes, she's upset now, but she's strong willed. Trust me, *that* Raine will be back." Hammer shook his head, willing Liam to understand. "She hides behind bluster and sarcasm, but under it she's so fucking fragile. I worry someone else would break her."

"And you don't think you are? I mean no disrespect, mate, but if any other Dom was putting her through this emotional torture, you'd have kicked his ass by now."

Hammer would rather Liam had punched him in the jaw than flayed him with that truth.

"Who are you, Dr. Fucking Phil?" Hammer curled his hands into fists. "She's not wired for what I'd want. So drop it."

"I think you're bloody full of shit. You're protecting yourself because you're afraid that if you take even a taste of her, you'll get addicted and lose your heart. You're terrified she'll have the power to hurt you."

He hated that Liam knew him so well, but he wasn't about to admit that his friend was right. Instead, he clenched his jaw and glared. "I said that's enough."

"Listen, I've not gone back to New York because I won't leave when you're coming apart at the seams. Luckily, I can run my business from almost anywhere. I'll be here as long as you need me and I'll always listen." Liam's voice softened, his eyes holding more compassion than Hammer could stand.

He was the only Dom—the only friend—Hammer trusted, not only with his club and livelihood, but with his legacy. Liam didn't know it, but Hammer had named him the beneficiary of Shadows in the event of his death. There wasn't another person who understood the hell he'd been through or could advise him better.

Still, he couldn't fail to learn from Juliet. That would only dishonor her more.

"Thank you." He forced out a wry smile. "I can always use a friend." Then his smile fell. "But where Raine is involved, fuck off."

As nausea turned his stomach, he pivoted away, walked back into his private office, and slammed the door.

Chapter Two

Fuck off, was it? Liam watched Hammer shut himself away and shook his head. Through the past decade, he and Hammer had shared so many good times, so much laughter, untold quantities of liquor, and of course for a time, Juliet. The man was the closest thing he had to a brother. Sure, they'd exchanged a cross word or two, but never anything like this. Clearly, his friend didn't appreciate his interference. But he needed it.

Since Macen had moved to California eight years ago, Liam only saw the man every November seventh, but they'd talked on the phone often. Hammer had acted as if he'd grieved and moved on, and from their conversations, Liam had never imagined otherwise. So when Hammer had invited him to visit after his divorce, Liam had jumped at the chance, eager to avoid the coming winter and painful memories.

An hour after arriving at Shadows, Liam knew Hammer had hoodwinked him. Why the fuck hadn't he realized how truly damaged Macen was? About two minutes later, he'd discovered Hammer was in love with a girl he wouldn't let himself have.

Liam more than saw Raine's appeal. Besides being a striking beauty, she was smart, fiery, good with people. And terribly in love with Hammer. Liam had pulled her aside once or twice to ask about his friend. She'd been skittish but had guarded Macen and his privacy fiercely. They'd suit well.

Getting the thick-headed man to see that, however, was proving difficult.

Tiptoeing around Hammer's issues for the past two months had accomplished nothing. Talking about them this morning hadn't helped, either. Clearly, Macen wasn't ready or willing to exorcise his ghosts.

Running a hand through his hair, Liam paced down the hall. He missed the laughing mate he'd once known, one with life and vigor pumping in his veins. If Hammer didn't know how to move forward, Liam would give him a serious shove—starting with his size thirteen up Hammer's ass.

And Raine would provide the force behind that kick.

About her, Hammer was intensely protective and possessive—in a way Liam had never seen his friend behave. Macen hoarded the lass and snarled at any other Dom who dared to touch her. Liam had every intention of forcing him to choose between hiding behind his walls or watching Raine blossom under another man's dominance.

His own.

He'd been considering this for a few days now and was convinced he stood a good chance of healing not just one heart, but two. Though he hadn't spoken to her about anything other than Hammer, Liam sensed that Raine was broken, like the china she'd carried in her hands. And she was starved for affection. Any idiot could see that she needed caring more than discipline, but she would thrive for the man who gave her the proper measure of both. Granted, Raine might turn him down, but he could be persistent for both their sakes.

Then once she'd gained a bit of confidence and Hammer had pulled his head out of his ass, Liam planned to be on his merry way and let them live happily ever after.

But he had no illusions; the moment he took Raine under his wing, Hammer would see it as a betrayal. Their friendship could get ugly before common sense prevailed, but he'd risk it rather than standing aside and watching the man self-destruct.

As Liam crept further down the hall, he heard Raine bustling in the kitchen. Slowing his step as he reached the door, he watched her bowed head and shaking shoulders. A shuddering sob later, the girl reached for a stainless steel bowl, grabbed a few cups of sugar, some eggs, and butter.

A fond little smile curved his lips. Raine was rarely predictable—except in this. The short-fused firecracker often flew off in ways he'd never seen in a submissive, and Liam was never sure when or how she'd explode. Obviously, she'd had no formal training, and no one took her to task. But when she started thundering like a summer storm, Raine always came to the kitchen as if being one with the dough soothed her.

Seeing her tears and defeated posture, Liam itched to rattle Hammer into next week for closing himself off from the very woman who could save him.

Raine cracked an egg over the bowl and sniffled to hold in her tears. He drew in a bracing breath. What to say to the distraught girl? If he barged in, she'd bristle and give him a cold shoulder. He had to tread carefully since he didn't know exactly what ran through her wee head. And that meant he couldn't let her in on his plan. Raine needed to feel valued, not like she was simply bait. Nor would she truly learn to submit if she believed what lay between them was only an act for Hammer's benefit. It had to come from her soul or Macen would see straight through it. His friend's jealousy must spur him to act. Most of all, he didn't want Raine hurt. If he made her his conspirator and the ploy failed, the defeat would crush her delicate heart.

"Maybe I should just quit." She grabbed a wooden spoon and attacked the dough, adding in brown sugar. "Leave. There's nothing holding me here, that's for damn sure."

His gut clenched at the finality in her miserable words. He refused to let her go without doing everything in his power to persuade her to stay. He had to act now.

Raine yanked a fresh dishtowel from the drawer, pressed it to her face, and took a few deep breaths to calm herself. A long moment later, she threw the towel down, flipped on the faucet, and shoved her hands under the stream of water. She hissed in a breath, and he frowned. How badly had she cut herself?

"Except…this is home. Where would I go?" she muttered as she cut off the water. "But how can I stay here?"

That was his cue.

Liam raised his fist and knocked on the door. Raine whipped her head around, hope brimming in her eyes. It visibly died when she realized he wasn't Hammer.

She surprised him when she cast her gaze to the floor submissively. "Hi, Liam. Sir. Um, if you're here because you're worried or something, I'll be fine. I'll bake a batch of chocolate chip cookies and be as good as new."

So sweet. And lying. Eventually, he'd both soothe and paddle her until she learned to be honest, but for now he simply tried to set her at ease. "While I've little doubt about your culinary skills, since your baked goods are most excellent, I doubt they'll mend your woes, lass. Show me your hands."

Obediently, Raine held them out. Liam stepped closer, taking her wrists in his grip and examining her fingers. "You've a few wee cuts, but nothing serious." He gave her a smile and gently kissed her palm. "I think you'll live."

She stiffened. "I told you I'm fine."

"Your hands, yes. What about your heart?" He watched her shoulders slump. "I've come with a proposition. Would you hear me out?"

He had to win her consent—and give her hope—or she would leave and take Hammer's only chance of healing with her.

Raine sent him a wary glance. "I guess."

Liam sidled closer cautiously, careful not to give her cause to bolt. "Would you be adverse to me training you?"

At his words, her startling blue eyes widened, sucking him in like a whirlpool. He'd surprised her. Almost an instant later, she opened her mouth, regret already softening her face.

Before she could refuse him, he cut in. "How much longer will you let your own happiness be denied? Why not seek it with someone ready to appreciate the beauty you are?"

He watched her, following her every nervous gesture: her slight shrug, the tilt of her head, the rise and fall of her chest, the cant of her hip as she leaned back against the counter. Her innate grace and the subtle feminine scent he inhaled as he drew closer sent blood rushing to his cock unexpectedly. The primal reaction surprised him, but he was male, and Raine was lovely, after all.

As he looked into her haunting eyes, he knew yet another reason Hammer had kept this one for his own. Innocence. Fear. Hunger. A swirling mirror to her soul lay just beyond reach. Interesting. A heady challenge.

She bit the fullness of her lower lip. It only took that instant to make him want to comfort her. But that wasn't all. Lust to taste her sweet mouth, touch her, lay her back and—

He shoved the urge down and told his stiff cock to take a rest.

"I don't understand." She blinked up at him. "You want to train...me?"

"I think you need it. And you deserve it. I admire your spirit and your grace. I can't imagine that you want to wilt away, pining for unrequited love."

Her mouth pinched. "What's in it for you? You saw my stupid display earlier."

The girl needed reassurance. Liam reached for her and pulled her into his arms. The act nestled her pillowy breasts against his chest, her soft curves against his body. An intriguing musky lily scent wafted from her pale, smooth skin. A vision flashed across his brain of Raine beneath him, crying out as he fucked his way deep inside her.

Liam sucked in a shocked breath. He forced himself to think about something else—anything else. Absently, he rubbed her back, his thoughts racing. What the hell? Sure, he'd thought Raine was stunning when he'd first arrived at Shadows. Her inky hair and eloquent blue eyes turned heads every night. But now that he had her close, everything about her called not only to the Dom in him, but to the man as well. He needed to get his head screwed on straight, for Hammer's sake.

"It isn't your fault. You care for Hammer, and he's...well, he's got a few issues he needs to be sorting out, for sure. While he does, wouldn't you like to learn about true submission so you might be ready for him? Have you ever wished to stretch a bit, find out if you truly have the courage to submit?"

The way her breath caught before she blushed and jerked her gaze to the floor again suggested that his idea intrigued her.

Liam curled a finger under her chin, raising her face to his once more, and had to steel himself against another shocking jolt of lust. "You have, haven't you?"

"I want to be what Hammer needs, but I don't know for certain that I have the self-discipline to kneel and hold my tongue. I've never had the opportunity to try." She swallowed, honesty paining her expression. "But I still don't understand what's in it for you."

"You're a beauty, for sure. Touching you will be no hardship, lass." Right now, he hated how true that was. "From what I've seen, you can be a mouthy wench who would benefit from a red ass now and again." He forced himself to wink and grin.

After a split second of waiting for her reaction, her eyes flashed wide. Then she bestowed on him the sweetest sound he'd heard in months, her unbridled laughter.

"There's a girl." His smile became real. "Let me help you. I see your need. I enjoy molding and teaching." He cupped her cheek. "You should be cherished and nurtured, and I'd be honored to give that to you, Raine. Are you game?"

Indecision washed over her face. Liam found himself holding his breath, praying she'd say yes. Hammer needed her…and Liam staggered with his own need to touch her—at least once. It wasn't noble, and he wasn't proud of it. But she was so damn fuckable, and he was just a man. This lust would pass.

"You don't seem like the sort to do something halfway. You'll want to lay my soul bare, won't you? Make me show you all the broken parts?" She crossed her arms over her chest, nudging him back. "If I show you, are you going to run like Hammer, too?"

He uncrossed her arms and leaned closer. Now he could hear her softly indrawn breaths, see her fine trembling. Desire surged. Liam couldn't stop himself; he curled a hand around her shoulder, eliminating her personal space, and brushed his palm down to fasten on the curve of her waist. "I never run from a challenge I've set my mind on. Yes, I intend to split your soul wide open like a ripe peach, study you until I know well every piece of the intriguing puzzle you are, down to the last detail, lovely. Then, I mean to put you back together with my touch and make it worth your while."

Raine looked half terrified. "Wow, that's awfully honest."

"Best to set the expectation up front."

She let out a deep breath and fidgeted, trying to drop her gaze once more. He didn't allow it, lifting her chin again and bending until their eyes met. "Answer me, Raine. Yes or no?"

"I-I've wanted a good Dom. I thought it would be Hammer, but…" She closed her eyes and frowned.

Liam bit his tongue. She wanted to feel valued above all else—needed it. He tucked that knowledge in the back of his head and let her continue. "But?"

"I can't be less than honest with you. You know where my heart is. As much as I would love to explore everything you could teach me—really, I would—I don't know if I could give you the devotion you deserve. And I doubt Hammer would ever give his consent, even for you. It might be better for us all if I just left."

He trapped her against the counter in an instant, pressing his body to hers. Her lips parted in question. Her wide gaze jumped to his, then she focused on his mouth. An electric jolt rattled down his spine. Damn, she was potent.

Yanking her soft curves flush against the hard ridges of his body, he ached to dig his fingers into her hair, pull her lips under his, and eat away at her mouth until she moaned. Liam forced himself to stop. This wasn't about him, but Hammer. And Raine.

Dragging in a rough breath, he palmed her nape tenderly with one hand, fingers teasing the perfect pink shell of her ear with the other before trailing down to caress her throat. Finally, he settled his hand on her chest, just above her plump breast. Her breathing changed to soft pants. He could feel her heart beating madly under his palm. She wasn't immune to him. An intoxicating rush of power filled him.

Then he took her wrists in his free hand and brought her arms up slowly, bracing them against the cabinets above, her breath caught. A triumph he didn't welcome spiked inside him. Still, he bent to Raine, giving her ample time to push him away. She didn't. Her tongue swept nervously across her upper lip. His cock jerked. Then he couldn't stop himself from seizing her mouth with his own, capturing her gasp.

Soft. So fucking soft. And sweet. Bloody hell... Pleasure fired through his blood like a potent drug as he delved inside. She melted beneath him.

Curling his tongue around hers, he feasted on her addicting flavor, hungry to memorize it. One kiss melted into the next, and he devoured her, inhaling her into his lungs. She turned to liquid desire against him, wild and tumultuous. One leg slid surreptitiously around his, capturing his calf, pulling him in tighter against her small frame, splitting her thighs open. He should pass up that perfect invitation, but he didn't. Instead, he ground himself against her pussy, leaving her no doubt that he desired her. Despite Raine's little skirt, her flesh burned him. A low groan ripped from his throat. He didn't need air or space or tomorrow, just more of her. Right fucking now.

Liam imagined her body welcoming him, her cunt opening to him. He groaned. Lust thundered through his veins. The urge to possess her burst in his brain as she surrendered to the moment. To him. He curled his fingers into the top of her blouse, ready to rip it wide open. Her little startled whimper brought him back to sanity. He tore his mouth from hers, breathing hard.

Raine was his best friend's girl. But even knowing he must secure her trust if he intended to resurrect Hammer from the depths of the past, he couldn't deny that something about her had shaken him down to his very bones.

"Don't worry about Hammer's consent now," he managed to spit out. "I'll see to him. You need training, and I'll give it to you. Can you deny the passion sizzling between us?"

She swallowed. "No."

Good. He needed to kindle Raine's desires to keep her here, but the kiss had proven that arousing her would be a double-edged sword. The more she responded to him, the more he wanted her.

Liam pushed the thought away. "Be aware, lovely, if you say yes to my offer, I'll test your submission and expect you to give me everything, no less. You deserve some happiness. God knows, I could use a little myself. Think about it. Find me when you're ready."

Liam released her, turning away and striding out of the room as quickly as he had come. Nothing more he could do now. And if he stayed, he feared he would do far more.

The ball was in Raine's court.

Sleep was impossible, and Raine was tired of trying. The night was warm for November, and she couldn't get comfortable in any position in her bed. In fact, nothing about her life felt comfortable now.

Liam O'Neill had to be brave. He'd thumbed his nose at Hammer's no-touching rule and kissed her. Actually, he'd more than kissed her. In that shocking moment, he'd owned her, and she'd been desperate for his mouth on her own, to feel his naked body sliding against hers as he spread her legs with his powerful thighs and filled her completely. He'd do her the way he did everything else: well and with a single-minded purpose. She might love Hammer, but Liam was very easy on the eyes and he intrigued her. No denying it had been forever since any man had touched her, but Liam had proven he could more than take her breath away.

More importantly, he was offering her something she needed: A chance to see if the submissive path was truly right for her.

She swallowed. It was probably time to give up on the dream of being Hammer's. But Raine could barely remember a time she hadn't loved him. He'd not only taken her in as a runaway, but given her a roof over her head, food in her belly, and a job she loved. He'd also taught her to drive, urged her to get her GED, and helped her pay her way through college until she had earned her bachelor's degree. Hammer had held her and listened to the bits she'd confessed about her terrible childhood, then reassured her with his compassionate words that she wasn't to blame. In many ways, he made her feel safe and cared for. And utterly treasured.

Just not as a woman.

The painful realization that he didn't love her as anything more than a little sister made her soul bleed. And so her life had come to a fork in the road. Stay on the same path she'd dogged down for six years? Leave Shadows altogether? Or take a new trail to explore her submission with Liam?

Hammer probably wasn't going to suddenly fall in love with her, not when he had women like Marlie at his beck and call. But if she gave up before she ever gathered her courage to show him that she was a woman who could please him, wouldn't she always regret it? Could she say yes to Liam's offer in good conscience if she was always haunted by the thought that Hammer might have come around if she'd just waited a bit longer?

Then she had to show him. Now. And she couldn't do it halfway. No more coffee and muffins, like she was a damn waitress. She finally had to lay it all on the line and demonstrate that she could be everything he could ever want.

The clock said it was nearly four in the morning. She could take Hammer by surprise now, so he'd simply react, not think. His response when he wasn't guarded would tell her all she needed to know.

She showered quickly. After hair, makeup, and lingerie designed for seduction, she was ready. After adding silk stockings and a pair of sexy stilettos, she slipped from her room by quarter 'til five. Nerves scraped and knotted her stomach as she reached for her keys and made her way down the hall to Hammer's room.

Opening the door to his private office and bedroom with a trembling hand, she tiptoed to minimize the clattering of her stilettos on the marble tiles, wincing with each little click. She prayed he was alone.

It seemed like forever before she reached his sleeping form, looking so strong and male, moonlight streaming in across his bare torso. And not curled up with someone like Marlie, thank god. Silvery beams highlighted the ridges of his shoulders, chest, and abdomen. His black boxer briefs barely concealed his cock.

For a moment, she couldn't breathe. She rarely got the treat of seeing Hammer this bare. Her mouth was suddenly dry as she imagined sliding into bed with him and melting into him as he thrust inside her.

If she did this right, maybe she would finally know the joy of being Hammer's. Really, truly understand what it meant to be taken and satisfied by the man she loved.

She eased into the bed beside him. The incredible slab of male occupied most of the mattress, but she didn't let that deter her from curling against him and inhaling his scent. Musk, leather, sex, fresh cotton. Everything about him was so familiar, so sexy. Anticipation danced in her stomach as she trailed her fingers from the deep line between his rigid pecs, down his torso, watching his muscles bunch and flex with each touch. A curl of excitement pressed against her clit as she gently pushed his boxer briefs down to the tops of his thighs.

Her eyes widened. He was big, the head of his cock wide even while flaccid. His balls hung heavy. She wished she could see him better in the moonlight. But hopefully, they'd still be in bed long after the sun rose.

God, she'd dreamed for years of this...of him. She savored the moment, achingly aware of her pussy weeping.

Then, lowering her head, she licked her way up his shaft with the flat of her tongue, basking in the manly, salty taste of him, in the feel of his cock stiffening for her. In seconds, he was at full staff, and holy hell, he was a sight to behold. Thick, long, and ready, he would fill her needy body and then some. Raine shivered at the thought and closed her mouth around his cock, taking him all the way to the back of her throat with a groan.

As she sucked and laved her way up to the head, he arched his hips, slamming into her mouth. She engulfed him completely, and he cried out in agonized pleasure and wrapped his fingers in her hair, using his grip to thrust harder against her throat.

"Yeeessss. Deeper."

Raine ached to take him there, so deep that he'd never want to leave. She stretched her lips to open completely for him.

"That's it. Hmm…precious."

When she glanced up, his eyes were still closed. Her heart quickened. Had he ever called anyone that but her? Not that she knew of. Was he thinking of her? Maybe, deep down, he wanted her, too.

With a whimper, Raine hollowed her cheeks as she sucked harder, moaning appreciatively at his masculine taste. Marveling as he stiffened even more between her lips, she closed her eyes and shivered when his grip in her hair turned rough, then he plowed into her mouth with another unrestrained thrust.

She opened her throat and breathed through her nose, as she'd heard other submissives describe a thousand times, licking the entire length of his shaft with her tongue, circling the head and teasing the sensitive underside. All the way down, a slow, thorough cradling of his cock until her lips pursed around the base. Then she bobbed back up even more slowly, working toward the crest once more.

This was where she belonged, serving him, pleasing him. He seemed pretty damn pleased, too. Yes, he might protest that she'd taken matters into her hands—and mouth—but he couldn't deny how good this felt, not when his entire body tensed, his balls drew up, and his cock twitched on her tongue.

As she retreated and licked the head once more, she whispered, "Yes, Macen..."

He finally lifted his heavy lids, confusion evident in the shimmering moonlight. Then he zeroed in on her and recognition dawned. His eyes widened. He pulled harder on her hair, then slid deeper into her mouth as a moan tore from his chest. Raine clasped his shaft with her red-painted lips, lavishing all her attention on him, worshiping his cock as she looked up at him with her heart in her eyes.

Horror spread across his face.

"No, Raine!" He choked out between harsh breaths and shoved away from her as if he was on fire. "What the hell do you think you're doing? Christ!"

"I-I wanted to make you feel good. I was..." *Showing you how I felt.*

He leapt from the bed, his hard cock still glistening with her saliva as he yanked up his underwear and flipped on the lights. His eyes darkened like a thundercloud. "Why are you giving me head in the middle of the night? That's not the sort of relationship we have."

She looked at him hopefully, but felt exposed in her next-to-nothing lingerie. She found herself slinking under the covers to hide. "It could be."

"No, Raine...precious." His voice softened. "Never."

Hammer's gaze wasn't unkind, but full of a shaming mixture of alarm and finality. It crushed her. And it pissed her off.

Raine shot him an accusing glare. "You liked it. You moaned. You called me 'precious,' like you always do. You fucked my mouth like you were desperate for me, even after you knew who I was. I'm here because I need to show you that I can please you as a woman. Just one chance."

But Hammer was already shaking his head. His denial made tears stab her eyes. Raine tried desperately to shove them back. "Why not me?

Why every other goddamn woman who steps foot in this club except *me?*"

"I won't touch you, Raine. And I don't owe you an explanation. Leave!" He pointed to the door. "Go to your room and go back to bed. We'll forget this ever happened. Don't step foot in here again without my permission."

"I don't want to forget!" She jumped from the bed and stared. His cock still bulged hard and angry beneath his boxer briefs. Longing melted her. "It looks like you want me, at least a little. I'm not tall like Marlie or as experienced, but I'm eager and I can learn. If my blow job technique isn't good enough, then you can teach me. But I'll love you like she never will. Doesn't that mean anything to you?"

"Goddamnit, Raine! We're *not* talking about this. Later, when you've got some fucking clothes on, I'll determine a proper punishment for breaching my privacy and barging your way past boundaries you have no business crossing. Go!"

Every word stabbed her, and he didn't seem to notice. Or care. "I'm not a child. I'd be so good to you. Why can't you want me?"

"Stop trying my patience, and for fuck's sake, Raine, stop topping from the goddamn bottom. *Now go!*"

Raine tried to hold back her tears. Topping from the bottom. Yeah, she could see how he'd think that. Maybe she needed a different tactic...

She scrambled to her knees, dropping her gaze, palms up on her thighs, doing her best to appear supplicating. "I'm sorry, Sir. Let me make it up to you and ease your discomfort. Let me serve you." His big cock rested inches from her face, still hard and about to burst from his underwear. Her mouth watered as she craved another taste. "Please."

A growl tore from his chest. He wrapped his hand around her arm and yanked her to her feet. He didn't once look at her as he dragged her to the door, opened it, and shoved her out of his room. "Stop pushing me! It's never going to happen. Get that straight, girl."

He slammed the door in her face and locked it, sliding the deadbolt in place.

Blinking at it with horror and desolation, Raine choked on a sob, then sank to the floor and covered her face with her hands. She'd offered him everything with an open heart, and he'd brutally refused her. Apparently, he wanted the Marlies of the world, with their fake boobs and even faker intentions. Hammer excelled at fucking with a woman's head, not at treasuring her heart. Yet she'd hoped that his concern and caretaking for her translated into more. He didn't love her; he pitied her. And she'd humiliated herself in the most cringeworthy way by throwing herself at him.

Fine. So she would leave, start over. Yes, she loved it here. The people, the energy, the genuine concern the employees shared for each other—it was home. Shadows was the only place she'd ever felt safe. She had nowhere else to go, and Liam had offered her a reason to stay, along with most everything she'd ever wanted. But Liam wasn't Hammer. In fact, she barely knew him. How the hell could she devote herself to another man?

On the other hand, how could accepting Liam's offer make her hurt worse than she already did? Maybe she should grab what happiness she could and accept that she'd never have what she truly wanted. After all, it wouldn't be the first time. And if watching her with another man bothered Hammer at all, well…even better.

Hammer didn't take a deep breath until he'd locked the door with Raine on the other side. Knowing her, she'd storm away to lick her wounds. Then somehow, he'd have to repair them—but not until he'd gotten this fucking clutch of lust under control.

Furious and frustrated, he rammed his fist against the solid wood until his knuckles bled. If he'd allowed Raine to stay one second longer, he would have grabbed her, slammed her to the bed, and fucked her into next week—no question. As it was, he could barely stop himself from opening the door now, then dragging her back and beneath him.

The vision of her sinful mouth wrapped around his cock was burned into his retinas.

"Motherfucker!" He closed his eyes and curled his fist tighter, trying to shake the pain from his knuckles. They throbbed almost as much as his dick. Because of her. Damn it, and he still had to see her every day. Watch her smile, see the flash of her eyes, fucking smell her. He wouldn't be able to resist her if he didn't take care of this throbbing need now.

With a savage curse, he snagged a tube of lube from a nearby shelf and squirted a healthy dollop into his hand. Then he wrapped his fist around his aching cock and stroked it in rapid, graceless jerks. Visions of Raine sucking him into the mind-bending heat of her mouth were unraveling him. *Damn the little minx!* She'd stripped him of every shred of self-control and reduced him to jacking off, desperate for the girl he couldn't touch.

He pumped into his fist frantically.

At first, he'd been dreaming of Raine laying in a field of fresh cut grass, her raven mane thick and silky, draped over his stomach as she worshiped his cock. When he'd awakened, reality had been so much better. She'd tongued an enticing trail over the distended, throbbing veins of his shaft and taken nearly every thick, hard inch down her throat.

And fuck, then… Raine on her knees, offering herself to him to use in every rough, dirty, possessive way he could think of. A fiery streak of lightning slammed down his spine.

He panted her name as his body quivered, and his cock jerked in his grip. Stroking faster, harder, his head swam with desire so thick he thought he'd choke. Hammer chased pleasure, his elbow banging the door with every pull on his dick until he exploded with dizzying force and a hoarse groan. "Raine!"

Stream after stream jettisoned from his shaft, splattering onto the tile floor. He panted, gasping for breath. The immediate need for orgasm faded. But his yearning for her remained.

Then a feminine growl of fury broke the silence.

"Oh my...are you kidding me? You're masturbating!"

Hammer froze. Raine. *Shit!* She'd been listening outside his door? After the callous way he'd rejected her, it seemed unfathomable that she hadn't run to the safety of her room. But no, she'd stayed and heard every wretched moment of his self-pleasure, even the way he'd shouted her name so desperately as he came.

"How *dare* you, you bastard!"

The pain in her voice sliced him in two. Hammer slumped against the door, hanging his head with a sigh. What the fuck should he do now? What kind of bullshit excuse could he possibly give her?

Stepping over the mess he'd made on the floor, he donned a pair of trousers and hastily fastened them, trying to force his sluggish brain to come up with some halfway believable excuse.

Before he could, a crash and a clatter resounded in the dungeon. *What the...?*

Muttering a curse, he yanked the door open and raced down the hall. As he rounded the corner, he watched Raine reach into the bins of new and freshly sterilized toys, then throw them to the ground. They scattered everywhere, bouncing, breaking apart, and sliding across the decorative concrete.

Hammer tried to swallow back his shock as Raine heaved boxes of condoms and tubes of lube through the air like a rookie pitcher. Then she whirled on him with blue eyes blazing like a beacon through the shadowed room. He'd seen her angry before, but never, ever like this.

Hell hath no fury like a woman scorned.

"Fuck you!" she hurled at him. "No, never mind. Fuck yourself. You'd obviously rather do that than fuck me."

He swallowed down her barb and narrowed his eyes at her. "What do you think you're doing, besides throwing one hell of a fit?"

In her hand, she gripped a huge purple dildo. "Enjoy shoving this silicone dick into your little fuck toy Marlie's plastic pussy."

She raised the toy and heaved it at him, and Hammer barely jolted from his stunned silence fast enough to duck as the heavy torpedo sailed over his head.

His ire rising, he pointed to the floor in front of him. "Get over here, girl. Now!"

"Piss off. You had your chance."

Arching a brow at her rebellion, he watched her face tighten as anger rippled through her bristling form.

"Raine…" he warned.

She scoffed at him, the sound dripping contempt. "I'm not listening to you anymore. You wanted me, but you jacked off instead of coming in the willing mouth I offered, and why? I'm starting to think it's because you're not man enough for me. So if you want me over there?" She cocked her head in challenge and crossed her arms over her chest. "Make me."

Chapter
Three

"Really, precious? You want me to make you?" Hammer's voice lowered dangerously. She'd trampled over every submissive rule. Insulted him utterly. Challenged him in a way he couldn't let pass. And damn if he didn't want her even more. The girl had fire; she would burn him in bed.

The way she'd thrown herself at him told Hammer that she was crying out for attention. But if he gave Raine what she sought, she'd be damned. All he could do was punish her defiance and pray it drove some extra distance between them. Hammer didn't lie to himself. The thought of spanking her bare ass made the pervert in him get hard all over again. He'd do the job thoroughly, too. Sitting would prove painful for days.

With long strides, he prowled toward her, gripped her silky hair in his fist, and yanked her head back. As he pressed their bodies together, her lips trembled right beneath his. He fought the urge to kiss her. Why did Raine stir such insatiable hunger? What was it about her that drove him to crave her? Made him want to rip her clothes off and sink into her over and over?

As Hammer struggled for control, he stared into her tumultuous eyes and looked past her anger, through her soul, all the way down to her shattered heart. He'd done that, and her agony split his chest. He wished to fuck they could go back in time, when his relationship with Raine had been easier. Guiding her had given him great joy when she hadn't been quite a woman. But he'd been unable to ignore her passionate beauty for long, and thoughts of claiming her had begun to plague him relentlessly. Rejecting her now made him feel like a first-class asshole. This was hardly the first time he'd questioned whether he was protecting her from himself or simply hurting her more, but the answer was always the same. Keeping her at arm's length was for her own damn good. Her dented pride would heal faster than her crushed soul.

So he had to step carefully. If she suspected for a second how close he was to throwing all caution to the wind, Raine would never stop trying to break through his walls. The tenacious little vixen would wear him down because he wanted her too badly to fight her off for long. And that would make him a completely selfish bastard. Despite what Liam thought, he was never going to be whole again. He didn't deserve to be.

Raine would have to be content with his guidance from afar, and he'd pray that someday, she found the right Dom to treasure her as she deserved. Even if the thought made him homicidal.

"Just what do you think you're going to accomplish by throwing toys at me? Have you lost your mind?" he demanded in low tones. "On second thought, don't say a word. You want to be treated like a submissive? You got it," he snapped, releasing her abruptly. "Strip!"

Yes, he was a stupid bastard, testing his already precarious control. But any Dominant would have to peel back the defenses she hid behind so desperately. He needed her naked, physically and emotionally. Exposed. Maybe then he could make her comply.

Her eyes widened, then suddenly narrowed as she glared daggers at him, crossing her arms tighter. Her breasts lifted in a mouthwatering offering. Forcing himself to ignore the view, he snatched her wrists, flung her arms to her sides, then wrenched the skimpy black lace bra from her chest. It hit the floor. Her breasts bounced free.

Raine rushed to cover herself with her hands, but he blocked her—and tried not to stare at her luscious breasts with their perfect rosy nipples. "The rest, precious. I said strip. Not when you feel like it. Not when it suits you. Now!"

Her plump red lips pursed as she scowled. "You let your opportunity pass, sport. Since you have no intention of doing anything more than pulling my hair and stroking your own cock, we're done here."

She jerked free and turned her back to him, revealing her lacy thong and delectable ass as she marched away, leaving her bra on the floor between them. The infuriating minx was on a roll, using every tactic imaginable to challenge him. Hammer wasn't having it.

He sucked in a deep breath and snagged her by the neck, then spun her around. She crashed against him, head snapping back. Her gaze, silent and furious, locked on his. Fuck, all the ways he wanted her raced through his head...

"Enough! This defiance ends here and now." Hammer hoisted Raine over his shoulder.

At her shriek of indignation, he smacked her bare ass and carried her through the deserted dungeon, down the hall, and back into his private bedroom. The second they cleared the portal, he kicked the door shut, tossed Raine on the bed, then tore the black lace thong from her hips. And stared.

Shit! Her pussy was bare, plump, and pink. As her heady scent filled his nostrils, he nearly staggered back. The room swayed. His cock throbbed painfully. He couldn't fucking breathe.

Gritting his teeth, he sat on the edge of the bed beside the little hellcat, forcing himself to remember that she was mostly naked in his bed for her punishment, not his pleasure.

In one fluid motion, Hammer flipped her over his knees and gripped her hair. He ignored her yelp while he threw her shoes across the room, then shredded her silk stockings impatiently.

Now she lay completely bare across his lap. Swallowing back the thick swirl of lust as he stared at her smooth, supple ass, he drew back his hand. He hesitated, fantasizing that he could slip his fingers into her pussy, collect her juices, then slide them back to her puckered rosette, properly prepare her like a Master should—like he fucking wanted to—before driving balls deep into her ass and claiming her. That fantasy had played over and over in his head a thousand times.

Not happening, man!

Dragging in a steadying breath, Hammer closed his eyes to center himself. A responsible Dominant always handed down punishment in a calm, cool manner. It didn't matter that Raine had taunted the sexual beast seething inside him. He'd be damned if she'd provoke him into something he'd regret.

He silently counted to ten, then focused on the lesson she needed to learn. "You will count for me, precious, loud and clear. I have no qualms about spanking you hard until you follow instructions and respect the boundaries between us."

"No…you…won't!" she vowed as she wriggled to work free of his hold.

She squirmed all over his cock, her alluring scent assailing him with every twist of her body. Hammer glimpsed the delicate folds between her thighs and cursed under his breath. Raine was drenched.

"Don't you even *think* of—ouch!" she yelped as he landed the first stinging blow across her ass.

As she struggled to get away, he felt her molten honey seep through his trousers, scalding his thigh. Her intoxicating scent breathed more life into his already painful erection.

"Count," he snarled.

"One, you rat bastard. You've made your point. Now let me go!"

"Rat bastard? Oh, precious, I haven't even started to make my point, and you have no idea how big a bastard I can be. Just wait." Landing another blow on her silken backside, he clenched his fist to quell the burn she blazed across his palm. "Now count, without your smart-assed commentary."

THE BETRAYAL | 93

She hissed as she struggled over his rigid cock. Damn it, Raine was going to massacre every shred of his control before he finished her punishment.

"Fine. I'll count." She slipped into a sing-songy voice dripping sarcasm. "One, two. I don't belong to you! Three, four. Go fuck your little whore. Five, six. Oh, look who's got a hard dick. Seven, eight. If you want me, asshole, guess what? It's too late."

Hammer barely managed to smother his stunned bark of laughter. Only Raine would still be dishing out insults while he smacked the hell out of her ass. This punishment wasn't going to put a dent in her attitude. He was pretty sure the only way to strip her sass was to settle himself between her legs and fuck her blind. As incredible as that would feel, once he started, he would never stop.

Landing two more quick blows to her bright red ass, he leaned down to whisper in her ear, "Nine, ten, guess we'll have to start again."

She screeched in fury, and he swung his hand back to land another blow. Then her supple thighs fell apart—and his mind went blank. Before he could summon his sanity, he drove two fingers deep into her seeping cunt. *Oh god...* Tight. Slick. Swollen. Everything he'd ever imagined. His lust raged, melting his brain and good intentions. *Fuck.*

Gasping, she rocked against his embedded fingers. The sound of her pleasure cut into him like a white-hot spike. He'd never touched Raine sexually. Now his cock pulsed in time with the pounding of his heart.

Driving his fingers deeper, he turned his hand and brushed his thumb over her pebbled clit, his heart galloping as she melted against him. "Am I a bastard now, precious?"

"No," she whimpered and bowed her head in surrender. "Please..."

It was the singular most arousing moment of his life. God, she looked so beautiful, her dark hair spilling around his thighs, her nape exposed, her bare ass reddened by his hand. He fought hard not to roll her over, pin her to the bed, and shove himself inside her wet, snug cunt.

"Do you think I don't know what you want?" Strumming her clit as she mewled so beautifully, he inhaled a ragged breath. "See, precious. I do. Now, who is the Master?"

"You, Sir. Please... You. You're all I've ever wanted."

Christ, she'd sliced open her chest and shown him all the feelings she'd been holding inside. Unlike him, she had the balls to confess everything in her heart. His pride swelled at her courage, even as his heart seized. Maybe for this—for her—he could try to heal the past... but then he'd have to confess his greatest failure to Raine. *Fuck, no.* He'd rather have her idolize him from afar than loathe him to his face. Or worse, fear him.

"You'll always have me, just not on your terms." Unable to stop himself, he arched his hips, driving his steely cock against her soft belly. "I won't deny that you make me hard when you're naked and poised over my lap, your soul open and raw. But I won't give you anything more. And you can't demand it, as if it's your right. Don't pin your hopes on me, precious. I'm not good for you."

Now that he'd made his point, he should pull away, set her on her feet, and send her out the door. But with the feel of her silken pussy clutching his fingers, making his cock scream in need, he couldn't bring himself to dismiss her yet. Just a few more moments to savor her... It was unlikely he'd ever touch her this way again.

Calling himself a fool, Hammer squeezed another finger into her sodden cleft and found the bundle of nerves hidden deep within. He massaged the soft, sensitized tissue, his body stiff, breathing harsh, as her nectar spilled over his hand. "Do you want to come for me?"

Raine panted and nodded frantically, whimpering in desperate need. He felt her folds flutter as she tensed like a tightly drawn bow, her entire body humming.

"Please...Yes," she begged. "I want it. So badly. From you."

Probably every bit as badly as he ached to give it to her. But he had to do what was best for Raine. She *needed* a lesson about respecting the boundaries between them—or there'd be disaster in their future.

Steeling himself against her soft pleas, he withdrew his fingers from her sweet cunt. "No, you may not. That's the punishment for your bratty behavior, your insults, your brazen seduction, and most of all, your blatant manipulation."

As he set her on her feet, she cried out in frustration. He resisted the urge to growl along with her. But he couldn't stop his gaze from sweeping over her naked body. Her glistening pussy, those red nipples puckering in the morning chill, her hypnotic eyes lost in sexual splendor, all tempted him. And he'd put that look on her face.

Swallowing back his desire, he stood and handed down the rest of her punishment. "You're denied orgasm for three days, girl."

Her jaw dropped. "You drive me to the brink of madness with those big fingers, then expect—"

"Yes." He tilted his head, silently warning her not to defy him. Her mute stare gratified him. "Go pick up your mess in the dungeon, precious. We're through here."

Turning his back and dismissing her, he strode into his private bathroom, locking the door behind him with a ragged breath. Shoving his trousers off and flipping the shower on, he looked down at his angry cock throbbing—again.

Cursing, he leaned against the cool tiles. But now he had new fuel to add to his fire, the feel of Raine draped over his lap, her intoxicating pleas as she begged him to let her come. Squeezing his eyes shut, his mind filled with more images of her. Regretfully, he soaped up and began stroking his shaft once more, the distended veins and swollen head aching for attention.

It didn't take long. His overloaded brain threw in a replay of her sucking his cock, and he was done for. Heart drumming, Hammer threw his head back and pressed his lips together to smother a hoarse cry.

Still panting, he washed himself, then turned off the water and wrapped the towel around his waist with a heavy sigh. Having to jack off like a pubescent teen, not once but twice, totally pissed him off. "And whose fault is that, dumbass?"

His own.

He prepared himself to act as if she hadn't ruffled him a bit when he saw her around the club. If not, it would encourage her. He couldn't risk that. Raine had proven that she could wear his restraint down to nothing. He hoped like hell her unruly antics were over because if he had to punish her again—touch her at all—he would cave. He'd spread her open, sink deep, and fuck her into oblivion. Nothing would stop him, least of all his regrets.

Raking a hand through his hair, he opened the bathroom door in a cloud of steam and stepped out—then froze.

In the center of his bed, Raine lay naked, her sleek legs spread in decadent invitation with a hot pink vibrator thrust into her pussy, her head thrown back in sexual abandon. Fuck, she looked so beautiful. His nostrils flared. His jaw locked and his heart pounded. And holy shit, his unruly cock sprang to life again.

Hammer stumbled to the edge of the bed, where her feminine fragrance filled the air and enticed him. He swallowed tightly. He should stop her, but instead, he sank to the mattress, mesmerized, as the toy disappeared between her slick folds.

She squeezed her eyes shut. As her back arched, she dug her heels into the bed, then cried out and shattered before him in a stunning display of pleasure. Hammer could only stare.

After years of pampering him with coffee, his favorite baked goods, and other little gestures meant to please him, this brash behavior, while sexy as hell, came across loud and clear as a giant "fuck you."

It was obvious that she needed sterner punishment, but it couldn't be by his hand.

"Before you strive for orgasm number two, I'll take that." He swatted her hand out of the way and withdrew the toy from her pussy. His mouth watered. He craved a taste of her.

Raine collapsed on the bed and flashed him a languorous stare. Then her gaze dropped to his tented towel. "Are you going to try to tell me you didn't enjoy the show as much as I liked putting it on?"

At her razor-sharp question, he speared her with his sternest glare. "I'm very disappointed in you. You've blatantly disregarded my punishment."

Scrambling to her feet, still naked, she blinked away the tears starting to form. "Maybe I'm disappointed in you, too. Somewhere in there, you want me and you won't admit it. At least I'm honest! I came to you with a genuine desire and revealed exactly how I felt. I gave you every opportunity to take what you want from me. But no! You made me feel like a child, then jacked off because you want it and aren't man enough to take it. You know what? That's fine. I think I know someone who *is* man enough. Thanks for absolutely nothing, Hammer."

Cut to the core, he wrapped his fist in her silky mane and led her to the wall by her hair, lifting her to her toes. "Hands behind your back. Nose against the wall, girl. Don't say another goddamn word. Listen to me," he demanded. "Did you ever think that maybe if you stopped acting like a child, I'd stop treating you like one? I'm not sure what prompted this bratty behavior, but I don't like it and I won't tolerate it. Do I make myself clear?"

She didn't reply, but he knew she'd heard. It was enough for now.

"Tell me, precious, would your mythical Dominant save you from living in an alley, give you shelter and food, put clothes on your back, then finance your education, and never demand a goddamn thing in return?"

The starch left her body instantly. Fat tears trailed down her cheeks, and every one of her sniffles was a blade to his heart.

"My attitude has nothing to do with you rescuing me. I've always been grateful. I always will be. Did you need to hear that? Is it not enough that I owe you everything I have? I'm just so goddamn tired of being ignored. Every freaking day, I'm here. You see me, but you don't *see* me. Why? Am I not obedient enough? Pretty enough? Smart or cultured enough? Or is it because I'm not a carbon copy of one of your plastic whores?"

Every word broke his heart a little more. Raine finding him with Marlie had, no doubt, kindled this defiant fire. Her insecurities and his own rebuffs had fed it. Was Raine really so broken she couldn't see that everything about her put Marlie and those like her to shame?

With a sigh, he brought her around to face him. "None of that, precious. I don't ignore you or look through you. Why would you think such a thing? Because I won't let you bring me to my knees? Because I won't give you attention the way you want it? I see the gorgeous, vivacious woman you've become, but your behavior suggests that you're only willing to submit to your own desires. If you're the one setting the bar, how can you ever blossom into the submissive that yearns inside you? If your tantrum today is because I spent the night with Marlie, then I regret if that hurt you, but you don't get to choose what or who I do."

Raine bowed her head and closed her eyes. He could feel a palpable hopelessness wash over her.

"But I can't compete. I have almost no experience."

Her little, broken voice ripped at him. Hammer couldn't stop himself from cupping the back of her head and caressing gently. "It's not a competition."

"It is! I don't get a chance to submit and learn and grow," she went on with a sob. "No one will touch me because they won't cross you. I've had sex twice in the last five years. I've never really scened. Every man here avoids me. I feel...damaged and ugly. If you don't want me, show a little mercy and let me go."

Each brutally honest word that tumbled from her mouth burned him like acid. In allowing other Dominants to look but not touch, he'd kept her captive, like a bird in a gilded cage. He could hardly blame her for her submissive shortcomings. How was she supposed to flourish if he constantly impeded her growth and refused to give her up? Liam was right; he'd done her a huge injustice.

You've known for years she's in love with you, and you, you sick, twisted fuck... How long have you cared for her? Ached for her? Guilt burned bitter on his tongue.

Goddamnit, he wasn't what she needed. That truth hurt like a bitch. Furious at himself for not being the man she deserved, Hammer knew he should set her free.

But letting go would be so fucking hard. Fear that she would, indeed, find a better Master punched him in the gut. The pain didn't bring out the best in him, and at the thought of losing her, he lashed out, knowing exactly how to scare her into obedience.

"You want a taste of someone else's dominance? I can arrange that." He gritted his teeth. "You're due a punishment. How about an evening with, say...Beck?"

As soon as Hammer spoke the threat, he wished he could call it back. Jesus, he had to stop letting his emotions take over, but Raine had him so unhinged that he was acting more like a bully than a Dom.

Her eyes flew open wide and her body shook. "But he—he's..."

A tremendous sadist who took pleasure in torturing submissives. Raine was not a pain slut. Still, Hammer had to ensure that she ceased pushing him for what he couldn't give, no matter how much her lesson hurt them both. And he couldn't take his threat back now without undermining his own authority.

She tore herself from Hammer's grasp and glared at him with panic in her eyes. "Dear god, haven't you hurt me enough? Would you hand your perfect little Marlie to him? Of course not. You give a fuck what happens to her. You care whether he terrifies or marks her. Me? Oh, let's just throw the little girl to the big bad wolf. Will you stand there and laugh while he marks me?"

Her angry taunt shamed him to the core. "Since you've never acted out this seriously, I'll show you mercy and rescind your punishment if you say you're sorry."

Hammer prayed that she accepted his leniency. Instead, her eyes bulged in shock.

"You want me to apologize because I was dumb enough to confess my feelings so you could tear them to shreds? No. You know what? I'm done! *So* done."

Just when he thought her temper tantrum couldn't get any worse, she stormed out of his office, hell bent on...what? He had no clue. She disappeared into her room at the end of the hall, slamming the door until the walls shook. Then she reappeared a minute later, barely dressed in a miniscule skirt and a cleavage-hugging halter top, sans bra. Without warning, she launched her office keys at him. He caught them before they smacked him in the chest.

"I won't be in your way anymore. I won't stare at you with stupid puppy dog eyes. I won't bake for you. I won't do your filing. I won't order your booze. I sure as hell won't masturbate to thoughts of you. Just erase me from your memory bank because I'm gone. And I'm never coming back."

No. Fuck, no!

Before she could blaze out the door in an F5 cyclone of fury, he chased her and snagged her arm, his fingers staying her in a desperate grip.

"Stop! Are you really going to act like a child and threaten to run away from home because you're not getting your way?"

"Since you just had your fingers up my pussy, I would have hoped that you'd figured out I'm a woman. I'm also perfectly within my rights to leave. Buh-bye."

Leave it to clever little Raine to throw his stupidity back in his face. He had to bite back the urge to shout at her. As it was, they'd already been so loud that the other Doms and subs sleeping nearby in their private rooms were getting one hell of a wake-up call.

Instead, he gripped her harder. "You cry because I'm not paying attention to you, but when I command you to hold your orgasm to drive your submissive needs, you defy me—on my own bed. You swear that you want a Dom, so I give you one. But oh, he's not the one *you* want! See a pattern here? You're only willing to submit to your own bratty self. Guess what? It. Doesn't. Work. That. Way!"

Suddenly drawn by movement down the hall, Hammer glanced over Raine's shoulder to find Liam watching them, slowly buttoning his trousers and wearing an unmistakable scowl.

Chapter Four

Hammer turned his attention back to Raine only to find her looking toward the stairs, already planning her escape. Even as she defied him, he fought the urge to press his lips to hers. Claim her up against the wall, fuck the attitude, insecurities, and every ounce of hurt out of her. Leave her no doubt that she was *his*. Even if she wasn't.

Glancing over her shoulder once again, he was pleased to find Liam had wisely stepped back into the shadows, but had no doubt the other Dom was still listening.

"So I'm just supposed to let Beck do whatever he wants to me? Whatever happened to safe, sane, and consensual?" Raine challenged. "He isn't safe, and you know it. You've thrown him out yourself more than once for taking a sub too far. Putting someone who's never tested her pain limits with a sadist like him isn't sane. You know he terrifies me, so any scene between us wouldn't be consensual. With this mood you're in, I think you'd be happy to watch me bleed."

"Is that what you think?"

"What else am I supposed to think? I pushed some button of yours that you absolutely can't stand. It's made you mean. But you can't force him on me or keep me here against my will. I told you, I quit. And I'll consider myself lucky to have made it out of here with no more than a broken heart because Beck will break everything else."

She was right, damn it. The urge to reach up and trail his fingers over her cheek, reassure her and apologize, gnawed at him.

"Have a nice life." Tears rolled down her face. "I really hope you figure out someday that women like Marlie are too shallow to fill the big heart I know you have."

Panicked and unwilling to let her go, he pressed his body against her, pinning her back to the wall. With one hand braced above her, he looked into her stormy eyes. "Do you really think that after sheltering you for six fucking years, I would *ever* allow Beck to break you? And you have no idea what's in my heart, so please don't waste time guessing."

Her hard little nipples drove into his bare chest, surging electricity to his cock. Wanting her even as he turned her inside out made him a terrible bastard, and his self-loathing grated.

"I don't share your confidence in Beck. Right now, I have even less in you. You'll give your attention to condescending fuck dolls, but when I come to you with pure intentions, even if I might have gone about it the wrong way, you stab me through the heart." She shook her head and sniffled back fresh tears. "Enjoy little miss Botox. If Marlie and her ilk want to play head games, I don't know a man more equipped."

Raine shoved free and brushed his shoulder with her own as she stormed past him, giving him a look that warned him touching her again might mean the end of his balls.

God, he couldn't let it end like this. Not with anger and bitterness, blame and so fucking much regret. He'd crushed her fragile soul…but what else could he do? He couldn't explain his rejection without revealing all his nastiest secrets.

Ignoring her silent warning, he grabbed her again and slammed her to the wall, pressing his body so tightly against hers that escape wasn't possible. His cock jerked. "I told you, I'm not good for you, precious. I hate that you're hurting, but I won't let you waltz out the door when you belong here. Get that through your thick, stubborn skull."

She squirmed in an attempt to get away, shoving at him and stomping on his foot. But he refused to budge. He watched as she drew in a huge sob.

"You're not at all who I thought. I fell for a giving, gracious man with a spine of steel and a kind heart. You saved me once, but now…I'm already crying, and you've gone out of your way to make me feel both stupid and delusional." She shot him a scathing stare. "It's taken me a long time, but I finally figured it out. You're the fucked-up one, not me. All this time I thought I was broken, but your issues run deeper. At least I want to grow past my ghosts. You seem awfully content to let them haunt you."

His heart clenched. After all the years of shielding her from his demons, she'd still seen through his façade. He'd failed her. A red haze clouded his vision. *Fuck!*

"What happened to you, Macen?" She shook her head. "Forget it. You'll never tell me." Raising her chin rebelliously, she seared him with her blazing blue eyes. "Thanks very much for the last six years, Sir. Now please, let me go."

Impossible. But now what? No fucking clue.

Anger permeated every cell in his body as he slammed his fist into the wall right beside her head. Drywall exploded and rained onto the floor.

"Damn it, Hammer!" Liam barked in rebuke, tearing down the hall toward him. "Just what the hell do you think you're doing?" When he reached them, he pried Hammer's biting hands off Raine. The instant she was free, his friend pulled her shaking body into his arms, and she buried her head in his shoulder. "Look at yourself, man. Have you lost your bloody mind, then? Leave the wee lass alone. You're scaring her to death!"

Hammer clenched his jaw. Liam was right. How had he ever allowed things to get so out of hand? And why did she nuzzle against Liam so quickly, so naturally?

Raine eased away. "I'm sorry if we woke you. I was going to say goodbye as soon as Hammer let me go."

"Are you all right?" He stroked the side of her face with a gentle hand that made Hammer want to punch the wall again. When had they started speaking? Why had Liam gotten the idea that Raine would allow him to touch her?

"I'm fine." A sad smile curled the corners of her mouth. "Thank you for trying. I really wish..." She shook her head. "But I wouldn't be good for you, Liam. As Hammer pointed out, I'm nothing but a strong-willed brat. Consider that you've dodged a bullet. I wish you the best."

Wouldn't be good for him? As if...they'd done more than shake hands?

"What the hell are you talking about? I never fucking said that, girl!" he growled. "Did you not hear a single word I've said?"

Liam sighed. Then with a patient voice, he tucked a strand of midnight hair behind Raine's ear, fingers sure and soft, as if he'd done it before. "Go down the hall to wait for me in my private room, would you? I'd like to talk to you before you go." When she would have protested, he added, "Don't be making decisions about your future when you're upset. Let me talk to Hammer. I'll be in to speak to you soon. Will you do that for me, lovely? This won't take a minute."

She bit her lip as her gaze bounced between Liam's calm demeanor and his own furious stare.

Raine sighed. "All right."

Hammer didn't miss the ease with which she submitted to his friend. A silent string of curses filled his head as both he and Liam turned and watched her disappear down the darkened hall and into the other Dom's room.

Once she'd gone, Liam whirled on Hammer, like Raine's fucking knight in shining armor, his eyes incredulous and damning.

"What is going on between you two?" Hammer growled.

"What's going on between the two of *you*?" Liam countered. "I've no idea what ruckus caused you and Raine to reach this point, but it's obvious you've gone mad. Do I have to point out that a wee, raven-haired female is undoing you, Hammer?"

Oh, he knew that. As if dealing with Raine wasn't enough, Liam had joined the fucking bandwagon. To do what, see how much more he could take before he imploded?

"Do you have a point to make? Or should we just step outside so I can break your jaw?"

"I don't wish to embarrass you as I mop the car park with your face. That won't solve a bloody thing. Pull your head out of your ass, mate. You're worried you'll hurt her with your needs, but you're afraid to try because Juliet hid how she felt about them."

"I never said that," Hammer snapped. *Perceptive bastard.*

"Not in so many words, but you're thinking it. After all I heard tonight, do you think Raine is the sort who would hide her feelings from you? If she wasn't happy, do you think she'd keep that to herself?"

Hammer bristled. "She's so damn independent. Do you see her living Juliet's sort of life? There's no way she's ready for that. She wouldn't let me tell her what socks to wear, much less pick her entire wardrobe. And you know that's just the tip of the iceberg."

"So you want a more trained submissive, but you're unwilling to do anything to help her become what you need. That makes perfect sense," Liam drawled.

"I'm saying I don't think she'll ever get there. She'd take on the responsibility of trying and it would go against her grain. We'd both be miserable. Not only is it too much to put on her narrow shoulders, it would damage her. I can't do that."

"Then stop holding her to you when she tries to leave."

"It's not that simple. Every time she walks into the room, I come to life. Every time she leaves, I fucking fall apart. I'm not trying to hurt her."

"But do you really think you can order her to stay at Shadows after this? You said yourself she's impulsive. You told me that she left her home when she was barely more than a babe. You think she won't do it as a woman grown? And before you let your temper talk, think for a moment about a Shadows without Raine. Honestly, how would you feel?"

He couldn't fucking breathe. Hammer clenched his fists as panic surged through his bloodstream.

"This will blow over. In an hour, she'll be fine."

"Is that what you're telling yourself? Bloody christ!" Liam shook his head again. "Not this time. You've kept Raine on a leash so tight, she's all but strangling. She's done with that, I tell you. She's more than half out the door."

"Over my dead body."

"Then how badly do you want her to stay? Because I guarantee she'll be leaving before the sun's even up."

Hammer drew in a rough breath. He hated Liam for butting in and confronting him. Mostly, he hated his friend for being right.

"Goddamnit." He swallowed the scream inside him. Raine leaving Shadows was never going to be an option, at least not one he could live with.

"Use your head," Liam urged. "If you let her leave, you'll regret it for the rest of your life. The pain of Juliet might well pale in comparison."

Liam voiced his worst fear. Hammer swallowed.

"What the hell do you want me to do?" he demanded, tossing his hands in the air. "Since you have all the answers, tell me how I unwedge myself from this rock and the hard place I'm in?"

"Well, if you're not able or willing to help her down the submissive path, I guess I could." Liam shrugged nonchalantly. "She's pretty enough."

"Don't you *dare*!" Hammer saw red. "You're far more than Raine can handle, too."

"And Beck isn't? You said that giving her a red ass wouldn't fix her. Changed your mind, then? You think a sadist would do better?"

No. But Hammer wasn't trying to fix her…just make her hate him. "Maybe."

Liam rolled his eyes. "Give her to me to straighten out. I understand she's got under your nettle and deserves discipline, but for christ's sake…What in the hell possessed you to bring that sadistic son of a bitch into the equation? He'll break her for sure."

"No. Raine deserves punishment for her deplorable actions this morning. I'll make sure she gets it."

"And what about your behavior? Raine was dead on the money when she told you that you'd never allow Beck to touch any of your usual subs. Yet the one you've protected and nurtured for years, you'd toss her to him like a goddamn bone to a Rottweiler?"

He tried not to wince. "I've already handed down the punishment, and I can't go back on it. She's undermined me enough. Raine spends a session with Beck. That's final."

Liam turned a scrutinizing gaze on Hammer, as if trying to read his soul. "Very well. But if I can persuade her to stay, I insist on being there. Neither of us should risk Beck losing his head and drawing blood, or forgetting to heed her safe word."

Liam and Raine's lack of trust made him fume. Did they both think he'd simply turn Beck loose to do his worst on her? "Fine."

With a nod, Liam turned away abruptly, striding down the hall to find Raine. Hammer just watched. How the hell had everything turned to shit so quickly? With a sigh of disgust, he watched his friend disappear into the bedroom with the woman who'd consumed his soul, hoping Liam could work a miracle.

Liam entered his darkened room. Raine twisted around on the bed to watch him. The lighting from the hallway illuminated her big eyes as they fell on him. The silvery paths of tears stained her cheeks. Her nose was a bit red. Her little-girl lost expression made him want to stride across the room, take her in his arms, and soothe her. But he couldn't yet. She was nervous and distressed. First things first. He had to calm her, then find out where her head was at.

"Are you all right?" he asked, shutting the door behind him, then lighting a candle on his nightstand.

"I said I was fine. I'm sorry we woke you. What happened with Hammer? Is he mad at you? Or me? Yeah, that's who he's really mad at. Damn. Sorry, I'm nervous." She drew in a shuddering breath. "I didn't mean to babble. I'll shut up now. It really won't take me long to pack up and be gone."

"Stay, Raine. I'd like to talk to you." He put just enough command in his voice to induce her to respond. "I would hold you, listen, help if I might. Tell me what happened."

Her face closed up instantly, and Liam tamped down his frustration. He had to reach this girl if he was going to use her to help Hammer. And damn it, Raine was one unfulfilled need after another. It simply wasn't in his Dom DNA to let her suffer like this.

"Tell me." He drew closer, sat on the edge of the bed beside her. As she turned her face up to him, he cupped her cheek in his hand. Even in her sorrow and heartache, her delicate features drew him in.

She stiffened, swallowed. Bloody hell, if Hammer was going to be jealous, Liam knew she couldn't be wary of his touch. He had to fix that quickly…and forget how much he liked putting his hands on her.

"It's all right," he assured her. "You've had a rough morning. You need to get this off your chest."

"Thank you, but you don't have to trouble yourself. This morning just proved that I need to grow up. I'm sorry. I should probably apologize to Hammer, too, once I get my pride out of the way. But talking about it is pointless. I just don't belong here anymore."

With a heavy sigh, she rose from the bed. His stare fell on her soft curves, and Liam was suddenly aware of how little she wore. As she leaned down to him, she cupped his shoulder—and the tempting valley of her cleavage drew his gaze. To his shock, she brushed a kiss across his cheek. He had to fight the urge to touch her. "Some sub will be very lucky to have you. I'm kind of sorry it won't be me. But thanks for your offer."

He tried to stay calm, think, tread carefully.

"Now don't leave yet. Sit and tell me what happened." He'd give her a more direct command if he must, but he didn't want to come across as the enemy, so he kept his voice coaxing—for now.

She hesitated, then plopped down on the bed, looking somewhere between embarrassed and miserable. "I thought that before I could really consider your offer, I had to see if there was any chance that Hammer could…" She stopped, sighed. "But there isn't. I went to his room dressed in a lot less and tried to seduce him. Even when I had my mouth on his—" She looked away with a grimace, and Liam had a vivid mental picture of what she'd done to get Hammer's attention.

"He still turned me down. It hurt. We fought. I lost my temper. It got ugly." She shrugged. "Here we are."

A smile pulled at his lips. "No doubt you startled the hell out of him. Awakening to the soft, wet heat of a woman's mouth wrapped around one's John Thomas is generally something to appreciate. I'd say you surprised him, and he reacted poorly. Surely you'd not hold that against him."

She jumped to her feet. "I should have known you'd take your pal's side. I surprised Hammer, all right. And I aroused him. But he didn't want to deal with *me*, so he tossed me out of the room and jacked off. He had the nerve to shout my name when...well, you get it. You'll probably say it's his Dom's right or whatever, but I got so mad, I saw a red haze. I went to the dungeon and threw everything I could find on the floor. Okay, so it was stupid. But from that, Hammer decided that I needed a spanking. And to stick his fingers up my—" She shook her head. "He's not dictating to me when I can have an orgasm, and I made that clear."

Raine was like an angry wee bird, feathers bristling as she emphasized her words, her hands waving and breasts heaving. She was glorious.

He gave her a genuine smile, picturing only too well the scene she described.

She rolled her eyes. "And you think it's funny. Fuck, I am so leaving."

When she marched for the door, Liam leapt up, grabbed her wrist, and pulled her back against him. He surrounded her completely, stroking her back lazily to offset his unyielding hold.

"There now, lass. Christ, I'll bet the orgasm he gave himself was an empty regret compared to one he'd much rather have had between your lips."

She snorted. "No. I'm like a sister to him. He doesn't want me. He never will, and I don't think I can stay and watch him with women like Marlie anymore." She fidgeted in his grasp. "Can you let me go?"

Not a chance in hell, and if she thought Hammer truly wanted anyone but her, then someone had to pull back the man's curtain and show her the truth. Words wouldn't do it, but actions… Hammer in a jealous rage ought to convince her.

"You can't really want to leave home and all you know?" he said softly. "My offer still stands. Hammer hasn't done a good job teaching you or making you feel valued as a woman. So let me do that. Aren't you even a little curious to see what you might gain?"

She hesitated, considering. Liam wanted to push, but he didn't. The time wasn't right. Instead, he cajoled.

"C'mon lass. You're ready. Any responsible Dom gives the sub what she needs, and you've gone too long without that since Hammer has stifled you."

Raine stared at him, biting her lip. He could practically see her thoughts working. Time to lean on her a bit.

"Be brave, lovely. Take what I'm offering. I'd be good to you."

"That sounds great and all, but you're Hammer's best friend. And it's taken you a couple of months to reach the conclusion that I need…whatever it is you think I'm doing without. Plus, you never really told me what's in it for you. Yeah, you said I'm pretty, but I don't think that alone would motivate you to spend the weeks or months it will likely take to train me. Not to mention that you danced around telling me what you said to Hammer a few minutes ago. So forgive me if I'm a little suspicious."

Clever girl. She was smart to be wary. But he couldn't allow it to continue.

"It seems to me that you have more to gain than to lose by giving me a go. Hammer has already rejected you, and I'm sorry for it. But should you have to lose your home, as well? Rather than leaving, why not take this opportunity to try something new? Test your limits and grow." He stepped back and put a bit of distance between them so she wouldn't feel crowded or threatened. "You seem to think I have some ulterior motive, but I'd be lying if I said your plight doesn't grate at my need to protect and teach you what I believe you crave."

She sent him a considering stare. "If you have nothing to hide, then what did you two talk about before you came in here?"

He forced a casual shrug. "I'd have thought that would be obvious. We discussed why he was allowing you to get under his skin and create an uproar. Both of you were hot enough to fry eggs. He's my friend. Why wouldn't I be concerned?"

"About him, sure. That makes sense. But me? I'm nothing to you."

Just like Hammer had said, trust was going to be a major issue for her. Earning it while he wasn't being totally honest was an added challenge. But his plan would ultimately benefit Raine and Hammer both, if it worked. While he trained her, he would have to separate his ploy from her progress and focus on giving her exactly what she needed. She would eventually trust that he wanted her happiness.

"Because my concern for Hammer extends to his responsibilities as a Dominant. If he's unable to manage them, for whatever reason, then I will. That includes you."

Her nose wrinkled in distaste. "I'm tired of being someone's responsibility."

"That's not all you are to him. You're wrong if you think he doesn't love you. It may not be the way you want him to, but he cares." He cocked his head. Talking to her was a bit like playing a chess match. He had to carefully consider his every move. "I'll be more honest than I should when I say you won't be simply a responsibility to me. You're an untested submissive. That makes you a very attractive proposition. I'll enjoy coaxing your surrender. You'll be a lovely challenge."

She flushed. "And it won't bother you that I love him?"

Liam crafted his words carefully, then took a half step closer to cup her cheek and delve deep into her eyes. "I don't need your love, lass, just your trust. I've said I'd be willing to help you become the submissive you're wanting to be. Leave, don't leave. The choice is yours. But know this, Raine: Regrets are a heavy albatross to carry around your neck for the rest of your life."

She turned her attention from him to her own thoughts. He watched her face, practically saw her mind start to spin and race. Fascinating, really. He'd grown so used to women with towering walls guarding their thoughts, especially his ex-wife. Raine was so new, a blank slate in so many ways. Fresh. The idea of molding her excited him. The idea of touching her excited him, too—far more than it should.

"I see your point," she finally conceded. "What's the catch to your offer?"

Slowly, but surely, he was reaching her. "Hammer insists that he'll have his pound of flesh. I can't stop Beck from punishing you on his behalf. But if you agree to let me train you, I won't let him touch you. Either way, I'll be by your side to lend what support I may."

She lifted her chin. "If I stay, I'll manage Beck. I'm not a coward."

Liam fought a smile. Raine was many things—a minx, a smart girl trapped in a woman's body, a submissive without a Dominant to guide her—but he would never call her a coward.

"That you're not. Come." He took her hand. "Let me give you a taste of what I think you need. You can hardly say yes to what you don't fully understand."

He gave her a gentle tug. This time, she hesitated only an instant before she complied. He settled back on the side of the bed, pulling her onto his lap, facing the dresser mirror. She diverted her gaze.

"Look at us," he commanded, his words barely above a whisper.

This time, she didn't hesitate, but peered through the shadowy room to meet his stare in the mirror. As he held her back against his chest, he felt how small she was in his lap. When he brushed the shell of her ear with his lips, she shivered.

"Excellent," he told her. "You need discipline, and I don't disagree with Hammer's idea of giving you a red ass for your antics earlier."

When she stiffened and opened her mouth to protest, he held up a finger and sent her a stern glance. "Not a word. Let me finish."

When Raine sagged against him with a sulky little pout, he fought another smile. She'd be a handful, this girl. Something about her enchanted him. God knew that looking at her scantily-clad curves in the mirror was taking an uncomfortable toll on his self-control. He had the urge to find every one of her defenses and plow through them as fast as possible so he'd have her entire soul open to him. The idea was exhilarating. The mental image of her naked and bound, looking up at him with trust and longing… Fuck if that didn't make him hard. Well, harder.

"What you need more than discipline is understanding and affection. When was the last time you had someone you could truly talk to?"

Panic flitted across her face. "Don't you just want to tie me down and spank me and…"

Oh, he did, eventually. "Without trust, that's just abuse. And I'll never be treating you like that."

She fidgeted again. "But talking?"

Pain creased her features, as if he'd said he intended to drive stakes under her wee fingernails. He smothered another smile. The amusing little vixen was going to keep him on his toes. "How do you think trust is accomplished?"

Now Raine openly winced, and he didn't bother to hold in his laugh.

"Oh, that's right. Laugh it up at my expense." She gently elbowed him.

But her tart words didn't hold any heat. She teased rather than sassed. The ghost of a smile on her face pleased him.

"I said I intended to split you wide open like a ripe peach, didn't I?" He raised a brow.

Her smile fell. Slowly, she nodded.

"If you accept my offer, you'll quickly learn that if I say it, I mean it." Liam drilled his stare into her through the mirror, willing her to believe him. But he knew that would come in time. "And I need you to be honest with me as well. Can you do that, lass?"

"I'll try." She sounded hesitant.

Any other sub, he might punish. This one needed a different approach. As Hammer had admitted, she was fragile. Beneath her sometimes-saucy surface lay a woman who could easily break, and he wouldn't risk that. Raine was a potent mix of vulnerable femininity, intelligence, and strong will unlike any he'd met.

"You'll do more than try. If you feel you can't be honest, you'll say that. But you will not lie to me. Can you agree to that?"

"But if I tell you I can't be honest, you're only going to want to talk about it."

"I am."

"Ugh!" She rolled her eyes and sighed like a teenager talking to a probing parent. "I don't like to talk."

Neither did Hammer, and that was part of their problem. Both found it painful. Both were going to have to change if they wanted more in life than they had now.

"I gathered that." A smile tugged at his lips. "But that doesn't change anything. Tell me, when was the last time you had pleasure you didn't give yourself?"

"Ouch!" Her jaw dropped. "Don't go for the jugular or anything."

"Neither of us gains a damn thing if I dance around your pretty feet. Answer me."

She frowned and crossed her arms over her chest. Before his very eyes, he could see her walls rising, watch her forming a flippant answer.

"Whatever you're thinking now, stop." He infused the words with a sharp whip of demand. "Honesty. Not whatever you were digging out of your sleeve. Now, the last time a man gave you pleasure?"

Raine hesitated for a very long time, her face anxious. The truth was on the tip of her tongue. He just had to work it out of her.

Liam eased a hand under her little cotton halter and rubbed a thumb over her nipple. It hardened in seconds under his touch. She gasped but didn't push him away. Her pulse began hammering at the base of her neck. His body surged. Earning her trust an inch at a time was going to be arousing as fuck. And he didn't dare let up. As long as he did this, she would be too distracted to think up smart-assed replies.

"Tell me," he breathed in her ear.

With a little whimper, her head fell back, and she melted into him. Bloody hell if that wasn't one of the most arousing sights he'd ever seen.

"Two years ago."

"Where is he now?" He pinched her nipple, then soothed it with a caress.

She gasped. "Gone."

"What happened?" He lifted his free hand to her other nipple, giving it equal attention.

Raine arched, thrusting her lush breasts deeper into his hands. God, how had Hammer resisted her for so long? Already, Liam was hungry to fuck her. But hell, she needed his guiding hand far more than sex.

"Hammer always hunts down any man who touches me and sends them away."

So Hammer had been hoarding Raine. Yes, he'd begun by protecting her, but…the road to hell was paved with good intentions. And as her little backside squirmed in his lap, Liam realized he'd better keep that in mind, too. No way she could mistake his throbbing cock for passing interest.

She twisted around to look at him. He shouldn't…but he couldn't fucking stop himself.

Liam cupped her face, then captured her mouth. She opened hesitantly, but that was all he needed to deliver her a deep, drugging kiss. Then Raine went wild, turning toward him, throwing her arms around his neck, and straddling him, pressing herself tightly against his body.

The lass was indeed starved for touch. A groan slipped free from his chest as he gave it to her with a wicked onslaught of his lips and tongue. Her breath caught, and she wriggled her pussy against him like she'd caught fire.

Normally, he might not think she'd earned an orgasm. She hadn't been formally punished for her defiance yet. But Hammer had hurt Raine far more with his rejection than if he'd opened her skin with a whip. What she needed now was a reason to stay. And Liam needed a way to bind her to him so he could keep her here. He meant to use every weapon at his disposal: kindness, affection, pleasure. He'd steep her in orgasm until she had no interest in leaving. Then, once she'd learned a bit, once he'd displayed her pleasure with him and given Hammer the opportunity to go insane with jealousy, and once his friend had claimed the woman he loved…well, then Liam figured he'd consider it a job well done.

Raine clung to Liam, ground herself into his thick, steely cock, and whimpered. Every kiss between them was fireworks and rocket launchers. God, he felt incredible. Hot, muscled, persuasive, determined. He kissed like a god. With one seductive whisper, he could distract her utterly. One touch, and she felt her defenses crumbling. But those lips could capture her soul. Yes, she loved Hammer, but…Liam set her on fire.

Why? Why wasn't her body following her heart?

She pulled away and blinked into Liam's dark eyes. Why did that matter if Hammer didn't want her? Liam had given her a host of reasons to consider his proposal. Maybe she should.

"Was that a yes to my proposition?" His gaze drilled into her as he waited for an answer.

Raine could actually feel his desire when he touched her, surging toward her like a tidal wave, big and strong and sure. But what if he got tired of her after a few days? What if he fucked her once or twice then got her out of his system? What if she ended up alone again?

Liam brushed his fingers through the hair at her temple, then palmed her neck—a silent reminder that he waited. Did she have it in her to submit, really and truly? Did she trust him enough to try? Maybe. She wanted to. But she'd probably fail. As tempting as his offer was, she should save them both the trouble now.

On the other hand, what if she said yes? Raine suspected she'd be out of her clothes and flat on her back in less than a minute. Would that really be so bad? Besides being sexy as hell, Liam made her feel like a goddess. And she really needed that now. Kink aside, he seemed like a gentleman. Maybe he'd give her time to learn and adjust…get used to him.

Raine drew in a shuddering breath. "You heard my argument with Hammer. I'm not very good at being submissive, I don't think. When I lose my temper, I'm awful at controlling what I say. I mean to be good… I think I'm doomed to disappoint you." For whatever reason, that thought nearly made her cry again. Her throat closed up. Embarrassment stung. "For my own selfish reasons, I want to say yes. But you've been beyond fair. I can't be less so. The truth is, I probably can't be what you want or need."

He smiled gently. "We'll never know unless we give it a whirl. I've the desire and patience to help you. What have you got to lose, lass?"

Hammer was already lost to her. "Nothing, I guess."

"Precisely. We'll have an enjoyable battle of wills, you and I. I promise, you'll not be bored."

A tremor passed through her when his broad hands surrounded her waist. This man could never be boring, not when he ignited every red-blooded cell in her body with a single touch.

"Take a chance, Raine," he coaxed. "Have you not shed enough tears from these lovely eyes? You could do worse than a big bastard like me." He chuckled, clearly trying to lighten the mood. "I'd try my best to make you feel good about yourself and the two of us together."

With every word he spoke, she grew more tempted—and confused. He said all the right things. He echoed so many of the sentiments she'd longed to hear from Hammer. Raine wondered if she should pinch herself…or wait for the punch line. But no denying that Liam made some great points. The idea of taking a chance with him made sense, even though it scared the hell out of her.

"I hear you. I just I don't know how to take you. You sound like you're for real, but I keep coming back to the question, why me? You must want a proper submissive. And I… Look, if you just want sex, that's easy. I'd be interested. We could do that now and call it a day. You don't have to take me on as a 'project' for that."

Raine couldn't pass up the chance to feel good and focus on nothing but the pleasure Liam could give her for an hour. She reached for the hem of her halter top, ready to yank it over her head. It wasn't like Hammer would care.

"Now hold up there." He stayed her with a light grip on her arm and a shake of his head.

She froze. Shame flooded her. Crap, she'd done it again, thrown herself at a man who had no intention of taking her up on her stupid, impulsive offer. Once more, she'd been put in her place. Though Liam had done it differently than Hammer, the result still made her feel the same. Rejected. Embarrassed. Uncertain. She'd thought Liam wanted her, but...

"I-I'm sorry. Oh, god." She felt sick. "I d-didn't mean to presume... I'm going to go."

When she tried to scramble to her feet, he tugged her back against him. "Stop. I want you, lass, something fierce. But if it were just a fucking I sought, do you think I'd even be talking to you now, hmm?" He cocked a brow. "Why would I seek out a distraught woman for sex who's been through the wringer when I can find a compliant sub?"

With that deep, lilting voice that turned her on, he made a really good point.

"What are you saying?"

"Let's go about this the right way, shall we?" Liam lifted her from his lap. "Strip and kneel on the floor here at my feet."

Raine hesitated. "B-but I *was* stripping."

"Carelessly and without a single thought of submission in your head. That's not acceptable. That's not how it's going to be. Go on now. I want to see you bonny and bare."

With trembling fingers, she locked her gaze on his as she lifted her shirt over her head. Then she eased her skirt down her hips. With a pounding heart she sank, naked and on her knees before him. Breasts thrust out, she knelt with legs spread.

Liam silently praised her with a soft hand down her hair. She could feel the heat of his stare all over her. "You look lovely. What's your safe word?"

She barely had time to bask in his praise before his question hit her. She blinked. "Do I need one? Are you going to…hurt me?"

"You always need one, no matter what. Tell me yours."

Her mind went blank. She'd never needed one before, and she'd heard many over the years of working here at Shadows. It had to be something she could say easily, but not something she'd shout in the midst of pleasure or pain. "Paris?"

He raised a brow. "Beautiful city. Is that why you picked it?"

"I've never been, but I'd like to go someday. It just popped into my head." She shrugged.

"Paris it is." A little smile played at his mouth. "Now, tell me why the devil you would think you're a project. You're a woman, beautiful and feisty. But you don't see that in yourself, do you?"

She grinned a little. "Is that your polite way of saying I'm pretty but a brat…Sir?"

"Maybe a wee bit." His rich, deep laugh caressed her before he fell serious again. "Raine, you know I can only take what you give me. Submission means you have the control. Always. Like now. Stand up and turn back around. Look at yourself in the mirror. What do you see?"

His voice turned deeper, more controlled. Finding the courage to look in the mirror was difficult. She couldn't force herself to face her own reflection. She bowed her head, fretful that she'd annoy or displease him. Something in her seemed to shrivel up at the thought.

He walked across the room and flipped on the bright, glaring lights overhead. In the terrible hush, she didn't know what to say. Feeling his silent will, she followed his command and raised her head. She frowned as she got a good look at her tear-stained face.

"Oh my god, I'm a mess!" Raine couldn't stand to look at her splotchy cheeks, swollen eyes, and wild hair under those intense lights for a second more. She glanced away.

"No, none of that, lass. You're a beauty. Look again, past the tears. What do you see?"

"I don't know," she murmured as she forced herself to gaze at her own reflection, trying not to flinch. "Someone lost. Someone who's been lingering where she probably shouldn't. Someone everyone in this club probably thinks is pathetic."

Liam cupped her face in his hand, raising her chin. Side by side, their faces reflected.

"There's a wee bit of a lost soul here, but you're no longer the frightened child you once were. You're a woman grown, and you need more than Hammer has allowed you. But you haven't found the Dom willing to give it to you." He wrapped an arm around her. "Until now."

Maybe Liam could give her more. Hammer had watched over her, helped and protected her, which was more than she could say for her own family, but he hadn't nurtured her as a submissive or a woman.

Liam palmed her heavy breasts. She sucked in a shaky breath as his thumbs lightly brushed over her nipples. As she liquefied beneath his touch, she watched the heat grow in his eyes.

"There's my beauty, right there. Just a little trust... Give me that, and I'll make it better."

Or make it worse. In seconds, he'd set her entire body aching and yearning.

"Liam," she whimpered, arching her back, legs shifting restlessly, silently begging for more.

"There now. Softly does it, lass. Put yourself in my care. I know what you need and I want you to let the longing you've kept inside you free. But you've got to be still for me."

Damn it, that voice of his deepened again, turning her on even more. As his fingers pinched her tight nipples, she writhed. Her hips bucked. Her pussy wept. She wanted to close her eyes and savor every sensation, but his demanding stare held her prisoner.

Suddenly, his hands settled gently on the curve of her waist. "I know you've been hurting. But if you want me to help you, you've got to be still and give yourself over to me."

It wasn't easy, but Raine forced herself to relax, stop her movements, and look at the two of them in the mirror.

His smile made her glow. "Excellent. For your effort, you deserve a little reward."

He lowered one hand, aiming between her thighs. His caress brushed down her abdomen agonizingly slow, but his intent was clear. His other hand continued to torment her nipple as his warm breath skimmed over her neck.

"Please, Liam," she whispered, struggling to remain still under his slow, teasing touch.

His hand lingered over her, his hovering fingers taunting her. "I feel the heat of your cunt, Raine. I smell you, too, sweet and ripe."

She couldn't speak, only look into his eyes with a beseeching hunger. Her hips jerked involuntarily toward his touch. His fingers grazed her bare heat. He quickly removed them.

"Now what did I tell you?"

"To stay still." She bit her lip. Would he punish her now? "I'm trying, I swear."

"Try harder. Your will is strong. Be brave enough to surrender your control. If you can do that, you'll get what you need."

He was right; she knew that. She'd watched enough scenes to know how it worked. She closed her eyes, focused, not on the way he made her ache, but on hearing his voice in her head and heeding his command. *Be still.* It took a moment. The urge to lean closer to him, sway into his mesmerizing touch was strong, but she forced her will to be stronger. With a deep breath, she raised her chin, opened her eyes. And didn't move.

"Now there's a pretty sight. I knew you had it in you, lass. You're pleasing me so much. Let me show you."

His fingers plunged into her swollen, weeping folds, and she arched back, crying out as her pussy gripped his digits tightly. "That's a good girl. You are one of the most lovely creatures I've yet laid eyes on. Feel what I do to you. Center yourself around my touch. I mean to draw you to me, little by little, Raine. I'll take everything you give and always want more. Are you strong enough to handle that? Do you crave more of the feeling I'm giving you right now?"

It was as if he could see into her soul and know everything she wanted to hear. Liam's tender dominance made her feel so alive. So free. If this sensation was what all submissives felt…god, no wonder women flocked to this club. No wonder so many wanted Liam.

"God, yes." On fire and feeling like a desirable woman, the words were out of her mouth before she could think. He devastated her with his voice, his deft touch. Her body reacted as though he plunged his cock deep and sure inside her. And her defenses began to crumble.

When his thumb circled her little pebbled clit, her dormant body ignited, the fire so painfully scalding that she couldn't hold back the torrent of release rolling inside.

As if sensing the rushing wave cresting higher, he brushed his lips up her neck. "Feel me, my warmth and sincerity. Feel with your heart, not your head. Yes…" he moaned. "You're surrounding my fingers like a hot, silken glove. Come for me, Raine. Let me feel how the woman and the submissive long to be freed. Shatter for me hard!"

Inside her, the wave of ecstasy crested and broke. She was helpless to do anything but give her pleasure over. Here, in this moment, she felt more protected and cherished than she ever had. Her mind and body splintered, fracturing to pieces before him. Screams of joy tore from her throat and with it, the blissful hope that he would never let her fall.

He held her in his arms as she trembled in the aftermath, gently brushing back the hair from her face and whispering praise. He smiled warmly as she slowly focused back to their images in the mirror.

"Beautiful, lass. Your submission is a bounty beyond compare. I'd all but resigned myself to the status quo of subs here at the club. But a bonnier woman with such fire I've never seen. If you let me, I will comfort you and cherish your submission. Hold your head high for me."

She raised her chin.

"Yes, like that. Now wipe your tears and be brave. Stop your worrying about whatever it is you think I need. Give me all you can so you can be whole."

No doubt he must see that she was a bigger challenge than he'd intended…but it wasn't turning him away. If anything, he seemed more determined to have her. She had no idea why he'd turned his goodness her way if it wasn't for the sex. Maybe he wanted to stick one in Hammer's eye. Maybe he just liked helping wounded doves. Whatever. She was done looking a gift horse in the mouth.

He wrapped his arms beneath her breasts and pulled her tightly against him. The warmth of his body enveloped her with a comforting promise of protection. His hard, thick cock burned into her lower back, but he made no move to ease himself.

She closed her eyes and savored his touch—the touch of a man who seemed to both want and appreciate her. It was far more than she'd ever had before. Than she'd dared to hope.

"Thank you." Raine didn't know what else to say to express all the gratitude in her heart. This man would be so easy to kneel for.

"Will you give me a bit of your trust, then?"

Whatever happened next, Liam had given her a precious gift: hope. She had to stop being so defeated and hold her head up. Face life. She'd always done that before. If Hammer didn't want her, she wasn't going to let the son of a bitch break her.

"I need a bit of time to be sure. I'm not in the best frame of mind to make decisions. A day or two... Is that too much to ask?"

"No, that's wise. Take a couple of days, then give me your answer. For right now, come. Lay with me on the bed and let me hold you. Try and get a little sleep."

He stepped away, taking the soothing veil of body heat with him. Shivering softly, instantly missing his reassuring warmth, she watched as he held out his hand. She turned and took it, allowing him to lead her to the bed. "Just sleep?"

He settled against the sheets, bringing her close, then stared into her eyes. "You need it, but I'm still a man. I want you naked against me. Rest your weary head for now. We'll work everything out."

Chapter Five

With less than an hour to go before this travesty was set to begin, Liam prowled into the bar, looking for Beck. Hammer had avoided him all afternoon, knowing Liam would do his best to talk him out of this public humiliation. It was meant to strip Raine of her considerable pride, and Liam understood. But tearing the lass down wasn't the way to correct her. And if his friend wasn't going to listen, maybe Liam could convince Beck to see reason. Raine certainly didn't deserve what the sadist would dish out in Hammer's name, and unless Liam missed his guess by a mile, Raine wouldn't like it, either. He'd held and reassured the girl enough all morning to know that the last thing she needed was more pain.

And with every moment he'd cradled her in his arms and slid her soft skin over his own, he'd only wanted her more.

Seated at the long, sleek bar, Beck nursed a glass of whiskey in one big hand. A coiled whip dangled from his hip. Instantly, Liam saw a vision of Raine's blood trailing down her fair skin, pooling in the small of her back, in the crooks of her knees, just like that of the masochist Beck had worked to oblivion last weekend. Every protective instinct came off its leash. Even if Beck was skilled enough never to scar his subs, Liam would *not* have Raine's perfect, milky skin cut even once—and he didn't want to think too hard about why he felt so insistent.

Beck turned and watched his approach with a welcoming smile. At Liam's glare, the sadist's expression turned puzzled.

He didn't give Beck the opportunity to say a word, just growled at the man in barely controlled rage. "Don't be thinking you'll mark wee Raine. I'll be there watching you like a hawk. If you make her bleed, I'll take your fucking whip and shove it up your ass!"

Beck raised a brow at him, eyes glittering. "Who flipped your bitch switch? First of all, Hammer already talked to me about what I'm allowed to do to the princess. And second, it's none of your business. She's been under Hammer's protection for years. His choice, his punishment. My pleasure. Piss off."

Liam leaned in, pointing his finger directly in the other man's face. "I mean it, Beck. Don't mark her, or you'll answer to me."

Now that he'd gotten that off his chest, Liam tapped the counter. The bartender set a shot of whiskey before him. Liam slammed it back, needing it to calm his nerves. He tried to think of any other way he could spare Raine this degradation, but his options were limited. He couldn't help her unless she chose to help herself.

Beck lifted the whip from his hip and arched the long leather single tail above his head, splitting the air with a sharp crack. Looking over his shoulder, he smirked at Liam. "Don't worry. The marks from this little beauty won't last long. She can handle it. She might even like it. And if she doesn't..." He shrugged. "Well, that's why it's punishment."

Liam charged Beck, fury boiling his blood. "If she so much as breaks a fucking fingernail while she's with you, I'll break your goddamn face."

Beck looked somewhere between annoyed and amused. "Okay, so the whip is out. How about a nice, thick leather paddle? It won't break her skin, but the bruise it will leave. . . Hmm, yeah." His grin turned to a leer. "That deep purple hue on her lily white ass will make your dick hard."

Liam knew a hundred ways to get off, but bruising a pretty sub wasn't one that tripped his trigger.

"Listen to me. Not your whip. Not your fucking paddle, or any other cutting, bruising, intense pain giving, sharp-knotted flogger you have touches her skin. I don't give a flying fuck what you and Hammer have cooked up. I'm telling you, I don't want her marked, period."

"So basically, you just want me to kick back and have a manicure?" Beck threw up his hands. "Maybe I should just flog her with cotton balls. No, wait! You probably think that would be too damn brutal." The sadist grinned slyly. "I guess I could beat her with my tongue."

Liam saw red. Vaguely, he realized that Raine was tying him up in knots—like Hammer—but that didn't stop him from wanting to protect her. "Your tongue best be kept to yourself, along with your pecker, if you've a mind to keep them attached. You've been warned."

Beck yawned. "Go bark at Hammer. Believe me, I'd rather get this over with, so I can find a *real* sub who will—"

"Fuck you, Beck. Raine *is* a real sub."

"Yeah? When has she ever submitted to anything or anyone?"

This morning, and it had been delicious. Her soft sighs. Her tentative, trembling trust. Bloody hell, he got hard just thinking about it. He was walking a dangerous line with Hammer's girl…

Beck was deliberately baiting him. Raine was none of the man's business, and this pissing contest was getting them nowhere. Riling up the sadist just before he meted out the lass's sentence completely defeated the purpose of trying to spare her.

"Just remember what I've said."

As he pushed away from the bar and headed for the stairs, Beck laughed. "Christ, this is funny. You and Hammer have both got a boner for the princess."

Fuck the wanker for being right.

Gnashing his teeth, Liam ignored Beck and stomped back to Raine's room.

If she'd only agree to his training, then she'd be under his protection. But she wanted and needed time to make a decision. Maybe she sensed that she shouldn't take his offer at face value. Maybe she feared what opening up her soul to him—or any man—would mean. It was that trust problem Hammer had warned him about. And it chafed. Ordinarily he'd be happy to let her weigh the pros and cons and come to a sensible conclusion. But Beck could very quickly get out of hand, and with Hammer not in his right mind where Raine was concerned, Liam had no option but to convince her to reconsider.

When he knocked, she bade him to enter. He found her sitting quietly on the bed, waiting in a ruffled, black baby-doll nightie. The top two triangles were completely transparent as they hugged her heavy breasts and tight nipples. Just beneath her bust, the fabric turned silky. He couldn't see through it, but it shimmered as it parted and played peekaboo with her navel. Beneath that, Liam caught a little scrap of silky black underwear. She rounded the seductive look with fuck-me stilettos that, despite her short stature, made her legs look a mile long.

Liam sucked in a breath. What had possessed her to wear *that*? She looked stunning and completely fuckable, but not at all ready for the sort of attention Beck had in mind. *Christ!* And, no doubt, she'd chosen that get-up to flaunt her every curve at Hammer. Raine's expression looked surprisingly resigned, even calm, but already he could distinguish fidgeting and stuttered breathing that revealed her agitation. Liam cursed.

She drew her knees up to her chest, covering her breasts, and he wondered why she sought to show everything to Hammer…but hide from him.

Because she loved the stupid brute. And that bothered him more than it should.

"Did you find Beck?" She bit her lip. Something on his face must have given the answer away because she suddenly groaned. "Don't tell me, let me guess. He didn't want to hear a word you had to say."

"Precisely, lass. Sorry."

"That's Beck." She smiled. "It was sweet of you to try, but we should go. Don't want to be late."

"Hold up." He grabbed her hand, squeezing it. "It doesn't have to be this way. I could protect you if you wore my training collar. Agree, and this foolish business stops here and now. You'll still be punished, but it'll be by my hand."

She hesitated, dropping her gaze, then sent him a soft stare. "In a way, it's really tempting. But if I'm truly going to say yes to you, I want to do it for the right reasons, not because Beck scared me enough to hide behind you. And maybe I shouldn't care what Hammer thinks, but six years of habits die hard. If I walked in wearing a training collar, he'd know I took it simply as an out. That would make me both a coward and the brat he accused me of being."

"You're nowhere near the brat everyone has convinced you that you are. And personally, as much as I'd enjoy color flushing your face and striping that perfect white ass, I'd rather it came from *my* hand."

Suddenly, she lowered her legs, exposing her breasts again, and he forgot what else he'd meant to say. He stared at her loveliness and imagined his cock fully seated inside her snug little pussy. The erection he'd been enduring all day got harder.

Damn it all. Fucking her wasn't the plan. He'd begun all this for Hammer…yet he could barely think of anything now but having Raine to himself. He'd better shut that down and get his head on straight.

"But if you'd rather face Hammer…" Liam pulled her upward. "Let's get this over with."

With a nod, she followed him into the corridor, around the corner, and into a public area of the dungeon. Word obviously traveled fast, because a crowd had gathered, and it seemed to him that every man in the place turned to look at Raine's breasts. Beck lounged against a spanking bench, staring at her with a predatory leer that Liam wanted to punch off his face. Hammer stood nearby, body stiff, mood ugly.

His stare drilled into Raine, bouncing between her big eyes and her nipples. The stupid bastard must be tempted by her. He'd have to be dead not to be.

Raine stood defiantly, without an ounce of submission in her "fuck you" expression. Liam would have smiled if not for the fact that she crossed her arms over her chest, fingertips squeezing her biceps tightly. Under her bluster, the wee thing was terrified.

As Hammer approached Raine, his eyes narrowed in silent warning. She glared back. Liam watched protectively, gut knotting with an overwhelming need to keep her safe.

"Lose the baby-doll and the attitude, precious. You're here for a reason," Hammer drawled.

"Let me see to her punishment," Liam said quietly. "Beck looks like he's going to enjoy this way too much."

Hammer sent him a scathing glare. "Beck knows what I want."

What was Hammer trying to accomplish? He wouldn't take the girl as his own, yet with this stunt, he'd keep Raine at arm's length while maintaining his hold over her.

Beck nodded with a dirty grin, his five o'clock shadow spreading over lean cheeks. "Oh, yeah. I know *exactly* what to do."

That set Liam off. He grabbed Hammer by the arm and yanked him to the far side of the dungeon. "Stop this! You're not punishing her for her behavior, but because she makes your cock ache and you're too much of a pussy to take her."

"Is that what you think?" Hammer hissed. "Did she neglect to tell you that she came into my room uninvited while I slept and wrapped her mouth around my dick?"

"She told me."

Hammer's jaw tightened. "And when I spanked her for crossing boundaries, she fought me. I denied her orgasm for three days, so she masturbated *on my bed*. As soon as I found her, she chose that moment to come."

Liam hadn't known that. "You hurt her feelings, mate. It's no surprise she lashed back."

"Instead of talking to me, she made a fucking mess on the floor that someone else had to clean up. I even gave Raine an easy out of this punishment. All she had to do was apologize, but the girl was too stubborn to do it. I don't answer to you, *mate*, so get your hand off me."

This confrontation was accomplishing nothing except getting Hammer's back up. Liam uncurled his fingers from the man's arm and strode back through the parting crowd to Raine.

She stiffened, looking so brittle, it was a wonder she didn't shatter. "Can we get this over with?"

"Yeah." Beck prodded, uncoiling the whip at his side and rolling it, the tattoos on his biceps bunching with movement. "Is this fucking gabfest done?"

Liam opened his mouth to warn Beck off, but Hammer cut in. "Absolutely. Do it." He stared Raine down. "Strip, girl. Now! Your safe word is 'lesson.'"

"Oh, that's clever." She rolled her eyes.

"Keep up the insolence. You'll get extra punishment." With a clenching of his jaw, Hammer strode away and settled into a nearby chair. Everyone around them fell utterly silent.

Liam turned to Raine, whispering in her ear. "I'm here, lass, and I'll not be leaving you."

At her tense nod, he plucked at the ribbon holding her baby-doll together and eased it off her shoulders. God, the sight of her bare skin and pretty nipples nearly made his knees weak. She turned her gaze to her own reflection in the mirrors surrounding the padded table, holding her head high, even as she shivered. So bonny and brave…and stubborn. He cupped her shoulders and brought her forward to face Beck, who sidled closer with a burning stare that looked a bit too happy to promise anything but pain.

As Liam released her, he glanced down the graceful line of her spine, to her pert backside, then reared back in surprise. She wore nothing beneath the nightie, except minuscule black boy shorts. Emblazoned across her ass in bold print were the words Fuck You Very Much.

"Bloody hell!" Was she trying to incite Hammer to turn Beck loose on her?

Liam saw now exactly what the man had meant about the brat's claws coming out when she felt threatened.

Raine peeked over her shoulder at him from beneath dark lashes, flashing him an anxious look. "Um, that wasn't meant for you, Liam. Sorry."

Normally, he wouldn't condone disrespect, but as far as he was concerned, Hammer had earned it. He spun Raine around so his friend could read her sassy message.

Immediately, Beck chuckled. Half the crowd gasped. That only seemed to set Hammer off more.

With a low growl, the dungeon owner narrowed his eyes. "That's going to cost you a few more, precious. Beck, rip those damn panties off and begin."

"It'll be my pleasure. I'll make sure she pays." The sadist flashed a broad smile as his big steps ate up the floor. Then he tore the panties from Raine's ass with a loud rip and snaked his big hand around her arm, yanking her from Liam. "Up on the bench, brat. Time for me to have some fun."

As Raine swallowed and glared at Hammer one last time, she positioned herself on the padded apparatus, head up and eyes forward in the mirror as she draped her slender body over the top and lifted her tender white ass in the air. Liam would have appreciated the view more if he hadn't been so riled.

Circling her, Beck inspected her with a critical eye. Letting loose a hearty laugh of satisfaction, he reached between her knees and shoved them apart. Raine yelped. Beck didn't pay her any mind, just locked her ankles in the cuffs.

"Remember what I said to you," Liam growled in Beck's face as the man sauntered past and restrained her wrists.

Beck snorted as he ripped off his tank to reveal his wide, muscled chest. The idea of him unleashing all his strength on wee Raine made Liam insane. She hadn't been without blame in the spat with Hammer, but she didn't deserve the kind of beating Beck would give her.

The sadist raised a mocking brow. "Before I start, you want to make sure she can tug her wrists out of those cuffs so she can reach back and cover her ass? We wouldn't want her butt to sting or anything."

Bloody wanker! His hands were tied unless Raine safeworded out or said yes to his proposition. Given the lift of her chin, he didn't think for a moment that she'd tell Hammer she'd learned her "lesson." She'd rather saw her own head off. Nor did she seem ready to commit to his training collar. Liam cursed under his breath. All he could do was scrutinize the restraints to ensure they weren't too tight.

Beck grabbed his damn whip and cracked it sharply in the air. Raine gasped, stiffened. Her big blue eyes went wide with fear. The goddamn sadist grinned, and Liam had to force himself to stand down when he would have gleefully knocked Beck on his ass. But Raine needed him now more than he needed to unleash his anger.

"Don't worry," he whispered in her ear. "I won't let him hurt you."

She sent him a shaky nod and a grateful expression. To everyone else, she'd shown defiant anger. But on some level, she trusted him—and him alone—with her vulnerability. She was trying. It was enough for the moment.

"Get on with it," Hammer snapped at Beck, drilling a cold, hard stare Liam's way. "I've told you what to do. Now fucking do it!"

"On it." Beck dropped the whip, and it slithered to the ground. Liam didn't have time for relief before Beck raised his beefy hand in the air, then dropped a menacing whisper in Raine's ear. "Count, princess. I want to hear you loud and clear."

The words had barely passed his lips before he brought his hand down. Obviously, Beck had decided to skip the warm-up. Instead, he began with a brutal blow across her left cheek.

Raine's head snapped up as she jolted and hissed. Then she glared at Hammer in the mirror. Her stubborn pride kept her from admitting aloud that Beck's spanking hurt like hell, but her pinched mouth and tense glower said it anyway.

"I told you to count," Beck growled.

Turning to look at the sadist, she glared. "Are you too busy being Hammer's bitch to remember what comes after one?"

"You'll pay for that, brat," Beck thundered at her as he threw his hand back in the air, aiming brutally for her ass again, landing an even harder blow on her right cheek.

Liam watched her bite her lip to hold in a cry. She dug her teeth in so hard, he wasn't surprised when it started to bleed.

Storming over to Beck, Liam grabbed his wrist. "You should never touch a sub in anger."

The other man yanked away, rolling his broad shoulders. "You think I don't know that?"

"Then act like you do." Liam went to Raine and leaned down to brush his lips over her ear. "Enough. You've made your displeasure known. Don't bait the bear anymore. Take your punishment, then it will all be over. I know you're mad at Hammer, but try to remember that he's the man who kept you safe all these years. If you—"

"This is my punishment of a sub under *my* protection. Back the fuck off," Hammer snarled at him, leaping from his chair and striding across the room. When he reached Raine, he gripped her chin, forcing her to look up at him. "Girl, you either accept this punishment without another mocking outburst, or I swear I'll throw Liam out and unleash Beck to do whatever he wants on your ass. Playtime is over, and I'm out of patience. Do you understand me?"

"Yes, Sir." Her tone was more insolent than obedient.

Things had gotten out of hand far too quickly. Liam could either sit back while Beck beat the shit out of her or he could try coming up with a plan *B*. Hammer wasn't going to stop this. It didn't take a bloody rocket scientist to see that Raine was never going to yield her submission through pain. Boundaries would help her feel safe, yes. But she needed affection to blossom.

More than anyone, Hammer should understand that. If his friend didn't want to hear the truth, then he could go fuck himself.

Reaching Hammer was a long shot, but Liam had to try again.

"We both know she'll learn nothing from this punishment except to hate you," he whispered in Hammer's ear. "You've spent years protecting her, and now you're going to scare the bloody shit out of her? Surely you can see she needs a different direction. I know you want me to shut up, but the sub's needs come first. Think about hers."

Hammer's eyes turned molten. His face flushed with anger. "If you question me again during this punishment, I'll ban you from the club." He gestured to Beck. "Continue."

Liam swallowed his incredulity as Hammer returned to his throne. Rage followed. He'd expected that Hammer wouldn't appreciate his interference, but they were friends. The man who had all but given him the shirt off his back once or twice had threatened to throw him out. Liam wondered if he knew the man at all anymore.

Shoving aside his confusion, he focused on Raine. Riling up both the executioner and the Dungeon Master wouldn't help her. He dragged in a shuddering breath, trying to find some calm. Fuck, what a balls up! Seeing Raine so apprehensive made his Dominant heart growl with the need to protect. He had to start thinking with his head or he'd leave her vulnerable.

The girl clung to her bloody stubborn pride. Hammer hadn't left her with much else, so she wouldn't cede it without a battle. Earning her trust and teaching her to curb her temper would be a full-time job.

And god help Beck if he didn't stop behaving like a barmy fuck. The sadist obviously enjoyed the power of toying with everyone. Personally, Liam didn't know why Hammer let the man in the club, much less seemed to like him. Whatever the reason, Beck bore watching.

So did Hammer. The man's famous cool-under-pressure façade seemed to be crumbling under…what? Frustration? Guilt? Longing? Probably a potent cocktail of all three—not that Hammer would admit it.

Beck smiled smugly, and Liam did his best not to bristle. Instead, he focused on the eerie quiet around them. The dungeon lacked the usual sounds of paddles, whips, sighs, and moans. Even the music seemed muted. It felt as if time had stopped, and every eye was on them.

The crowd held their collective breath with bated anticipation, eyes glued to the drama. Crossing his arms over his chest, Liam forced himself to stand and watch, determined to see this through for Raine, no matter what.

From the corner of his eye, he saw Beck reach into his toy bag and withdraw something oblong and red that looked like a colorful paddle. Liam started forward, but he wasn't fast enough. Beck crossed his arm over his body, then brought the paddle down with a quick *whoosh* in a backhanded swat.

Someone in the crowd gasped. The legs of Hammer's chair scraped the floor as he leapt to his feet and shouted just as Beck whacked the back of Raine's thighs.

The telltale whiff of rubber assaulted him. Then agony erupted across her face, as if Beck had split her very flesh open down to the bone. Her wee body jolted as she stiffened every muscle and screamed. And screamed. And screamed some more, even when she'd run out of air and her mouth hung open in horrific silence. Her face looked shocked and wounded, eyes wide with distress.

Furious, Liam twisted around to Beck. The man's expression gleamed with satisfaction—almost pride. His smug grin widened again when Raine hung her head and sobbed, tears pouring down her cheeks.

"What the hell are you doing?" Hammer snarled at Beck, his face blazing with rage.

Exactly what Liam wanted to know. His hand curled into a brutal fist, and he charged toward Beck. Suddenly, Hammer's attention snapped Liam's way, and a warning scowl dominated his face. Fuck, if he did anything to Beck, Hammer might really throw him out. Didn't his friend fucking see that Beck was abusing the girl?

Rushing back to Raine, Liam grabbed her face. A glance down into her eyes—so blue, wide open, and terrified—kicked him in the gut. Silently, she pleaded for help as the tears kept running. He wanted to take her in his arms.

"You've got a safeword. Use it," he demanded.

"Won't let them win." She gritted her teeth, holding herself together by pure will.

The *whoosh* filled the room again as Beck lifted the paddle. Raine gasped and grabbed the table, obviously bracing for another brutal blow. Liam glared at Hammer incredulously. The air stopped. He wondered if his old friend would really let this continue.

The Hammer he'd known once upon a time, never. But this one was miserable and tormented. Liam didn't know where this man's head was at all.

"Then say yes to me." He bent to Raine and stared into her eyes, willing her to understand and accept. "Say yes, and all of this stops."

"What?" Beck barked. "The only thing the princess gets to say is, 'thank you, Sir. May I have another?' And I've got plenty more where that came from."

Raine's eyes darted from Liam to Beck's reflection in the mirror.

She flinched and breathed, "Yes."

Relief and a dizzying thrill flooded Liam's veins.

"Put that goddamn paddle down now," Hammer barked at Beck. "Rubber? Are you out of your fucking mind? She's not a pain slut."

"Don't be a pussy," Beck sneered, fingering the rubber paddle, clearly eager to bring it down on Raine's tender flesh again. "A few good whacks will pull the starch right out of her bitchy attitude and make her pliant as a kitten."

Liam couldn't disagree more, and neither man seemed to have heard what she'd said.

"If you hit her with that again, I'm going to chain your ass to a cross and beat you with it myself," Hammer threatened.

"Louder," Liam demanded. "Let everyone hear you."

"Yes!"

Raine wailed out the word, but it was finally enough.

Suddenly, Hammer whipped his stare to her. His narrow-eyed glare fell back on Liam. "What did she say 'yes' to?"

Right now, Liam didn't owe Hammer a goddamn word, not where Raine was concerned. Nor did he have time. Only Raine herself mattered. He shook off Hammer's questions and knelt to her wrists, prying them out of the cuffs one at a time before he jumped to the restraints around her ankles. A glance at the backs of her thighs proved an angry bruise was already forming where Beck had struck her.

Worry and fury hit him in equal measure, but he buried both for Raine, wrenched her ankle cuffs off, and pulled her into his arms. He cradled her, limp and sobbing, against his chest.

"What the fuck are you doing? Give her to me." Hammer strode toward him, arms outstretched to take Raine away. "*I* decide when the scene ends."

"Not anymore," he growled. "Raine just accepted my training collar. She is now *my* submissive. So it's *my* scene, and *I've* decided this bloody farce is over." He pointed at Beck. "Get the fuck out of here. Now!"

Disbelief fell across Hammer's face. It quickly turned to cold rage, shadowing the sockets under his eyes, emphasizing his icy stare. A fury Liam had never seen in all the years they'd been friends blared there. "You planned this, you son of a bitch!"

"I did what I needed to keep you from hurting her more."

Hammer ripped his biting gaze away and settled on Raine. Stark pain consumed his expression. "Precious…"

The devastation in Hammer's voice as he called out to Raine would haunt him, but he refused to worry about that now. He shoved aside what might have been if Hammer had just listened. Would have, could have, and should have been. *Waste of fucking time…*

As far as Liam was concerned, the only one who had set Hammer up for a fall was the man himself, the minute the stupid fuck had allowed a sadist like Beck anywhere near the woman he supposedly loved.

Raine lifted her head to stare at Hammer. Betrayal and hurt filled her eyes, then she hid from her mentor, burying her face in Liam's chest once more. He cradled her head.

"She was so precious to you that you let a sick wanker like Beck abuse her," Liam sneered. "No more."

He'd never meant for this to happen, but he'd been forced to choose between the man he'd thought was his friend—whom he didn't seem to know anymore—and the girl who needed him. The woman who was making him feel alive again.

He hugged Raine in his arms, tight to his chest, and turned away from his old pal.

In the glass, he caught sight of Hammer, shock and denial spilling all over his face. Then he grabbed Beck by the arm with a feral growl and yanked the big tattooed sadist away. "I told you to scare her a bit, not to hurt her, you stupid fucker. Go wait in my office."

A million thoughts careened through Liam's mind. Even if Beck had taken the punishment farther than Hammer intended, his friend had still allowed the sick bastard in the same room with a naked Raine. She'd suffered a terrible blow—and not just physically.

Giving Raine his full attention once more, Liam soothed and petted her, calming her tears and gentling her with his voice. With his touch. "There now, lass. Your punishment is done, but I need you to stay brave a bit longer. I'm determined to claim you as a Master should. And I intend to see it done properly, here and now. So no one has any doubts." Her startled gaze bounced up to his face, and she glanced at the crowd. "Do you understand me?"

It wasn't strictly necessary, but he didn't trust Hammer not to hurt Raine anymore. Even if the man rushed in to claim her now, Liam didn't have any faith in Macen after today. As far as he was concerned, Hammer best learn that Liam was in charge of the girl now. Yes, he wanted to fuck her, which still made him feel vaguely guilty, but with this act, he'd give Hammer a vivid picture of the new reality—Raine was off limits.

She looked bewildered and anxious, unsure. He gave her a moment to digest, comprehend. He watched as the light dawned. Finally, she nodded. Sheer will emanated from her. Fuck, her determination amazed him.

She didn't once look Hammer's way as the man walked back in the room, alone now, clenching and unclenching his fists.

Liam helped her to her feet, making sure she had two steady legs beneath her. He didn't release her until she sent him a sure nod. "I'm fine, Sir."

He cocked a little smile at her. He wasn't usually much for protocol, but he appreciated her effort, especially in front of the others. "Then back on the bench."

At his words, she allowed him to help her onto the padded contraption. As he gave her a gentle push between her shoulder blades, she bent over the bench. Her show of trust warmed him, and he was determined to make this good for her.

The angry red stripe across her thighs, mottling into a terrible purple, made him murderous, but now wasn't the time to let his fury loose.

Crouching behind her, Liam urged her legs apart and cuffed her ankles again. She tensed, understandable given how helpless she'd been against Beck's wrath.

"Shh. Give yourself over to me. I'll make it worth your while."

Then he gently kissed each thigh where she'd been abused by the rubber strap, ignoring Hammer's stare that all but singed the skin off his back. Liam dismissed him even as another part of him wanted to plant his fist in the bastard's face and scream that he deserved every bit of what was about to happen.

As he moved up and reached for her wrists, her soft voice curled in his ear. "You know how long it's been since..." Her anxious glance willed him to understand. "And I've never..." She drew in a shuddering breath. "Will it hurt?"

He'd be the first Master to claim her, and that made him swell with pride—and even more potent desire. Hell, what a boon. Liam was mightily glad she hadn't let some other potentially inept fucker have this part of her.

"No. There now. Close your eyes. Pretend it's just you and me here. Take a deep breath and give me your worries. Will you do that for me?" He petted her hair gently. "Yes, that's it. Just like that. Now open yourself, Raine, and trust that by the time my cock is buried in your ass, you'll be feeling nothing but pleasure. I'll awaken a more submissive side of you and give you something you've never felt."

Liam ripped off his shirt and concentrated completely on claiming Raine as his own. He had to fuck not just her body, but her mind, too. She had to surrender her will in front of all these people and open herself completely to him.

As he wound behind her again, he gently stroked her thighs to soothe her with one hand. With the other, he signaled to a watching slave for ice and a towel. Within moments, he pressed the cooling terrycloth to her. It wouldn't stop the bruising, but it might numb the area enough so he could take her mind and body elsewhere.

A tall order for the troubled woman, but he had the desire and patience. This was his first act as her Dom, and he would not fail her.

Minutes later, Liam set the towel aside, and Raine stiffened.

"Shh, lass. Breathe in and out. Like that, yes," he crooned. "Relax for me."

And she listened, the starch left her body by degrees. Liam breathed across her skin, then followed with a languid brush of his fingers. He caressed his way up her hips, her back, over her tense shoulders, all the way to her neck, until she warmed for him. He worshipped her body, getting lost in her softness, her heady feminine scent. Her perfection.

By the time he delved between her thighs, Raine was gasping her readiness. He trailed his fingers along her bare slit. So wet. The scent of her arousal slammed his brain and his cock with equal force. Liam eased a finger inside her and groaned as her swollen, silky pussy squeezed him. Fuck, she was going to feel so good enveloping his cock, so small and tight. He couldn't wait.

But first things first.

Liam bent and rimmed her little virgin rosette with his tongue. She gasped, trying to squeeze her cheeks together to keep him out. Clearly, she wasn't accustomed to anyone touching her there. He couldn't help but smile at the thought that he'd make damn certain she both got used to it and loved it.

Dragging his lips over the fleshy part of her backside, he lapped his way up her body to murmur in her ear. "Don't forget to relax for me. Let yourself feel. Sink into the sensations. They'll be new, but I promise, they'll be ones you come to crave."

At her shaky nod, he slid down her body back to her small, untried hole and pried her open. He laved and circled around her sensitive flesh until her breath caught, until she flushed, until her body tensed and she was grabbing the edges of the table again, this time not anticipating pain, but bracing for pleasure. Then he added to it, his questing fingers seeking out the swollen bundle of nerves at the top of her weeping cunt.

With a soft little cry that made his cock harder, Raine undulated as she sank into the slow, insistent rhythm he set. She was nearly ready to take everything he intended to give her. Then all this pale, silky skin...his. This virgin ass...his. All her will and fire and need...his.

Intently watching her, he reached into Beck's bag of tricks under the bench and found a new tube of lube. He squeezed some onto his fingers, massaging and pressing lightly at the puckered rosette of her ass. She tensed again. Liam shushed her, giving her his calm so she could surrender and let him take over. Fear hovered under her surface. Yet he also saw anticipation growing in her eyes. They heated and softened, like the entrance he stroked. Her cheeks flushed. The little sounds in the back of her throat told him that she was ready. No other penetration could make her feel quite so submissive, so owned. He wanted to be the one who gave her that experience.

Liam looked at her with a fierce stare, barely managing to hold back his urgency as he savored the control she slowly surrendered to him. He intended to nurture and strengthen the new connection between them, starting here and now. He'd do whatever necessary to allow her trust to grow so she would seek him out for all of her needs. That he expected her to. He hadn't wanted anyone like this in years, maybe ever, and he was determined to make her crave him.

Somehow, she'd become important—like warmth and food and air. Liam didn't understand it and he didn't want to rationalize it. He just couldn't deny how deeply he wanted her. Even if her need for him was only physical for now...well, one step at a time.

As she cried out again, Liam knew the time to claim her had come. This was his chance to make her see him, feel the promise of what could be. He had no intention of wasting it.

He slid a finger inside her ass, waited until she pushed back, tentatively seeking. Then he gave her more, easing in another with teasing strokes. She groaned, her eyes still pinned to him in the mirror, glazed in a smoky blue. And he watched her, listened to her roughening breaths, waited for her to relax upon his fingers. Finally, she did, sweetly giving him more of her trust.

Attempting to stretch her sinfully narrow opening, his cock wept, hungry to replace his fingers. The need inside him started to snarl and growl. He dragged in air and forced himself to be gentle.

"Breathe. There's a good lass. Trust that I won't hurt you. I feel your need growing. Give it all to me. I promise you, I will indeed put that fire out. Then I'll stoke it again."

She gasped, mewled, skin sheening under the lights, eyes closed. *So sensual…*

Removing his fingers, he gathered more lube, generously slathering her slightly expanded opening. "Just a little more. You're ready." Inserting his fingers again, he spread the digits wide, gliding his knuckles back and forth against her thinning rim.

Attuned to her every nuance, from her soft whimpers to the way her eyes fluttered open and closed as she desperately tried to focus on him, Liam exercised every ounce of his patience. Pleasure played across her face with abandon, thrilling him. Very soon, he'd fill her wee, lush body to the brim with exquisite need and drive her to orgasm under his command.

"That's it. You've got my cock bursting at the seams, desperate I am to be inside you," he whispered for her ears only as she breathed out her pleasure, her muscles rippling and clenching around his fingers. "There… Stay with me, Raine. We'll do this together. Let me help you touch the stars."

Plucking a condom out of his pocket, he tore into his zipper, then slid his trousers down. With his teeth, he tore into the foil package and slid it over his turgid shaft, biting back a groan. Dripping more lube onto his cock, he stroked the slick gel over it, coating the latex completely.

"Look at me. Focus on me now and me alone. Don't look away. I want to see your eyes as I fill you. I intend to watch you come for me."

Her eyes widened, but still contained a dreamlike blue haze. Removing his fingers, he wrapped his fist around his throbbing shaft as he set the crest against her readied opening. So small, so delicate everywhere. Pulling her cheeks wider still, fighting every god-given instinct to plunge balls deep, he sucked in a stuttering breath and eased the bulbous tip inside, as far as her tight band of muscle allowed.

Suddenly, she gasped. Apprehension filled her eyes when he met them in the mirror. Desire lurked there, too. "Shh...there now. Don't fight me, lovely. Take a deep breath. As you release it, push back and let me in. Let me turn it into the most glorious pleasure you've ever felt. Can you do that for me?"

Liam paused as he waited for her answer. Reaching beneath her, he stroked her clit again. The moment throbbed. He itched with the need to press in and drive into her welcoming softness and be burned alive. He resisted and watched her in the mirror. A movement in the glass caught his eye. *Hammer.*

The hot, fierce eyes that glared at him promised retribution. Another problem for another time. Raine needed him now.

Lowering his gaze to her once more, he teased her clit with another light stroke as he sank a bit deeper inside. Finally, she relaxed, pushed back to him. And he slipped past her tight ring of muscle and began to fall into her.

Oh, fuck. The burn, the grip, the perfection of her flesh...Liam couldn't hold in a groan as he pushed into her, little by little. Filled her. Melded with her, not stopping until his balls rested against her weeping cunt, until every inch of his cock filled her blistering ass. Her hiss turned to a sigh as he claimed her.

He gave her the briefest moment of respite, then he began to thrust in slow, friction-filled strokes. The sweet burn soon had her trembling on his cock and wailing for relief. Biting back a curse, and fighting the urgency gathering in his balls, he gritted his teeth and focused on Raine.

She welcomed him as he plunged into her over and over again, trying to burn himself into her soul. She came alive, grew wild. With every sensation he drew forth, she melted and gave up more control to him. He felt the fragile connection he forged all the way to her glorious soul.

Brimming with thrill, he laid over her back, dragging his lips across the curve of neck. He raked his fingers through her drenched folds and over her hard clit.

"Now you're mine, lass. Feel my cock stretching you, filling you. This is the cock that will grant your every pleasure," he growled hungry and raspy in her ear. "Feel my hands on you. These are the hands that will mold you, stroke you, guide you through the journey you've been craving."

Raine didn't answer exactly. She tossed her head back, eyes a wild blue, and cried out.

Excellent. Gorgeous. Now to crawl in her head some more. "You're so hot and tight, lovely. I could stay buried inside you 'til the end of time and not get my fill."

She moaned and rocked her hips, eager for more, her little whimpers driving him higher.

"Yes, that's it. This is where I belong. Now that you've let me in, I'm going to consume you. Let the sensations set you ablaze. Take everything I give you."

Watching as he stretched her more with every thrust, groaning with a pleasure he'd not felt in too long, he drove his cock deeper, filling her tight passage again and again.

As he pinched her clit between his fingers, she cried out, "Liam!"

That desperate plea, that longing in her voice, called to his Dominant soul. She'd screamed his name. Not Hammer's, but...*his*! The man wasn't even on her radar right now.

He wanted to cradle her close, protect her from heartache. So deep inside her, he longed for things he had no right to ask of her. But that wasn't going to stop him. She'd trusted him, given him her power. He was going to use that. The conflagration threatened to consume them both with its intensity. And at this moment she was his to will, to own.

"Tell me how it feels."

"It stings. Burns. I feel stretched so wide." She hissed, then wriggled her hips, arching her back, forcing Liam to slide even deeper and moan as he greedily claimed the new space she'd granted. "Yes! It's... I..." She clutched the table in a white-knuckled grip. He saw her soul as she met his gaze with pleading eyes, panic-stricken as her orgasm threatened to consume her. "Liam? Please."

Every pulse, every squeeze, every tremor that rippled along the length of his cock was exquisite agony. She relinquished all control, and he reveled in his possession of her. His balls drew up hard, primed to erupt.

"I knew you would feel like this, lass. So tight. Fuck, so perfect. And the taste of your surrender is headier than anything I imagined," he whispered against her ear. "Let yourself go and fly. Come *now*, Raine!"

As if they'd choreographed it, as if he'd timed it perfectly, she did. Her panting little cries filled the room as her body bucked, jerked. Then she screamed, and Liam soaked in her power as she soared with rapture. He gasped for breath and self-control as she shattered all around him, but orgasm barreled toward him like a freight train. He tensed, gritting his teeth, desperate to stay lost in the moment just a bit longer. He gloried in every pulse of her body, was captivated by each cry from her lips. He couldn't look away from her blossoming under him, opening to him as if he was the sun.

At the thought, he fell head first into an exquisite abyss stronger than anything he could remember. The wonder of it—and her—nearly brought him to his knees as she continued to convulse, milking his cock with the blistering power of her pleasure.

Raine dug her nails deep into the padded table as she screamed again. Thrusting and grunting powerfully, he rode the waves of her delirium to a blissful, shuddering end. Everything and everyone fell away except Raine as he poured himself into her, wishing he could mark her with his seed instead of the condom he filled.

Slowly recovering from the earth-shattering climax, he saw Raine blink, breathe…then close her eyes with a little smile. He kissed her shoulder and wrapped his arm more tightly around her. *Mine!*

Hammer's stare in the mirror scorched him. Liam glanced up and tensed. He refused to allow Raine to shoulder Hammer's rage or guilt herself.

"Eyes on me," he whispered roughly as he withdrew from her body and uncuffed her. "You're so gorgeous. You pleased me so much. I've got you…"

She sagged against the bench, and Liam stripped off his condom and tossed it in the nearby bin before he zipped his trousers, patently ignoring Hammer. Instead, he picked up her baby-doll and eased her into the garment, then back into his arms. The crowd melted away as he swung her up against his chest, gratified when she clung to him, burying her face in his neck.

"That's a love. Let me get you back to my room where I can take care of you."

As she nodded tiredly and kissed his jaw, he smiled in triumph. Already she sought him for comfort and put herself in his care. He'd known she'd bloom under affection.

Then a wave of anger and pain emanated from the man he'd called friend for a decade. It reached inside his chest, yanked and twisted.

Gouged deep. Liam did his best to ignore it. Hammer had made his choice. Liam would rather have saved the girl than lost them both.

And now he was wondering if he'd somehow lost his heart in the process.

He studied Raine as he walked from the room, his eyes softening on her sheer beauty. She was his…at least for now. But she'd warned him where her heart was. When he'd been scheming to win her solely to prod at Hammer's possessive streak, that hadn't mattered. Now? He grimaced. Raine was like smoke, seemingly so real when captured in his arms and searing his lungs. She stole his very breath. Yet something about her was elusive. Only time would tell how this played out, but right now, he refused to let go. And he'd not give her up without a fight.

Chapter Six

Fuck me running.

Hammer couldn't believe his best friend—no, his *ex*-best friend—had the balls to trick Raine into a training collar. Not only that, but he'd claimed her virgin ass in the middle of the goddamn dungeon, right before his eyes. The cold-hearted fucker. Liam knew how he felt about the girl, even if he hadn't admitted it in so many words. And the Irish prick had still taken Raine from him.

That knife in his back would leave a deep, bloody wound for a long time.

Even as he'd watched Liam sink deep into Raine's backside, Hammer's own cock had engorged. Fuck, she'd looked beautiful in her submissive surrender—everything he'd imagined she would be once she finally started to trust and let go. But in his fantasies, she'd always come undone under his hand, by his cock. Tonight, he had to face the reality that she'd given herself and her power to Liam. And just how the hell had the asshole managed to coax her so quickly? Like he did everyone else—he'd fucked with her head.

So now Hammer could no longer chide or punish, praise or stroke the beautiful girl without crossing a terrible line. Jealousy sludged through him like ugly black tar, hardening his veins, darkening his mood.

He turned away from the padded bench on which he witnessed Liam give Raine such sexual splendor. It didn't matter what the fuck he looked at. He saw her anyway. Her phantom cries rung in Hammer's ears. The memories sucker punched him.

God, would he ever be able to look at this part of the dungeon again without wanting to kill that fucking O'Neill bastard?

Worse, Hammer couldn't deny that while Liam had heaped pleasure on Raine, thoughts of how incredible it would feel to have his cock buried deep in her little cunt while Liam squeezed in and out of her tight backside crept through his brain. It wouldn't have been the first time they'd shared a woman.

But no. That was impossible. The risk of damaging Raine—of losing her forever—was too high. All it would take was once. The moment he started pounding his cock into her tight, hungry body, he wouldn't stop.

He refused to risk another colossal fuckup like Juliet's.

A glance back showed Liam clutching Raine in his arms and heading for his private room. The vengeful part of him wanted to throw the son of a bitch out and ban him from Shadows…but what if he persuaded Raine to leave with him? What if Liam took her back to New York, played more head games with her, and she found herself alone? What if she needed him and he wasn't there for her… Hammer swallowed. He couldn't take that risk. Seeing them together would gut his insides every fucking day, but he'd do it, just to keep her close and safe.

That still left him between a fucking rock and a hard place, but now he could add a brick wall to that. Goddamnit, he hated not having palatable options. Bitterness iced his veins.

He turned and stalked back toward Liam. He should let it go. He should…but he couldn't.

Hammer grabbed Liam's arm, refusing to look down at Raine curled in his embrace. "You motherfucker. I hope you're happy. You've been duped by a pair of big blue eyes and a great rack." He shoved a superior smile on his face even when he didn't feel it. "In about three days, you'll realize that she played you to get back at me. She'll have your balls tied up in knots. And when you go to ease them by shoving your cock into her sweet cunt, don't fool yourself into believing that she'll be thinking about anyone but me."

Liam's eyes narrowed, but before he could respond, Hammer pivoted away from the pair. He didn't feel any better. In fact, he felt far fucking worse. What if Raine didn't think of him at all? What if she didn't love him as much as he adored her? God, then he'd be both pathetic and a fucking joke.

Then again…what if tonight had been a ploy? It wasn't like Liam to latch onto a woman this quickly, but it was like him to concoct some little plot to make him let go of his hangups. What if Liam and Raine had schemed together to crack the hard shell around him? What if they were plotting even now their next step to make him fall?

He shot a glare toward all the club members with their curious, pitying glances, then stormed through the dungeon, refusing to make eye contact with anyone. Seething, he made his way to the security room. Punching in the code, Hammer swung the door open so quickly, the employee manning the numerous rows of monitors jumped, then shot him a nervous stare.

"Out!" he ordered.

Without a word, the computer geek dashed out of the room. The door slammed behind him.

Hammer took a deep breath, then sat at the control desk. Adjusting the dials, he zoned in on Liam's room. Enlarging the image from the security camera, as well as raising the volume of the audio, he could see and hear Liam and Raine's conversation as if he were there.

Leaning forward in his chair, Hammer glued his eyes to the screen as Liam ministered to Raine tenderly in silence. As she lay across his bed, he soothed her well-used rosette with a cloth as he kissed her back and shoulders. Raine moaned a contented little sigh.

Hammer forced himself to watch, hope still flickering in his chest. It burned in painful contrast to his dread. The thoughts kept spinning in his head. *What if…? What if…? What if…?*

"You were beautiful, lass." Liam showered her in praise. "The way you let go... I know that was difficult for you, and that giving yourself to pleasure after Beck's pain can't have been easy. But you trusted me, and I'm honored."

"I did." She rolled over and blinked up at Liam with those big eyes that always seemed to melt him, and Hammer's gut clenched. "I do."

"You're mine now, and mine alone. Do you understand?" Liam gripped her chin gently.

Hammer held his breath.

"Yes." She licked her lips. "Sir."

Liam smiled down at her with tenderness. Hammer's heart exploded. So much for the hope that they'd cooked up a ruse to reel him in. Right now, the way they were looking at one another, he might as well not even exist.

His old friend might be a motherfucking bastard, but Hammer knew himself to be a fool. He'd let Raine slip through his fingers. Seeing the seeds of worship in her eyes, hearing her address someone else as her Sir...it was too painful to watch.

Before he could turn off all the security equipment, Liam urged Raine flat on her back. She curled her arms around his neck, and that blasted Irishman put his hands on her. Raine peered up at Liam, so focused, looking at him almost as if he was a goddamn god.

Hammer's stomach twisted. He should fucking leave now. Voluntarily watching his former best friend caress Raine's soft skin made him masochistic. Hell, now Liam dropped a soft kiss on her pillowy lips and thumbed her nipple slowly through that sexy-as-fuck baby-doll nightie, back and forth.

Raine gave Liam a shy, almost secretive smile. "Thank you for making tonight incredible. I was afraid at first, then I realized you were there. I knew you wouldn't let anything bad happen, so I did what you said. I relaxed and I let go." She sighed. "And it was everything I could have wanted."

Hammer gripped the counter tightly until his knuckles turned white, until his fingers went numb.

Liam palmed her breast again, looking down into her eyes like an indulgent lover. "It was beautiful."

Fuck, that should have been him. It should *be* him now. But it couldn't be, and Hammer knew all the fucking reasons why.

Still…he could hardly believe that Liam had swooped in and stolen Raine from him in less than two days with his fucking head games. But Hammer knew he hadn't given her what she needed, and Liam would.

A bitter pill. It clawed his throat raw as he swallowed it down.

"We'll be good together, you and I, lass. Just keep giving me all you can."

She nodded solemnly. "I will. I want to. To really submit for the first time was amazing. I'd tried to imagine it so many times, but actually doing it? It both eased me and sent me soaring. I don't know how to explain."

"You're doing fine. Keep talking. Tell me how the crowd made you feel?"

"I didn't notice them. I was focused on you, like you said. They just fell away for me."

"You did perfect. And what about Hammer?"

He saw her body stiffen at the question, the way she diverted her gaze from Liam. Hammer turned up the volume again and leaned in once more.

"I'm…torn." She drew in a trembling breath. "You want me to be honest, right?" At Liam's nod, she frowned. "I'm so angry at him. I mean, Beck? And Hammer did nothing to stop it. I don't understand. I thought he cared at least a little. He's taken care of me so diligently for years. But tonight…he seemed like a stranger. Even so, I'm realizing that my feelings for him aren't like a switch I can turn off at will, but I'll keep trying."

God, her words hurt more than anything. She was going to try to put him out of her heart. Yes, it was better for her. And yes, he wanted her to be happy. But he would be alone again, just like he'd been for the last eight long fucking years.

Hammer reached up toward the screen and traced his fingers over the image of Raine's cheek. His eyes stung, and he blinked quickly to stave off unmanly tears. "I'm so sorry. If I'd known what Beck planned to do… He'll pay. Trust me. But go ahead and hate me, precious. It will be so much better for you."

Regrets were like assholes; everyone had one. Hammer wished again that he could be what Raine needed, but he'd only break her in two.

Liam brushed away the baby-doll from her body, then tore off his trousers and grabbed a condom from the nightstand. Hammer knew by the gentle way Liam covered her what was coming next and he didn't have the fortitude to sit and watch his ex-best friend make love to the woman who'd grown to become his everything. He muted the audio and killed the video feed from Liam's room. Closing his eyes once again, he drew in a deep breath, then unleashed a primal scream of rage until his throat burned. Until he realized his machinations had backfired in his face and he could do nothing to take it back now.

Resigned and furious, he stalked out of the room to find Beck.

Tearing back through the dungeon, Hammer stared straight ahead, ignoring everyone in his path. But he felt the eyes of the club members on him, boring into him, silently wondering how he had lost control of that scene. He looked through them, not about to give anyone the benefit of seeing him care.

Down the corridor to the private rooms, he opened the door to his office, expecting to see Beck waiting. Instead, he found the room empty. His blood pressure spiked. *Goddamnit.*

Stomping down the hall again with long, heavy strides, Hammer heard the prick's deep baritone instructing a submissive to strip. He didn't bother knocking on the door, just barged in. Beck spun around as Hammer's stare zeroed in on a startled sub kneeling at the sadist's feet.

"You! Get your clothes on and get the fuck out," he snarled to the scared woman. Then he turned his attention back to Beck. "You. Stay put."

The little blonde looked between the two men. With a sigh, Beck gestured her out the door, and she scrambled away.

"Do we have a problem, Hammer? Whatever it is, couldn't it wait until I got my dick wet?"

"Getting your dick wet should be the least of your concerns, you son of a bitch! What happened to our plan? You were supposed to be on *my* side. Why the hell did you deviate? Don't tell me you didn't understand when I told you not to mark or hurt Raine. You hid that paddle with your body so I couldn't see what you were holding until it was too late. After seven years, I know a lot of your secrets. I also know you're not stupid. What the fuck were you doing?"

Beck shrugged. The smirk on his lips pissed Hammer off even more. "Oops."

What the fuck kind of answer was that? Launching toward Beck, Hammer wrapped his hand around the Dom's beefy throat and squeezed. "You think that's funny? I don't find it the least bit amusing, motherfucker. You did exactly what I told you not to do. So now, you get to deal with *me*!"

"Don't take your frustration out on me. You should have taken care of the princess yourself and you know it. It was your punishment to hand down, yet you dragged me into it. The bigger question is, why didn't you save her from me, instead of that Irish ass? I gave you every opportunity to be a hero, and you let O'Neill steal your thunder. What the fuck is wrong with you?"

Hammer didn't owe Beck any sort of answer. "Right now, what's wrong with me is you."

"Raine is just another sub, man. No different from any of the others around here, right?" Into Hammer's telling silence, Beck's lips curled up. "C'mon. Admit that, for you, she's not. You're crazy if you think nobody knows you've got a serious thing for that girl. You treat her like her cunt is made of gol—"

Beck didn't get the chance to finish his sentence. Hammer's fist snapped out and plowed him in the jaw. Then he landed another blow to Beck's chin. "You don't get to talk about any part of her body, fucker!"

Beck's powerful right hook caught him off guard, but Hammer welcomed the pain. After watching Liam fuck Raine, he felt hollow, like the life had been sucked right out of him. The red-hot fire boiling beneath his jaw was proof that he wasn't completely dead.

With his hand still cinched around Beck's throat, he slammed the bastard up against the wall and drove his knee into the man's balls. The air left Beck's lungs in a deeply satisfying rush. Then Hammer unleashed a blistering round of blows to his mouth, nose, and jaw.

With an angry growl, Beck finally shoved Hammer back, then charged at him, blood bubbling from his nostrils. Not about to let up, Hammer drove his fist into the man's stomach.

"Holy fuck!" Beck coughed and sucked in a deep breath. "I don't think I've ever seen you so pissed. So I slapped her thighs. Big deal! It's not like she didn't deserve it." Beck landed another blow to Hammer's jaw and kept on growling out the tough love. "Does she scare you so much you can't even slap her ass to keep her in line? You're afraid to touch her, aren't you?"

"Not another word. I came to you for a simple favor, and you fucked everything up. Because you terrified her so much, she's paired off with Liam now and is convinced that I'm a monster who plotted to have her beaten way beyond her pain threshold." He clocked Beck in the jaw again, then shook the sting out of his knuckles. "Thanks so much, pal."

Beck took a step back and narrowed his eyes at Hammer. "You can hit me with your purse all night long, but I'm nobody's bitch, Hammer."

His patronizing smile fueled Hammer's anger all the more. "Fuck you. You hurt her because you could, and that's not acceptable around here."

He punched a fist into Beck's kidney. The big Dom wrapped him up, and they tumbled to the floor. He felt Beck's determination as he began to unleash an equally violent wrath. Both men rolled on the concrete, taking turns punching, each striving to gain the upper hand until Hammer found himself pinned beneath Beck's muscular legs. The sadist leaned over his face, blood and sweat dripping from his brow.

With a wicked sneer, he winked. "You stupid bastard. You lost her to Liam because you were a pussy. Good luck trying to get some sleep tonight. I bet all you'll be able to picture is Liam buried inside your little princess. I doubt you'll be able to find a bottle deep enough to drown in."

Hammer bucked Beck off him, then rolled to his feet, fury like a volcano inside him, primed to erupt. "You're banned from the club for a week."

"Again?" Beck chuckled, then stood and grabbed a bottle of Jack Daniel's from a low table against the wall. He unscrewed the cap and tossed it to the floor, then took a long gulp and hissed through the burn. He thrust the bottle toward Hammer.

"Yeah. Again, asswipe," Hammer snarled as he took the bottle and swallowed a healthy swig.

"A week? That'll work. I need a break, anyway. You do know that you hit like a bitch, right?"

"Yeah, that's why your lip is bleeding and your eye is already turning black," Hammer snarled. "You hurt her. I can forgive a lot of things, man, but it's going to take a while for me to get over that."

"You really need to work out your shit when it comes to her. She's eating you up inside because she means something to you. Admit it, or one day you're going to wake up and you won't even recognize the man in the mirror."

Hammer bristled, crossing his arms over his chest. "Is that your professional diagnosis?"

"You should have fucked the princess out of your system. Been done with her already."

"Never going to happen."

Hammer stormed away and headed to the liquor room. He grabbed a bottle of Patrón and stalked back to his office, slamming the door behind him. He ripped off his suit coat and tie, tossing them on the bed as he walked to the bathroom. As he rinsed the blood from his knuckles, he raised his head, catching his own reflection in the mirror above the sink. Blood oozed from a cut above his brow, but what startled him most were the haunted eyes staring back.

He splashed cold water on his face, then watched crimson swirl down the drain.

Hammer turned off the faucet. As he reached for a towel, the sounds of sex filtered through the walls. It was Raine's tender moan of passion. Liam's familiar Irish lilt coaxed, melding with hers. Frozen like a statue, he stood listening to the sounds of their lovemaking. It gnawed at his gut.

Swallowing down the scream boiling in his chest, Hammer marched from the bathroom. Uncapping the tequila, he tipped the bottle back, guzzling it like water. Even so, the moans resounded in his head, burning their way into his brain. Beck was right—there wasn't a bottle deep enough for him to escape this pain.

Sitting at the foot of his bed, he thought he'd put enough distance between himself and the sounds of Liam and Raine's ardor, but her sultry cries still bled through the walls. He covered his ears—anything to drown out the reality of another man giving Raine all the pleasures he ached to grant her himself.

All four walls seemed to close in around him and sweat sprinkled his forehead. He gulped more alcohol, then hung his head. The entire day had been a fucking Greek tragedy. All because he'd taken Marlie to bed. Didn't Raine get that he would—and had—fucked almost every other woman in the club to keep himself from taking her to bed and ruining her life? Of course not. He'd never been honest with her. Hell, it was hard to be honest with himself. But right now, the real sounds of Raine screaming Liam's name as she shattered for the backstabbing prick was more reality than he could take.

Sweat dripped from his face and down his back. Hammer stood and stripped off his shirt and threw it to the floor. He walked from the bedroom to his adjoining office, praying the walls would provide enough of a buffer to find some goddamn silence.

He sat at his desk and wrapped his thick fingers around his coffee mug, then peered inside. Clean as a whistle. Through all the tears, bullshit, and drama, Raine had still made sure his mug was clean.

With a terrible roar, he heaved the ceramic cup across the room, and as the sound of splintering shards hit the floor, he tipped back the bottle of Patrón and guzzled. When he came up for air, he flopped down on his buttery-soft leather couch and rested the bottle on his knee. Studying the clear liquid sloshing inside, he hoped it would at least dull the brutal pain slicing through him...but he wasn't betting on it. Fuck Beck for being right.

Beside Raine, Liam snored softly in her ear. Spooned into his chest, his arm curled around her waist, his warmth surrounded her, protected her. She closed her eyes. He made letting go so easy. That tender voice... The caress of his eyes... He might still be something of a stranger—what did she know about his past, his goals, his life—but with him, she found it unsettlingly comfortable to let her guard down and believe him. Trust him. It was exhilarating...and scary as hell.

She snuggled up to him, astounded by the turn their relationship had taken so quickly. But tonight, he'd shown that he would be there for her, just as he'd promised. That he would care for and protect her. He'd broken his long-standing friendship with Hammer to defend her when he barely knew her.

Why?

Raine didn't know, and the question unsettled her. Liam had claimed her tonight, once publicly and gently, showing everyone his tender dominance. Then he'd brought her to his bedroom and...what? More than fucked her—and more than once. His every touch and look had been rife with some meaning.

Raine had never really had a man make love to her, but she imagined it would feel a lot like what Liam had done. Thorough. Gentle. Consuming. If he'd wanted to reach deep into her, he had succeeded. He'd ripped through her protective walls and totally exposed her soul. In the aftermath, she was finding it hard to fortify herself with those barriers again. Besides being sexy and caring, Liam had been *there* for her in a way very few ever had.

Why?

She didn't know. And damn, the day had rushed over her like a flash flood, and she hadn't found high ground fast enough to take cover.

For so long, her ever-present desire for a fierce protector had burned inside her. But so did her craving for a firm Master. Hammer had been the former for the past six years, sometimes shielding her too much. She knew he could be the latter, if he wished. But she couldn't make him love her. Maybe he did, on some level. Maybe that would explain why he'd tried so hard to keep her from leaving Shadows when they'd fought. Maybe that was his guilt talking. Or maybe just another one of his games to control her.

It didn't really matter anymore. Hammer had given her to Beck to punish, rather than touch her himself. And if he wanted to believe that she'd tricked Liam into caring, then screw him. She was done. She belonged to Liam now.

Raine thrust aside the memory of Hammer's decimated face just before Liam carried her from the room. Her heart clutched. Despite everything, she was stupid enough to love him still. Sadly, some part of her probably always would.

But what about Liam? If he was everything he seemed to be, he deserved a woman who could submit her entire being to him, heart and soul.

God, she could think in this endless circle all night long.

Raine rolled over and looked at the clock. 3:30 A.M. Did Hammer know or care where she was? Did it matter to him at all?

Glass shattering suddenly splintered the night. It sounded like it had come from upstairs, in the bar. She sat up, her heart starting to beat faster. The club was closed, and all guests should be long gone. So what the hell was that sound?

She was still analyzing it in her head when something heavy clattered to the floor from the same vicinity, skittering over the stained concrete above.

She turned to Liam, hand outstretched to wake him. Shadows darkened under his eyes. He'd been through the wringer tonight. The noises upstairs were probably from a drunk member or maybe another one of the staff had just dropped something while cleaning up.

Whatever it was, she could handle it.

Raine stood and slipped Liam's navy silk robe over her naked body. She should probably wake Hammer, too. Had he heard the ruckus?

But when Raine padded into the hall and reached his bedroom, she found it empty. She fought back surprise, then anger. Bitterness eventually won. He was probably with Marlie somewhere. Inside Marlie, pounding deep into her— No, damn it, she wasn't going to finish that thought. She had no control over who Hammer liked or fucked. If he didn't want her, she had to let her thoughts of him go.

She stood for a minute, trying to decide what to do. Then silence pervaded again. Whatever disturbance had been upstairs had stopped. Maybe it had been nothing…

Raine was about to turn back to Liam's room when she noticed light spilling from Beck's open door.

With eyes narrowed, she sauntered down the hall. After this evening, she had a few things to say to the dirtbag.

When she peered into his room, she found every light on. He chugged on a fifth of Jack Daniel's and packed a few things into a duffel bag. As he turned with a flogger and a pair of cuffs in hand, he caught sight of her. Despite the fact that he had a black eye—where had Beck gotten that?—he had the balls to wink at her.

Raine lost it—her temper, her hold on her emotions, her will to hear his side of the story. She charged into the room, straight at him, and slapped him across the face. "You bastard!"

"Watch it, princess." He rubbed his offended cheek, then she caught sight of another bruise there, along with a split lip. It was no less than he deserved. Thunder rolled across his face. "I'll let you have that one. I earned it."

Meaning...? "Did you do what Hammer asked you to do to me?"

"Nah." He took another swig of Jack, then grimaced, absently tonguing his busted lip. "Motherfucker, that hurts."

"So do my thighs!" she shot back. "Why did you smack me with a rubber paddle if Hammer told you not to?"

He sent her a considering stare, then a grin spread slowly across his mouth. "A couple of reasons. Hammer warned me off you years ago, but hey, I'm just a man. You're my kind of wet dream, and I had to know if there was any chance you might be a latent pain slut so that... yeah, maybe we could live kinkily-ever-after."

Why would he imagine that for a minute? "I think we can safely say somewhere between no and hell no. That really freaking hurt. And no warm-up?"

"Not your bag, I get it. But I wasn't going to do you any lasting damage."

"How do you know that, Beck?"

Dark eyes glittered as he sent her a mocking tip of his head. "If you're never going to call me Sir, that's Dr. Beck to you."

Doctor...? "Surely not as in M.D.?"

He nodded, smiling as if he was really enjoying her surprise. "Dr. Kenneth Beckman, board certified vascular surgeon, at your service. I know exactly what's happening with your veins right now, princess. Trust me. I didn't really hurt you."

Holy shit. Shock was an understatement. Beck the Sadist was actually Dr. Kenny, who healed people's circulatory systems for a living? Raine blinked at him. Blinked again. She'd always known he was smart. In his late thirties, she supposed he was old enough to have achieved that level of education and experience. But hearing that the Jack-swigging, leather-clad sadist swaggering through these halls and melting the panties of every pain slut had a medical degree and practice just didn't compute for her.

"Keep a lid on this, will you, princess? Don't want the vanillas freaking out that their doctor enjoys inflicting pain. Hammer knows, too, in case you're wondering. But he's one of the few. He picked me to administer your punishment because he knew I'd scare the hell out of you and because if anything went wrong, there was a doctor in the house."

So Hammer *had* been looking out for her...in his way. And she hadn't trusted that he'd been looking past his anger enough to care for her. He always had, and her lack of trust now shamed her a bit.

"Thanks." She lost her starch. "I needed to hear that."

Beck shrugged a pair of massive shoulders. "You also need to hear why I threatened to hit you again."

"You're a sadist. Duh!"

That made him laugh outright. "Besides that. After the first blow, I knew you were never going to come over to my dark side. But I wanted to do a little test."

Fury needled her. "To see how much of your shit I could take?"

"Low opinion of me much?" he drawled. "No, Hammer's told me a little bit about your background. Remember when he took you to a rash of doctors shortly after you arrived?"

Yes. Lord, there had been a dozen. An internist, a dentist, a gynecologist, a plastic surgeon to repair some scarring her father had left behind. Even a shrink. Now that she thought about it, Beck had been lurking in the background a lot then. "You referred them?"

"Every one. From that, I know you're not like the others. The pain sluts I see…" He shrugged. "Most haven't had to endure what you have. They come to me for the release pain gives them. But yours was non-consensual. I've guessed that pain isn't going to free you, just make you determined not to cow down to anyone again."

Beck might as well have read her mind. "Exactly."

"You're a survivor, standing here so goddamn vibrant that you draw everyone to you. I've known Hammer for a long time. He needs you. I threatened to hit you again to see if he'd rescue you and finally fuck you, like he's dying to."

"He's not." Beck might be shocked to know how diligently she'd pursued that path, only to be rebuffed…

"Yeah, he is. Everyone else is a way to pass the time. You, he takes care of. He watches over. He guides. He loves. Don't let him bullshit you into believing different. But I honestly didn't see Liam O'Neill coming. That man has a serious hard-on for you."

Yes. She'd been feeling it most of the night. Raine flushed.

"I wanted to see if Hammer would save you from me." He grinned. "But I think it will be much more fun to see if he fights Liam for you instead."

Raine opened her mouth to shoot off a snappy reply, but a yell interrupted her. Angry. Wounded. Unmistakably Hammer's. Another heavy *thunk* of something wooden hitting the floor followed.

"Why don't you go see what he's up to, princess?" Beck suggested. "He sure as hell doesn't want to see me."

She didn't bother answering him, but turned and jogged into the hall, heading for the stairs. Was Beck suggesting that Hammer needed her help?

Darting up, Raine ran as fast as she could to reach him, before he woke everyone up or did something reckless, like put his fist through a window.

Then she skidded into the bar and saw a shirtless Hammer lift a solid wooden barstool over his head. The muscles of his back and arms bunched and flexed as he hurled it against the wall with a mighty growl. It landed with a loud *thump*, then crashed to the floor. He cursed again, something really ugly that made her flinch. What the hell was wrong with him?

She was still puzzling out the answer when he zipped behind the bar and grabbed a bottle in his fist. He unscrewed the cap, then pitched the little plastic disc across the room with so much rage, Raine stared wide eyed.

Hammer took a long swig and prowled into the open room. Moonlight streamed in through the window, falling silver and bright across his face. An angry red cut marred his brow. He sported another just above his eye. A bruise formed on his left cheek and on the right side of his jaw. His bottom lip looked a little swollen.

He'd been in a fight. With Beck?

"Macen, what the hell happened to you?"

Hammer's stare zipped over to her. He said nothing, just sawed angry breaths in and out as he drilled holes into her with an exacting gaze that promised…something she couldn't put her finger on. Fighting the urge to take a step back, she stood her ground.

"Raine." His voice finally thundered through the room as he slammed the bottle of liquor on the bar so hard the contents spewed from the neck like a geyser. In three long strides, he ate up the distance between them. Snarling, he gripped her arms tightly as she smelled tequila. "You honestly didn't think I'd let him get away with that, did you? The fucking bastard!"

Raine tried to block out the zip of desire at the feel of Hammer's closeness and his grip on her. Which fucking bastard did he mean? "Beck?"

"Yeah, Beck. Though I wish to hell it had been Liam's face I'd rearranged. But he was too busy fucking you. Yeah, I heard you scream his name."

His condemning tone made her feel a little sick. Not with shame, exactly. Not just embarrassment. And he sounded…jealous almost. But Raine held her tongue. What could they say that hadn't already been said?

"Want to tell me why you're throwing things and trying to wake everyone in the place up?"

"Leave me alone and go back to bed. Let Liam sink into your hot little cunt some more. I'm sure he hasn't gotten his fill of you yet. In his place, I wouldn't have," he snarled. "But then I've got six years of ache for you to fuck out of my system, and I could never sate that in one goddamn night. I'd tie you to my bed and devour you for weeks. Months. Until you were sore. Wrung out. Exhausted and begging me not to fuck you again. And that still wouldn't stop me."

This from the man who had thrown her from his room for trying to seduce him? Raine stared at Hammer as if he'd spoken a foreign language. His every word burned desire into her. It sizzled her belly, seared her pussy. She couldn't let herself be swayed. Crap like this was easy to spew when one was nursing tequila.

"Bullshit. You're drunk. I'm going back to bed." Raine whirled away, knowing she should leave the room, but just couldn't let his little speech go. She turned back to him, hands on her hips. "Just when I think you've still got a decent bone in your body—Beck told me that he's a damn doctor and that he wasn't supposed to hurt me—then you try to *B.S.* me. When I came to your room, I gave you every opportunity to work out any ache you might have for me. But no. Because you don't have one. If this is some effort to save my ego or whatever, just...stop. I know you're never going to tie me to your bed."

And she didn't want to hear Hammer confirm that fact, so she belted Liam's robe around her more tightly and, shoulders stiff, pivoted toward the stairs again.

"Goddamnit, don't turn away from me. You look at me. Now!"

The force of his demand sent a startled glance over her shoulder. Where the hell had his anger come from?

"Am I drunk? Fuck, yeah. Because of you! Don't think I'm doing anything to save your ego, precious. I'm saving your goddamn life."

She turned back to him and crossed her arms over her chest with a snort. "Riiiight... I know your reputation, Hammer. You trying to warn me away from your big, bad Dom self because you want me to worry that you'd tie me to your bed and what? Fuck me to death?" She rolled her eyes. "Please... You're so full of shit. I don't even understand this game, but I'm done playing it. Put the cap on the bottle and go to bed. And try not to throw any more barstools."

He rushed toward her with a burning glower, then pulled her to his broad, hard chest. His steely erection throbbed against her, prodding her from beneath his trousers. "You think I wouldn't tie you to my bed, precious? Trust me, given the chance, I'd live out every nasty fantasy I've hidden for the past six years. I'd make you my dirty little whore and you'd beg me to use you in ways that would make the devil blush."

Raine went wide eyed. She barely had time to process his silky threat before he grabbed her hair and tugged, forcing her gaze to his. His stare delved, branded, commanded.

The truth hit her. She swallowed—hard. *Oh god...* "You're serious. All these years, you've wanted..." She gaped at him, trying to reconcile everything she thought she knew with the dark thunder of desire pounding across his face, charging up the air between them. "Me?"

"Every fucking hour of every goddamn day. Do you have any idea how insane I was when I found out you'd given your virginity to that piece of shit, Zak? He won't be back. Ever. I made sure of it." Something dangerous and lethal flashed in his eyes.

Pieces of the puzzle started snapping together. "I know you've made everyone who ever touched me go away."

"That's right. And I always will. I've wanted you almost since I took you in that hot August night six years ago. You weren't quiet eighteen yet, and I called myself every name in the book: pervert, pedophile, dumb fuck. None of it stopped me from wanting you."

God, she didn't understand this complicated man. "I've been here all this time. I'm not a teenager anymore."

"I noticed. When you grew up on me and blossomed into the incredible woman you are now…" He stopped and trailed his thumb over her bottom lip.

Raine found it hard to breathe. His information was almost more than she could absorb. Reconciling it in her head was like suddenly hearing that the sky wasn't actually blue.

He. Wanted. Her. The shock of that just kept rolling through her system. After hiding it for years, why admit how he felt now? Because he was drunk enough to finally be honest?

The way his thumb kept brushing her lip and his stare lasered in on her mouth made her insides jumpy, her folds turn damp.

"Wait. You've always treated me like a child." Remembering all the hurt and anger, she jerked out of his embrace. "Like your sister. What's changed? Did you watch Liam fuck my ass and suddenly decide I'm grown up and, therefore, fair game?"

"You've been grown up in my eyes since you turned eighteen. In some ways, even before then. As for Liam…" He curled his lip in a condescending sneer. "He can't handle you. You're going to walk all over him, precious. You need a strong Dom who can keep you under his thumb and your sexy ass in line. I'm the only one who could ever give you those boundaries you crave. Don't kid yourself. He'll be a fun play toy, but that's all. You'll always hunger for me to be firm with you and push your limits."

Oh, she understood now. Same song, different verse. "Before, you told me that I wasn't mature enough, good enough, strong enough. *Now* you're going to dangle that cock in front of me because I'm taken, so I still can't have you. Then what's the point to this dazzling truth?" she spit at him. "You're never going to touch me. Malign Liam if it makes you feel better, but he's tender and wonderful and has the guts to treat me like a woman."

She stalked over to the bar, grabbed the bottle, and guzzled from it. The tequila burned going down, and she welcomed the fire as she slammed the bottle aside and fastened her stare on him again. Her blood sang. Her body buzzed, and not for anything would she admit that to him. "And you never will. So take your boundaries and shove them up your ass."

Before she could draw in another breath, he pursued her, pressing his hot body against hers. His bare chest heaved and his lips were drawn in a tight, angry line.

He glared down into her eyes. "I *never* said anything like that. You're the one who conjured up self-depreciating reasons, not me. If I were going to dangle my cock in your face, I'd sure as fuck instruct you how to suck it. Trust me, it's not *my* ass that's going to get reamed, and it's not boundaries I'll be shoving up yours."

Grinding his heated arousal against her, he closed his eyes and moaned, making her shake all over. When he opened them again, she saw savage hunger blazing there. "Hammer, I…"

"Not another fucking word, Raine."

He slanted his mouth over hers, his lips seizing her own, taking, claiming, demanding everything from her. Shock pinged through her. Raine's head spun. Her heart roared. Her pussy wept. And she opened her lips to him, couldn't help but kiss him back.

He grabbed handfuls of Liam's robe in his big fists and dragged her even closer. She hadn't known that was possible, but every inch of her was covered by him. His brutal grip parted the silk, and she felt nothing but his trousers against her swelling folds as he all but inhaled her, stabbing his way into her mouth like he owned her.

Raine melted, her head swimming, dizzy. She moaned and opened wider to him, arching against him in a silent pleading for more, just like she always had…

How long before he put a stop to it and pried himself away this time?

Tearing herself from his kiss and jerking from his grip, she panted and stared at him through the shadows, backing up until she hit the bar. "Stop. I'm not playing this game. I'm Liam's now."

But he wasn't looking at her face. His hot stare was fixed decidedly lower, on one of her breasts he'd bared by clawing at the robe. The pale orb hung heavy in the moonlight, nipple drawn up tight. She reached for the lapels of the garment to cover herself, but Hammer, with a muscle ticcing in his jaw, was already on her.

"No game, precious. Tonight, you're *mine*!" He fastened his mouth over her exposed peak, sucking her deep. His teeth sank into her tender flesh as the tip of his tongue flicked over her nipple, immersing her in a blistering combination of pleasure and pain. He cupped her breasts in his big palms and teased her distended tips, alternating from one to the other with his teeth, lips, and tongue.

The sensations drowned her instantly. Macen touching her was everything she'd thought it would be and more. Pleasure dragged her under to a dark, lovely place. She tossed her head back, clenching and unclenching her fists. It was her only defense against the need to wrap her hands in his hair and hold him to her. But it didn't work for long.

Suddenly, a moan slipped from her throat, and Raine cradled his face as he tongued her nipple. She felt the jolt straight to her clit. Her back arched. She curled her leg over his hip. God, she was all but rubbing against him. And she still didn't really understand why he wanted her now. Just because he was drunk enough not to care about tomorrow? Well, she cared.

Raine twisted her body, breaking his suction on her breast. "If you had wanted to show me yesterday, fine. But today... And Liam..." She shook her head. "I said yes to him. I made a promise."

Nipping at the tight tip of her breast with his teeth until she cried out, he finally released the throbbing nubs. "Fuck Liam. He made you believe he was saving you from Beck. He mindfucked you into thinking he was the only one who could. I've saved you for years, Raine. I will always be here to save you. *Always.*"

The vow in his eyes was fierce, and a tremor passed through her. Without another word, he smoothed his palms over her shoulders, sliding the robe from her body. Naked and more exposed than she ever imagined she could be, Macen wrapped his hands around her narrow waist and lifted her onto the bar. His eyes never left hers as they laid claim to her soul. His nostrils flared, and she could smell her own arousal in the air between them.

"Lay back. I've wanted to know the flavor of you on my tongue for a lifetime."

Chapter Seven

She should stop him. She fooled herself into thinking that she could. But Patrón had ripped away his veneer of the passive protector, of civilization. If she'd thought she wanted Macen before, it was nothing compared to the ache he filled her with now that he'd finally, truly kissed her. Maybe a smarter woman would have been able to close off her feelings after the public punishment. But she wasn't that woman. Right or wrong, she still wanted him, felt him in a huge corner of her heart.

The choice was hers; she knew that. But was there really any question? The man she'd wanted forever was offering her a fantasy. All she had to do was lie back and let him do his worst.

But Liam… Had he really mindfucked her? Had he worked the situation to his advantage to sleep with her? To stab Hammer in the back? Whatever the reason, he'd barely known she existed, beyond trying to extract Hammer's secrets from her, until two days ago. He didn't love her. And she didn't love him.

Hammer would sober up tomorrow and likely regret this. If she gave up her one opportunity to be under him, she'd kick herself for the rest of her life. She was rationalizing, yes. But it all boiled down to her certainty that she'd never be whole without knowing his touch at least once.

"Yes, Sir." She lay back against the bar and shyly parted her legs a bit, craving his approval.

"Jesus," he breathed thickly. "Wider. I want your sweet pussy splayed opened just for me so I can breathe you in, taste every drop."

Her breath caught in her lungs. How long had she dreamed about hearing him command her?

Spreading her legs as wide as she could, exposing every slick fold for his pleasure, she sucked in a quivering gasp as his warm lips hovered just above her swollen pussy.

"Yeah...mine. Look at you, so stunning. I've imagined you like this, but now that you're here... Fuck, my precious one, you're breathtaking," he praised. "Don't come without my permission. You won't disappoint me." He raised a sharp brow at her. "Will you?"

Disappoint him? She didn't want to, ever. But just being in the same room with him aroused her, much less having his face in her pussy, a breath away from tasting her. Already she felt dangerously close to orgasm.

Trembling, she took a deep breath and tried to steady herself, then grabbed her knees and held herself open for him. "I will try. For you, I will always try."

He trailed his fingers up the inside of both thighs, his breath feathering over her aching slit. "Oh, precious, you'll do a hell of a lot more than try. Anything you set your mind to, you accomplish. You'll find the strength. The desire to submit burns brightly inside you, and I'm determined to make it blaze even hotter for me."

He lowered his head and drew his hot, slick tongue through her swelling folds and up to her clit. Unable to stop herself, her hips arched as his lips captured her clit and sucked at the turgid bud. She cried out. With slow, deliberate strokes, his tongue caressed and toyed, driving her higher and faster than she'd ever experienced.

The way he worshipped her pussy melted her. The way he knew her psyche undid her even more. God, how badly she wanted to please him, more than anyone else in her life. The feel of his tongue rasping over her sensitive flesh, trailing in long, sinful laps to swipe at her clit had her wailing. She gasped when he did it again. Arched higher. Lifted to him. Keened out her need.

"Please, Hammer. Please... God, yes. I want to please you. But I don't know how to fight this pleasure. No one's ever..." She panted, unable to form more words as his thumb prowled over her little button and he stabbed his tongue inside her, all the way to her fluttering center.

Then he eased back and slid two fingers in her slick slit. "My sweet girl, I've longed to be your first at something. Fuck, yes. I'm dying to give you this ecstasy. Look at me, Raine. Look into my eyes."

Forcing open her heavy lids, she blinked as she tried desperately to focus.

"That's it," he cajoled. "Don't look away and don't close your eyes. I want to watch you struggle to hold that orgasm back for me. It's big, isn't it? Yes. And your desperation is going to taste so sweet."

A slow smile crept over his lips before he moved his thumb and concentrated his skillful tongue on her clit again. His stare penetrated as surely as his fingers as they dragged in and out of her wet pussy with deliberate, measured strokes, curling and brushing the sensitive patch of nerves deep inside. Those sensations mingled and quickly merged to create a massive ache. She struggled to process it. Containing it was impossible. His unblinking stare still held hers captive, just as he did her body, telling her without a word how much he was enjoying her sensual distress.

Still, she marveled at the fact that Hammer touched *her*, that he found her woman enough to want. That he looked at her with a hunger that promised to devastate and consume.

The feelings jumbled together and tore away at her restraint. She dragged in huge gulps of air, trying to keep herself centered, but the heady pleasure of it just kept unraveling her. She didn't know how much longer she could hold on.

"Hammer..." she whimpered. "Please, I'm begging you. It's so big. It's going to pull me under. I can't—"

"You can. And you will. Just a bit longer." His words reverberated over her pulsating nub and shards of lightning zapped her spine. She cried out as she struggled to control the towering need building, faster and harder. He eased his mouth away, but his eyes never relinquished his hold on hers. "Tell me how badly you're burning."

"Help me. I'm at the edge, dangling. The sensations keep getting hotter. Please. Please...let me come."

"Soon, precious. I'm savoring the sounds of you begging for me. They make my dick so hard."

She panted, her entire body tensing to hold her orgasm back. Dizziness swirled in her head. In the face of this much need, her will to fight him and his mastery dissolved. "Hammer, I'll do it. I'll beg. Please, I'll be good. I'll give you anything you want."

"You'll give me *everything*. Keep your eyes on me, even if my image blurs in your ecstasy." With a frantic nod, she whimpered, clinging to her resolve by a thread. "I want to feel it fucking *now*, Raine. Come!"

Hammer fused his lips to her clit as he slid another finger into her sweltering cunt. Stretching. Driving. Demanding her orgasm. He pressed her hard clit between his teeth and tongue, insistently sucking as he hurtled her over the edge.

The sensations overwhelmed her. Raine slapped her palms on the bar, her body arching and surging up to his demanding mouth. He prowled her pussy, probed every nerve, and shoved such electric pleasure on her that she wailed his name. Sensations crested and threatened to drown her. But she didn't look away. Her eyes pleaded with him, while the gleam in his only promised her more of the sublime torture.

He devoured her, dragging out each second to infinity, stimulating her every nerve until her body jolted. She squirmed to escape the insanity. He wasn't about to let her off that easily. With a tight grip, he held her hips down and forced her to keep taking the punishing lashes of his tongue as he lapped and drank her essence. And that sharp, hungry stare of his told her that he'd let her know when he was done.

After an agonizing stroke of his tongue up her center, an indulgent smile curled his lips. "That was a delicious appetizer. I'm going to need another taste."

She hadn't even comprehended his words when he assaulted her with his fingers and mouth once more. It was not a slow coaxing. Now he sent her climbing with exacting precision. Fingers. Tongue. Teeth. He ate at her with single-minded determination.

It was too much sensation. Too much demand. Too much to even breathe. She pushed at his head, trying to dislodge him. He only grabbed her wrists and pinned them to the bar, then ate her voraciously again, driving her up, up, up with no respite. She plateaued quickly, at a place where need swelled and beat at her, where her body and mind raced to catch up as blood rushed and churned, but the peak was just beyond her reach.

"Stop. I can't," she sobbed. "I can't."

Hammer tightened his grip on her. He had to see the tears swelling in her eyes. But his masterful stare simply kept demanding more as he nipped her clit with his teeth.

"I know you can, Raine. Stay with me. I've got you." His voice was a low rumble, but the power in his words spiked inside her. "Climb to the edge and wait for my command."

Tears fell, streaming from the corners of her eyes as Raine fought for the pleasure. He wanted it. She wanted it—desperately. Yet her body hung suspended above the roar. She closed her eyes as her hips undulated helplessly with the building fire.

"Open your eyes, precious."

Her lids fluttered open. Their gazes connected, and all the tears in the world weren't going to stop him from doing whatever he wanted—in his time, in his way. Then he slapped the pad of her pussy before shoving his fingers right to the one spot designed to send her soaring toward the peak again. And suddenly, it was hard to hold back. "Hammer!"

Jerking his head back, he crooned, "I know, precious. You're right there and you're so beautiful. Stay here just a bit longer so I can watch you writhe for me."

"But I *need* it."

As the mournful wail tore from her throat, he stood and scooped her in his arms. Automatically, she wrapped her legs around him, desperately grinding on his thick shaft. He stilled her with a harsh grip on her hips as he carried her down the wide staircase.

"You think you need it now? Aww, precious, you haven't even begun to ache for me." His lips claimed hers as he stormed down the long hallway and into his private room. Kicking the door closed behind him, he rushed into the bedroom and splayed her across the center of his bed. "Eyes on me. Tell me what you want."

She watched him. Blinked. Her heart raced, and the slam of his door still resounded in her ears. She knew what she wanted from him, almost from the moment he'd taken her in, fed her, listened to her story, and promised in his fierce voice to keep her safe. She'd fallen a bit in love with him then. And in six years, she'd never stopped falling. Never stopped wanting. Never stopped waiting for this.

"Please, Macen. Fuck me."

Never before had those words slammed him with such force. They burned across his brain, searing away rational thought. Because they came from Raine.

Tearing at his trousers, he yanked down the zipper until his cock sprang free, thick and so engorged he felt as if it might burst. Raine's smoky blue eyes widened as she stared at the broad crest, dripping for her.

He took himself in hand, stroking slowly, loving the way her gaze followed and her mouth fell slightly open, as if waiting. "Oh, baby, I'm going to fuck you hard. Deep. And so thoroughly, you will *never* again doubt how much I've wanted to be inside you."

Standing over Raine, her tempting scent filled him again. *Christ*. He couldn't get inside her fast enough. He'd never sink deep enough. But he'd fucking try.

"Spread wide for me, Raine." he commanded. "I can't wait another second."

He'd never felt so out of control in his life. This alluring vixen who'd tempted him all these years was now his. Legs open, inviting him to sate every salacious longing he'd struggled to contain for a goddamn lifetime.

He climbed on the bed, prowling to her like an animal stalking its prey, crawling right between her thighs, then fusing his stare to hers. "I'm going to fuck you all night long."

"Yes," she whimpered.

Hammer covered her body with his. He wanted to howl at the feel of her hot, silky flesh under his own. The floral scent of her hair melded with the spicy aroma of her cunt into an intoxicating mix that fueled his demand even more. He slanted his lips over hers, taking everything she offered. He drank in her gasp as his cock pressed against her bare, swollen folds.

She felt like velvet against the screaming skin of his crest. Wet. And so fucking hot. He took her lips, parting them wide while he grabbed her hips and began to push inside her.

Fuck, she was swollen from her last orgasm, folds thick with the need for another. She squirmed and tensed against his invasion.

"Wait, Macen. I—ouch. Just a second. I—"

Goddamnit! He forced in a calming breath. Before tonight, Raine hadn't had much sex. His cock was so hard and his desperation to be inside her so relentless, he couldn't fucking see straight.

"Relax, precious. Let me make it good."

He worked in a bit deeper only to be stopped short again by her tight pussy. Hell, even with inches left to slide inside her, Raine staggered him with the amazing feel of her closing around him. His fucking eyes nearly rolled into the back of his head. She was both heaven and hell, and he wasn't willing to give up a second of her.

Gritting his teeth, he forced himself to back off for a moment. "If you want me to fuck you, baby, you have to let me in. Take a deep breath. Now let it go. Just relax. Yes..."

Slowly, she forced in choppy breaths before they shuddered out. But every muscle in her body still clenched, leaving him no way to breach her cunt.

His mind raced. Was he going to be able to work himself inside her? Was she so inexperienced that her little pussy couldn't accommodate his cock? No. Somehow, he would make it fit.

Leaning down to her breasts, he laved her hard berry nipples as he slid a hand between them and circled his thumb over her clit. Instantly a rush of hot cream covered the head of his shaft, and he eased back slightly to lubricate himself. He groaned. Her body relaxed, and he suckled her nipple as he pushed against her once more.

His crest bore a bit deeper through her slick folds—until she tensed again. "Easy."

Driving a little deeper, she gasped. He stilled, letting her body grow accustomed to his girth. But it was fucking excruciating.

Raine clawed at his back, shoving her hips up at him. "More…"

"I know. We'll get there. Just take a deep breath and let go. I'm not going to break you, Raine, but I fully intend to use you. I'll try to be gentle, but… God, I've waited."

"Me, too," she cried out in his ear.

But words weren't going to work her pussy open fast enough. He was going to have to get ruthless before he went insane.

He wrapped his lips into that tender spot between her neck and shoulder, sucked hard, then nipped. She drew in a sharp breath. But she directed all her focus on his bite and stopped tensing against his demand on her cunt.

And he slid into her fiery channel all the way to the hilt.

Oh, fucking hell. She was snug—and every bit as sinful as he'd imagined, especially when she clenched on him again. A long, low groan tore from his chest. After six endless years, Raine enveloped him, surrounding him everywhere. Her spice filled his nostrils. Her little cries sang in his ears. Her fingernails dug in his shoulders. She was so far beyond anything he'd fantasized about.

"Did I hurt you, baby?"

"No," she panted, her gaze clinging. "You're inside me. It's…incredible."

All he could manage was a jerky nod. "You're killing my control."

Balancing his weight on his elbows, he watched her, refusing to miss a moment as he eased back, then plowed his way deep inside her pussy again. Her eyes went wide. Her plump lips made a sexy little *O*. Her body jerked. Her breasts jiggled.

As he stroked in and out of her again, he fixed his mouth on her nipples, sucking, drawing her in. And hell yes, she tightened on him again. Jesus, every sensation with her was so damn intense. She fucking ignited his cock.

As he withdrew once more, he realized that was because he wasn't wearing a condom.

"Are you on the pill, precious?" he choked.

But he feared he knew the answer.

"No." She tensed for a moment.

He was stupid and probably going to regret this later, but Hammer wasn't going to stop fucking her. In fact, he'd be goddamned before he put anything between them again.

As soon as he slid inside her once more, Raine moved with him, eyes half closed, her body surging against him in a sensual dance that made him even harder.

"You need to get on it. We need you protected. Today."

She didn't respond, just gasped as he fucked deep inside her again, putting his weight behind the thrust and shoving her up the bed.

"Do you hear me, Raine?" he pressed. "I'll drive you, help you take care of it."

Because he didn't know if he could ever give up fucking her bareback.

"Yes." She wrapped her legs around his hips with a cry. "I will."

She was close, struggling to hold back. That, along with her fluttering cunt and her ragged breathing, were all the signs he needed. This was Raine. And imagining how she would feel contracting around him—because *he* had driven her to climax—made him ready to shed his self-control and come inside her.

Gritting his teeth, he held on, trying not to focus on the slickness of her clutching pussy or her breathy, escalating cries, just on giving her all the pleasure he could.

"Come for me, baby," he growled in her ear. "Give it all to me."

Hammer squeezed her clit between his finger and thumb as her body arched and he slid deeper.

"*Macennnnnnnnnnn.*"

Fuck! He'd waited a lifetime to hear her cry out his name while he fucked her.

"Yes!" He pounded into her, dying a bit more with every spine-melting thrust.

As she screamed, he struggled again to hold back. He stared down in awe as Raine clawed at him, desperation in her cry. Her body moved with him, rolled and molded against every inch of him. She grabbed him as if he was the center of her universe as the mighty orgasm rolled her under.

Then it took him along.

"Yes! Fuck, yes! Raine!" *My Raine.*

She'd imprinted herself on him. A corner of his soul would always belong to her, and rather than scaring the hell out of him, the thought took him higher. His cock jerked, and he let go, unleashing a torrent of his seed to splatter her silken, clutching walls.

Hammer panted and bellowed through the orgasm as she fluttered around him once more. Coming inside her felt so fucking good. His body hummed with the excruciating pleasure, like a million pinpricks along his skin bleeding satisfaction.

Part of his fulfillment was that he'd marked Raine in more than one way. His fingers biting into her tender hips would probably bruise her. His mouth on her neck had drawn a trail of love bites over her skin. His seed scalding her womb could leave her with something more lasting. God, he was playing a dangerous game with Raine, but now that he had her naked and open to him, he had to know if there was even a sliver of a chance that she could handle the demands he'd make on her body. On her soul.

A rosy flush spread over her face as she breathed heavily, eyes closed. Peaceful and recovering. Her breasts pressed against him, her legs still wrapped around him—and that's all it took for him to need her again. He didn't have to work to get demanding. With Raine, the urge was like breathing.

He withdrew, rolled to his feet, and walked to the other edge of the bed, pausing near her head. Then he filtered his fingers through her hair. He tried to be gentle as he tugged her head back.

Her blue eyes flew open and fixed on him, so wide and dilated. Even her startled gasp aroused him. Given half the chance, he'd surprise her all the fucking time.

"Scoot up and tilt your head over the side of the bed."

Raine blinked, then edged back on her elbows.

"That's it," he purred. "Open your mouth, precious. I need you to suck my cock. The memory of your hot little mouth all over me has plagued me since I woke up to find you swallowing me." She obeyed, and he groaned with anticipation. "God, yes."

The need to feel her everywhere rode him so hard, and Hammer told himself to ease up, but his desire to claim her in every way possible clawed its primal way through him, obliterating all else. Shit, he had to get himself under control.

But the moment she extended her tongue, laying it flat over that pillowy lower lip, and he slid his cock into her hot, silky mouth, he knew control wasn't happening for a long while.

Almost instantly he got hard enough to drill holes in concrete, as if all the blood in his body had rushed south. As if he hadn't come just a few minutes before.

He savored the hot stretch of her lips around him, clinging to him. But he either had to come down her throat now or step back and fulfill another of his fantasies with Raine. Gritting his teeth, he pulled out and walked to the far side of the bed.

"Move down here, precious. On your hands and knees."

She presented her lush white ass to him, and he got a good look at the terrible bruises Beck had left on the back of her thighs. He fingered them gently, regretfully, then kissed them slowly.

"I'm sorry," he murmured. "I swear he wasn't supposed to do that to you."

"Beck told me."

Hammer pressed his lips to the small of her back, then he reached into his nightstand and grabbed a tube. He slathered lube all over her rosette, plunging a pair of fingers inside the ass he was dying to claim.

"Are you sore here?"

"A little, maybe."

Raine gasped, squirmed. She didn't try to get away, but he got the distinct impression she fought the urge not to. The thought that she'd want to put any distance between them only made him more unrelenting.

"I'm sorry, precious. I'll do my best to be gentle. Arch your back and push out for me. I'm dying to take you like this."

With one hand gripping her hip, he stroked the slick gel over his shaft, then lined up the head with her tiny puckered ring. Pressing through the tightly drawn tissue was nirvana. As he watched the crest of his cock narrow into her, streaks of lightning slammed up his spine. *Christ!* He couldn't plunge into her the way he longed to or he'd rip her fragile tissue. Panting to calm his raging demand, he slowly fed each inch of his throbbing dick into her ass as he stroked her pebbled clit. The silken vise of her sweltering softness made him want to explode.

"Feel me, precious. Feel every thick, hard inch." He increased the tempo of his thrusts. "For you."

Raine whimpered and lowered her shoulders to the mattress, head thrown back so that mass of dark hair blanketed the pale skin of her back. She was fucking stunning.

"Yes!" He could hear the need consuming her in her little feminine growl.

She was adding fuel to his raging fire.

Anchoring his palm on the small of her back, he unleashed the beast clawing to be set free. Slamming his cock in and out, marveling at the strangling tissue surrounding him, he knew he'd never be able to last in her heavenly ass.

"Come, baby. Come again for me." He caressed her clit with insistent fingers.

Her tight passage gripped his expanding shaft. His restraint burst free, and he let go deep inside Raine as she convulsed around him with a cry. Jesus, so fucking good that his eyes crossed, his body hummed.

But still, he wasn't done.

Before she could sink to the mattress, he lifted her into his arms and carried her to the bathroom. Sitting her on the cool marble counter, he turned and started the shower. When he looked over his shoulder at Raine, she was slumped against the mirror with a little smile. Her eyes looked glassy, her skin flushed, those cherry nipples drawn tight, legs draped limply in the aftermath of his demands. To him, she was the most gorgeous woman on the planet.

His cock twitched. Fuck, everything about her made him hard. He stepped toward her and caught sight of his savage smile in the mirror. He tried to offset it with a soft caress to her cheek.

"Up, precious. We're not done yet."

Chapter Eight

She raised her heavy lids to him, exposing her dazed eyes, and damnit, he burned to be inside her pussy then and there. Instead, he lifted her, wrapped her limp arms around his shoulders, then hoisted her up from the counter and into the hot shower.

He wanted to bathe her and pamper her, let her know he treasured all she'd given him. But as soon as his soapy hands began cascading over her satiny flesh, the ravenous animal inside him leapt to life once more. Quickly washing his engorged cock, he rinsed the soap away as he gripped her hair and guided her to her knees.

Sliding back inside her hot, slippery mouth, he eased his cock to the back of her throat, holding her there for two beats of his pounding heart. Then he pulled back.

"I need more of you." He bared his teeth. "Suck my cock, precious. Swallow every drop."

And she did with a sudden burst of gusto that made his heart swell with pride. Roaring in pleasure, he praised her with gruff words and splintered commands, cradling her face in his hands. His vision blurred, and as his balls drew up tight and painful, he erupted down her throat, watching as she drank everything he gave her.

Afterward, she lapped at him like a little kitten, eyes closed, a little grin on her delicate face. The wrecking ball of his feelings for Raine slammed him right in the chest. God, she meant the world to him. He could almost picture every day and night with her like this, the need fevering up their blood, her obeying him as she surrendered to his rough demands, then him laying her down so that he could stroke her tenderly and curl her against him as they slept.

With a smile, he looked down at Raine. His cock slipped from her mouth, and she rested her head on his thigh, eyes closed. Oddly, her contentment revved up his blood until he was fired up and ready for her again.

Damn, he was demanding most any night, but this need was over the top, even for him. And it was all because of her.

Hammer lifted her to her feet. Bleary-eyed, she blinked at him, body limp. Her legs didn't seem able to support her, and she stumbled. He caught her with one arm and turned off the shower before grabbing a towel. Wrapping her in it, he lifted her onto the vanity and patted her dry, squeezing the excess water from her hair that continued to drip down her smooth back. A bolt of something deep and burning pierced his chest as he watched her pale cheek resting on his shoulder. He stroked her soft, soft skin.

With his arms wrapped tightly around her, he carried Raine to the bed and laid her on the cool, wrinkled sheets. She gave herself over to exhaustion like a child at the end of a long day, tumbling almost instantly toward sleep.

He stepped to the foot of the bed and gazed at her naked body. Unconsciously, she spread her legs for him. Inviting. Pliant. Once again his cock jerked to life, stiff and hungry for all she offered. In the muted light, he saw more of his markings on her, and that damn violent urge to take, mark, claim even more slammed him. He should leave her alone, let her rest. But why start pretending now that he was anything other than a horny bastard who would fuck her constantly?

Sliding onto the bed, he wedged against her side and sucked her nipples, toying with her clit. Her eyes fluttered open.

"Macen?" she whispered weakly.

"Yes, precious. I have to feel you again."

"So...tired," she whimpered.

Yeah, she'd had an eventful twenty-four hours. He'd used her hard. Liam, that fucking bastard, had taken her before him. He tried to tell himself that her fatigue was normal. But he knew that whatever Liam had done to her wouldn't be any less demanding than what he would have done himself if he'd been fucking her all day. Than what he'd do to her tomorrow or the day after…or the day after that.

"I know. It's just that… I don't know if I'll ever get enough of you."

As his fingers teased her pussy, Raine lifted her hips to him, searching. She was wet. She was ready. She could take him again.

Calling himself a stupid bastard, he climbed on top of her and spread her wider with his thighs. A slow smile of contentment curled her lips. Then he sank into her sweet, so swollen cunt, and she gasped. Thrusting with deep, long strokes, he rode her hard. All the while she whimpered and clutched him with the last of her strength. As he demanded her next orgasm, tendrils of worry licked his brain.

All too soon, her arms and legs gave out, and she lay splayed beneath him, wilted and almost still. Occasionally, she winced. Hammer knew she had to be sore. Just one more orgasm with her, then he'd let her rest…at least for as long as he could stand not touching her.

Her whimpering cries of discomfort filled him with guilt, and with a curse, he pulled from her pussy, gripped his cock in a rough fist, and worked it until he showered her full breasts with his come.

He collapsed against her, panting, kissing her closed lids, her temple, her jaw. Then he forced himself to roll away. If he stayed here, pressed against her softness, with his seed marking her, her face inches from his own, he'd only try to fuck her again.

Jerking away from Raine, he cleaned her up, then showered again, dressed in a pair of sweats and sprawled out in the chair in the corner, hoping he could give her some time to rest…and wondering how many more nights might be spent exactly like this, watching her sleep as this insatiable need to fuck her again clawed at him.

Hours later, Hammer felt strung tight enough to snap any goddamn second. He'd ventured onto the bed sometime during the night and slept for a few hours. Now, he laid on his side, watching Raine in slumber. He'd been clenching his fists since he'd awakened. His rigid dick still craved more of her.

Gazing at the soft curves of her face, his heart swelled. She was so gorgeous, more beautiful than any angel in heaven. And he couldn't deny for another moment how he felt.

"Raine?" He called out to her as dawn began to color the sky, but she didn't stir. Damn it, there was so much he wanted to say to her…do to her.

"I've tried damn hard to shut you out of my heart, but you stole it so quickly after I laid eyes on you. I love you, precious. I always have, and damn me to hell, I always will."

It had fucking killed him to deny her day after day for years. He'd helped her, yes. But he'd also brought her so much pain.

And today wouldn't be any different.

"I'm so sorry, my sweet girl. I'm a pathetic excuse for a protector. I've tried to shelter you from everything that can harm you. That includes me."

Goddamnit, the pain of constantly wanting her had finally grabbed him by the balls and squeezed hard. And he'd given in. But Raine was so deep inside him, he'd felt the relentless ache of trying to live without her for months and years…and it had been slowly driving him out of his mind.

Even as he called himself every kind of pervert, his cock jerked as he stared at her red, plump lips. Skimming his gaze over her alabaster flesh, a bittersweet smile curled upward. The marks of his possession colored her milky flesh. She'd be wearing them for days and have no choice but to remember this, remember him.

Wasn't regret a bitch? And he had so much of it. That he couldn't be the sort of man who'd be good for her. That he couldn't, in good conscience, mold her into what he needed. That he was so goddamn warped he couldn't settle for less.

Her raven hair spilled across his pale sheets, and Hammer reached out, threading his finger through her soft mane. Need clutched him with a desperate grip as he squeezed his hand in her hair and pressed his lips to hers.

She moaned in a dreamy whimper, eyes still closed, then nuzzled her cheek against his.

As much as he longed to slip inside her pussy one more time, he had to back off. He'd exhausted her. She couldn't endure his unquenchable sexual need, which she only seemed to exacerbate. And that was only half the problem. Dread flooded his veins.

With a silent curse, he shook his head. He'd known from day one that Raine would never be able to acquiesce to the beast inside him. Not the way he needed her to. She was too innocent. Too fragile. Too headstrong in ways that would keep her from bending to all he'd demand. It would break her, just as it had Juliet.

His stomach twisted in a rancid knot. Knowing what he had to do, he swallowed down the bile rising in his throat and pulled her against his chest instead. He needed a few more minutes to hold her, feel her warm supple flesh on his. Feel her heart beat next to his. Feel her breath feather over his neck. He needed a few more selfish moments to savor her before he destroyed every feeling she had for him.

She rolled over as sunlight flashed brightly through the window, hitting her eyelids. Every muscle in her body ached, like she'd been in a fight. No, like she'd been run over by a truck. In a good way. It wasn't like having the flu, thankfully. This was delicious, and a smile curled her lips. But as she stretched and arched her hips, the sore folds of her pussy rubbed against one another. She hissed in a breath—and smelled Hammer all around her.

Her eyes flew open. Hammer's room. Hammer's bed. The night rushed back. Hammer using her over and over. Hammer...now not lying beside her.

She turned over, struggling up to her elbows, and found him sitting on the bed beside her, in sweats and a T-shirt, staring. Regret lined his familiar, beloved face. Resignation dimmed his eyes.

"No. Whatever you're going to say, don't. Just don't," she spit out between clenched teeth. "Don't you dare tell me that you made a mistake or changed your mind or feel like you fucked your sister."

He only sighed and shook his head, and it made her angrier. She knew that her words weren't going to change his mind. He'd never listened to her. Why couldn't he do it just once now?

"Raine, listen to me. Last night *was* a mistake, precious."

His words hit her like a bullet to the chest. Agony ripped through her. All she did for this man was yearn and hurt. For six years of pain, she'd only gotten a few hours of ecstasy, and now he was going to rip her open again? "You didn't seem to think that when you had your cock inside me."

"Christ, I'm so sorry, but this isn't going to work. Goddamnit!" He jerked to his feet and paced the room, raking a hand through his hair. He didn't look at her.

"But…I never refused you anything. I gave you every bit of me. We were amazing together. I know you enjoyed it. You can't fake that."

"You're right, I loved every fucking second. Feeling you was all my most sinful fantasies come true. I won't lie to you anymore. But you couldn't handle everything I'd do to you." He spun back to her, torment choking his words from his throat. "You have no idea what I'd demand. Fuck, Raine, you passed out on me after I'd barely gotten a taste of you. You're not wired to deal with my needs. Look at you. Look at the marks I've left. You're already bruised and...fuck! They almost didn't stop me. You're built for a tender Dom who can give you that picket fence you crave. I can't be anything but an unrelenting Master."

"What kind of bullshit is that? So I got tired? I'm here this morning. Use me." She tossed off the blankets and spread her legs, trying to hold in her wince of pain...and failing. Hell, she was so sore. And Hammer's stare flicked over her, settling on her pussy for a long moment before drifting back to her face. His cock grew hard in his sweats, but he didn't move a muscle toward her.

"Whatever you want, I'll get used to it. Give me more than five minutes to adjust! Bruises are no big deal. And I never said anything about picket fences. Can't we just...be together right now and see what happens? Make love, have breakfast, work together, grab a nooner, then a nice dinner before the club starts hopping and—"

"No." He silenced her midsentence. "You don't understand. I'm not the kind of man who shares a relationship. I demand one. On *my* terms. There's no vanilla give and take."

None of this made sense to her. "But...you're great with everyone. Employees love you. Patrons all say you're flexible and fair and—"

"Because they don't wear my collar. Let me tell you what I'd expect if you did, because it's a far cry from what you're imaging." He spun back to the bed, eyes blazing into hers. "In the morning when you wake up, I'll unchain you from the bed." Her eyes flew open wide in disbelief. "That's right, unchain you from my bed. Then I'll force your mouth to my cock and you'll suck me off before your feet even hit the floor. Then you'll leave the room to fix my breakfast. There won't be any sweet talk at the table unless I wish it. Most likely, you'll be on your knees at my feet while I eat. I'll spoon-feed you what and when I decide. You'll be naked twenty-four/seven, unless I take you out in public. Then—" His grating scoff sliced into her skin, up her back— "you'll wear what *I* choose. You'll cut your hair the way *I* want it. You'll wear the fragrance *I* like. Your pussy will be waxed at all times. Your fingernails will be short with clear polish only. Most of all, you'll take my cock anywhere, any way, and any time I decide without so much as a peep of protest. If I want to fuck you on the sidewalk in broad daylight, you'll let me. And if I want to share you? Yes, that's right, I said *share* you, you'll spread yourself wide and welcome another man's cock into your pussy, ass, or mouth at my command. None of this is negotiable. You *will* tell me every day that you accept and crave my every desire. Because that's what I need to be happy. And don't blow smoke up my ass and tell me that what I've described is your dream, too." He jerked upright as his frustration poured through the room. "I need a slave, Raine, not a sub. And you have no idea the toll that would take on you. I've already been through the havoc it can wreak on a woman ill prepared, and I'm not willing to live through it again. That's fucking final."

"Seriously? This is the lie you're going to tell me to get away from me? I've seen you every day for the last six years. I've even watched you scene when you thought I wasn't looking. You've never treated a woman like that." She rose with a stomp of her feet and looked around for her clothes, only to remember that he'd dragged Liam's robe off her in the bar, and they'd left it there. And she'd be damned if she would put anything of Hammer's on her body right now. "You would have had more success just telling me that you'd fucked me out of your system and are done with me. This slave bullshit is pathetic. But whatever. You want me gone? I'm gone. I should have left yesterday, like I planned. At least I'd be minus a few hickies, bruises, and a sore pussy. But I get the message. You're just a miserable fucking bastard who wants to be alone. No problem."

Stark naked, she marched for his bedroom door.

"It's not a goddamn lie!" he bellowed. "Go ask Liam. He was there. He knows exactly what went down. He was fucking her, too, for christ's sake. Yes, precious, that's right. I shared my wife with him. And it ended in disaster. I won't fucking do that to you."

Gasping, she stepped back from him in horror. "Wife?" Oh dear god, she'd fucked a married man? Raine didn't have many boundaries, but that was one she held sacred. She never stole another woman's man. "You asshole! Why didn't you tell me you're married? I would have never... And where the hell has she been all this time?"

God, she was going to be sick. Raine grabbed the comforter from Hammer's bed and used it to cover herself as she backed toward the door.

He ripped it away from her body.

"My *late* wife. She's dead because she couldn't handle life with me." His stare seared her flesh. "And if you think you can, then you have to start understanding now that when we're alone, you won't be allowed even this." He tossed the cover back on the bed. "But if you think you're ready to be my slave, precious, then get on your knees. Or get the fuck out!"

Her head spun. His wife. His slave. Dead...how? How did not handling Macen's demands lead to a grave? She stared, struggling to comprehend. Hell, she'd never known—even remotely suspected—that he'd ever been married, much less lost a wife. And Liam had been there, sharing her?

"What's it going to be?" he asked. "I'm not a patient man when it comes to sex with my slave. Open your mouth. Finger your clit and get yourself wet so I can fuck *my* pussy again. For your dithering, you won't get an orgasm. I'll probably want your ass again, too. Hell, we may not see daylight for a week. Now hurry up!"

"You're trying to be a vile asshole," she accused. She'd never seen him be this wretched to anyone. This wasn't him.

"Nope, I'm finally being myself. You've got five seconds to decide. Either kneel and stick out your tongue or get the fuck out."

She'd suffered abuse as a child when she'd been powerless to stop it. As a woman, she understood finally that she didn't have to stay in any situation that made her feel less than valued. She'd had enough therapy to know she was worth more. Even if he was telling the truth, the relationship he described sounded like a one-sided nightmare. She'd never be happy like that.

"You're a selfish son of a bitch, Hammer. Go suck your own cock."

Head held high, she whirled to the door and yanked it open, feeling Hammer's heavy stare all over her.

Raine stormed out into a wall that shouldn't be there. She looked up—right into Liam's face. His blue robe draped over his bare shoulder. His stare raked her up and down, coldly furious, as he catalogued every bruise, scratch, and love bite. Her heart plummeted to her stomach. Guilt strangled her throat.

Oh, Liam… All he'd tried to do was save her. And as she always did, she'd ruined everything.

She tried to dart past him and run to her room. Instead, he grabbed her arm, then shot Hammer a glare full of rage and loathing. "Let's go."

Chapter Nine

Liam led Raine to his room beside Hammer's, rage still pinging inside him. She'd spent the night fucking Hammer, damn it. He tamped the anger down, compartmentalizing it for later, and shut the door behind them with a quiet click.

He looked at her standing naked in the middle of his room, lost, her shoulders curled self-consciously as she wrapped her arms around her middle. Fuck, bruises and marks covered her everywhere. What the hell had Hammer done, tried to fuck her to death? He'd rarely seen so many marks on a sub. Damn if he didn't want to punch his "friend."

Later. Now had to be about processing this logically, figuring out what the fuck had happened, and deciding what to do next.

Because the bruises she wore weren't marks of tender passion at the hands of the man she loved, but were brands from a bastard who'd meant to betray him by marking her as his possession. *Message received loud and clear, Hammer.*

Liam fully intended to mark her, too, but his would be deeper than the flesh. And he knew exactly how to do it.

He approached her and draped the robe over her shoulders. "You have ten minutes to wash Hammer's stench from your body and be dressed to leave."

Raine looked like she wanted to shed guilty tears, but she held them back. "I'll just go. You don't have to—"

"I don't recommend arguing with me just now. Shower and dress." A muscle twitched near his eye as he shoved down more anger.

She swallowed and dropped her gaze. But she finally nodded. If she wanted to know where they were going, she didn't ask.

"And be quick about it."

With guarded posture, Raine obeyed. The wild tangle of her dark, silky hair was the last thing he saw before the bathroom door closed. He heard the water come on. She stepped in a moment later, interrupting the spray. Sobs followed.

Fuck if that didn't piss him off all over again.

But he had other things to do besides stand about and listen to her cry her heart out for another man. At the end of the day, he'd wanted to believe she was different. Didn't that make him a fucking idiot?

Exiting his room, Liam backtracked down the hall and shoved the door open to Hammer's domain. The man just stared like a statue, unmoving. He wore the same shell-shocked expression as Raine.

Everything he'd believed about Hammer, everything that had happened past and present, converged to just this moment as the silence beat heavily.

What the fuck had happened? That's what he'd like to know. He'd awakened to an empty bed hours ago and heard Hammer and Raine fucking like bloody rabbits. It was what they'd both wanted. What he'd originally sought for them. From the cries of Raine's ecstasy and Hammer's roars of passion, Liam had assumed they were happy together. That he was out, and Hammer was in like Flynn. And her betrayal had hurt far more than it should for a woman he'd taken to bed once or twice. Everything about it had poked his most miserable insecurities.

But Hammer knew that.

After listening to them fuck half the night, hearing Raine scream Hammer's name, Liam had packed, fully intending to walk away from the pair of them. Let them bloody well tear one another apart.

Looking at Raine's ravaged body and her mournful face...his anger had spiked. He shouldn't feel sorry for her, but goddamn it, he couldn't help it. She'd been hurt enough.

Raine had gotten under his skin. Caring about her hadn't been part of his plan. How the bloody hell had it backfired so quickly? Despite Hammer's mocking reproach, she'd already become more than a pair of blue eyes and a great rack to him. Far more.

Hammer had hit him where it hurt most. By god, he intended to do the same.

Cold fury curled like a wild thing inside him, itching for release, as he stared at Hammer. He forced it down, delivering every word with control. "I remember Juliet being marked now and then, but nothing like what you've done to Raine. Your own wife couldn't handle it. How do you think the girl will cope? You used her with a ruthless selfishness, but I shouldn't be surprised. You have the audacity to think you love her? Like you 'loved' Juliet?"

Again, Liam clenched his fists at the thought of all the bruises, of her pain as she'd tried to walk back to his room. Of the betrayal Hammer had dealt him, doubly vile because the man *knew* how it would push his buttons.

Hammer seethed, rage in his haunted eyes. "I do love her. God help me, even more than Juliet. Not that I owe you an explanation."

Liam sneered. "Not that I believe you. Take a look at your wretched mug in the mirror. You're a pathetic motherfucker who destroys women to make himself feel big. You're not fit to call yourself a Dominant, let alone *her* Dominant."

"I told you yesterday that I wasn't good for her, but you wouldn't listen." The man lunged in his face. "Who the fuck do you think you are? You're not my life coach. You're not God. You sure as hell aren't my friend."

"I could say the same to you."

Hammer's eyes turned to ice. "You thought this up, didn't you? Of course. How fucking like you. You 'collared' her to trick me into claiming her. And now you're pissed that it almost worked? Asshole," he hissed. "I've seen you play people for years. I just never imagined you'd do it to me."

"Fuck you! I tried to help. You could have taken Raine as your own any time before last night, but you chose not to. Now I agree with your reasons. You *aren't* good for her, but you conveniently forgot that, didn't you?" Liam accused. "You waited until Raine became *mine* to fuck her. For the pleasure of cuckolding me? Were you trying to crawl under my skin? You broke the Dominant code of conduct. Don't you ever think of touching Raine again. I'll be taking her and going now. And after the way you've treated us both, I'd best not be hearing a word from you."

"Don't you *dare* preach to me about the code of conduct. The honor of your training collar means shit! Only you would collar a sub with ulterior motives. Stellar job, asshole. Don't deceive yourself; you're going to fuck up her head." Hammer shook his head in disgust. "Oh, and you're not taking her anywhere, motherfucker!"

"Watch me." Liam raised a brow, then turned and walked away. He left the door open in his wake as he headed back to his own room. And to Raine.

She sat on the bed with a towel still wrapped around her, staring at her feet. Her eyes were red. At least she smelled of soap now rather than the animal who'd used her sorely.

He shut the door. Seething, he made his way to his dresser, yanking out a fresh robe. He helped Raine to her feet and gently removed the towel. Wrapping her in the robe, he picked her up and grabbed his suitcase, then carried them both from the room, past a gaping Hammer, and out of the dungeon. He didn't stop until he'd reached the car, tossed the case in the boot, and secured her in the seat beside him. Only then did she turn to him.

Her big blue eyes filled with tears, and Liam gripped the steering wheel as he peeled away from Shadows. A glance in the rearview mirror showed Hammer panting in the door, looking all but ready to run after them. Well, after her.

Liam reached behind Raine's seat and extended his middle finger in the air. Hammer wouldn't miss it through the back window.

She was oblivious to the drama taking place behind her. She dropped her gaze to her clenched hands folded in her lap. Her delicate profile was taut and so fucking sad...

He gritted his teeth. She'd chosen to fuck Hammer without giving her supposed Sir so much as a heave-ho first. But if his former mate had treated the girl carelessly before he'd taken her to bed, he'd treated her far more wretchedly afterward. Liam didn't need to be a mind reader to see Raine was breaking.

"I'm sorry," she said so softly he could barely hear. "I know it's not much. I don't have a good explanation, except that I was stupid. Impulsive. And I thought it was love." She drew in a shuddering breath. "I'll answer whatever questions you have. I owe you that. Then you can take me back and wash your hands of me. I'm going to leave Shadows. I have an old friend who might be in Vegas. I'll find her, and I'm sure she'll take me in...help me find a job."

How long would she be homeless in the meantime? The very thought filled him with anxiety he probably shouldn't feel. He clenched his jaw.

"Never mind." Her face closed up even more. "I'm sure you don't care."

She paused, and he sensed that she worked up the courage to look at him again. When she did, the pain on her face stabbed him. Liam cursed under his breath.

"For what it's worth, I really appreciate everything you tried to do," she whispered. "I wish I could have deserved you more."

Some logical part of him thought he should be happy at how bloody the girl was beating herself, but it only burned anger through his veins. And made him want to take her in his arms more. For now, he'd use it to his advantage.

"I'm not so sure I'll be taking you back there, Raine. Whether you meant it or not at the time, you gave me your commitment to be my submissive." He felt her gaze again, but this time he stared straight ahead, paying attention to the traffic. "You and Hammer both seem to have had no compunction whatsoever about letting that wee fact slip your minds. But now you will submit to me. Have no doubt that you will learn well what it means to be mine. *That's* what you owe me."

"Why would you want… I did everything wrong, just like I always do. I would have thought you'd want to sever the collaring and tell me to go to hell."

The lass was defeated and self-blaming, and he'd have to fix that over time. "You weren't listening when I told you that I don't back down from a challenge, were you? Best mark my words from now on."

She went a bit wide eyed. "Oh. Okay."

Liam could read her so easily. She didn't think he'd last long with her, that he'd grow tired of her after a few days or weeks and cut her loose. Raine didn't know him well yet, but she would.

"You know damn well that you need not fear me. Every time I touch you, you'll have your safe word, but by christ, I'll not be played again."

"I never meant to—"

"I'm not finished." Of course she hadn't meant to cross or upset him. She hadn't thought of him at all last night. And that burned bitter in his gut. She meant far more to him somehow than she should after a handful of days. And he wouldn't let her go until he figured out why. "You and I will spend some time together, just the two of us, until we share an understanding. Do you hear me, Raine? I was as clear as I could be yesterday when I told you that you were mine and I would *not* share you with another."

She just nodded, her face a mask of guilt.

"I meant every word. Now lay back and get some rest. We've a long drive ahead of us."

"Why would you bother?"

He turned to stare at her, raised brow, silently chiding her for her disobedience. She bit her lip and looked down.

The truth was, he usually made every decision logically. But this he couldn't explain.

Her eyes were soft and contrite. "I don't mean to question you, but yes, you're right. I owe you and I didn't stop to think enough. I never thought you'd really care...but when I hear myself say it, it sounds lame. I am more sorry than you know. I don't expect you to forgive me, so don't worry. Can I just ask that if you want to spank me that you try to avoid the bruises? But if you'd rather not, I understand. I've earned it."

"I'll answer this, then you'll stop with the questions and rest. And you'll obey." As she started to speak, he stopped her. "Nod, Raine. Take a deep breath and just nod. Don't disappoint me. Listen, then you'll sleep. I've a place that's remote and beautiful this time of year. We'll be alone there, and we'll sort this out. That's all you need to know now. Do you understand?"

"Yes." The word held a vast quantity of remorse, but she'd said the one word he wanted to hear.

"I 'bother' with you, as you say, because I'm a Dominant. Because you need what I can give you." But Liam was painfully aware that wasn't the only reason, just the one that made the most sense and would be more likely to win her cooperation. "By the time we're ready to face...others together once more, you and I, I promise that you'll not forget what it means to be truly owned. And you will never mistake my kindness for weakness again."

She looked like she had a hundred more questions, but she held her tongue, laid back, and tried to rest. She curled into herself, and he couldn't help but notice that she shivered. The November morn was nippy, and with her wet hair and bare feet, the lass had to be chilly. He turned the heater up, questioning again why she mattered. But the answer remained the same. This damaged girl needed someone to care for her, take her in hand. For some reason, he wanted to be that man—and it wasn't because he pitied her. Because he didn't want to lose at the infidelity game again? Maybe… But he could picture her now naked and waiting for him in their bed, her big blue eyes welcoming him before she spread her legs and invited him into her lush body, or kneeling before him, head bowed, offering him her submission…

Liam jerked his gaze back to the narrow mountain road.

When she finally fell asleep, he placed a call to Adam, the caretaker of the cabin he'd inherited last year. He hadn't visited the place in years. Best of all, Hammer would never find it.

He made the necessary arrangements to have everything ready for their arrival, and Adam assured him that he and his wife, Ngaire, would collect some clothing for Raine, as well as lay in food and provisions. He hung up, checking that task off his mental list, then he allowed his thoughts to drift back to the morning as he drove steadily onward.

Hammer's incomprehensible behavior still had him shaking his head. And the conflicting rage and protectiveness Raine had instilled standing before him both bruised and dazed stunned Liam. Then, not surprisingly, his thoughts turned to the moments he'd claimed her in the dungeon and again in his bed…followed by the memory of his crushing disappointment. Waking to find her gone from his bed and hearing her cry out in passion from Hammer's… *Fuck!*

His past come to haunt him all over again.

Why in the hell hadn't he just walked away from her and Hammer and the whole sordid saga before it had come to this? After all, he'd had ample opportunities to leave. It wasn't as if the man had asked for or wanted his help. Hammer's assertion that Raine had only used him to get her boss's attention flitted through his thoughts. It was possible. Probable even. But Liam knew without a doubt that Raine felt *something* when she was with him. She might love Hammer, but her responses when she'd been with him had been all innocent gasps, clinging arms and legs, sugary-spun kisses, and welcome. He didn't have much certainty about anything right now. But two things he did know: Raine wanted him, and he wasn't ready to let her go.

By the time he pulled up in front of the lodge a few hours later, she was waking. "We're here. Stay where you are, and I'll fetch you inside. We'll get you warm soon."

She glanced up at the lodge, clearly puzzled. But she banked her questions—for him, that much was clear. But her meekness wouldn't last. Guilt would wear off, especially once he started to confront her issues. Then…Liam knew he'd be in for a battle.

He was fast coming to realize that Raine knew well how to fight fire with fire. Hell, sometimes she started the fire all by herself. But when someone lavished her with consideration and caring? She had no weapons—and unless he missed his guess—no experience with that. When showered with tenderness, she all but whimpered like a kicked puppy. But she needed it, and using that weapon would help him get answers. Though he probably shouldn't care, he didn't have the stomach to see her so tormented and ill-treated again.

As he jumped from the car, he blocked the caretaker from opening Raine's door. "Thank you, Adam. I'll help her in. She's had a rough time of it. If you'll just take my bag…"

The caretaker nodded and pulled his suitcase from the back.

As the man turned away, Liam helped Raine from the car. She winced and walked slowly, obviously tender and sore all over, as Liam led her toward the warm lodge, wrapping an arm around her wee waist.

What exactly had happened between Raine and Hammer? Why had she been crying as if her world had near ended yet be furious to boot? And why was she always determined to leave when trouble rolled around? Liam sensed that her waters ran deep and her secrets deeper. If he wanted to hang onto the lass, he'd best be getting smart and coax some answers from her.

After watching a few of her ginger steps, he swept her into his arms again and strode inside. A fire burned brightly in the hearth, warming the cavernous room, while the yeasty scent of fresh-baked bread made his stomach growl. Raine trembled in his arms, but he merely held her closer and mounted the staircase beyond the open lounge.

Inside the master bedroom, he laid her carefully on the bed and continued to the bathroom, then set about filling the massive tub. As he approached Raine, her eyes followed him. Though she watched him mutely, he knew she'd find her moxie again soon enough. But he was ready.

"Use the bathroom, if you need. Once you're finished, get in the tub. Let the water and Epsom salt ease your aches and pains. I've added some oils to soothe you. Away you go. I'll be there in a minute. I want to check on our lunch first." He waited until she'd carefully moved from the bed and into the bathroom before he headed downstairs and to the kitchen.

Bless Ngaire! She'd prepared some hearty sandwiches with lots of fruit and a bottle of wine, crusty bread, cheeses, a jar of fine pickles, and an unexpected treat. He put together a platter, grabbed two glasses, and headed upstairs once more.

Liam poured her wine, then stripped and sauntered into the bathroom to join her. She lay with her head back against the tub, eyes closed, immersed in the scented water.

As he stepped in the hot tub with her, Raine started, sitting up and gathering her knees to her chest, watching him wordlessly with wary eyes. He handed her the wine as he sank down and leaned back against the opposite edge of the tub, lifting each of her legs in turn and spreading them open and over his own.

Steam swirled softly around them as his stare bore into hers. "Take a drink of your wine, Raine."

She did, and Liam picked up one of her feet and laid it against the hard flesh of his belly. He had to lower her guard, convince her that she had nothing to fear. So he kneaded her gentle arch with his hands, smiling at her little moan.

"What are you thinking? Tell me what's on your mind."

He could tell by her silent consideration and sudden tenseness that she was trying to figure him out and decide how honest to be.

Liam leveled a fierce stare at her. "No editing your answers. Spit it out."

"I don't know how to take you." She tucked a strand of hair behind her ear. Tears sheened her eyes, and she took another sip of wine to hide it. "Hammer had six years invested in me and he let me leave with barely a word. You spent a few hours with me and yet you're still here, despite…everything." She took another sip of wine, then set it on the window ledge beside her. "I can never tell you how much I appreciate what you've done for me. I needed to get out of there. But if anyone should have been happy to see my ass getting smaller in the distance, I would have thought it would be you." She smiled, trying to lighten the mood. "You have a knight in shining armor fetish?"

He didn't respond right away, simply kept kneading and pressing, circling and gentling the foot he cradled in his hand. How the fuck should he answer her? Certainly, he couldn't tell her that he'd first approached her, because he'd schemed to use her to make Hammer jealous. Nor could he confess that something he couldn't explain had happened along the way. That their first kiss had blown his plans to hell. That he couldn't imagine letting her go now.

"Knight in shining armor, not exactly. But a Dominant who can't stand seeing a sub so starved. The guilt is written all over your face. And I won't say I'm happy with your choices. There will be consequences. But you can repay me by learning, and this time, giving me your trust and honesty. Can you do that, Raine?"

"I don't know. How I can be afraid of something I've wanted so badly for so long?"

He watched her struggle to hold in her tears. She tossed her head back, furiously blinking them away with sheer will.

"If you need to cry, then cry, lass. Let it out."

She shook her head, her mouth tightening mulishly. "If I'm going to cry over anything, it's going to be because I was stupid. I'd rather learn from my mistake and move on."

"Fair enough. Why do you think you can't give me your trust and honesty?"

Raine didn't answer right away. "I'm not…very good with either one. I never learned as a kid. I haven't had much practice at Shadows. I even lied to myself that Hammer could love me as more than a little pet. I don't think he knows how to be honest, either. To get rid of me, he spouted a bunch of crap about having a wife who was a slave that you shared with him. I wish he'd have saved the *B.S.* I could have filled in the blanks with a better lie of my own."

"What makes you think he lied? Juliet was lovely, but sadly flawed, like most of us. She seemed the most devoted slave to Hammer." Liam kept talking into Raine's stunned expression. "Yes, we shared her on occasion, but the lesson you should take from her tale isn't obedience, though that would be nice… But what you should learn that she tragically never did is communication. We rely on it in the power exchange. It's as essential as the air we breathe. You'll learn to give me your tears and your broken heart. I would have your pain, just as I will your pleasure."

Liam lifted her then, as easily as he would a child, and sat her on his lap. Holding her to him and surrounding her with his strength, he rocked her, stroking her until the terrible pain she'd been holding in for so long couldn't be silenced a moment longer. She wept long, hot tears.

"Get it all out. Just hold on to me tight and let it go."

She hid her face from him, but couldn't stop her sobbing. "I don't know how to do this, cry and bleed in front of someone. I feel too exposed. It hurts too much." She shook her head, struggling for each shuddering breath as she fought to contain her emotions. "He didn't tell me what happened to Juliet—god, she even sounds pretty—but I'd lay money I'm far worse at communicating than she was." She sat back from him, curling her arms around her middle. "And I'm not going to be good for you. You'll split me open like a ripe peach, all right, but you won't like the rotting core underneath. I can't stand that, without meaning to, I've come between you and your best friend. I'm like an atomic bomb everywhere I go. Destructive. Stupid. Thoughtless. You should cut your losses and let me go. I owe you too much to stay and screw up your life." She yanked from his grip altogether and climbed from the tub, then raced for the door.

The pain in her voice told him that her terrible guilt only fed her inadequacies. She would dart, even naked, into the cold. Yes, to save herself. But everything about her expression said she actually believed she'd be saving him, too.

Liam acted quickly. Chasing her put the control in her hands. Time to wrench it away.

"Stop! Present yourself, sub."

Her body froze. Liam could almost hear her determination to flee fighting with her need to submit to his Dominance. He waited a moment, letting his command sink in. Then, with a sob, she fell to her knees on the tile and assumed the pose. Her shoulders still shook, and her breath still shuddered. He waited as she composed herself, soaping his body and rinsing. He saw the moment she chose to heed the submissive within. Her breath evened out. Her body relaxed. Her mind seemed to quiet. And Liam just watched.

Raine giving him her power was intoxicating.

He stepped from the tub and squatted beside her as steam rose upward from their heated flesh. "As I said, you will learn to give me everything inside you, Raine. Easy or hard, that's up to you. But you *will* learn." Rising, he extended a hand and helped her up. "Come, before you get a chill. Let's dry you off. Then I intend to feed you."

Raine trembled, her knees aching from the cold tile. But it was the power of his whip-like commands still lashing through her brain that made her shake. *Oh god, oh god, oh god.* He'd found one of her weaknesses and he was too smart not to know it. With that voice, somehow sharp and velvety at once, he'd revealed himself a Dom in gentleman's clothing.

Biting her lip, Raine risked a peek up at him. One look at his face told her that he'd brought her here not just to rescue her and let her heal, but to unravel her utterly. Here on his turf, in his bed, under his control, she'd have no place to hide. And no Hammer to interfere.

Anxiety bloomed in her stomach.

Liam reached back for a towel, but did he give it to her or cover her with it? Of course not. He gently dried her, then wrapped it around his waist before leading her, stark naked, to the bed. There was a message in that, and she couldn't fail to understand.

She eyed the food spread out on the nearby dresser. Not that she was hungry, but eating would buy her time. Because not for one second did she imagine that what came after the meal would be easy.

"Kneel on the floor facing the bed, Raine. Get comfortable. You might be there a while," Liam said with an arch in his brow.

She watched as he moved to the thermostat in the room. He stared at it, nodded, then turned back toward her, clearly ready to unleash whatever he had planned. So maybe he wasn't waiting until after the meal to make her life difficult.

Prowling to the dresser, Liam removed something from one of the drawers and set it aside, out her line of vision, before selecting food for them both. Then he returned to the bed and sat in front of her. "Hands behind your back."

Why? She wanted to ask the question, but knew how BDSM worked. He commanded; she obeyed without question. That didn't mean she always liked it…but she wanted it. Reminding herself that Liam wouldn't really, truly hurt her, even though he must still be angry, Raine slowly wound her hands behind her.

"That's not bad. A little faster would be nice. Try hard not to think so much. Trust, not logic. Do you understand?"

She watched him, her stomach dancing with nerves, then she nodded.

"Answer me with words. I'll not be relying on a bob of your head."

Raine had a hard time getting the word out, as if it implied more trust than she was ready to grant, but she knew that he'd likely make her spend all day on her knees until she complied. "Yes."

"Yes, what? What do you call me?"

"Yes, Sir."

"Better. Now open your mouth. Let's feed you a bit."

"I'm not actually hungry."

He crossed his arms over his chest. "I didn't ask if you were hungry. You skipped breakfast, and you won't be skipping lunch. I told you to open your mouth."

Raine eyed the little platter in his hands, then watched as he picked up a piece of buttered bread and brought it toward her mouth. She leaned away and turned her head. "I can feed myself."

"I assume you've been doing that for years. But I'll be feeding you today. No arguments."

She should probably let it go, but…damn, she found that hard. When she opened her mouth to argue, he merely shoved the bread inside.

"Chew now. Swallow."

Reflexively, she did, then he followed with a sip of red wine. A chunk of pineapple after that, then a bite of succulent roast beef. Wordlessly, she allowed him to place the food in her mouth, squirming as he watched, the flavors mingling on her tongue while she consumed every bite. It was intimate and weirdly arousing, taking food from his hand. She didn't hate it.

Until he came toward her with a dill pickle spear. Then she backed up quickly, almost springing to her feet to avoid him. "No."

Liam paused. "Are you allergic to them?"

She scrunched up her face. "No, but they're disgusting. They reek like fermented gym socks."

He smiled. "That's quite an analogy."

She gave him a hesitant grin back. "Well, they do."

"So it's safe to say you'd like to be avoiding them, then?"

"Absolutely!"

"Keep that in mind as we go on. And last…" He popped a piece of chocolate into her mouth.

What wasn't to like about chocolate? But *this* chocolate? Positively divine. Something baked by the angels and sent down from heaven. The best she'd ever had in her life. As it melted on her tongue, she moaned.

"Like that, do you?"

"This qualifies as love. Oh my god…"

He grinned at her again, and was probably laughing a bit at her expense, but she didn't care. That chocolate was worth whatever bit of fun he poked at her. She'd almost crawl across glass for more.

"Well, then, you should also keep that in mind as we move on."

Raine wasn't quite sure what he meant by that statement, but if there was more chocolate involved, she could deal. "Yes, Sir."

"Excellent. Now close your eyes."

The command made her frown. He wanted to feed her when she couldn't see? "Wait. Is this one of those 'trust' exercises? Wouldn't it be better if I let you stand behind me while I tipped back and waited to see if you'll catch me?"

"Another day, maybe. Not now. Yes, this is about trust. Everything is. Close your eyes."

His voice had dropped another octave. A fresh swarm of butterflies emerged in her stomach. She didn't like it. Not being able to see made her feel wretchedly exposed.

"If you don't hurry, I'll be taking everything back to the kitchen except the pickles."

Raine slammed her eyes shut.

"About time. Keep them shut and hold still."

She heard the bed squeak just a bit, then felt the rush of cool air on her arm as Liam walked past. His gaze on her back seemed to singe her skin. Then something cool and silky fluttered in front of her face before he settled it over her eyes and knotted it at the back of her head. A blindfold. *Oh, hell.*

It scared her a little. But she was also able to focus on the sounds of his movements, the warmth in the air, the humming of her skin. Anticipation. Everything he did to and for her felt almost like a seduction.

His footsteps trailed away from her, then a drawer opened, closed. He returned, and Raine felt his grip settle around her wrists. A moment later, he snapped something around them snugly. Leather? A gentle tug proved the cuffs were attached.

"Restraints? What the… I said I wouldn't try to feed myself."

"I heard you. Think of these as my insurance policy. Beside, you look fetching all bound."

He was a Dom. Of course he'd think so. Besides… "You pervs just like it because it makes a sub's boobs stick out."

"That, too, you mouthy wench. Now focus. Pay very special attention to everything I say. There's going to be a test."

Great. She'd failed plenty of those in her life. She wasn't keen to fail this one now. Somehow, she was pretty sure he'd make that really unfun. And the idea of failing him again upset her even more.

"I'll do my best."

"Glad to hear it," he sounded almost amused, but she didn't believe for a second that he wasn't taking this seriously. Yesterday, she might have believed that he'd dance to her whim. Now…not so much.

"What's your favorite color?"

Liam had not dragged her out of Shadows and up a mountain to find out if she liked green more than blue.

"Red," she said tentatively, hoping like hell there wasn't a wrong answer.

"A nice color. Open your mouth."

The demand made her pause, wonder what the hell he was up to. But maybe there would be chocolate. She parted her lips. Between them, he stuck more bread and followed that with a sip of the sweet, rich wine.

She smiled. This might not be a terrible game, after all...as long as the questions didn't get too difficult.

Yeah, she didn't hold out a lot of hope for that.

"And what's your favorite pizza topping?"

Was this a getting-to-know-you exercise or a quiz for dinner? She didn't know exactly where they were, but she gathered he'd brought her to basically the middle of nowhere. Doubtful anyone delivered out here. "Mushrooms and extra cheese, but I'm not that picky. Avoid bell peppers and anchovies, and I'll probably eat it."

"Good to know. Open up again."

This time she did so quickly, hoping for a bit more of that lovely melting heaven on her tongue. Instead, she got a bite of a really rich cheese. A little tart, a tad smoky... He followed it with more bread. Raine sensed his eyes on her, felt her nipples getting hard. Wow, this game was way sexier than she'd first thought. She licked her lips, then plumped them a bit. "What's next?"

Absolute silence. She could hear him breathing. His body heat poured toward her in a warm wave. His displeasure wasn't far behind.

"Sir," she corrected quickly. "What's next, Sir?"

"When matters get tough, why do you always run, lass?"

His question slammed her in the chest like a semi chasing the land speed record. She had to force her answer out. "I-I don't run; I just leave a situation when I'm making it worse."

"I see. Open."

Raine couldn't get a read on his tone, but she dutifully parted her lips.

"Stick out your tongue."

She frowned, hoping he was in the mood to give her chocolate. She could hope it was melting.

Instead, something slimy slithered across her taste buds. That awful smell hit her next. She curled inward as her stomach bucked. Damn, she didn't have her hands free to clutch it, but she did something even better; she spit the pickle out.

"Stop. That's not acceptable! Open again. By god, you will chew and swallow."

"B-but I answered you."

"As answers went, it was a weak one, and well you know it."

"No, that's the serious, honest truth. Why would I stay where I'm not wanted? Where I just seem to fuck everything up?"

That wave of his displeasure came at her again, this time like a towering tsunami. "You will not use that language, Raine. Do you hear me?"

Seriously? She was supposed to amend her vocabulary, too? But that strict voice…even without seeing him, Raine knew he'd unleash something really unpleasant—like a whole jar of pickles—if she didn't cooperate.

"Yes, Sir. I'm telling you the honest truth, Sir."

Liam paused for a long moment. "All right, then. If that's the truth as you see it, we'll let that go for now. Open."

"Am I getting the pickle?" She cringed.

"Open now!"

Raine did, knowing she probably looked like a toddler spitting out its vegetables. Sure enough, he plopped the pickle on her tongue again.

"Chew and swallow."

Crap, she felt like she might throw up. But she managed to hold her breath and choke it down.

"Wine?" she croaked.

He placated her, putting the glass to her lips and letting her take a few long swallows.

"Thank you." The flavor of the fermented grapes was a relief.

"Who are you thanking?"

What was his sudden preoccupation with formality and protocol? "You, Sir. Thank you, Sir."

"Better. Who taught you to cook?"

How did they get from running away to knowing her way around a kitchen? "I taught myself, Sir. It's better than starving."

"Fair enough."

For her effort, he rewarded her with a juicy bite of the roast beef that did a blessed shitload to remove the terrible pickle flavor lingering.

"Why were you in the alley the night Hammer found you?"

What kind of question was that? "Because I had no place else to go and the one behind Shadows wasn't crowded with drug addicts and pimps searching for fresh meat."

He grabbed her jaw in his hand. He didn't squeeze hard or hurt her, but his grip let her know that he could. "Are you willfully misunderstanding my question?"

"No. Sir," she added hastily. "If you want to know why I chose Hammer's alley over another, that's the reason."

Liam sighed, and she sensed him re-gathering his patience as he released his hold on her jaw. "Let's try again, then. Why, at seventeen, were you spending the night in an alley rather than under your parents' roof?"

"I ran away. I was making the situation there worse, according to my dad. So I left."

Those were some of the hardest words she'd ever spoken. Funny how the awful man's rejection still had the power to hurt her years later. She needed to get over it, but Raine had discovered telling herself that logically and actually being able to do it weren't the same thing.

And on top of Hammer's rejection… It was like a can being crushed, then recycled, only to be crushed again.

Her breath hitched as she choked back a sob. Crap, she'd been a teary mess all morning. Maybe she really should just move on. This wouldn't be the first time she'd lost her place in the world. She'd survived after leaving home and found something better. Maybe she could do that again. One door had closed, then she'd opened another, right?

Right. But Hammer had been the first man to break her heart. Getting over that *and* the loss of home at once wouldn't be easy.

"I believe that's how you see the situation," Liam murmured softly.

She leaned forward to lay her cheek on the bed, but found his thigh instead. The human comfort was too much to resist, even knowing that giving him control now only gave him the power to hurt her later. But when he started softly stroking her hair, she couldn't resist nuzzling him a bit more.

"That's a good lass." He caressed the side of her face with his fingers, then nestled them at her nape and lifted her face to him. "Mouth open."

Dutifully, she complied. The sinful flavor of that good dark chocolate burst over her tongue. She moaned long and low, smacking her lips.

Suddenly, Liam bent and took her mouth in a ravaging kiss, stealing inside and ransacking, taking her tongue. Immediately, she tasted the roast beef, pineapple, and wine in his kiss. Then they shared the chocolate flavor, and he ate at her mouth hungrily before suddenly lifting away.

"Watching you eat is a sensual experience, especially when I give you that chocolate. Christ, you make a man hard."

Raine felt a happy little flush crawl up her cheeks.

"What's your favorite, gold or silver?"

She got the game now. Innocuous questions followed by zingers. One was supposed to lull her into false comfort before he hit her hard. The food either rewarded or punished her, depending on how completely and honestly she answered.

Well, hell. She had to give Liam credit. It was damn clever. He could dig into her psyche while he established his control over her, all without laying a single swat anywhere on her bruised body. She was so used to Hammer, who was all glowers and demands, all thunder, and strict, and as subtle as his moniker. Liam was good with misdirection and confusion. He coaxed. He would sneak under her defenses if she wasn't careful.

Raine cleared her throat. "I like gold and silver. Why choose?"

He tapped the end of her nose with his finger affectionately. "I shouldn't have expected a different answer. Why, indeed? You'd look stunning in either."

Maybe he meant it. Maybe he didn't. But she could get used to compliments like that. "Thank you, Sir."

His palm cupped the side of her face. "Spoken so beautifully and naturally. Good."

He brushed something slightly textured and sweet over her bottom lip. She smelled the pineapple and opened her mouth automatically, allowing him to plop it on her tongue.

"Very nice, lass. You're coming along and pleasing me."

The praise warmed her. It shouldn't, really. God, she'd only given him a common courtesy and eaten a bite of fruit. But Raine knew the drill. He was pleased because she'd called him Sir and because she'd trusted him enough to eat willingly from his hand without being told.

Even so, she couldn't deny that his kind words made her glow. She smiled at him, and in return, he brushed a little kiss over her mouth.

"How sorely you tempt a man…" he groaned, then popped a piece of the roast beef on her tongue. He followed that with another, then gave her a pinch of bread and some wine to wash it all down.

The warmth seeped deeper in her bones. She could really get to liking this game as long as it stayed friendly.

"What's your happiest memory?"

The question flicked across her skin like a knife so sharp she almost didn't feel the cut. God, she hadn't allowed herself to dwell on this in years. It made the hell of the next decade that much worse. But she also hated the thought of Liam imagining that she was just a miserable woman whom no one in her life had ever wanted. Useless, discarded, forgotten.

"When I was six, my parents sent me to spend the holidays with my grandparents in Wisconsin. Just me. There was a big tree, and Grandpa lifted me up to put the star on top on Christmas Eve. There was snow. Grandma baked, and the house always smelled heavenly."

"Does baking now calm you because it reminds you of that time?"

Raine froze. She hadn't thought of it quite like that, but when she baked, she could close her eyes and be transported back to the moment she'd first awakened in the big, warm bed they'd given her and everything smelled like cinnamon and yeast and happiness.

"Maybe… Yeah, I guess."

His thumb slid over her bottom lip, and she parted, opening for him without thought.

"Lovely, lass."

More chocolate. It sat on her tongue, sweet and firm, until she sucked at it. Slowly, it broke apart and melted inside her mouth, making her taste buds sing.

"That is the best chocolate ever. I would eat that all day, every day, if I could."

"And give yourself a stomach ache." He chuckled. "Probably best if I dish it out to you a bit at a time. Don't you think?"

Probably. Otherwise, she could outgrow her entire wardrobe fast.

She wrinkled her nose. "It pains me to say it, but you're probably right, Sir."

"That's a good girl."

He fed her a bit more of the roast beef and pineapple. As far as he tipped the glass up, it seemed as if she'd finished the wine. The relaxation curling through her seemed to suggest that, too. The smile on her lips was probably a bit too happy for the moment, but it was as if getting away from Shadows for a bit, then having a good cry and a good meal with a man who seemed to care about her was cathartic. She felt a bit lighter, her soul not so weighted down with regret. She still had plenty, of course. But at least now it might not drown her.

"What happened to you as a child, Raine?"

Chapter Ten

The question came out of nowhere, like a heavyweight's punch to the stomach. Raine gasped, couldn't breathe. Her mouth opened, but no sound came out. She got to one knee, then leapt to her feet, backing away from Liam.

"No!" She shook her head frantically, well aware that she couldn't see him or anything else. But she'd rather risk bodily injury than answer that question. "If you want to know, ask Hammer. That's the last time I've spoken of it, at least to anyone important. And it's the last time I will."

She sensed Liam's closeness before he grabbed her arm. His grip wasn't harsh, but it was unyielding.

He growled in her ear. "I didn't give you permission to rise. Back in front of the bed, on your knees." He jerked her in place again, guiding her so she didn't stumble. The carpet was even still warm beneath her knees. "And I won't be asking Hammer a damn thing. You will tell me yourself."

The hell she would. Raine tightened her mouth mulishly. He wasn't getting her to talk. And he wasn't shoving more pickles in her mouth.

"Do you understand?"

"I'm too tired for this heart-to-heart."

"Answer my question and I'll let you sleep."

No, once she gave him this answer, he'd just keep digging into her psyche. He'd want details. He'd want to know how she dealt with it all. He'd want the stuff she hadn't even shared with Hammer.

"Ask me anything else."

"No. I've asked what I wished to know."

Panic welled inside her. "Don't I get a safe word around here?"

"You always have one," Liam assured. "It hasn't changed. But I'm not hurting you."

"You are!"

"Think carefully about that. Mental discomfort aside, am I physically hurting any part of your body?"

No. But she couldn't just shit out all of her crappy past like she had verbal diarrhea. Instead, she tugged at her arm. "Your grip is tight."

It wasn't, but she had nothing else.

He paused for a long minute, then loosened his fingers just a touch. "Am I hurting you now?"

Raine listened to his voice drop even lower. He'd chosen his words very carefully. His tone itself was a warning. He was about at the end of putting up with her, and he'd probably only let her get this far because he felt sorry for her. *Poor dumb, broken-hearted girl, too fucked up to be honest...* That's what he had to be thinking. It made her sick. But she didn't know how to change.

"No, Sir," she muttered.

"Good. Let's be clear. I'm not letting you put up more walls between us. Do you understand me?"

God, he was so patient. Could he just get mad and scream at her already? She could ignore that. But he never once raised his voice... and he still managed to get his point across with as much subtlety as a neon billboard.

"Yes, Sir." She fidgeted. She was running out of ways to avoid answering. Now what?

"I expect you to answer me now. What happened to you as a child?"

She flinched at the question. A thousand images rushed her all like a fist to her psyche. She shook her head, fighting tears. She'd rather take her punishment than open up this can of worms. After all, it's not as if this would be the first time she'd endured.

"Just spank me and get it over with."

"While you're bruised? While you're hurting?" His voice was so gentle now, it was like an ice pick straight to her chest. He shoved it in deeper as he stroked her hair. "No. I have no wish to cause more pain. Nor will I give you an easy excuse to defy and resent me. There's a lovely reward for you, if you'll just trust me."

More chocolate? But even for that, she wouldn't answer his question.

"I'm sorry," she choked out.

"Me, too," he said with regret, then he grabbed her hair and tugged. Her head snapped back. Her mouth fell open.

He slid a big chunk of pickle on her tongue and pushed the heel of his palm under her chin, forcing her mouth closed.

Raine's taste buds protested loudly. Her eyes watered.

"Chew," he demanded. "You're going to eat it."

Crap, there was no escape. She couldn't get out of his grip without losing a chunk of hair and she couldn't open her mouth to spit it out.

Quickly, she chewed it into large chunks and forced herself to swallow them down. But the pieces were still too big, and she choked. Liam let go of her hair immediately and braced one hand around her waist. The other slapped her between the shoulder blades. The last of the terrible pickle slid down, but that vile taste lingered on her tongue.

"You can't make me tell you."

Behind her, he froze. Slowly, he withdrew his hands from her. Instantly, she felt cold, alone.

Raine felt more than heard Liam sit on the bed. "You're right. I can make your life unpleasant enough until you want to, however."

"A steady diet of pickles will only make me puke."

"It might. I'll hold your hair and aim you over the toilet."

Was he kidding? "That's disgusting."

"It's not my first choice, but if that's what it takes…" She sensed that he shrugged. "You seem to think of me as the enemy. What have I ever done to make you believe I would hurt you?"

Nothing. In fact, if anything, he'd gone out of his way to earn her trust, rather than simply trying to take it.

"Whoever hurt you in the past… I'm not one of them, lass."

Her shoulders drooped. Raine couldn't see anything, but if she could, she'd be looking at nothing but floor.

Liam slid a palm up her back, under her hair, then cradled her neck. "I'm not giving up on this question, Raine. I want you to think about the fact that you'll never be happy if you can't share this pain and fear inside you. And you will never be able to truly bond with a Dom—or any other human being—until you do. Until then, you will always be alone." He stroked her hair again. "You have so many wonderful gifts to share. I'd hate never to know them. It disappoints me to see you waste them."

His soft condemnation was so fucking hard to take. The words lashed her like a whip cutting through flesh and opening her to the bone. Why didn't he just punish her already? Paddle her bruised butt… But he'd explained that. He couldn't force her to change, but he wouldn't let her hide easily.

"Liam…" she began.

"Yes?"

Raine had nothing to say. She couldn't make herself spill her past. Even thinking about it made her bleed. Shame. That she hadn't been strong enough to stop it. That she hadn't been smart enough to avoid it. And now she was left with the wound that just wouldn't seem to scar over. Instead, it just kept infecting everything she touched.

"Nothing."

He sighed, and she heard his disappointment. It hurt so damn much as he took hold of her arms and released her wrists. Her shoulders were a bit stiff, and she rolled them. Liam massaged them so tenderly. Oddly, the moment she got free of his cuffs, a part of her felt as if she was free falling inside, like some safety net had been taken from her. Without thought, she reached out for him.

He didn't deny her touch…but he didn't put the cuffs on her again.

"Climb up here on the bed and lay on your back. Arms wide, legs together." He helped her onto the cushy mattress, and she sank immediately onto what felt like a fluffy towel over soft cotton blankets. "That's it. Bring your knees up. Now relax them and let them fall open for me."

So her pussy was exposed?

Still, she did it. He'd seen and touched it all. He wasn't going to hurt her.

"Yes. Just like that." He released her and stood, retreating and returning quickly. "I've fetched a tray of lavender, tea tree oil, and rosemary. The caretaker's wife mixed it with pure olive oil and heated it for you. It will be a soothing medicinal balm. Don't be alarmed as I pour it on you. Just relax. Keep yourself open for me, and not just your body, Raine. It's your mind I speak of, too. This won't be painful."

With that, Liam began by massaging her methodically from head to toe, paying particular attention to her breasts, hips, and thighs—anywhere she was already bruised. He avoided her pussy, and unconsciously she rose to his traveling hands. But he didn't touch her there. Instead, he drifted farther down, slowly lulling her into a blessed calm.

He drizzled the oil directly onto her skin now, over her breasts, then trailed it to her mound. "This will help with the healing. It'll not alleviate the bruising, but it will soothe your skin. Does it feel warm and cool at the same time?"

She started to nod, then stopped herself. He didn't want her to answer him that way, and it seemed a simple thing to give him the words he wanted when she'd denied him almost everything else.

"Yes, Sir."

Raine sensed his sadness and wished like hell that she could see his face. No, that she could put her arms around him. The last thing she wanted to do after hurting Liam last night was make him even sadder now.

He stroked and caressed her breasts, massaging and kneading the tender flesh in concentric circles, drawing smoothly toward her areola, squeezing the nipple gently, again and again until she moaned.

Liam had found another of her weaknesses. Her nipples had always been sensitive, and his slow, slick touch with the oils was awakening her. As much sex as she'd had lately, everything south of her waist should be dormant, if not dead. But no. The warm oil spilled down her bare mons and over her sore folds, adding another layer of sensation.

And Raine couldn't miss his hardening cock growing thick and heavy as he leaned against her. She was probably far too sore to actually have sex with him right now...but some part of her really wanted to be as close to him as two people could be.

Blindly, she reached up for him, felt her way from his wrist to his shoulder, then looped her arms around his neck. Her clumsy lips groped from his jaw to the corner of his mouth before she opened for his surprise onslaught. He dove into her mouth, seemingly willing to drown in her for a nearly perfect moment. She needed someone, and Liam was here with and for her. Raine clung tighter. Her rock. Her life preserver in an angry sea. Her someone to believe in?

A long moment of union later, he eased his lips from hers. "Raine, whatever's hurting you, share it with me. Tell me what happened when you were a child. Let me comfort you."

Raine couldn't rip off this Band-Aid for him right now. She flinched and dropped back to the bed, tearing the blindfold away from her eyes.

She wished she hadn't.

Such soft pity… God, it curdled her stomach.

"Don't feel sorry for me. Don't you *dare*!"

His eyes narrowed, and he moved so quickly, it stunned her, stole her breath.

Liam straddled her, his hands curling around her wrists, his big thighs pinning her hips to the bed. She kicked and shrieked until she realized that she wasn't going to budge him and that she probably sounded like a willful child. She shut up and glared.

"Listen and listen well. You can't tell me how to feel, any more than I can tell you. If pity was all I felt, I wouldn't be trying this hard. You've got such fire in you. Are you really going to let something that happened years ago cripple your heart? Rob you of a satisfying future?"

He spoke the question in silky tones. It hurt all over. With his stare and his questions probing her, she felt so exposed. Vulnerable. She wanted to curl her knees to her chest, cross her arms protectively over her body, and keep everyone out.

Liam wasn't about to let that happen.

She searched for a clever way to put him off or skirt the truth, but his invasive stare and her aching nipples handicapped her brain. Her body was every bit as confused as her head. She'd barely slept, didn't know where she belonged or what to think.

Raine turned away. "I'm done. I'll volunteer all day long that I hate mustard, love reading, and that I'm allergic to antibiotics. But don't talk to me about my childhood again." Damn it, why couldn't she stop sobbing? "Please..."

"No, Raine. You don't get to call the shots here. My training. My rules. You've had it tough. I understand that. I also know the last few days have been...extreme. But I promised I'd split you open like a ripe peach. At some point, you'll know that I always keep my promises. You also need to learn to behave properly for a Dominant. All this arguing isn't showing me your desire to please or convincing me that you want to share a part of your soul."

"I do..." She blinked back his way. "I just...can't we work up to the worst? I've barely thought about my past in years. We've only been speaking for a handful of days, and now you want in the deepest recesses of my soul, a place where I thought I'd only show Hammer. But the man I've loved all these years doesn't think I'm good enough. Eventually you won't, either. Can't I just keep my goddamn secrets until you get bored?"

"No." His answer came back like the crack of a whip. "You'll watch your language, too. If I have to warn you again, once your ass is healed up, I'll make sure you won't be sitting pretty for a week at least. And you'll never bore me. *Never*," he growled emphatically. "You don't believe me yet, but I won't let up until you do." She opened her mouth to argue, but he put a finger over her lips. "Not another word. I'm bloody tired of arguing. You must be sleepy. Let's see if anything looks better after a nap."

"I don't want to sleep." Ugh, didn't she sound like a spoiled toddler? She had to shut up.

"Well, I do. Indulge me. I intend to nap cuddled up beside you."

He unwrapped the towel from around his waist and wiped the sheen of oil from her body, then padded toward the bathroom in absolutely nothing. The view of his backside walking away from her was…wow. Firm, narrow, not the least bit flat and…yeah, wow. He dropped the towel on the counter and headed back toward her.

The view from the front nearly had her eyes popping out. Even flaccid, he was large. Muscular thighs dusted with dark hair framed heavy testicles. An intriguing trail of hair climbed up to his navel. The chest above was lean and rippling with muscle. And his broad shoulders… She licked her suddenly dry lips.

Liam shook his head and gave her a wicked grin. "I see what you're wanting. None of that now."

The words came out of his mouth, but his cock said otherwise, rising quickly until it looked big and ready and demanding. She eyed him hungrily, remembering all the ecstasy of his gentle claiming in the dungeon, then his softly fierce loving in his room afterward. She didn't want Hammer any less than before…but she definitely wanted Liam more.

Raine didn't understand how she could have feelings for two such different men. And she probably wasn't going to figure it out in the next five minutes.

As she sighed, he slid between the covers and took her with him beneath the sheets, nestling her at his side. His erection lay against her hip, but he didn't make any move beyond kissing her lips softly. "Close your eyes. Breathe deep. Stop worrying for now. We'll solve everything later."

She did as he bid, her heavy lids sliding shut. She focused on his breathing, the comfort and warmth of his arms around her, and clearing her mind. With Liam's body protectively against hers, she could almost pretend that all was well.

Peace began to carry her away. She felt weightless, floated in a carefree bliss.

"That's a good lass," he murmured. "Someday, you'll tell me your secrets, every one. And after, I promise I'll still be here."

She slept like a child, deeply, finally letting go of all the trauma and fears. The pain and anxiety left her face and body at last as she let sleep take her. He watched her. Wasn't it ironic that, despite everything, he'd gone from using her to "fix" Hammer…to coveting her as his own? He gently stroked her skin and drew her closer. She looked all mother-of-pearl and satin soft. Her hair, a dark raven's wing, curled over her shoulders and shrouded her breasts.

A delicate pink nipple peeked through, and the memory of her under him, her breasts pressed against him, made Liam ache to lay claim to her once more, without Hammer watching, hovering, and jealous. He shoved the thought aside. Despite what tomorrow might bring, right here and now she was in his bed and lying in his arms.

But if he didn't get up now, he'd likely shove his aching cock into her. And he'd hurt her.

So he reluctantly eased from the bed, used the bathroom, and returned. He picked up a book and settled into the corner armchair where he could watch Raine. He tried to read, but spent far more time staring at her.

Until his phone chirped softly.

He jumped up, finding the device in his pants pocket. He silenced it, checking to make sure the chime hadn't disturbed her. He need not have worried. The lass was exhausted and hadn't moved one muscle since drifting off.

Turning his attention to the phone again, he saw a slew of messages from Hammer. Each revealed the man's mood. First, wildly angry and accusing, spewing fury. That gave way to stern demands, then a foolish attempt to negotiate. Finally, an obviously drunken Hammer who'd forgotten how to spell had begged him to bring Raine home.

Not bloody likely.

He set the phone aside, jaw clenched, texts unanswered.

With a sweep of his gaze, he studied Raine's battered body. Every visible mark on her ate at him. He couldn't yet answer Hammer without losing his temper. He wasn't sure he'd ever be able to.

Picking up the book again, he read a bit more, despite the phone's soft vibrating buzz over and over on the table beside him. Liam ignored it and watched over Raine.

The sun finally set. As the dinner hour approached, he made his way to the kitchen, fixed a cup of sweet, hot tea, and brought it to her.

Setting it by the bed, he roused her with a gentle hand on her shoulder. "Time to wake. You all but died on me, you slept so heavy. How are you feeling?"

Raine rolled over, looking disoriented and bleary-eyed. Her limbs hung heavy, moved slow. She rubbed at her eyes, clearly fighting to keep them open. "Tired."

"Here, then. Stretch a moment and let this tea cool, then take a wee sip. It'll help wake you up, then we'll see about going downstairs and finding some food."

She watched him through the shadows as she rose up on her elbows. He heard her stomach growl.

"How long did I sleep?" Raine yawned as she glanced out the darkened windows and stretched, then eyed her pillow consideringly.

"Four hours."

"Oh, wow…" She struggled to sit up.

Chuckling, Liam set the tea aside, wrapped his arms around her, and helped her. The blankets dropped, revealing her plump, soft breasts. The cool air beaded her nipples, and he fought the urge to lay her back and take them in his mouth.

When she reached for the blanket to cover herself, he shook his head. "Stop. I like you bare. Have a sip of your tea, then let's head downstairs." She leaned out for the mug, and he shook his head. "Let me."

With only the slimmest of hesitations, she nodded.

He smiled faintly, then blew on the steaming brew before lifting it toward her lips. "If it's too hot, I expect you to tell me."

"Yes, Sir," she said softly, letting her gaze fall to her lap.

Oh, sleep had made her soft and a bit mellow. She'd needed it. He liked it.

A pleased smile curled his mouth as he put the china to her lips. She sipped once, twice, then moaned.

"How is it, then?" He brushed the hair from her sleep-soft face. Everything about her drew him—innocent blue eyes, rosy cheeks, graceful shoulders…glorious breasts.

"It's sweet. A little foreign and fruity. I don't usually drink tea, but I like that."

"Excellent."

About half the cup later, he set it aside on the saucer, then helped her to her feet. She stretched again, every lovely inch of her bare. Liam nuzzled her neck, hands on her hips, fighting the urge to cover her body with his, and get reacquainted with the feel of her cunt gripping his cock and her fingernails in his shoulders. But she wasn't ready. Hell, at the moment, she was still half asleep. And he shouldn't give her the impression that he'd swept her infidelity under the carpet by making love to her now. Nor should he distract her from answering the question she'd put off before her nap.

"Come on then, lass. My belly thinks my throat's been cut, and I love your cooking. The kitchen is well stocked," he said to entice her.

That perked her up. "I'd like to cook for you." She looked around the room, then headed toward the closet. "I didn't have time to pack any clothes. You got a robe in there?"

Before she reached the door, he hooked an arm around her waist and hauled her back against him. "Not so fast. As I said earlier, I like you bare."

She stiffened. "I'm supposed to cook…naked?"

"Indeed. It's a sight I've looked forward to." He sent her a lascivious lift of his brow.

"But—"

"I'll give you an apron if you're expecting splattering grease or boiling water."

"But—"

"Stop." Liam sighed at her protests. Did the woman not understand the meaning of the word submissive? "The caretakers have gone. No one will see you but me." She hesitated for another long moment. "What now?"

"Um…my feet are cold."

Was that all? "Easy enough." He strode to his suitcase and pulled out a pair of socks. "Sit on the bed."

She did, watching him with those eyes. He slipped the large men's tube socks on her feet. They hardly fit, but they'd keep her warm.

She stood and moved toward the door. No way he could miss the socks flopping with every step.

Liam laughed. "That's a fetching look on you, lass."

Raine turned to him and propped her hands on her hips. "Do you want arsenic with your dinner?"

He sent her a measuring stare. So the kitten didn't always have her hackles up and her claws out. Liam grinned. He liked this side of her. A pity he wouldn't see it much until they'd worked through her issues. "Absolutely not."

"Then no more making fun of me." She stuck out her tongue.

"My lips are zipped. Now come on, you, before I find other uses for that tongue." He swatted her backside gently.

Raine made the kitchen her own in about five minutes flat. She came alive in this room, content as she explored the large walk-in cooler for meat and produce, then took stock of the pots and pans in the cupboards. He sat on a high stool, adjusted his aching cock to lie more comfortably, and enjoyed the show as she moved and bent to her task…and added a bit of wriggle for his delight. The saucy minx.

"I know we never got the chance to grab a bag for you before we left. Did we leave behind anything you need? Glasses? Birth control tablets? Any other medicines? I should have asked sooner." With her back to him, she stilled completely. "What is it?"

She didn't answer, and he jumped off his stool and approached her, dread coiling in his belly as a sudden thought occurred to him. "Raine? You *are* on the pill, right?"

Absolute silence.

"Talk to me. Since you reeked of Hammer's seed this morning, it's obvious he didn't use a condom, but tell me that you're protected."

Raine turned around, her eyes wide and terrified. "No. Last night, he told me to get on the pill today and I…" She slapped a hand over her mouth. "Oh god. I was so stupid. I thought…" She shook her head. "But I was wrong, and I fuc…really messed up in so many ways." Her shoulders dropped and her gaze followed. "It seems I always have to ask you to forgive me, and I'm sure you're going to get tired of it. If you want me to go, I'll find a way down the mountain and out of your hair. I really am so sorry." She huddled as if waiting for a blow.

A pang hit his chest as fury fired his belly. Another selfish act Hammer had so fucking thoughtlessly committed. True, Raine had said yes to the bastard, but he could have done the proper thing and protected her. The consequences, especially for Raine, could be far reaching.

Liam took the stricken girl in his arms and rocked her gently, while his anger with Hammer multiplied. What the fuck was wrong with the prick that he could be so careless with the woman he supposedly loved? Hammer had gone at her wee body both drunk and gloveless, knowing she had no way to prevent conceiving? It was beyond Liam's comprehension. And if Raine ended up pregnant, Liam knew all too well that Hammer would run a fucking mile.

Fresh resentment raged within him. He struggled to contain his wrath, but he did for Raine's sake, concentrating on what the shell-shocked woman needed. *Christ!*

Cupping Raine's face, Liam made her meet his gaze. "It's all right. We'll figure this out together, one step at a time. But you've got to stop running for the damned exit every two minutes. I'm not leaving, and I'm not letting you go without a bloody good reason. We'll get you seen by a doctor directly and get the birth control issue taken care of, as I'll be damned if I'll be wanting latex between us, either. But I'll have you safe first. If there's anything else to consider, we'll cross that bridge when we come to it." She nodded, but he sensed her quietly falling apart. "Come on now, lass. It's not the end of the world. Dry your tears and get this into your head: I'm not going anywhere. I will be here for you. I won't pack up at the first sign of trouble. But I'm trusting you, too, Raine. After last night, that's going to be hard, but let's find common ground and focus on us."

Liam brushed away a few stray tears and kissed her soundly. Raine eased back from his embrace and stared up at him. Part gravity, part wonder, as if she might actually believe him. "Thank you, Sir. Very much. You're...amazing."

"And I'm famished. Now feed me, woman. Those steaks look good!"

She sniffed back the rest of her tears. "Steaks coming up."

It didn't take long. The salad came out of the refrigerator and onto the table, as she pulled the toasty garlic bread from the broiler and the juicy fillets from the oven. Lovely asparagus emerged next with olive oil, bacon bits, and other goodness that smelled divine. She arranged everything on the table while he opened another bottle of wine.

As he poured two glasses, she smiled at him tentatively, gratefully. She'd obviously expected him to be furious with her that Hammer hadn't worn a condom while she wasn't on the pill. She'd expected him to leave her. Granted, she should have told Hammer to glove up. But Macen was a grown man who knew better, by god.

A bigger question circled in his head: Did she truly run away when she thought she made a situation worse...or because she feared someone else was going to leave her and she wanted to beat them to it?

Liam watched Raine, wondering how many people in the girl's life had abandoned her to make her so skittish.

He'd planned a peaceful dinner, but now...now might be the time to keep digging for answers. It would likely put her off balance again, but if he'd be better equipped to help her later, he could sacrifice one harmonious meal.

Sauntering over to the refrigerator, he grabbed what he needed and set it on the counter behind him. Then he helped Raine into her chair. All the delicious food on the table was making his stomach growl.

"Everything looks wonderful, lovely. I hope you're hungry."

She nodded as he scooted her chair in. "I am. All the smells while I cooked got my appetite going."

"Good to hear." He grabbed her fork and her plate, lifting them away. She'd barely started sputtering at him before he set the jar of dill pickles down in front of her.

"What the—"

"You determine your own dinner, Raine. Now, what happened to you as a child?"

Mouth agape, she blinked up at him incredulously. She stared at the jar of pickles, then at her plate in his hand.

A million reactions crossed her face then. Anger right off the top. Consideration...with fuming undertones. She appeared to be weighing how much she hated pickles against the rumbling of her belly. Then some of the starch left her body, and he could almost guarantee that she was finally factoring in that she owed him, along with his vow to stay.

"You can put the pickles away. I'll tell you."

Chapter Eleven

Liam set the jar on the counter behind him. "I'll determine if your answer is enough to put the pickles away." He pulled up the chair beside her and leaned in. "I'm listening."

She drew in a bracing breath. "Long story short, my home life sucked. My mother decided the grass really was greener elsewhere. My older brother thought boot camp would be better than life at the Kendall house. My much smarter older sister ran off to college the second she got a dazzling scholarship overseas, leaving me alone with a guy who would never win father-of-the-year awards. It wasn't like I loved high school. And I hated being reminded everywhere that I wasn't as good as my siblings. Since dear old dad wasn't shy about telling me that I wasn't worth the food he had to feed me, I made his miserable life better by taking a hike." She grimaced, then gulped down half her wine. "God, every word of that was like ripping out my entrails and lighting them on fire."

While he could have done without the snark, in reading between the lines, her explanation told him a great deal. Everyone she'd ever cared about had left her. "How old were you when your mother left?

"Nine."

"And...?"

"And...before that, things hadn't been rosy, but they hadn't been terrible, either. My grandparents had died the year before, and she'd been really depressed. Then I woke up one morning and she was gone. Never called, never came home. Just packed a bag and walked out. To this day, I don't know what happened to her."

"Were you close to her, lass?"

Raine took a really long time answering. "I thought so."

And the fact that her own mother had simply left without a word had blindsided her. "What about your father? Did he abuse you physically? Mentally?" Liam paused. "Sexually?"

"Gee, don't want to pry me open all at once or anything?"

He raised a brow at her and started to open the jar of pickles. She winced.

"Sorry. Sarcasm is a reflex. I've used it to drive people off for a long time. Just..."

Liam set the jar aside again. "I'm a patient man, but I'll warn you to watch your tone. Answer me now."

"My dad didn't...touch me like that." She swallowed, looking down, face nervous. "He actually didn't do much more than belittle everyone. At least that's what I thought. My brother always had bruises, but he'd say that he'd gotten into fights after school. Then my sister started getting them after my brother had gone to boot camp. But she'd just tell me that cheerleading was tougher than it looked. When she left, too... I found out that I shouldn't mess with Dad's temper. I just never got good at holding my tongue.

"One night after we fought, I got a concussion and a broken wrist. He told the people at the *ER* that I'd fallen, but they didn't believe him. He dragged me out, mad all over again. He said he wouldn't go to jail for disciplining his stupidest, most willful..." She dissolved into silence, looking at her hands wringing in her lap. The sight tore at his heart. Then she shook her head. "You get the picture. I'm not hungry after all. Can I go back upstairs?"

So she could escape again? He bent to her and adjusted her to face him, then tilted her chin upward, forcing her to look his way. "No, don't shut me out." He kissed her forehead and rubbed her arms lightly. "Thank you for the trust you've given me so far. I'm so proud of you right now. I know that was difficult. I promise you, I'm right here and not going anywhere."

"Thank you," she murmured, not meeting his gaze. "I'm so grateful... and more, but I don't know how to say it."

Just as he wanted it. He'd keep chipping away at her barriers until he found a place in her heart. She seemed to have made one in his already.

"I trust you'll find the words eventually. Eat here with me now. You did such a wonderful job of preparing us a feast." He smiled. "Let's share it."

With a tired nod, she focused on the plate he set in front of her before he tucked the pickles back in the refrigerator.

Liam sat and dug into his steak. "Perfect, as always. Thank you, lass."

Everything she'd cooked was superb. The bread crunched just enough when he bit into it. The salad was crisp, the meat savory. The vegetables had a burst of flavor. Raine was at home in the kitchen. Hammer's words about her being made for marriage floated through his brain again. At the time, he hadn't given it much thought, but Liam could see now that she would flourish with stability, with a man who committed to her and would be there day in and out.

He had no desire to marry.

A problem for later. No sense in borrowing trouble now.

"I think it's time I shared something painful from my past with you, Raine. I rarely do this, but you've been such a brave wee beauty. I would have you know more about me. It might help you understand. Don't get ideas, mind you. This is something I'm choosing to give."

She nodded solemnly, and he knew that he had her attention.

"As you probably know, Hammer isn't the only one who was married..."

She watched him with unblinking eyes, her questions lurking in her gaze. "I'm listening."

"After Juliet passed away and Hammer moved out here, I met Gwyneth, a seemingly lovely English rose from an aristocratic family on holiday in New York. I was rich. She was pretty. We had similar interests and appetites. So I married her. It seemed that we had found that elusive something idyllic for a time. Then…I discovered Gwyneth cheating. I returned home unexpectedly after a business trip to find her on her knees as her supposedly gay personal trainer fucked her while she gave his life partner head."

Raine paled. "Oh my god…"

Liam took a long drink of his wine, cut another slice of the moist, succulent steak, and savored it for a moment. "To say I was shocked would be an understatement. I thought we were happy, that she'd be the mother of my children. I had plans for our future. In an instant, I buried them. I realized that I'd married her because it seemed logical, not because I'd loved her. When she wanted a divorce, I let her go. I didn't care enough anymore to fight. But that sour taste of betrayal is something that, even now, triggers me…" Again, he paused, allowing his words to sink in. "You're not the only one with trust issues, Raine. So seeing you with Hammer this morning…"

"Brought it all back." Guilt tortured her face. She dropped her fork. "I'm so sorry."

Actually, Gwyneth's perfidy had enraged him. Raine's had fucking torn at his heart, so much that Liam barely understood. But he kept that to himself.

"I didn't realize…" Her face pleaded for forgiveness.

He leveled a considering stare her way. "I understand that what happened between you and Hammer was not just two people fucking for mere sex. He wanted you as much as you wanted him. I'd like to, but I can't blame you for giving yourself to the man you've long believed that you loved, though your timing was frankly lousy. Whether intentional or not, you agreed to something that I hold dear, then tossed it aside without so much as a backward glance when Hammer looked your way. Understand, Raine, that trust will be hard won from me, too. And if you ever violate it again like that, we'll be done."

She swallowed, looking stricken, and he realized that she'd stopped eating long ago. "I understand."

"Finish your steak." He waited until she picked up her fork again.

"Liam…I truly never meant to hurt you. I really am sorry." She looked at her plate, face filled with contrition. It was on the tip of his tongue to reassure her, but it might be good for her to think about what he'd said. He wanted this to work, but she needed to understand what would kill their growing relationship faster than anything.

Liam shook his head, thinking about the slew of messages from Hammer. Had the man been trying to get Raine pregnant as a way of tying her to him, even unconsciously? Or maybe fucking her without protection had been completely premeditated, to get him back for claiming her as his own. Liam gnashed his teeth.

"Does something not taste good?" Raine asked quietly from across the table. "I'll remake whatever it is."

"It's all lovely, lass. Excellent, as always." He noticed that she'd set her fork aside again and her napkin on the table. Her plate was still more than half full. "Why aren't you eating?"

"I'm not good at that when I'm upset. Maybe I'll reheat it later. Do you want seconds of something? I'll get it for you."

And there was the natural submissive. She wanted to feed him. It was her way of comforting and serving. Though the thought that Hammer may have gotten her pregnant made him violent, he could see that she'd make a wonderful mother.

"No. Thank you. I'd see you eat another few bites, though. You've scarce eaten enough for a bird."

"I don't think I can. Please... Not now. Maybe my stomach won't be turning later."

"You'll eat a few more bites of your meat and salad."

Raine wrinkled her nose, but managed to choke back a few more mouthfuls, then she started turning green. He stopped her with a raised hand.

"Enough. Is there something on your mind?"

She wrung her hands. "I should have thought far more about who I was affecting and how it might hurt you before I said yes to Hammer. But I didn't think much past the fact that I'd waited and loved him for so long, and if I said no, then I'd never know…"

"What he felt like? If he could love you in return? If it could work with him?" he leveled a heavy stare that told her he'd already guessed every one of her reasons.

Raine sank even smaller into her chair. "All of that."

"What had you planned to say to me the next morning?"

"I don't know. I didn't…" *Think.* Yes, he'd gathered that much. "Before we…" she sighed and looked down, guilt pouring from her. "I said no. I objected more than once. I told him that I belonged to you."

Liam froze. That was more consideration than he expected. But he wanted to make certain there'd been absolutely no misunderstanding. "So he forced you?"

"No."

Raine squeezed her eyes tightly shut, as if wishing she could escape. He gave her points for not lying to him.

"I didn't stand my ground as I should have."

Because she'd wanted Hammer so damn badly. Liam wished he could say otherwise, but it rankled.

"I won't ask if you feel guilty. I see that you do. Instead, I'll ask you to remember this feeling, so we don't cross this bridge again. I can be a patient man, but not always a forgiving one."

"Yes, Sir." She took a bracing breath and worked up the courage to meet his gaze. "In your shoes, I'd be furious, devastated. I would have run and done my best to disappear forever."

"Where I couldn't hurt you again." It wasn't a question; he was beginning to understand her well enough to know the answer.

"Yeah." She sent him a shaky nod. "But you…you've confronted this head on and actually listened to my side of the story…such as it is." Her question hung unspoken. *Why?*

And there was his clever girl again. She wanted to know why he'd chosen to give up on his wife, but would fight for her. In some ways, Liam wasn't sure himself. Maybe because he didn't want her to go the way of Gwyneth. Or because he didn't want to fail again. And yes, because she meant more to him than she should.

"I have my reasons," he said cryptically for now.

She nodded, as if accepting his vague answer. "Can I ask how long you've been divorced?"

He sat back in his chair. "Officially, just over a year. We were separated for nearly a year before that."

She hesitated, seeming to grapple with her next question. "Why didn't you tell me about all of this sooner?" She frowned. "And why are you telling me now?"

"Answer me this first: What difference would it have made? I doubt it would have changed a damned thing. You'd heard the rumors I was divorced. I didn't know how much Hammer might have told you." He shrugged. "What we can do now is communicate. I volunteered to share something of myself with you, Raine. But your way is to brush me aside at every turn. Quid pro quo."

She sucked in a breath and looked down, mired in more guilt. "It's not my intent to brush you aside. It's just...my mom didn't stay around to hear what I had to say. My dad never wanted to hear it. Hammer..." She swallowed. "He couldn't handle it. I assume that when most people ask, they're just being polite, but they don't really care. So I save us all the trouble." She shrugged. "You're the first person I actually believe wants to hear it. Problem is, I've kept it to myself for so long, I don't know how to say it."

Liam watched as she rose, rounded the table, then knelt beside his chair and grabbed his hands. "I swear, I didn't do it to hurt you. It was thoughtless. And selfish. After wanting someone so badly for so long, I didn't try hard enough to say no. Hammer kept telling me that he wasn't good for me. I'm starting to think maybe he was right." She squeezed his fingers and looked at him with earnest blue eyes. "I'm probably not going to be very good at telling you how I feel. But if you really want to hear it, I'll try."

She took a deep breath, and he realized that, for her, it was a big concession. And a big clue that she was willing to put some effort into their relationship, as Gwyneth hadn't been.

"Raine..."

Pushing the dishes back, he lifted her on the table in front of him. "Lean back, lass. You've earned a reward, and I've a mind to give it to you."

He lifted her legs, cradled them gently over each of his broad shoulders, then stroked his palm across her belly softly. She sighed as he kissed his way from her knees up to her inner thighs, paying tender attention to every purple mark Hammer had thoughtlessly left behind.

"Bloody hell, woman, you smell so good, like sin, so hot and feminine, utterly irresistible. I would taste you, Raine. Give you pleasure. Just relax and let me hear your cries."

Soon, she melted like butter beneath his warm tongue. He teased her clit and stroked her sweet, ripe nipples. As she undulated, her essence burst across his taste buds, overloading his brain with her flavor. And sealed her fate as his.

Her body grew tense, and she grabbed the edge of the table, anchoring herself as he drove her up higher. When she mewled, straining for the bit more stimulation she needed to tip her over, he slid a finger into her pussy. Groaning as her tender flesh squeezed him, Liam wished he could replace it with his cock. Then he drew her clit back into his mouth, all but inhaling her, pressing and flicking the swollen nub until the cries of climax spilled from her throat. Cream flooded his mouth.

Slowly, her grip softened, her body still quivering. Raine panted, her breasts rising and falling with each breath. God, he wanted to fuck her. But her eyes were squeezed shut, the aftermath still rippling through her. Liam tried to be patient, give her a minute to recover, but he couldn't stop himself from kissing the swollen pad of her pussy and looking up the length of her slender curves with a hungry stare.

He clutched her waist and dragged her into his lap so she straddled him. He moved to kiss her, but Raine reached him first, eyes closed, a soft joy on her face as she laid her lips over his. He tangled his hands in her hair and tilted her head to take her mouth deeper. Even in her kiss, he tasted her welcome. She wasn't just more open, but giving, and it was heady. God, he could get drunk off her. That he alone had tasted this sweet willingness spilling from her heart made it all the more thrilling.

Breathing heavily, he frowned when she broke away. He started to grab her closer and command her to stay when she lifted from his lap and squirmed to the floor between his feet, under the table. She reached for the zipper of his pants and looked up at him, silently asking permission.

He shook his head. "As much as I'd like to fuck you, you're not healed enough. And I've no condoms in the kitchen."

"I understand." She bit her lip, then looked up at him through the dark fringe of her lashes with coquettish eyes. "I wasn't asking if you would fuck me." She licked her lips.

All the blood rushed from his brain to his cock.

"Yes, lass. I've been dying to feel your mouth around me."

He'd never been harder in his life, nor more miserable with wanting. The need to have Raine in every way tormented him. Just the sight of her shiny pink tongue sliding over her plump lips made his heavy balls draw up and his thick crest leak. He fell into her blue eyes and gritted his teeth, fighting for control as her wee hands drew the zipper downward. She was giving this to him of her own free will. The significance of it not lost on him for even an instant.

As she pulled his cock free, his breathing grew harsh. And when she wrapped her hot, sweet mouth over the throbbing crown and sucked him deep, he sighed out a long groan of toe-curling pleasure. His nipples drew up tight as pebbles as she worked him in and out of her heavenly mouth with a slow worship that set him on fire and burned him to his soul.

The unrelenting pull and release of her mouth on his cock threatened to unravel him. Liam clutched his thighs, terrified that he'd succumb to the urge to grab her without restraint and force himself down her throat. He gasped, fighting to hold back. He tensed, but the overwhelming pleasure was about to drown him.

Liam was dying to make every second of it last, yet desperate to fill her throat with his seed. He had to see it, had to see her swallow him, needed to see the submissive glow on her face. "Raine... Oh god, Raine! Look at me. Take it all. I'm coming!"

She raised her stare to him. Their eyes locked as he uncurled his grip on his thighs, fisted his hands in her hair, and drowned in her stare as he released every drop in his balls on her tongue. Her joy as she drank him deep transfixed him until he felt his heart become hers, and Liam let out a long sigh. This hard road he'd been down to reach here with Raine… He no longer had a shred of doubt that he'd done the right thing.

Hammer paced. Though Raine and that bastard, Liam, had only been gone twelve hours, it felt like twelve fucking months. In that time, he'd exhausted every avenue he could think of to locate them. Mutual friends hadn't heard from either. He'd talked to a private investigator, but even his mad skills hadn't turned up a clue as to Raine or Liam's whereabouts in that short timeframe. The fucking Irish prick was no doubt using cash and an alias to keep her sequestered far from big bad Hammer's reach. *Son of a bitch.* Liam had to know that he'd leave no stone unturned until he found Raine, but the man was still ignoring his phone calls and texts. So was Raine. The woman-thieving son of a bitch Hammer could understand. But *his* Raine?

Unless… Racing to Raine's room, he saw her purse sitting on her nightstand. *Fuck me!* Liam hadn't even let her grab it before he'd kidnapped her and disappeared.

Diving into the bag confirmed his worst suspicions. His hand squeezed around her cell phone as his stomach tightly knotted. Raine was lost to him unless Liam allowed her to call. And what were the odds of that? Sure, she might leave the bastard…someday. But would she ever come back here?

"Motherfucker!" He resisted the urge to throw her phone across the room.

Hammer set the little colorful bag back on her nightstand, staring sightlessly at the wall. He grabbed her pillow, drawing it up to his nose to inhale the intoxicating fragrance still clinging to the linen. Closing his eyes, he breathed in the remnants of her scent. Remorse clogged his throat, but the lump was so damn big, Hammer felt as if it might choke him.

The sound of someone shuffling near the doorway snagged his attention. He set the pillow in his lap and found Beck staring at him, shaking his head. No way Hammer could miss the concern in the big man's eyes.

"What?" Macen barked.

"You need to get it together, man." Beck frowned and walked away.

As much as Hammer hated to admit it, the guy was right. Moping and mooning wasn't going to accomplish a damn thing. Problem was, he'd never mastered the art of not thinking about Raine even when she was here. Now that she was gone, her ghost lingered everywhere, haunting him.

"Fuck!" Hammer threw Raine's pillow back on the bed and stormed from the room. He might feel like a pathetic bastard, but he wasn't going to act like one.

Striding into the dungeon, he was determined to focus on work. Raine wasn't here to complete some of her tasks, and he needed to find a willing slave to take care of those duties until she returned.

Hammer wouldn't let himself think that he'd never see her again.

He found a pair of lounging subs only too happy to do his bidding. He knew their names and vaguely remembered playing with them in the past. Neither had made a huge impression on him, but he was grateful for them now. Since Raine's disappearance, no one had bothered to wash the coffeepot or organize the dungeon. Neither should have been a big deal, but because she always took care of those tasks, they stabbed him with her absence again—and made the hole in his chest bleed more.

As they ran to do his bidding, he looked about, watching others scene. He hadn't done that since that fateful night with Marlie. Shit, he didn't really want to, and Hammer felt a bit guilty about shirking his responsibilities to the others here today. But he couldn't bring himself to voluntarily take the hand of another sub and…

"Sir?"

Someone tapped his back, and a soft, sensual voice broke into his thoughts. He turned to find Crystal. She sent him an inviting glance. The single sub had few reservations about the Doms she chose to give her power to and even fewer boundaries. He usually strapped her up and pushed her to the edge about once a week. Often, he fucked her afterward. But he hadn't been interested enough to even look her way lately. She wasn't Raine. No one was. And the last thing he felt like doing now was Crystal.

"What is it, girl?" If he was lucky, maybe she had a complaint he could fix or trouble with another Dom whose head he could bash in.

Instead, she reached for his hand, prodding his fingers open with something cool and leathery. He looked down to find her giving him a single tail, then sliding to her knees. "Please, Sir. I need to feel the kiss of the whip."

Fuck. Guilt pressed down on him. He'd neglected her, and it wasn't her fault.

Since the blowup with Liam and Raine's departure, he wondered if the grapevine was working and members would start talking, whisper that he'd lost control. Would they wonder if they should play elsewhere? Speculate that he might not be able to run a safe place?

It would be better for everyone if he put the possible rumors to rest. He never wanted to use a sub in anger…but he wasn't mad at the nubile woman. In fact, anger had fallen far down on his list of emotions. Panic and desolation seemed to be vying for the top spot.

Confident that he wouldn't take Crystal past a place she could handle, Hammer nodded and gestured across the room. An eager smile spread across her lips as she headed to a suspension frame near the back wall.

Hammer untied the little bow holding her sheer, nude baby-doll together and flung it away. Compliantly, she raised her arms to the dangling cuffs, and he secured her in. Then he grabbed her little thong in his fist and gave a mighty yank. It tore from her body, and Hammer tossed it aside. The actions were familiar. He'd done this a thousand times. But nothing felt the same. None of it excited him.

Against his will, his eyes traveled across the dungeon to the infamous spanking bench Raine had perched on for her punishment with Beck…and where she'd given herself to Liam. God, he could still see her there, angry and frightened and determined, at least until Beck had fucked it all up. He didn't have the first clue where she'd gotten those *Fuck You Very Much* panties. At the time, he'd been furious. Now, he smiled a bit fondly. Only Raine…

How the fuck was he going to heal this gaping wound in his chest? How long was he going to miss her and need her and regret every second of the way he'd so fucked up.

"Sir?" Crystal stared at him over her shoulder.

Hammer could give this woman what she craved, and it didn't cost him a thing. Why couldn't Raine be as easy? Why did she want his heart and soul? Love he didn't have to give?

Gripping Crystal's long auburn curls in his fist, he jerked her head back as his lips whispered over her ear. "Your safeword is 'power,' girl."

"Yes, Sir. Thank you. But you know I won't need one." She sent him a dreamy smile.

"You might," he warned.

He smoothed a broad hand over her creamy flesh. Immediately, thoughts of Raine filled his head. His blood surged, boiled. Closing his eyes for a brief moment, he allowed himself to remember how her soft ivory flesh yielded beneath his hands.

Tightly, he gripped the leather-plaited handle of the whip and got ready to inflict pain.

But he was good at that, wasn't he? He'd brought so much pain down on Raine with his actions. His gut seized at the thought of inflicting more, even on a pain slut who craved it. Visions of the marks he'd left marring Raine's sensual body flooded his mind, and he liked the idea that those were the last marks he'd left on a woman. The memories of her slick, swollen pussy and how fucking epic she felt wrapped around his cock consumed him.

Shit, he had to focus.

Opening his eyes, he stepped back, arching the whip high above his head, and with a flick of his wrist, a deafening crack filled the air. Sweat broke out along his brow and trickled down his back. The room spun and a sickening taste filled his mouth. Staring at Crystal's unmarred ass, the canvas he was expected to paint with wicked red welts, he clutched the handle of the whip with both hands. His body trembled as he fought for control.

Raine had left him. His uncompromising needs and his goddamn fears had driven her away, leaving him with no way to harness the overwhelming panic.

He shook his head and closed his eyes.

Suddenly, a strong hand gripped his forearm. Snapping around, he growled at Beck, who stood next to him looking deeply concerned.

"I'll take care of her, Macen," he whispered in a voice that only Hammer could hear.

"I got it," he assured Beck.

"You don't. Pull your head out of your ass," Beck murmured for his ears alone, obviously trying to save Hammer the embarrassment.

He shrugged Beck off. "What the fuck are you still doing here? You've been banned."

Beck snorted. "Banned. Yeah, right. Sorry, chief, I'm still here because I'm the only one who will risk standing up to you. You're dealing with too much. Go unwind in your room. I'll see to Crystal's session."

The asshole was treating him like a BDSM invalid. "Go the fuck away."

"No. Look at yourself. You're white as a fucking ghost. If the members truly knew how much you were falling apart, the ramifications would be disastrous. I can't let you scene with Crystal, not while you're half out of your mind over her."

Hammer didn't have to guess which *her* Beck meant.

"I don't want to talk about it. Get your shit and get out."

"I'm not leaving until I know you're stable enough to be let loose among the subs. Now give me the whip and go unwind in your room."

Who did Beck think he was talking to? He clenched his fists and narrowed his eyes, ready to knock the fucker's head off.

"Ah-ahh, don't start swinging here. It'll ruin your fine, upstanding reputation as the bad ass Dom in charge now, won't it?" Beck taunted with an arch of his brow.

Hammer looked up. All eyes were on him. Even Crystal had turned to see the reason he hadn't started working her over yet. Hell, the sadist was right. "Shit."

"I got this," Beck assured. "I'll give Crystal whatever she needs."

With a sigh of defeat, he clapped Beck on the back. "Her safeword is 'power.' Don't forget it."

"No sweat. You worry about figuring out if you're going to get yourself together or self-destruct. Now that Raine is gone, man, those are your only two options."

With a disgusted sigh, Hammer slapped the handle of the whip into Beck's hand, then clenched his jaw and walked away. The club members' nervous looks did not escape him. Inwardly cursing for being such an idiot, he headed down the hall, to his room, picking up a bottle of Patrón on the way.

As he stripped off his clothes, Hammer stared at the wild tangle of his bed, the sheets still strewn from his night with Raine. If he closed his eyes, he could picture her naked and willing, legs spread, offering him every part of her without an ounce of reservation. God, she'd been all his wildest fantasies come true.

After all he'd put her through, Hammer couldn't blame Raine for taking Liam up on his offer. If Liam's ploy unraveled and she returned broken, he'd be there to pick up the pieces…like he always did. But for now, he was stuck here, alone.

Raine's scent lingered here, driving him mad. He could still feel her in this room. Hear her. Taste her. But it was a mirage. His eyes blurred.

Liam wasn't going to call suddenly and cough up their fucking location. But even if he could talk to her, Hammer wondered what he could really say except that he was sorry. Anything more would only hurt her.

Numb and empty, he unscrewed the top from the bottle and guzzled the clear liquid, relishing the burn down his throat.

As the tequila tore past his control, he allowed himself to drown in memories of Raine. The party he'd thrown for her eighteenth birthday, the night she'd cried to him after losing her virginity, the triumphant day she'd received her college degree—he'd been there for her. Her constant. And Hammer hadn't realized until now how much he needed her to need him.

Would Liam be taking his place?

Hammer had no idea how long he'd been sitting in the middle of his bed, clutching the pillow she'd slept on, but by the looks of the nearly empty bottle of Patrón, he figured it had been a while. How many more bottles would it take before he passed out? He'd drink an entire case if it would ease this ache.

Lowering his head to the pillow again, he caught a whiff of her waning scent. But he wanted more. The fresh reminders of her would make him continue bleeding, and he welcomed it.

Crawling out of bed, he stumbled down the hall to Raine's room. Yanking open her closet door, he pawed several shirts suspended on hangers and hugged them to his chest. Closing his eyes, he inhaled deeply. *Ahh, there she is.* Her scent filled him, made his mouth water, and a stunning visual of her swirled in his head. Much better.

He nearly tripped over his own feet as he turned and wandered back to his room. Sinking to the bed, he clutched her clothing against his face, breathing in her sweet floral and feminine musk, wishing he could hear her tender voice. Look into her big blue eyes sparkling with undeniable love.

God, he'd taken so much of her for granted. An agonizing scream tore from his throat.

"Christ, Macen. What the fuck is wrong with you?" Beck's dark eyes narrowed with pity as he stood in the doorway, eyeing the near-empty bottle of tequila. "Patrón didn't help you before. What makes you think it's going to change anything now? Pull yourself together. Seriously, dude, you're scaring the natives more than I do."

Yanking Raine's shirt away, he tried to stand, but just fell back to the bed. "You think I give a fuck what anyone else thinks? You're not a shrink. Go find someone else's spurting artery to repair and get the hell out."

He laughed. "Jesus christ, you're pathetic. You didn't want Raine enough to fight for her, despite fucking her all night. Loudly, I might add. You two lovebirds made it impossible for me to get any damn sleep." A smirk tugged on his lips. "And now you're going to cry in your beer? I thought the Irish lug was your bosom buddy. You just stood there while he swept her out the front door. It's over, man. She's gone. Stop weeping and start taking care of your business."

"I didn't have a fucking choice. How can I love her when she can't be what I need—when fuck, I can't be what she needs, either? This shit is..." his voice trailed off. "Yeah, Liam is my best friend. Hell, he's like my goddamn brother. So why did he do this to me? He knew... The bastard reads me like a fucking book. And he still stabbed me in the back." Hammer shook his head, staring into the bottom of his bottle. "He's going to fuck with her head. It's his *MO*."

With a sigh, Beck strolled into the room and picked up the bottle between Hammer's feet. He drained the last gulp in one healthy swallow. As he set it on the nightstand, he pulled up a chair, flipped it around, and straddled it. "Let me ask you something. Besides last night, when did you ever treat Raine as anything other than a kid?"

"Probably never. I wanted to protect her, and it just fucking took over everything else."

"Then you can't possibly know if Raine is incapable of being what you want. One night with her isn't going to tell you shit! You didn't try before. You're still not."

"You don't understand." Hammer scrubbed a hand through his hair and sighed. "I don't want a submissive. I need a slave. You *know* she never will be."

"You love her," Beck said quietly.

Hopelessness plowed through him like a freight train, and tears closed up his throat. "Yeah," he choked out. "And I have no fucking clue where to find her or how to save her before Liam turns her inside out."

"I think he cares about her, too."

"But he'll never love her like I do. No one will." He hung his head.

"You didn't show her that."

"The hell I didn't! Maybe not in the way you mean, but I've always taken care of Raine. The night I found her in the alley, I didn't dare look at the terrified girl as she tried to hide by the dumpster. I didn't know anything about her, but one look, and I had to protect her. I was frantic that she'd take off down the alley and be raped. Or shot full of drugs or bullets. I wanted to scoop her up in my arms and lock her away to keep her safe. She was so tiny and falling apart. Then fuck, I looked into her eyes… She seemed so damn lost. Hell, the first few weeks she was here, Raine jumped every time I raised my voice. But I refused to give up on her. I still can't."

"She's not that waif from the alley anymore, man, and if you think that…you've got the whole river of denial running in your veins. I have no doubt that you had your cock in every one of her openings last night. It's no big secret that she wanted you just as badly. As far as being a slave, it's not like a submissive can blink her eyes and presto, she's grown to that level. If you were giving yourself advice, you'd tell yourself that it takes time to train her. You'll teach her to drive, but not to be what you need? You won't even give her a taste. Why?"

"I told her this morning," he slurred. "I explained what to expect as my slave. She ran screaming."

"Do you seriously not know how to compromise? Ease her into it? Maybe it's time to wise up. Your so-called friend has collared Raine now. You're going to have to get at least as clever as Liam and figure out your shit to even think about winning her back."

A wounded growl erupted from his chest. "Even if she wasn't wearing his collar, I'd still be too much for her to handle. I almost broke her last night." His shoulders sagged as he sighed. "Where the hell did he take her? Do *you* know? I need her back. I've got to know she's okay." Tears blurred his vision, and Beck just shook his head. "Help me. Please?"

"God, you're a pussy when you get drunk." Beck rolled his eyes. "I don't know where she is. You think I've got a crystal ball? Did you try to call her? Call Liam?"

"Her cell phone's still here, and the son of a bitch won't answer his. I've sent messages, a shitload of them," Hammer mumbled, trying to quell the panic swirling inside him.

"I'll bet, but have you tried leaving a sober message he might understand?"

Hammer just glared. "Some fucking help you are."

"You need to sleep it off. Booze won't help, trust me. I've been there. But if she's still what you really want, then I'll help you figure out a way to fight for her."

"I can't." His voice cracked. "What if I won, then what? I'd just end up killing her. Then I'd have the guilt of two deaths to live with. Living with one is hard enough."

"Raine isn't Juliet. You've been so focused on what you think she can't do that you've never stopped to consider what she can. Or what you want now. You aren't the same person. Your wife died years ago. Try a little. It's time."

Launching toward Beck, Hammer grabbed him by the shirt. "Help me find her, Ken. I can't live without knowing she's all right. What if she needs me?"

"Fuck, you whine more pitifully than a damn dog. Rest. I'll see if I can find her."

"Thank you, man." He slumped to his side on the bed. His eyes felt like weights as they slid shut. Every minute Raine was gone chafed his soul. "Make it soon."

Chapter
Twelve

Raine stared at the darkened wall. Liam's body warmth kept her cozy in the big bed, despite the chilly night. He'd grabbed her in his sleep and cradled her head on his shoulder. She'd gone to him wordlessly, gratefully.

But her head was still spinning. After her long nap, sleep wouldn't come.

It had been confusing enough to love Hammer and want Liam with that rush of undeniable passion. But now to wonder how or if she could stop herself from falling in love with Liam, too... Devoid of answers, she closed her eyes and nuzzled her cheek against him.

Hammer's passion for her had been a flickering flame, probably snuffed out by the time morning had rolled around. Curiosity satisfied, he'd likely moved on.

But Liam's devotion to her... He'd taken her from a painful place and showered her with care. He'd demanded to see inside her past and her soul, not because he wanted to decide if he'd be arrested for harboring a minor, like Hammer. Liam had done it purely because he wanted to know. He'd given her ecstasy with no expectation of anything in return. He'd taken the news that she could, even now, be pregnant by Hammer with a steadfastness that blew her away.

He just cared. It wasn't an act. It wasn't a trick. Raine had no idea what she'd done to deserve him, but she wasn't going to continue second-guessing when it only made her crazy.

She'd always assumed love was a grand blaze, an all-consuming conflagration that would burn her soul...like she felt with Hammer. As she'd worked through college Lit, she'd read Shakespeare's sonnets, never quite understanding one hundred sixteen.

"Love is not love which alters when it alteration finds," she whispered in the dark. "Or bends with the remover to remove." *O no! It is an ever-fixed mark that looks on tempests and is never shaken...*

Suddenly, that made sense. Because of Liam.

"But bears it out, even to the edge of doom..."

Raine held him tighter. She had no idea how she'd begun falling so hard and so quickly. Her heart had been seemingly set, then fate had thrown her a curveball. And she understood now that love wasn't just wanting, but a steady devotion, no matter what.

As much as Liam had given her, she wanted to give back. But she had nothing to give him except herself.

She brushed her palm down his chest, his ridged abdomen, then traced her fingers back up.

Liam caught her wrist in his grip. "I hear you awake. Are you talking to yourself? You're thinking too hard."

Moonlight flooded the room as he gazed down on her, brushed her hair aside, and stroked the tender bud of her nipple so softly that she sighed and pressed herself into his palm.

Liam smiled as he rose over her and covered her with his big body. She clung to his shoulders and trailed her hands down his arms as he leaned in and devoured her mouth.

"I want to make love to you, Raine, not as a Dom, just as a man. But I've no wish to hurt you. Are you too sore?"

Everything in her body said yes. She opened her lips to him, sliding her hand between them to grip his shaft and squeeze. "Please…"

He moaned at her acceptance, and she writhed beneath him impatiently. Yes, she was still sore, but the need to be closer to him, drown in their connection, drove her.

Liam didn't let her rush him. Instead, he buried his face in her neck and nipped at her skin, palming and stroking her body until she mewled and clawed at him like a kitten. His thighs spread her wide as his cock slid through her wetness, teasing along the length of her slit.

"Am I crushing you? Sure you're not too tender?"

Now he was just toying with her. "You could only hurt me if you stopped."

He bent and captured her nipple, drawing it into his mouth and sucking as he cupped her breast. Liam seemed to know every sensitive note of her body and he played her well. She felt surrounded, cherished, desired... Nearly every fantasy she'd ever held dear when lying alone in her cold bed had come to life.

Same fantasy...different man.

Some things simply weren't meant to be, and she had to accept that. Besides, it wasn't as if she didn't want Liam, didn't like everything about him. Just the opposite. Because of that, they'd quickly moved beyond teacher and pupil in the blink of an eye.

"I want to be inside you, lass. You *will* tell me if I hurt you." It wasn't a question, but a gentle command.

"I will..." she promised. "But you won't."

Liam grabbed her against his body and took her mouth as if he owned it, as if it was his right to devour every part of her. "Bloody christ, woman, you make me hungry."

He broke away just long enough to reach his pants on the floor and fish in his pocket for a condom. He rolled it on, then she was on her back again. He pushed his way between her legs and held himself at her wet, clenching opening.

His breathing was fast, his face harsh, his stare into her eyes insistent. "Take all of me, love."

Raine spread herself wider and lifted to him. "Everything you'll give me."

After a calming breath, he worked inside her one slow inch at a time. He held every muscle in his body under such rigid control that she could feel him trembling to hold back.

Finally, he slid completely inside her with a long, low groan. Raine felt that penetration all the way to her soul. It wasn't just sex. They joined—thoughts, breaths, skin...hearts. The moment was almost reverent. She clung to him.

"Love, you're like melted chocolate around me. So slick and smooth. I've got to fuck you."

"I'm not made of glass, Liam. You won't break me," she promised. "Please fuck me."

Liam withdrew, then drove into her again, gripping her hips with unmistakable ownership. "Normally, I'd paddle you for your language, but when you're saying it to me like that... Bloody hell, it makes me want you more."

His words melted her, and her body welcomed him inside, immersed in the sensations of being with him. Shock pinged her when she felt a deeper fastening between them, the moment so pure and visceral.

"How wet and juicy your wee cunt is. There's no one like you. I can't wait 'til you're healed. Oh, my sweet lass, the things I'll do to you..."

He buried his face in her neck as he plunged his cock to the hilt again, wringing a gasp from her.

"That's it. Give me every little sound. Christ, you're so perfect! Come for me, Raine. Let me hear you."

He adjusted himself, lifting his hands under her ass, raising her hips to him. Then he delved into her in earnest, one pounding stroke after another, no pause, no respite, no way to hold back the spiraling orgasm.

She cried out, and he gave her a wolfish stare, then looked down their bodies in the moonlight, watching as he drove in and out of her pussy."

"That's it, my beauty. You like that? Yes… I can feel you squeezing me tighter each time I fuck my way into you," he moaned in her ear, making her whole body shiver. "Oh, it's so good."

Liam made her feel feminine and small…but so powerful. The way he stroked her now, even deeper than before, had her stretching to the stars.

And Raine couldn't catch her breath. "I'm going to—"

"Look at me." He grabbed her hair in one fist and fused his gaze to hers as the crash of pleasure splintered her. Her back arched. Her scream echoed off the ceiling. Her pussy clamped down on him. She couldn't look away as she unraveled under his touch, his cock, his control.

"Raine!" he cried out, buried deep inside her, then growled out his completion.

Gradually, his fingers released their grip on her hair. Their breathing slowed. Her heart stopped its mad beat. But neither of them looked away or said a word in the exquisite moment.

It hung silent, infinite, its gravity so stunning. Tears pricked her eyes.

"How did this happen so fast?" She'd only meant to think the words, but the surprise on his face said she'd spoken them.

"I'm not really sure, love." He brushed his fingertips over her cheek. "One minute we were talking, and the next…I couldn't stop claiming you as my own. But I'm not questioning it anymore. I—"

The emergency chime on his phone interrupted whatever he'd been about to say. With a curse, he slid free of her body, grabbed the device, and padded to the bathroom. A moment later, he returned with a warm cloth and sat beside her, holding the mobile to his ear. "What do you want, Beck?"

Raine sat up, watching Liam intently. For Beck to call a man he barely liked in the middle of the night, something terrible must have happened. *Hammer.* Her heart chugged with fear.

"What are you going on about?" Liam demanded. "What's wrong?"

"What the fuck do you think is wrong?" Beck shouted the words so loudly, she couldn't fail to hear. "You come here and fuck Hammer's girl in front of the whole goddamn dungeon, make a fool out of him, then steal her away without so much as a 'fuck you.' What problem could there be?"

"I wouldn't change it if I could because I don't regret it." A tick beside his eye twitched. "And since you hurt Raine, I've nothing to say to you except fuck off."

"Don't you hang up on me! Your best friend has been a basket case ever since you took her away." he shouted. "You listening? Get the girl's ass back here pronto and sort this fucking mess out!"

"He's no longer my best friend, and I'll not be taking her back."

He didn't wait for a reply, just hung up.

Raine's heart seized. "Liam…we have to go."

Calmly, he added a few drops of tea tree oil to the hot rag and smoothed it against her swollen pussy. It might have eased her if she hadn't been so worried.

"Liam?"

He ignored her.

"Then you stay. I'm going. Hammer needs me."

She tried to push the cloth away, but he gripped her hands and finished the job without a word. The intimacy was startling, but she was about to decide that was the norm with Liam. Still, she couldn't quite focus with the panic burning her veins.

"Did you hear me?"

"Yes." Liam's answer was clipped, almost angry.

"I have to go back home."

"What makes you think I have any intention of taking you back there? I'd intended to send for your things eventually, but I'd never planned for either of us to darken his door again."

"But it's my home. I..."

In a way, she supposed his resolution made sense. Nothing would ever be the same between Hammer and Liam again. And she bore the guilt for that.

Nor would anything be the same between her and Hammer. And she didn't think for a second that seeing him would be easy.

"That's not your home anymore, lass."

Raine gasped and wrangled free, scrambling back on the bed. "It is. It will always be home."

"One you were ready to leave just days ago. Why the sudden change of heart now?" He narrowed his eyes, as if daring her to say Hammer's name.

"I threatened to leave, but it was killing me inside. I didn't *want* to go. I just didn't see a choice, but now...I have to help him."

"Hammer is a grown man. He can take care of himself."

"Clearly he can't or Beck wouldn't be calling in the middle of the night. I owe Hammer." Liam looked at her impassively, and she balled her hands into fists. "I goddamn owe him!"

"Language, or I've got a bar of soap with your name on it."

"Fuck that! We're talking about a man we both care about, not a little bit of protocol. I can't let him self-destruct. He could have let me do that years ago. But he refused. He saved me. I have to repay the favor. I'd rather do it with your help, but I'll do it without you if I have to."

He clenched his teeth and stalked over the bed, taking hold of her arm and hauling her against him. "Are you repaying a debt…or are you still holding out hope for him since he's going mad with missing you?"

Even she didn't know the answer to Liam's question with absolute certainty. Hammer really missed her? Surely, he wouldn't be falling apart because she'd gone, right? Raine licked her lips. Her head told her anything with Hammer was hopeless, but she couldn't desert the man.

"Think whatever you want. You're going to anyway." She jerked out from under him and marched into the bathroom.

Her hands trembled as she started the shower. Exhaustion pulled at her. Every muscle in her body protested, screamed at her to lie down and rest.

Ruthlessly, she yanked the shower door open and stumbled inside. She had no idea what Liam would do now, if he'd wash his hands of her and take all his sweet caring away. As she stood under the hot spray, tears fell. She might lose him, lose everything. The thoughts crashed down on her, and she slid to the ground, head in her hands, sobbing.

But she didn't see another choice.

Liam pulled open the shower door with a heavy heart and hovered above her, watching Raine's body shake with every one of her tears. *Goddamn Hammer.*

With a sigh, he knelt. "There's no need to cry, lass. Your disrespect toward me is unsettling, but that's not what has me seething. It says a lot about your soft heart that you'd want to save a man who used you so badly."

"It wasn't terrible. I liked it," she confessed.

The words were like a slap in the face. He stood again, glared down at her, hands on hips. "Why did you come with me, then?"

A pregnant pause hung between them. He'd bet she didn't even know the answer to that herself. The only thing to brighten his life in years…and she didn't feel for him half of all the need bursting in him for her. *Fuck all!*

"Because…" she said finally, "with you I could have everything I want. You've made me feel like a woman, like I'm alive and pretty and worthwhile. Do you know how badly I've needed that? And for how long?" she shouted. "I had to stop chasing a dead end. I had to get smart. You've shown me so much about myself and what we could be together. How could I not want that?"

Liam digested her answer, prying it apart word by word. Her head told her that he was the better bet. But her heart…it still lay with Hammer. He'd been a fool when he'd told her that he only needed her trust, not her love. He'd been so fucking wrong.

He stared, held her gaze, not certain what to say. Possibilities rolled in his head. Two days wasn't long enough to make her fall in love with him. He might need weeks. Months. But he would do it. He would snatch her heart from Hammer's grasp eventually. One thing he knew to be true about himself…he could be patient. And ruthless.

The key was in giving her everything Hammer hadn't.

Liam sighed. "All right, then. I won't be keeping you here against your will. I'll take you back. Understand that you'll stay by my side. And you will follow my rules. If you're so bloody worried about Hammer, I suggest you not let him drag you off to his bed again." He allowed the implied threat to hang for a long moment. "I won't let him be driving a wedge between us. Is that understood?"

"Yes."

Time to reinforce his role in her life. "Yes, what?"

"Yes, Sir. Thank you."

Raine sat up on her knees and lifted her face to his. Liam bent to her. Christ, she smelled good. Even though he'd just fucked her, he wanted her again.

He let a heartbeat pass. Still, she didn't open her eyes. Finally, he palmed her neck and seized her mouth for a quick, desperate kiss. It wasn't enough, but all he could take for now or he'd be laying her down on the tile floor and sliding into her again.

"Don't be forgetting it." He stared at her, silently demanding acknowledgment.

She nodded. "I won't, Sir."

"After your shower, get dressed. I've arranged a few clothes for you. They're in the closet. I've a couple of calls to make, then we'll be going. Be ready in half an hour."

She breathed a sigh of relief and stared at him with gratitude that ripped him open. She was happy, all right—to go see her other lover. Liam shoved down his boiling blood and exited the shower.

Then he sat on the side of the bed with a curse, elbows on his knees, and let his head drop. How the fuck had all this come crashing perilously close to the end so quickly? He's wasn't thick ordinarily, but this…connection with Raine had felt so real, so much more than even his link with Gwyneth during their marriage.

He rubbed a big hand across his forehead, dug his finger and thumb into his eyes. Fuck if he knew what would happen once they reached

Shadows, but he'd be damned if he'd just let Raine go. If Hammer wanted her back…well, Liam wasn't above playing dirty.

Chapter Thirteen

Sunlight burned Hammer's eyes, and he squinted. What felt like a full brass band thundered in his head. *Fucking hangover.* All he'd learned was that he couldn't drink Raine away.

Rolling out of bed with a groan, he slumped into the shower, hoping the hot water might assuage his throbbing head. Even his eyes pulsed in time with his heartbeat, like they were going to pop from their sockets.

Bits and pieces of the night before filtered through his brain, and he vaguely remembered Beck playing armchair psychologist. And he'd spilled his guts like a fucking pussy.

"Great!" he barked as embarrassment clawed up his spine.

Washing quickly, he dried his aching body, then brushed the fuzzy residue of Patrón from his mouth. He groaned as he pulled on clothes, but at least he could find some aspirin and coffee now, in that order.

As he stood in the kitchen, Raine's kitchen, that familiar anxiety he'd been unable to contain grabbed him by the balls.

Willing the coffee to brew faster, he watched the *drip-drip-drip* of the little device. Before today, he'd only made coffee for himself once in the last six years, when Raine had fallen ill with the flu. He'd sat by her bed all night, watching her sleep fitfully, and helped her to the bathroom on cue. To keep himself awake, he'd fixed a pot of coffee, then took the steaming cup back to her room to watch over her some more.

But that was then…and now she was gone.

After downing plenty of pain reliever and pouring a hefty mug of coffee, he stepped into the deserted dungeon. All the members were long gone, and the cavernous room seemed cold and dead... much like his soul.

Weaving his way through the various stations, he wasn't surprised when he again found himself staring at the spanking bench on which he'd witnessed Raine's punishment. Had that just been two long, miserable days ago? Yeah, but it seemed like two lifetimes ago to Hammer.

Images of Raine cuffed to the bench punched him in the gut. Like the damned pervert he was, his cock jerked to life. Even as he'd wanted to kill Liam for claiming *his* Raine and stealing her out from under him, he'd been unable to deny how phenomenally gorgeous she'd looked bound and submissive and shattering. She'd looked even more beautiful in his bed, taking his cock.

But even if he didn't intend to ever touch her again, he refused to sit back idly and let Liam get away with stealing Raine. He would search the ends of the fucking earth until he found her, starting with Liam's house in New York. He was due to take his annual trip there anyway... and he didn't want to think about that task at all.

Sipping the bitter brew in his mug, he made a mental list of phone calls and arrangements needed. He had every intention of being on the other side of the country before dinner.

He trailed his fingers over the soft leather of the bench. "I'm going to find you, precious. And I'm going to bring you back home, where you belong."

Then what? An annoying voice in the back of his pounding head scoffed. With a heavy sigh, he shook the disturbing question away. He'd figure out something. Details weren't important, just finding her. Right now, he needed to pack for his flight. No, what he really needed was to see her beautiful face... feel her lush body warm in his arms... hear her sweet cries of pleasure resonating in his ears.

Goddamnit, no. He just needed to know that she was safe. End of story.

Tearing himself away from the bench, he marched in long strides toward his office. The sound of the front door opening stopped him dead in his tracks. It was far too early for guests to play or even for anyone to man the lobby.

A flutter of hope burst inside him as he raced to the staircase, taking the steps up two at a time. When he rounded the corner, there she was. Raine. Oh, thank god. She'd come home to him.

Barely cognizant of Liam hovering closer by her side, Hammer couldn't miss the resounding waves of anger rolling off him. Fuck the bastard. Liam could be as pissed as he wanted. All that mattered now was that Raine had returned.

Hammer's steps quickly ate up the ground between them. He couldn't get to her fast enough, couldn't touch her soon enough.

As he reached to pull her in his arms, Liam tucked Raine behind his back, his stance both protective and warning. The man's eyes leveled him with a glare that was flat, cold.

"Move. You have no right to keep her from me." Hammer skirted the other man and invaded Raine's personal space, staring his way into her eyes. But, for once, he couldn't read what she was thinking. What the fuck was happening here? He leaned down to cup her cheek.

"Don't you fucking touch her," Liam growled.

Hammer froze as he held Raine's gaze. "I need to talk to you, precious. Come with me to my office where we can have a few minutes." He glared at Liam. "In private."

She bit her lip, then turned away from him to look up at Liam with a silent question in her eyes. It felt like someone had kicked him in the nuts when he realized she was asking Liam for permission to speak to him. *Oh, fuck no!*

How the hell had Liam tamed her in little more than twenty-four hours?

Hammer gulped in a stunned breath. This had to be some kind of fucked-up episode of *The Twilight Zone*.

Liam shook his head. Raine's shoulders sagged with her sigh, but she nodded and cast her gaze to the floor.

"Motherfucker!" Hammer hissed as his heart clutched in shock and agony. "What did you do to her, you son of a bitch? Turn her into some kind of Stepford sub?"

"What you should have done!" Liam stepped in Hammer's face and lowered his voice. "And if she is pregnant, you selfish prick, I swear by all that's holy, they'll need tweezers to find all the parts of your body."

Liam's threat pissed him off, but her soft face erased the hurt. *Pregnant?* The logical part of him recoiled, but his primal side? That chunk of his psyche wanted to celebrate. Raine was too softhearted to ever end a pregnancy, and the notion that there would be a part of her and him melded together always felt right, as if the natural order of the world were falling into place. God, wasn't he a stupid bastard?

But if she was pregnant, he'd rip her from O'Neill's arms faster than the man could blink.

"How the fuck could you treat her like that?" Liam went on. "There's barely an inch of her body that isn't bruised, inside and out."

The stupid prick thought he'd abused Raine? Christ, Liam wouldn't know the marks of passion if they raised up and bit the end of his cock off.

"So don't be thinking for one minute that I'll be leaving her unprotected and alone with you," Liam continued. "Whatever you need to say, you'll say in front of me or you won't say it at all. Get it through your thick head, she's mine. If you shit all over the code of conduct again, she'll be leaving with me. Permanently."

There was no fucking way on this green earth that Liam would take Raine away from him again.

"I didn't give her anything she didn't beg for," Hammer snarled. "Over and over again."

Raine's jaw gaped open, and she sent him an imploring stare, one that begged him to stop throwing fuel on the fire.

Well, hell. And Liam's gaze drilling into him left him no doubt that the fucker was looking for an excuse—any excuse—to make good on his threat.

Shit. All right. He was prepared to say or do whatever necessary to keep her here. If Liam took her away for good...the last interminable hours had proven that he'd go crazy without her.

As if feeling her approach behind him, Liam turned to look over his shoulder. Most submissives would stare at the floor in silence when two angry Doms turned this much intent focus on her. Not Raine. She sidled around Liam and stepped between them. She put a palm to the Irish bastard's chest first. Hammer didn't have more than a second to let jealousy eat at him before she put her hand on him, too. Her touch seared him all the way to his balls, then eased him down to his soul. Liam could say what he wanted; she was still his.

"I know I'm speaking out of turn, and you can punish me later if you want," she said to Liam. "But I was thinking on the drive down the mountain... A lot has happened lately. Things have occurred, insults have been traded. But guys...you were friends long before me. This disagreement is just a momentary blip. I don't want to fight with my boss or my Sir. And I certainly don't want you two fighting with one another. It's the kind of toxic thing that can only hurt all of us and the club as a whole. And I know tempers are running high now. Just...think about it. For me."

Hammer feared that she was asking the impossible, but he remained silent when she faced Liam.

"I'm going to start tidying up and getting to work. It's my day to check supplies and complete the liquor inventory. You two should talk." She stood on her tiptoes and brushed a kiss over the man's lips before shooting him a little smile and walking toward the stairs.

"That's fine by me, but we should make a few things crystal clear, right here and now." Liam's voice filled the silence.

She turned back to them both, lashes blinking over her wary eyes.

"If you want to continue working here, then fine, but working is all you'll be doing, love. Hammer is capable of taking care of himself. Not only that, you know he has other submissives at his beck and call, should he require…extras."

Hammer smirked, barely resisting the urge to shake his head. Liam must be slipping to play Raine's insecurity card right off the top of the deck. That was fine by Hammer. The pompous prick only managed to remind Raine of her jealousy when he spent time with other subs. *That's it, asshole…keep that red-hot longing bubbling up inside her.* In fact, Hammer was willing to give Liam all the rope he needed to hang himself.

"You'll not be his maid, fuss after him, change his sheets, make his coffee, or bake him treats," Liam insisted. "You will stop all the other hundred and one things you've done quietly with such grace through the years, Raine. He'll not have the right to lay hands on you again. None of this is negotiable." He stared at Raine, brow raised. "Are we clear?"

Hammer watched Raine flinch, then swallow slowly. His blood boiled.

"Yes, Sir." She said the words, but no mistaking the sad note in her voice.

Apparently Liam didn't understand Raine at all. The asshole was ordering her to deny a huge chunk of her submissive nature. Liam had crossed the line from losing it to fucking idiocy. And in that mental state, what would he do to Raine? Without conscious thought, Hammer's fist curled into a ball and he lifted his arm.

Raine pinned a pleading stare on him and she shook her head. *Oh, fuck.* His violent urge goaded him to whisk her to safety and pound the hell out of his "friend."

I'm not worth this, she mouthed for him alone.

She couldn't be more wrong. But her beseeching blue eyes... Hell, he couldn't make matters worse for her.

Hammer sent her a fierce gaze that told Raine she was damn wrong. Then without sparing Liam a glance, he spun away, taking in deep breaths to get his rage under control.

At least Raine was safe and home. It was far more than he'd woken up expecting today. But she was still Liam's...at least for now. His calculating friend had been thinking with his head most every step of the way. He'd studied the girl, waited for a vulnerable moment, crafting a plan to convince Raine that he could give her what she needed. Liam had likely made himself the balm that eased her wounded soul. And Hammer had no one to blame but himself. He'd been thinking with nothing but his heart and his dick.

And that had to change now.

Because no matter what Liam said, he didn't have his shit together. The man had a dark side Raine hadn't seen...yet. Eventually, he'd chew her up and spit her out, and Hammer meant to do whatever it took to keep the bastard from hurting her.

Jogging down the stairs, he plotted, waiting for just the right moment...

Hammer paced his room like a caged animal. Liam's words rolled in his brain over and again... *If she's pregnant... If she's pregnant...* But what if she were pregnant and decided not to tell him? He'd know eventually, but that wasn't the point.

He scrubbed a hand through his hair as uneasiness ricocheted through him. Stepping from his office, he prowled the hall, checking the kitchen, then the liquor storage room, then the sanitation room. No Raine.

Hammer passed through the hallway again, pausing at Liam's closed door. Holding his breath, he pressed his ear to the wooden surface and listened intently. All was quiet. He spun on his heel and quickly rounded the corner into the dungeon and there she was, cleaning the equipment and readying things, like she always did, for the evening members.

Quickly scanning the room, a smile of triumph spread over his lips. She was alone. As he watched her work, calmness settled over him, and for the first time in two days, he was able to take a deep breath without feeling a knife slicing his chest. Beneath her short skirt, he eyed the ugly bruises on the tops of her thighs that Beck had left and clenched his teeth. As she turned to throw the cleaning cloths in the trash, he also saw the deep purple marks on her arms and neck that he'd left on her. His fingers itched to touch her again, to feel her silkiness upon his naked body once more.

Sucking in a deep breath, he quietly walked toward Raine, stopping a few feet behind her. As if sensing his approach, she turned and stared into his eyes for a half second before she lowered her gaze. She didn't look away fast enough to mask the guilt flitting through her blue eyes. He shouldn't be talking to her. Her body language screamed that she was dishonoring Liam. He should walk away and leave her alone, but he couldn't.

"I know I have no right, but I need to ask a favor of you, precious." He balled both hands into fists to keep from touching her as she raised her cautious stare to him again. "I'll do my best to respect your choice of Liam." His brain screamed a resounding *like hell*. "But if you miss your next period, I'd like to be the first to know, not the last. Would you do that for me, please?"

Raine hesitated, and his heart stuttered. He prepared arguments to convince her, but finally, she nodded. "It's putting me in an awkward place, Hammer, and you know that. But...this concerns you. You have a right to know."

Relief eased through his veins, and she looked like she had a thousand other things to say, but she fell silent.

Hammer hated the idea that she felt she couldn't talk to him anymore. Liam had done that. Well, Liam and his own stupidity. But if he wanted to at least keep the lines of communication open between them, he couldn't let her shut them down now.

"Whatever it is, precious, say it."

He saw the debate flit through her head, then she sighed. "I owe you my life, and I know that. But I owe him now, too. I'm going to do whatever it takes to make things right between you two again."

She licked her lips, and he noticed they were swollen, as if she'd been kissed a lot. Jealousy burned.

"You don't have to bother. I'm more concerned with you. Be careful, Raine. He's not what you think he is and—"

"Stop. I won't discuss Liam behind his back. Don't put me in that position." She stood and put her hands on her hips. "I don't know what's happening with you or why Beck had to call me home to help you. Don't make me regret my decision."

"Beck?" He had a vague recollection of begging the sadist for help. Had Beck called Liam to find her? Had Beck spilled how drunk Hammer had been? How much like a pussy he'd behaved. Now, he had one more reason to kill the asshole.

"Yes. Liam talked to him, but Beck was shouting and pretty damn…darn insistent that we get back here." She shrugged. "So Liam and I, um…talked about it and here we are."

Meaning Raine had put her little foot down with Liam? She wasn't going to confirm that now, but he'd dig into it a bit deeper soon. He had to think about the best way to do that without making the asshole suspicious. But fuck, all the thinking wasn't helping his hangover.

Raine reached out to touch him, then seemed to think better of it and jerked her hand back. "My famous hangover remedy? I can't make it for you, but…" She sighed. "Scramble yourself an egg and make dry toast, chase it with Gatorade, which you should mix with some of the Siberian ginseng in the spice cabinet. Take a B-complex vitamin. Then drink a lot of water today." She scowled at the coffee in his hand. "And stop drinking that crap. It dehydrates you and will make you feel worse. And I've said enough."

Hammer watched her go with a little smile. Raine hadn't exactly broken the rules, but she'd bent them. For him.

"Thank you, precious," he called after her.

As evening fell, Raine yawned and knocked on Hammer's office door. Since she'd seen him a few minutes ago mingling with guests upstairs, she didn't expect him here. Of course, he'd been holed up in here not thirty minutes ago with—*gag me*—Marlie. Blessedly, his "session" with the plastic skank was over for the day. Raine had stopped asking herself long ago what Hammer or any man saw in the Barbie doll.

When no one bid her to enter, Raine pushed the door open and dragged her trash bag in, then set about emptying the bins in Hammer's private rooms.

It was kind of a gray area of Liam's rules, but honestly, if she was in the office with a trash bag in hand, doing her job, why not take the extra ten steps to empty the bins in his personal areas? And okay, maybe she wanted to spy a little...

The trash cans in his bedroom and bathroom were both virtually empty. She tried not to imagine what it meant that, for once, there wasn't a handful of used condoms at the bottom of those bins after one of Marlie's visits, just a disposable razor and the box that had once held a bar of soap. Her ridiculous relief annoyed her. And made her feel guiltier than hell. She might have a future with a man who cared about her, who wasn't pushing her away at every turn. She had to stop thinking about Hammer as anything other than a boss. She definitely had to forget about him as a lover.

Easier said than done. She didn't care about Liam less. In fact, he'd shadowed her for most of the day, making her rest when she was tired. He'd also been there when she'd been too stubborn to stop and eat lunch. More than once, he'd demanded to know her emotional state, and he'd waited unblinkingly until she'd answered. She couldn't ask for anyone more watchful, and her heart gave a silly thump every time he smiled at her.

But Hammer and the sadness in his eyes haunted her. She didn't know what to do next, what to say to him...how to act. Every time their eyes met, she saw his carnal knowledge of her there, and her traitorous body tightened.

God, why couldn't she just figure all this shit out and live a normal life?

After emptying the little bin under Hammer's desk, she gathered trash from all the other private guest rooms, the main office, and the kitchen, then shoved open the door to the alley.

Raine had to gather her strength to toss the full bag into the dumpster. Damn, she was beat, and every bone in her body hurt. Tonight, she'd finally get a whole night's sleep...unless Liam had other plans for her.

And that idea didn't upset her at all.

Behind her, the door to the alley opened again, and she turned, half expecting to see him there, offering to help her lift the bag. But she was puzzled to find Marlie instead. The woman barreled toward her with as much of a snarl as she could manage around all that Botox. Marlie walked right up to her, eyes thundering, then slapped her cheek. Raine raised a hand to the side of her stinging face. Her mouth hung open as her thoughts raced. If she didn't work at the club, she would have hit the bitch back.

"What the hell is the matter with you?" she demanded of Marlie.

"You fucking cunt! What did you do to Hammer?" A howl of fury tore itself from Marlie's throat as she raised her hand again.

Raine warded off Marlie's oncoming palm with a shove. "I didn't do anything to him."

"You're a fucking liar! He was the best fuck I ever had, and you, you just couldn't stand the competition, could you? Now he's totally useless."

"What do you mean useless?" Raine frowned. "And don't ever hit me again."

"I'd rather scratch your batting blue eyes out. What do you think it means?" She railed. "I can't imagine why he would ever waste his big, gorgeous cock on you when he's got me. Like you'd know what to do with it..." She rolled her eyes. "But today during our session, he refused to touch me. All he wanted to do was chastise me for not being as kind as you, as sweet as you, as submissive as you. He wanted me to be more like you. As if I would lower myself, you good-for-nothing piece of white trash!"

Raine flushed and lunged into Marlie's face. "I might be white trash, but at least I didn't pay a doctor for my assets. And let me tell you something... Hammer *did* put his big, gorgeous cock inside me everywhere, and I have bruises all over my body to prove it."

She lifted her skirt to show the colorful marks on her thighs and up one hip. Marlie's eyes widened. Yeah, that news had clearly rocked her little country club world. Score one for the white trash.

"If he won't touch you again..." Raine couldn't help but smile. "I'll just consider that, since he's had better, he's no longer interested in a plastic whore like you. Go fuck yourself."

She tried to stride past the bottle blonde, but all of Marlie's time at the gym had apparently paid off. The bitch grabbed her arm, yanked her back, then shoved her against the dumpster. "Hammer should have left you here. It's where you belong. He felt nothing but *sorry* for you. I'm not worried. He'll get tired of slumming and come back to me."

He might, and Raine wanted to crumble just thinking about it. Still, she refused to give Marlie any credit or hope. "You hold your breath, honey, and see what happens."

Raine left a sputtering Marlie in her wake. Fuming, she jerked the club's back door open and stalked down the shadowed hall, headed toward her bedroom.

And here came Hammer, up the hall of private rooms. She could still feel her cheek stinging. No way it wasn't red. Once he found out she'd tangled with Marlie, he'd think they fought because she was jealous. And he wouldn't be totally wrong. She pivoted on one heel and turned back toward the kitchen, wincing and praying that he hadn't gotten a good look at her face.

"Raine?" The deep voice that always caused her heart to beat faster filled the small walkway. She turned to him halfway, shielding her blazing cheek. "All the way around, precious."

Nibbling her bottom lip and praying there wasn't an imprint of the plastic skank's hand, she jerked her chin up, then eased around to face him. He was on her in two wide steps, his broad hand cupping her chin as he tilted her head back, angling her cheek toward the light.

"What the fuck happened? Who did this to you?" A tremor of anger vibrated through his body.

"Nothing. No one." She closed her eyes as dread slid through her. "Just drop it. Please. If Liam sees us talking…"

"Fuck Liam, I don't need his goddamn permission to speak to you; I'm not a fucking sub! I asked you a question and don't you dare lie to me again!"

"But I need his permission to talk to *you*. I've already violated that rule twice today. Are you trying to fuck this up for me? You can't care about me, but you can't stand that someone else might?" She stepped back and clapped her mouth shut. "Forget I said that. Just…I'd rather not give Liam a reason to punish me. What happened isn't important. I don't think it will happen again."

"No. I won't forget you said that and we *will* discuss that later. I don't see how he expects you to work for me and not speak to me, but that's not your concern. I'll deal with him. Did *he* do this to you?" Hammer's eyes narrowed dangerously. "Is that why you won't tell me who slapped you? You're protecting him, aren't you? I'll fucking rip him limb from limb!"

"It wasn't me, you fucking wanker. Tell me now, lass. Who hit you?" Liam moved in front of Raine and tilted her chin up, mimicking Hammer's last move, but swept a gentle thumb over her lip. "Out with it now."

She seriously debated grappling for a story, but it wasn't like she could say that she fell onto someone's hand. Too many years had gone by, so she was out of practice lying about this sort of thing. And her dad had usually been more subtle about where he hit her. It rarely showed.

"It's just…" She shook her head and raised her gaze to the ceiling. Feeling their intent stares unraveling her, and there would be serious consequences for lying. Of course, there might be for telling the truth, too. And not for anything did she want Hammer or Liam to think she'd been in a jealous catfight with Marlie. "It was a misunderstanding and it's over. Really, I handled it. I'm fine. Problem solved. Thanks for caring."

Suddenly, Hammer gripped her arm and spun her around to face him. Even the snarl curled on his lips didn't stop the blast of arousal racing down her spine and pooling between her legs. God, this was so wrong. Liam was standing right here, and with a quick glance at the gorgeous Irishman, she was doubly turned on.

"No more stalling, precious. Tell us now. Who the fuck hit you?"

Liam growled with fury. "Take your hand off her now, Hammer, and step the fuck back. Raine, present *now*!"

She felt them both watch as she slid to the floor between them.

"Holy shit," Hammer hissed.

Liam ignored him and gently lifted her chin. "No more of your stalling. Out with it! Who. Hit. You?"

Raine sighed. She was damned if she gave up Marlie's name and damned if she didn't. Why the hell hadn't she headed straight to the kitchen instead of her room? Oh, she'd wanted to check her face and see if she needed makeup to conceal the fucking handprint, that's why.

"All right. I tried to save you this ugly shi—um, stuff." She shook her head. "Some things are just better buried, but whatever. It was Marlie. She followed me to the alley after I dumped the trash and wanted to tell me she was pissed about…" She stumbled. The truth served no purpose but to either annoy or embarrass everyone. "Her broken fingernail, her ugly plastic boobs, her period. I don't know. Whatever Marlie gets mad at. I told her to go fuc—" She looked over at Liam, who had a brow raised at her. "Perform an anatomically impossible act on herself, then I left. End of story."

He scowled at Hammer. "You need to keep your bitch on a leash."

A snarl tore from Hammer's lips. "She's not mine to put on a leash, asshole."

"More yours than mine. I was never stupid enough to stick my dick in her."

"Probably because she didn't want yours," Hammer sneered.

Liam rolled his eyes and turned back to Raine. "Broke a fingernail, ugly plastic boobs, or her period, is it? So who are you protecting with that lie? Can't be me, as I know fuck all about her, but if her Dom of the moment doesn't deal with her, I will. You, however, are my problem, and you promised me the truth. How quickly you forget. You won't like the consequences of compounding it further. So let's try again. Why did she hit you?"

She resisted the urge to cross her arms over her chest. God, all this ugly shit was going to come out, and they'd asked for it. Men just never listened... "Fine. I was protecting myself. I didn't want either of you to think that I got into some jealous tangle with the bitc...woman. She followed me out, slapped me without a word, then blamed me for making you useless, whatever that means." She glared at Hammer. "I didn't ask questions, since it's none of my business. And no matter how badly I wanted to, I didn't hit her back. She called me white trash and said you should have left me by the dumpster. So I called her a plastic whore and came inside, then I ran into you. That's it."

"I'll take care of this." Hammer's gaze softened as he looked down at Raine. "You didn't have to risk punishment to protect her, precious. She doesn't mean shit to me. Please, next time, just tell the truth."

He turned away, but stopped and glanced over his shoulder at Liam. "Should I demand to be present when you punish her, old friend? Maybe I can save her from you and offer her a collar, too."

With a scoff, he brushed past Liam, bumping his shoulder, then left.

Searching for the platinum blonde bitch, Hammer raced up the stairs and found her pouting at the bar, nursing a drink. Striding to Marlie, he grabbed her by the arm and plucked her from the barstool in an unyielding grip. She yelped in surprise, then flashed him a smile with her collagen-puffed lips, exposing her capped white teeth.

"Time to talk, Marlie," he barked in her ear. "You've stepped over the line, and I won't tolerate your behavior anymore!"

She bristled, her eyes growing wide with feigned confusion. "I have no idea what you're talking about. You're hurting me!"

He shot her a quelling glare and lifted her from the floor, then dragged her toward the stairs. "I'll explain in my office."

The shrieking shrew kicked and screamed. "She hit me first!"

"I thought you didn't know what I was talking about," Hammer drawled. "Show me."

"I-it was over my clothes. I dodged out of the way. It's not my fault if she's slower."

As they passed the dungeon, Liam stood in the hall, cradling Raine's cheek in his palm. It soured something in Hammer's gut, but at least the other man was taking care of her.

Hammer could feel hatred pouring off Marlie when she clapped her eyes on Liam's tender touch.

"Do you have something to say to Raine?" Hammer prodded.

Marlie glared at the pair. "I already said it and I meant every word."

Liam bent to Raine, kissing her cheek. "Why don't you go to our room, lass? I'll be along directly, after I've said my piece."

Raine hesitated before glancing at him, then back to Liam. She turned to leave as Liam's eyes fastened on Marlie. And suddenly, he unleashed his rage on her with a ferocity that had the woman backing up against Hammer in a hurry.

"You're a viscous, pathetic excuse for a human being, and if you were a man, I'd knock you into next week. How dare you lay hands on Raine? You aren't fit to so much as wipe her ass for her. You'll never have and never be what she is, and do you know why? Because she's real and decent, full of life. And she has a heart. How fucking dare you raise a bloody hand to her, you miserable plastic bitch! Get the hell out of my face before I forget you're female. Hear me well, though. If you come within a hundred yards of Raine again, I'll make you wish to christ you'd never been born!"

Marlie stared at Liam in abject fear. Hammer had never seen this side of his friend—ever. The calm, cool, collected Liam who never lost his temper was long gone. This startling transformation was something he'd best keep in mind.

Liam turned. Sweet Raine blinked at him with soft eyes.

"Damn it," he muttered. "I told you—"

She threw herself into his arms. He caught her with a groan and wound his arms around her, pulling her into his body. He didn't pause, but kept walking as she wrapped her legs about him and kissed him soundly before they disappeared into his room. The door slammed shut so hard the walls vibrated.

Suddenly, Hammer found himself alone with Marlie. He dragged her to his office.

It would be a long time before the image of Raine locking lips with the asshole and crawling up his body like he was some fucking hero left Hammer's mind. And damnit, he probably missed a golden opportunity to wrap Raine in his arms and shield her from Liam's tirade. But as pissed off as Liam was, Hammer was certain that if he'd jostled one hair on Raine's head, Liam would have gone berserk.

Mentally, Hammer sank to his knees. When had the fucking bastard fallen head over heels in love with Raine? The realization that she'd burrowed deep into Liam's heart disturbed him. It shouldn't shock him as much as it did; after all, Raine had captured his heart long ago. She still owned it.

Was all that tonsil-swabbing she'd played with Liam just gratitude…or was she falling in love with the fucker?

"Are you going to let him talk to me like that?" Marlie batted her lashes in a pathetic attempt to look fragile and helpless. She faked a sniffle. "She said that you fucked her."

"Nope. I didn't fuck her. I made mad, passionate love to her."

Marlie dropped the faux sadness. "Are you kidding me? Did you want to see how the unwashed performs in bed?"

Hammer gave her his sternest glare of contempt. "We shared something magical. Meaningful. Something I *never* had with you."

"She's so…gutter. How could you *want* her? All that dark hair tangles and hangs down her back in a disheveled mess and into her eyes. All that fake innocence…" Marlie made gagging noises. "Seriously, she must have fucked half the dungeon over the years. No polish, no class. She's so short and her boobs are too big to wear designer. I'm sure that's why she looks so thoroughly average." She shuddered, and Hammer felt his blood pressure rise. "That, and her grooming. Does she do her nails with a chainsaw? Cut her own hair wearing a blindfold?" Marlie curled her fake claws around his shoulder. Hammer shook off her touch, feeling a sudden, violent urge. "Macen, really. You're too sophisticated and smart to prefer that little urchin to a more worldly woman. You and I are so alike. We make sense. Be reasonable, lover…"

He'd never punched a woman before, but if he didn't get the conniving whore out of his office soon, he'd do just that.

Glaring at Marlie with a look that should have turned her to stone, he jerked the phone off his desk and punched in the code for security. "I need an escort from my office. Now!" He slammed the receiver back down and sucked in a deep breath, his body shaking in rage.

Clenching his jaw so tight he thought his teeth might shatter, he balled his hands into fists. "You're banned from Shadows until hell freezes over. But let me be clear. Raine is a beautiful woman who's real and warm. She's got a heart of gold. I don't know why, but she actually tried to protect you. Christ, I'm so damn glad we made her tell the truth. Don't ever darken my doorstep with your shallow cattiness again, you miserable cunt!"

"You actually prefer that unkempt whore?" Marlie stared, open-mouthed. "Oh my god, you're in *love* with her? Ugh! My opinion of you just went down ten notches. That 'heart of gold' won't look so good on your arm since I've seen better-dressed women who just crawled out of the projects. She wouldn't know the difference between Versace and Prada if someone held a gun to her head. But, oh, that's right. She won't be on your arm. She's busy fucking your what...best friend? So I guess that leaves you all alone." She smiled coldly as she grabbed his thumb. "Have fun with Polly and her four sisters. That's all the sex you'll be getting because you won't be getting it from me, you stupid ox!"

"You were nothing more than a convenient place to shove my dick. The only reason you came here was to spread your legs for cock, and the whole fucking club knows it. You're no more interested in being a proper submissive than I am! Don't concern yourself with my sex life. I'll manage just fine without you and your nasty snatch." A condescending smile curled on his lips just as two Dungeon Monitors appeared in his doorway. "Take this trash out and toss her in the dumpster. Literally."

Hammer shoved Marlie toward the two men.

"With pleasure, boss." A broad smile cracked the stoic face of one DM. "Come on, Marlie. Looks like you've worn out your welcome here. Thank fucking god."

Hammer sucked in a deep breath as he watched them take her away, still fighting the urge to knock her flat on her ass. It was over. Marlie couldn't hurt Raine again, and he needed to let her know.

Storming from his office, he headed toward Liam's room, the sounds of Marlie sputtering in protest fading in the distance. At Liam's door, he knocked. The thought of that bastard deep inside Raine seared across his mind. He was more than happy to interrupt.

Impatiently he knocked again, louder and harder. Finally, the door swung open with such force, Hammer thought it might fly off its hinges.

Liam stood there with his shirt open and his dick tenting the front of his barely-buttoned trousers as he licked Raine's glaze from his mouth and chin with a smacking smile. He didn't speak, just cocked his brow and waited.

"Jesus christ!" Hammer mumbled under his breath as the scent of Raine's essence assaulted his senses. His mouth watered, and he ached to push Liam aside and dive face first into her heavenly cunt.

Hammer took a steely breath, trying to restrain himself from driving his fist into Liam's gloating smile. "I want to speak with Raine."

"No. Maybe tomorrow. Maybe never. We're busy. Fuck off, Hammer."

"You're really loving this, aren't you? Okay, give her a message for me. Tell her that Marlie won't ever lay another hand on her. She's been physically removed from the club and banned for life," he bellowed loud enough for Raine to hear—along with most of the dungeon.

From the room behind him, he heard a chorus of applause.

Then Hammer backed away. To his surprise, Liam followed him into the hall and closed the door behind him, crossing his arms over his chest. "She insisted on coming back here for you, so am I loving this bullshit? No, not a lot." He cocked his head to the side. "Isn't it that time of year for you to visit New York and pay your respects to Juliet?" He dug into his pocket and flipped his keys in Hammer's direction. "I'm staying at your place. You can stay at mine." He shrugged. "I figure I owe you."

Hammer palmed the keys. "Well, free rent doesn't come close to compensating me for stealing Raine."

"You had six years, and all you did was bloody tear her apart. Are you going to begrudge her some affection?" His eyes narrowed. "Because you're not the one dishing it out?"

Hammer didn't have an argument for that. "Will Raine still be here when I get back from New York?"

"As long as she wants to stay, we'll be here. And trust me, friend, if she wants to stay, then I'll not be going anywhere either. Can you deal with that?"

Fuck no. "Oh, I can deal. It will take someone better than you to truly be competition," he sneered, then turned and walked away.

Chapter Fourteen

Raine scrambled back onto the bed. She hadn't caught every word by pressing her ear to the door, but enough to get the gist. Hammer had given up Marlie without a second thought, as well as banned her.

She shook her head. Liam had said she could stay at Shadows as long as she wanted. Maybe that wasn't smart. Hammer would always have a piece of her. He would always be a temptation. Seeing him every day wouldn't be easy, especially since he and Liam were at odds over her. But so much of her heart now seemed wrapped up in the tender Irishman who swaggered his way toward her and stripped off his pants to reveal a body that made her catch her breath.

Somehow, she had to fix their friendship.

"Everything all right?" She flashed a shy grin his way.

"Never better. You'll have no doubt heard, along with the rest of the dungeon, that Hammer's fuck toy will no longer be a problem for you. Now, then…" He stalked around the bed. "Where were we before we were so rudely interrupted, love? Oh, I remember now…"

He dove on the bed and scooped her up, lifting her legs over his shoulders.

She giggled and clutched wildly at his head. *"Liiiaaam!"*

Nuzzling between her thighs, he paused. "That's 'Sir' to you, my saucy minx. Be thankful you're still too bruised or I'd be spanking your ass." He laughed at her moan. "But you're utterly beautiful, and you taste so sweet…"

As he lapped at her folds, joy suffused her, along with a drowning pleasure. When she was with Liam, he never failed to make her feel special, significant to him. She'd never had that—ever—and she didn't know how to put her gratitude and everything overflowing in her heart into words that he might understand. But she'd promised to try and she would.

"You make me feel that way, oh great and powerful Sir. And you're incredibly wonderful yourself."

When he smiled indulgently, she stroked his hair. He made his way up her body and kissed her once. Twice. The third lingered. By the fourth, she met him open-mouthed and lost track of the number of kisses they shared, each longer and more intimate than the last.

She whimpered and hugged him tight, wishing again that she had the words to tell him how she felt. Everything about him made her heart glad. Hope buoyed her when he rolled her to her stomach and his body covered hers. Breathing his way up her neck, he skimmed his lips across her skin so lightly that she shivered.

Unconsciously, she spread her legs in welcome. "Liam, please! I want you inside me. I'm so wet. I ache. I..."

Raine gasped when she felt his hand slide under her, then onto her clit. The little bud had seemed sated just moments ago, but with so little effort, he awakened her all over again. She writhed, begged once more, then turned her head to give him better access to her neck so she could melt into him.

"My bonny wee lass. That's what you need, isn't it, love? But tell me, do my fingers feel as good as my mouth did? I can smell you. Still taste you. It's burned inside me." He laved her throat, bit and licked and suckled her as he ground his cock against her.

She lifted her ass to him, and his cock slid along her folds. He pumped harder.

"I'm dying to be inside you. Best let me find a glove." He flung himself off the bed and rifled through the nightstand. "Bloody hell, I can't wait until we've taken care of the birth control issue so I can fuck you the way I want, Raine. I want to feel you melting all over my cock and not have a single sensation dulled by latex."

Clutching a foil square, he sprawled across the bed and made short work of gliding the condom over his swollen shaft. "On me now. Slide my cock inside you, slow and easy. That's it." He held himself still, gripping her hands in his as she lowered herself onto his broad shaft. "You like that?" His voice was thick with lust. "Tell me."

"Yes!" She tossed her head back, eyes sliding shut as ecstasy filled her veins like a drug. "I feel you everywhere inside me. It's the most amazing…oh, god!" she cried out as he bucked up beneath her, sinking in deeper and hitting a spot so sensitive, Raine gasped.

He did it again, then used one hand to guide her hips, leading her up until only the wide head of his cock stretched her open. Then he shoved her down as he thrust up to meet her, hitting that spot in her pussy even harder. As he repeated the motion again and again, she balled her hands into fists while he held her wrists immobile. She felt deliciously restrained, and it sent her soaring faster.

"Liam!" she panted his name again. "I love the way you fuck me, control me. That's just…" Her breath caught as he flicked his thumb over her clit. The storm gathered, converged, then released its thunder. "Yes!"

Her entire body jolted, and he pumped deep inside her, rubbing that spot that sent her into the beautiful madness once more, until she lost her breath, screaming, and scratched her throat raw as sweet lethargy hummed in her veins.

Barely managing to open her eyes, she looked down at him, feeling so open and bleeding and earnest. Normally, she would hide that from everyone, but not Liam. He would understand it. He would treasure it. Just like she wanted to do to him.

"How can I make you feel every bit as good as you've made me feel, Sir?"

"You please me, love. Your surrender fills my heart." He drew her down to him and kissed her tenderly. Then his eyes darkened as he rolled her beneath him. "Reach back and hold on to the headboard. Don't let go. Lock your legs around me. Lift…"

He placed a pillow beneath her ass and drove in even deeper, then held himself there until she shivered and her body clutched him helplessly.

"That's it, love. That's what I need. Watch me now. See the pleasure you give me as I come. It's all you…"

He filled her with slow, torturous strokes that ignited her all over again. When her breath caught and she begged him once more, he finally increased his tempo. As he reached his zenith, Liam wedged his hand between them and stroked her clit.

"Stay with me," he demanded.

Then he came with a primal yell, sending her over the blissful edge as well.

As they floated down from the stars, he stared. She felt herself flush and smiled, reveling in their intimate silence that somehow managed to speak volumes.

She clung to Liam as he brushed a strand of hair from her face and looked at her as if she was the most beautiful woman on the planet. Amazing that such a man wanted her.

Peace settled in her veins. When she was with him, everything felt so close to perfect. Close…but not quite there. That mild bit of panic every time she thought about the growing distance between her and Hammer gnawed at her. But her girlish love for him wasn't healthy, and she'd come to realize that she couldn't devote herself to someone so trapped in the past that he couldn't build a future and love her in return. He clearly cared…but that alone wasn't enough. She didn't know for sure, but it sounded as if Juliet had committed suicide or lived recklessly because she had a death wish. Because Hammer hadn't been able to show his love?

It didn't matter. The here and now with Liam, ending the enmity between the men—that mattered.

"I know you wanted to stay at the lodge longer, but thank you for coming back to help me with Hammer. I know you're pissed at him. I am, too....but I think he needs friends right now. We'll be all right here, I promise. It will all work out."

"It will eventually sort itself out. Don't worry. I think I've got a plan."

Two days later, Raine woke to find Liam showered and dressed, shaking her gently. "Up with you, love. In the shower."

She stretched. The blankets fell away exposing her breasts. Liam caressed them with his gaze.

"Are you sure that's what you want?" she teased.

"Trying to fuck me to death, are you?"

She snorted. "As if I could. Probably the other way around."

He smoothed a hand down her hip, brushing the covers from her thighs. "You're healing up nicely. Less tender?"

"I told you, I'm fine."

"Who are you speaking to?" He crossed his arms in disapproval.

"I'm fine, Sir," she groused.

"Roll over."

It crossed her mind to resist, but that would only get her in trouble. She really didn't like disappointing Liam. With a sigh, she did as he bid.

"A bit slower than I'd like, lass. You're still bruised here or I might spank you a bit."

"You're just waiting, aren't you?"

He laughed. "Counting the seconds."

She wiggled her ass at him and sent him a coy stare over her shoulder.

"You look fetching, but that will cost you later."

"Promise?" she quipped.

Liam shook his head at her, then smacked her lightly. "Up, you little glutton. Shower, dry your hair, put on your makeup. I'll be back shortly, and I want you ready."

He didn't give her time to argue, just left. With a shrug, Raine strolled to the bathroom, letting the hot steam of the shower unwind the leftover kinks from her muscles. Every night with Liam was like an Olympic marathon.

When she emerged with a towel around her body, all softened by her scented lotion, she headed to her closet, then stopped short at the sight of a blood-red corset on the bed. Lacy. Provocative. Oh so feminine.

"Put it on, love."

The command in his voice made her shiver. He wanted something, and he wanted it bad. Raine blinked at him, but his face gave nothing away.

"All right, Sir."

Liam stood, stared, never taking his eyes off her as she pulled the thong over her hips, then laid the corset over her breasts. He cinched it up. God, the way he touched her, watched her, was beyond intimate. Like he had every right to eat her up with his gaze. Like he owned her.

Once she'd dressed, she approached him, head bowed.

He brushed her crown, smoothing her hair. "Look at me."

Raine did, wondering what the hell he was up to. What he was thinking.

"You look gorgeous. Come with me." He took her hand and led her into the hall.

He wanted to scene before breakfast? In the empty dungeon? Why? Did he want her all to himself?

They'd taken no more than two steps outside the room they now shared when he took hold of her arms and stopped her. "I need to talk to you. You've accepted my training collar, lass. But we haven't had time to fasten any symbol of your commitment to me around your neck. I don't like the fact that other Doms might think you're fair game. I think it's time we changed that officially. What do you think?"

A smile broke out across her face. She'd only wondered a hundred times a day if or when he might bring this up. To know that he hadn't forgotten, that he still wanted her to be his, warmed her through and through. "I think I'm thrilled."

"Grand. Glad to hear it." He swallowed, looking surprisingly nervous. She'd already said yes, so...what was the issue?

"It's more than that, Raine. I want a collaring ceremony with you, and not just for training. I want to formally collar you."

Raine opened her mouth, gaping. She'd expected a lot of things—everything from him wanting her to have her nipples pierced to trying a new flogger out on her. In both cases, she'd prepared arguments. But she hadn't been prepared for this. He wanted to skip training her under his hand to see if they would be compatible and simply make her his? It was the BDSM equivalent of a wedding ring.

"Really?" she breathed.

She couldn't deny being a little sad that Hammer had gone to make his annual pilgrimage to New York—finally, she knew why—and wouldn't be here to witness the event. It worried her that by accepting, she might be hurting him. But he'd pushed her away, made it clear that he couldn't or wouldn't be with her. Why should she throw away a chance at happiness to keep pining over a man who refused to love her? Liam made her feel beautiful and cherished. She fell a bit more for him every day. With him, she could learn and grow and...wasn't that what Hammer ultimately wanted for her?

A smile spread across her face as tears pricked her eyes and tingled at the back of her nose.

"Really." Liam smiled indulgently.

Amazement coursed through her again. He wanted her, really, truly. Wanted *her*. She didn't know why fate or the universe thought she deserved him; she was just glad he'd chosen her.

"Yes!" She threw herself into his arms. As Liam caught her and dragged her against him with a hearty laugh, she hugged him. "I'll do everything I can to make you proud. I know I need practice and work, but I'll make you happy, Sir."

He palmed her cheek. "I'm counting on it, lass."

On the flight back home, Hammer sipped his drink, swirling the ice in the plastic cup as he stared out the window, thanking god he'd taken an earlier flight home. He was desperate to get back to Raine.

Leaning back against the seat with a sigh, he closed his eyes. Making the yearly jaunt to New York to pay his respects to Juliet's grave was always depressing. The only saving grace over the years had been Liam. His best friend had never failed to accompany him to the cemetery and reminisce about the good times they'd once shared. Liam's support and jovial stories had often kept him from shedding tears while visiting his wife's final resting place.

This year, everything had been different. Different, hell. It was a clusterfuck of biblical proportions. He couldn't remember the last time he'd shed tears while staring at Juliet's tombstone. Though he'd tried to determine why, after all these years, he'd come apart so brutally, Hammer still didn't know. As he'd knelt, he'd stared at the barren soil. And he'd spilled a torrent of bitter tears.

Now, he took another sip of bourbon as his mind swarmed like a nest of angry bees. He mulled over the situation back home.

Had the fact that Raine had been swept out from under him played a part in his breakdown at Juliet's grave? Of course. It had to, at least in part. The sultry siren always had him grasping for the threads of his control. But the loss of his friend weighed heavy on him, as well. The feeling of hopelessness was damn foreign to him. He didn't fucking like it.

Liam had played him, manipulated him to steal Raine. It pissed him off. But after watching Liam verbally assault Marlie, Hammer had no doubt they were both hopelessly in love with the sweet girl. And he was amazed at how quickly Liam had brought out the stunning submissive inside her. The idea that Liam might be good for Raine burned his throat like a blistering fireball, all but making him choke.

After landing at LAX, he hailed a taxi and climbed in. His stomach swirled, wondering if Liam had kept his promise. He wasn't prepared to face Shadows without Raine again. It would be a daunting task to live without her. He'd already had a taste of that, and he'd rather fly back to New York and relive the hell of his past than cope without her again.

Sighing heavily, he resigned himself to the fact *if* she were still at Shadows, he would somehow have to carry on, as he had for the past six years. But this time, he'd have to watch Liam with her, touching her, possessing her. It made him violent.

Son of a bitch, could this be any more fucked up?

When Hammer walked in the door of the club, people milled around everywhere. What the hell? It was far too early for this sort of crowd. Shadows wasn't even open yet.

With a frown, he fell in behind a crowd heading downstairs, where an even larger group had gathered. His employees seemed to be smiling brighter than everyone else. He frowned. *What the...* If the club had opened for an impromptu event, why weren't they working?

Excitement hung in the air. For a reason he couldn't explain, the scene filled him with dread.

As he reached the bottom of the steps, he slipped into a dark corner and watched. At the center of everything stood Raine. He couldn't miss her. Red was her color, and the corset hugged her beautifully. His cock, dead for days, suddenly flared with life. He remembered every moment of that night with her, replayed it in his head over and over—

Beck tapped the side of a glass, jerking him from his thoughts. A hush fell over the room. Suddenly, Liam wrapped an arm around her waist and led her to the stage, in front of the watchful crowd. Then he urged her to kneel at his feet and face him. She was stunning in her submissive pose, beautifully poised and graceful.

Liam smiled, addressing everyone. "Thank you all for coming to share this joyous event with us."

Hammer froze. This better not be what he feared...

Reaching down, Liam cupped Raine's chin. "Look at me, love. With great pride, I offer you my collar. I promise to always be there for you, steady and strong. I give my protection and guidance, the shelter of my body, the care in my heart, and the joy in my soul. I promise to lead you down the path best suited for you, be it with praise or pain, and help you grow into the submissive that lives and breathes within you. I vow to honor our bond and nurture your submission. And to use you as I would see fit." There were chuckles from the crowd. "I will treasure and cherish you, and embrace that which you give freely.

In return, you will empower me with your emotional and physical well-being, communicate to me your every feeling, knowing I will show you compassion and understanding. Do you give me all this of your own free will and accept my collar without reservation?"

Hammer felt sick to his stomach. *Training collar, my ass.* Liam was making her his—utterly.

He wanted to kill the son of a bitch.

Was this what Raine truly wanted? Had she…fallen in love with Liam?

Instant denial and betrayal sliced his soul like a hatchet.

She stared up into Liam's face. The glow of desire and excitement—of love—in the other man's eyes nearly cut him at the knees. Their happiness seemed to spread to everyone else in the room, infectious and cloying.

Raine squeezed Liam's hand and spoke solemnly. "I would be honored to wear your collar. I give you the softness of my body, the comfort from my soul, and the obedience in my heart, to grow into the submissive you desire. I will respect this bond. I will give myself to you without reservation. I will serve you, honor you, strive to be a good reflection of you, as I embrace all you grant me, Sir."

Pride shined on Liam's face as he bent to fasten the thick collar around her neck. He extended his hand and helped her to her feet. Together, they faced the crowd, arm in arm, all smiles.

Hammer's stare fastened on the substantial collar. Nothing simple, of course. No, Liam had to make a big fucking statement, flaunt her in his face. Silver and gold entwined in knots with a filigree pattern before swirling down to embrace a heavy teardrop ruby, which winked under the light as it settled perfectly into the hollow of her throat.

"It's beautiful." She glowed with joy. "Thank you, Sir. I feel so honored."

And Hammer felt like pounding Liam's face as he kissed her again.

Everyone around them clapped. Jovial laughter and clinking glasses soon filled the air as Liam lifted his head and cupped her nape possessively. "I'll look forward to testing you, love."

That was it. That was fucking all he could stand.

Love? Hammer pounded his fist against the wall, then prowled out from the shadows with a roar. "What the hell is going on here?"

The crowd fell dead silent.

The stunned look on Raine's face, followed by her guilty wince, struck him like a slap. Liam tightened his arm around her as Hammer marched toward them, his furious gaze pinning the other man where they stood.

If Hammer could rip the asshole's heart from his chest, he would. How convenient that Liam had arranged this lavish ceremony while he was scheduled to be out of town. Hammer knew better than to believe it was coincidence. The calculating prick had planned every minute of this.

But Raine…poor Raine. She didn't have a clue how this would most likely end. She thought she was living the fairy tale that he could never give her, and how could he fault her for wanting the dream? For being naïve? The glow he'd seen emanating from her as Liam sealed their bond with a kiss both churned Hammer's stomach and took his breath away. Raine was so stunning.

"Macen…" An apology softened her eyes.

He lowered his lips to her cheek. "Congratulations, precious. You look…angelic."

Though he'd spoken the truth, he'd had to force the bitter words out. Then he took another step, edging closer to Liam. His eyes narrowed as his lips curled into a sneer. "Don't gloat just yet, motherfucker. This isn't over."

Then Hammer turned and stormed off the stage, striding into his office and slamming the door behind him.

THE END

Hammer isn't giving Raine up, especially not to his (former) best friend. Ready to see what happens when he punches back? Continue the epic, dark romance journey with Raine, Hammer, and Liam in The Break now!

One woman. Two lovers. Countless secrets…

THE BREAK
The Unbroken Series: Raine Falling (Book 2)
by Shayla Black and Jenna Jacob
NOW AVAILABLE!
(available in eBook, print, and audio)

THE BREAK
The Unbroken Series: Raine Falling (Book 2)
by Shayla Black and Jenna Jacob
NOW AVAILABLE!
(available in eBook, print, and audio)

One woman. Two Rivals. Countless secrets...

Raine Kendall has everything a woman could want—almost. Sexy, tender Liam O'Neill is her knight in shining armor, but is he too good to be true or could their growing connection actually last a lifetime? To complicate matters, she can't shake her feelings for her commanding boss, Macen Hammerman, especially after the mind-blowing night he stopped fighting their attraction, took her to bed, and ravished every inch of her.

Now there might be consequences.

While Hammer can't stop coveting Raine and counting the days of her cycle with glee, Liam resolves to keep her for his own. But she stubbornly refuses to open the corners of her scarred heart. Determined to win her for good, Liam risks everything. Though once he puts his plan in motion, she proves as elusive as smoke. It's a bitter pill when he needs Hammer's help to bring her home. And Liam can't help but wonder...will Raine ever be his again or will he lose her to his ex-best friend for good?

EXCERPT

Macen "Hammer" Hammerman stifled the mundane conversation with his assistant, Raine Kendall, and stood, bracing his hands on the desk between them. Though his office door stood open—he wasn't "allowed" to talk to her otherwise—they were as alone as they'd been in weeks. It was now or never. He had an important question to ask.

"Tell me something, Raine. Your period is what, five days late?"

Blood leached from her face. "Wha—I... How would you even know that?"

Because it was his business. After six years of being her mentor, caretaker, and employer, he'd recently given in to his gnawing hunger and fucked her in every way known to man. And recklessly, he'd done it without a condom. Since admitting how much he wanted her, he couldn't seem to stop. But the elaborate collar that now dangled from her neck strangled him with one indisputable fact: She was owned. Taken. Completely off limits. Property of another.

That son of a bitch, Liam O'Neill. His former best friend.

"Kind of blows your theory that I've always looked through you, doesn't it?" He smirked. "Since you came to Shadows, I've kept tabs on your cycle every single month. You promised you'd let me know if you were so much as a minute late. I've been waiting..."

THANK YOU

Thank you for reading The Betrayal! If you enjoyed it, please review and recommend it to your reader friends. That means the world to us!

If you'd like an easy way to keep up with the latest news, releases, and sales from Shayla and/or Jenna, subscribe to our newsletters for announcements about new and upcoming titles, series' previews, exclusive excerpts, teasers, random stuff about author life, and more!

Shayla's VIP Reader Newsletter or www.shaylablack.com

Jenna's Reader Newsletter or www.jennajacob.com

ABOUT SHAYLA BLACK

LET'S GET TO KNOW EACH OTHER!

Shayla Black is the *New York Times* and *USA Today* bestselling author of over ninety contemporary, erotic, paranormal, and historical romances. Her books have sold millions of copies and been published in a dozen languages.

As an only child, Shayla occupied herself by daydreaming, much to the chagrin of her teachers. In college, she found her love for reading and started pursuing a publishing career. Though she graduated with a degree in Marketing/Advertising and embarked on a stint in corporate America, her heart was with her stories and characters, so she left her pantyhose and power suits behind.

Shayla currently lives in North Texas with her wonderfully supportive husband, her daughter, and two spoiled tabbies. In her "free" time, she enjoys reality TV, gaming, and listening to an eclectic blend of music.

TELL ME MORE ABOUT YOU.

Connect with me via the links below. You can also become one of my Facebook Book Beauties and enjoy live, interactive #WineWednesday video chats full of fun, book chatter, and more! See you soon!

Website: http://shaylablack.com

VIP Reader Newsletter: http://shayla.link/nwsltr
Shayla Store: https://www.shaylablack.com/bookstore/
Facebook Book Beauties Chat Group: http://shayla.link/FBChat

- facebook.com/ShaylaBlackAuthor
- instagram.com/shaylablack
- tiktok.com/@shayla_black
- twitter.com/ShaylaBlackAuth
- bookbub.com/authors/shayla-black
- pinterest.com/shaylablacksb

OTHER BOOKS BY SHAYLA BLACK

WICKED LOVERS: SOLDIERS FOR HIRE
Steamy, High-Octane Contemporary Romantic Suspense

FREE! Wicked as Sin (One-Mile & Brea, part 1)

Wicked Ever After (One-Mile & Brea, part 2)

Wicked as Lies (Zyron & Tessa, part 1)

Wicked and True (Zyron & Tessa, part 2)

Wicked as Seduction (Trees & Laila, part 1)

Wicked and Forever (Trees & Laila, part 2)

Wicked as Secrets (Matt & Madison, part 1)

Wicked and Bare (Matt & Madison, part 2)

REED FAMILY RECKONING
Sultry, Angsty Family-Drama Contemporary Romance

SIBLINGS

FREE! More Than Want You (Maxon & Keeley)

More Than Need You (Griff & Britta)

More Than Love You (Harlow & Noah)

BASTARDS

More Than Crave You (Evan & Nia)

More Than Tempt You (Bethany & Clint)

More Than Desire You (Xavian & Corinne)

FRIENDS

More Than Dare You (Trace & Masey)

More Than Hate You (Sebastian & Sloan)

NOVELLAS

More Than Pleasure You (Stephen & Skye)

More Than Protect You (Tanner & Amanda)

More Than Possess You (A Hope Series crossover) (Echo & Hayes)

DOOMSDAY BRETHREN
Sexy Paranormal Romance

Tempt Me with Darkness (Marrok & Olivia)

FORBIDDEN CONFESSIONS
Sexy Bedtime Stories - Contemporary Romance

FIRST TIME COLLECTION

Seducing the Innocent (Kayla & Oliver)

Seducing the Bride (Perrie & Hayden)

Seducing the Stranger (Calla & Quint)

Seducing the Enemy (Whitney & Jett)

PROTECTORS COLLECTION

Seduced by the Bodyguard (Sophie & Rand)

Seduced by the Spy (Vanessa & Rush)

Seduced by the Assassin (Havana & Ransom)

Seduced by the Mafia Boss (Kristi & Ridge)

FILTHY RICH BOSSES COLLECTION

Tempted by the Billionaire (Savannah & Chad)

[Tempted by the Executives](#) (Marcus, Kate, & Josh)

Tempted by the Bosshole (Bella & Nathan)

THE WICKED LOVERS
Sizzling Contemporary Romantic Suspense

Wicked Ties (Morgan & Jack)

Decadent (Kimber & Deke)

Delicious (Alyssa & Luc)

Surrender to Me (Kata & Hunter)

Belong to Me (Tara & Logan)
Wicked to Love (Emberlin & Brandon)
Mine to Hold (Delaney & Tyler)
Wicked All the Way (Carlotta & Caleb)
Ours to Love (London, Javier, & Xander)
Wicked All Night (Rachel & Decker)
Forever Wicked (Gia & Jason)
Theirs to Cherish (Callie, Thorpe, & Sean)
His to Take (Bailey & Joaquin)
Pure Wicked (Bristol & Jesse)
Wicked for You (Mystery & Axel)
Falling in Deeper (Lily & Stone)
Dirty Wicked (Sasha & Nick)
A Very Wicked Christmas (Morgan & Jack)
Holding on Tighter (Jolie & Heath)
Devoted to Wicked (A Devoted Lovers crossover) (Karis & Cage)

THE DEVOTED LOVERS (Complete Series)
Steamy Contemporary Romantic Suspense
Devoted to Pleasure (Shealyn & Cutter)
Devoted to Wicked (A Wicked Lovers crossover) (Karis & Cage)
Devoted to Love (Magnolia & Josiah)

THE UNBROKEN SERIES
(co-authored with Jenna Jacob)
Scorching Ménage Contemporary Romance
Raine Falling Saga (Complete)
The Betrayal
The Break
The Brink

The Bond

Heavenly Rising Saga
The Choice
The Chase
The Confession
The Commitment

THE PERFECT GENTLEMEN (Complete Series)
(co-authored with Lexi Blake)
Steamy Contemporary Romantic Suspense
Scandal Never Sleeps
Seduction in Session
Big Easy Temptation
Smoke and Sin
At the Pleasure of the President

MASTERS OF MÉNAGE (Complete Series)
(co-authored with Lexi Blake)
Sizzling Contemporary Romance
Their Virgin Captive
Their Virgin's Secret
Their Virgin Concubine
Their Virgin Princess
Their Virgin Hostage
Their Virgin Secretary
Their Virgin Mistress

STANDALONE TITLES
Naughty Little Secret (Sexy Stranger/Office Romance)
Watch Me (Steamy Romantic Suspense)

Dirty & Dangerous (Sizzling Ménage Romantic Suspense)

Her Fantasy Men (Sizzling Reverse Harem Contemporary)

A Perfect Match (Sweet Opposites-Attract Contemporary)

THE HOPE SERIES (Complete Series)
Steamy Contemporary Romance

Misadventures of a Backup Bride (Ella & Carson)

Misadventures with My Ex (Eryn & West)

More Than Possess You (Echo & Hayes) (A Reed Family Reckoning crossover)

SEXY CAPERS (Complete Series)
Steamy Contemporary Romance

Bound and Determined (Kerry & Rafael)

Strip Search (Nicola & Mark)

Arresting Desire (Lucia & Jon)

HISTORICAL ROMANCE
STANDALONES

The Lady and the Dragon (Sexy Georgian Privateer Romance)

One Wicked Night (Sexy Regency/Forbidden Love Romance)

STRICTLY SERIES (Complete Duet)
Sexy Victorian Historical Romance

Strictly Seduction (Madeline & Brock)

Strictly Forbidden (Kira & Gavin)

BROTHERS IN ARMS (Complete Trilogy)
Angsty Medieval Romance

His Lady Bride (Gwenyth & Aric)

His Stolen Bride (Averyl & Drake)

His Rebel Bride (Maeve & Kieran)

BOXSETS/COLLECTIONS

Wicked and Worshipped (One-Mile and Brea duet)

Wicked and Forbidden (Zyron and Tessa duet)

Wicked and Enslaved (Trees and Laila duet)

More Than Promises (Reed Family Reckoning: Siblings)

Forbidden Confessions: First Time

Forbidden Confessions: Protectors

First Glance (A trio of series starters)

Summer Fling (Four sexy beach reads)

Unbroken: Raine Falling Complete Series

Unbroken: Raine Falling, Volume One

Unbroken: Raine Falling, Volume Two

The Strictly Duet (Victorian historical romance)

ABOUT JENNA JACOB

USA Today Bestselling author Jenna Jacob paints a canvas of passion, romance, and humor as her alpha men and the feisty women who love them unravel their souls, heal their scars, and find a happy-ever-after kind of love. Heart-tugging, captivating, and steamy, her words will leave you breathless and craving more.

A mom of four grown children, Jenna, her husband Sean and their furry babies reside in Kansas. Though she spent over thirty years in accounting, Jenna isn't your typical bean counter. She's brassy, sassy, and loves to laugh, but is humbly thrilled to be living her dream as a full-time author. When she's not slamming coffee while pounding out emotional stories, you can find her reading, listening to music, cooking, camping, or enjoying the open road on the back of a Harley.

CONTACT JENNA:

Website: www.jennajacob.com
E Mail: jenna@jennajacob.com
Facebook Page: https://www.facebook.com/authorjennajacob
Jenna's Jezebels Party Page: https://www.facebook.com/groups/jennajacobsjezebels
Instagram: https://www.instagram.com/jenna_jacob_author/
TikTok: https://vm.tiktok.com/ZMR8v5QWA/
BookBub: https://www.bookbub.com/authors/jenna-jacob
Amazon Author page: http://amzn.to/2Bmp0wP
Newsletter: http://bit.ly/JennaJacobNewsletter
Goodreads: http://bit.ly/2lZagNE

OTHER BOOKS BY JENNA JACOB

BAD BOYS OF ROCK (Complete Series)
Rock Me (Prequel)

Rock Me Longer

Rock Me Harder

Rock Me Slower

Rock Me Faster

Rock Me Deeper

COWBOYS OF HAVEN
Coming Soon:

The Cowboy's Second Chance at Love (September 21, 2021)

The Cowboy's Thirty-Day Fling (October 5, 2021)

The Cowboy's Cougar (October 26, 2021)

The Cowboy's Surprise Vegas Baby (November 16, 2021)

THE DOMS OF GENESIS
Embracing My Submission

Masters of My Desire

Master of My Mind

Saving My Submission

Seduced By My Doms

Lured By My Master

Sin City Submission

Bound To My Surrender

Resisting My Submission

Craving His Command

Seeking My Destiny

PASSIONATE HEARTS

Small Town Second Chance

STANDALONE TITLES

Innocence Uncaged

UNBROKEN: RAINE FALLING

(Co-authored with Shayla Black)

The Broken

The Betrayal

The Break

The Brink

The Bond

UNBROKEN: HEAVENLY RISING

(Co-authored with Shayla Black)

The Choice

The Chase

Coming Soon:

The Commitment (June 7, 2022)

Printed in Great Britain
by Amazon